Frankie Jemison

MY LORD OF WRYBOURNE

The Works of Jeffery Farnol.

MY LORD
OF WRYBOURNE

Being
an account of
his further perils,
grief and joy

by

JEFFERY FARNOL

LONDON
SAMPSON LOW, MARSTON & CO., LTD.

First published 1948

MADE AND PRINTED IN GREAT BRITAIN BY PURNELL AND SONS, LTD.,
PAULTON (SOMERSET) AND LONDON

CONTENTS

MY LORD
OF WRYBOURNE

CHAPTER I

WHICH INTRODUCES OLD FRIENDS—AND ENEMIES

I

SIR ROBERT CHALMERS, who had always hated solitude, sat alone as had now become his wont; this once formidable man who had lived for and borne himself so arrogantly amid the glitter and homage of great Vanity Fair, now merely existed—a sullen recluse shut away in a rustical isolation he scorned and detested.

Almost two years had dragged their weary length since the hour that had transformed him from a man feared, honoured or dreadfully respected, to the maimed, helpless creature he now was and for which he so bitterly despised himself.

Thus today, with the glad noon sun bright about him, he sat crouched in elbow chair brooding darkly on that merciless, oft-dreamed vengeance which had become his one object in life and only consolation. Very still he sat, gazing haggardly before him, powerful left fist tight-clenched upon his knee, right arm half-hidden in the breast of his coat—this mutilated right arm that shamed him and of which he was always so painfully conscious that it had become his torment.

Beyond the open lattice before him lay a wide and lovely prospect, for his house stood high,—a green down-land country rolling southward to the sea; but Sir Robert's burning gaze was fixed with a dreadful intensity in that one and only direction where, towards the west, some fifteen miles or so, rose the aged walls and towers of that house called "Wrybourne Feveril" where my lord the Earl was even now in residence.

And thinking of the Earl, this enemy whose blade in smiting off his terrible right hand had bereft him of so very much beside, Sir Robert plucked from breast his mutilated arm, this ghastly memento whose merest sight could always goad him to such wild furies of despair,—even as now; for, leaping afoot, he shook this hideous, silk-bound stump against that unseen, far-distant House of Wrybourne Feveril, while from back-drawn lips and gnashing teeth issued such breathless tirade of threats and curses that the tallish pallid gentleman on the terrace without, paused in his leisured approach to listen, his thin lips curling in cynical amusement until Sir Robert's furious outburst ended, then advancing silently, he leaned in at the open window to smile and say with airy flourish :

"Well, well, dear fellow, what a particularly lovely day; I wish you all joy of it."

Sir Robert merely scowled, then as if reading some subtle meaning in the speaker's look and tone, he clenched his remaining hand, saying :

"Ha, Twily! Curse you, Viscount; d'ye dare—can it be possible that you attempt to jeer and mock me—is it possible?"

"Eh, jeer you?" repeated Viscount Twily, mouthing the words. "Mock you? I? No, no, Robert, perish the thought—never think it. If I smile, which I do, it is for you, my dear Robert, with you, not—at you. Never that, no, no! And I am a trifle gay because I have succeeded——"

"Ah, fool Ralph sold them? You have secured the property?"

"Well, not exactly, but good as——"

"Did Scrope accept my money? Have you the title-deeds?"

"Well, n-n-no," drawled the Viscount, "not precisely. But all in good time, my dear fellow, for it seems his lovely wife—ah, that lusciously bewitching creature holds the deeds and refuses to part with 'em, but——"

"Then damn you, Twily, you have not succeeded!"

"Patience, dearest fellow, I cry you patience! For Lord Scrope needs the money so damnably that needs must. The deeds will be in my hands this time tomorrow despite all his so charming better half may do! And oh! Gad, how very much his better half she is—aha, Robert, what a golden beauty and how devilish alluring——"

"Scrope agreed to sell then,—at what figure?"

"Three hundred guineas. He took my first offer, jumped at it, in fact."

"Was he quite fuddled, very drunk?"

"Not more than usual. But, my dear Robert, though the property is a bargain at such price, what you can want with Wrexford Mill, that dreary ruin and devilish ugly pool, passes my understanding."

"Naturally!" retorted Sir Robert and with zest. "However, I want it for a purpose known only to myself. . . . That ruin, that accursed pool . . . these are the beginning!"

"You're devilish mysterious, dear fellow,—not thinking of —murder, I suppose?"

"Twily, what precisely do you mean?"

"Merely that it is a very murderous sort of place. The late Lord Julian Scrope was done to death there as you may remember. There have been others; and I should not be so vastly surprised if there should be others yet. For e'Gad, it strikes me as a strangely fatal or, shall I say, fate-ful place—ah yes, a place of doom, old fellow, and—destiny!"

"Hold your—infernal tongue!" gasped Sir Robert, making to leap from his chair, whereat the Viscount, always smiling, recoiled.

"Dear fellow," he murmured, "we are all of us creatures doomed, more or less, for this or that,—as saith the Swan of Avon: 'All unavoided is the doom of destiny', and, may I add, there is a Fate hangs above each of us ready to drop and extinguish us, dear boy, whenso it will, nor can it be eluded. Your fate dooms you for the present to a fury of solitude and mine to share it—compelling me to soothe you, cheer you, comfort and console you, my very dear fellow."

In each softly uttered word, in every look and tone and gesture, Sir Robert seemed to find something so altogether odious and unbearable that, with the inarticulate cry of a goaded animal, he sprang afoot brandishing his stump while the Viscount from safe distance surveyed him with expression of mild wonderment and enquiry.

"Dear boy," he murmured, "why—oh, pray why this perturbation?"

"Twily," said Sir Robert in voice strangely hushed, "I use you because nature meant you for a lackey, and you obey me because you must. Ah, but, Viscount, should you ever be so unwise as to rebel, defy me or cross my purposes —then, by God, you shall find I'm still to be reckoned with— though I am a maimed cripple. . . . Oh damn and curse him!"

"Certainly, Robert! Oh, by all means if you are alluding to Wrybourne's noble earl, as of course you are and very naturally—considering!" Here he motioned gently towards Sir Robert's stump. "So permit me to curse him with you and damn him as heartily. Ah yes, and the more especially as his so beautiful countess, as you may have heard, has lately blessed him with a son and heir. Indeed, Japhet Scrope, Earl of Wrybourne, should and would have been dead a year ago but for your—unfortunate lapse, dear boy. As it is, the cursed fellow enjoys life, begets children, has hosts of friends, while we, my poor, dear Robert, merely exist——"

"Damnation!" panted Sir Robert.

"Yes indeed—for him, Bob, for him! I was forgetting,— our Wrybourne has lately committed himself quite damnably in a speech to the Lords, defending this rebellious scoundrel Cobbett and thus has got himself into such disrepute, such an infernal mess he shall never get out of—if the matter is handled judiciously . . . a word here and there, letters to the papers, notes to proper authorities and so on,—these should prove his absolute social ruin and final damnation. Did you happen to see a report of this speech of his in the *Gazette*?"

"Not I."

"Ah well, I have a copy here. Take it, dear fellow; read, mark and inwardly digest; it should so inspire you that with my humble though zealous assistance you may at last pay your Wrybourne for"—here a graceful gesture towards that maimed arm—"past favours and bring him to—the so desired end. Meantime, dearest of all Bobs, I'll to my chamber, to snooze, perchance to dream how you, or we together, are his now approaching doom—and destiny, of course." And, with nod and smile, Viscount Twily ambled away.

Now scarcely had this too-too smiling gentleman taken himself out of sight than the door opened to admit a tall, grey-haired woman, somewhat run to bone and tooth, whose face would have been harsh but for wide, humorous mouth and eyes that could beam so gently whenever they lighted upon this grievous, sore-stricken man; she closed the door, crossed the room with the stride of a grenadier, shut the lattice with a slam and, folding long arms, met Sir Robert's scowl with one just as dark, shook her grey head at him and spoke in a Scots idiom, difficult to describe, thus:

"Oomph-hoomph! Syne yon black-hairted Viscount is awa' —de'il tak' him—'tis mysel' ye'll be needing the noo tae sweeten the air and yesel' forbye! Ay, 'tis Elspeth ye need, Rabbie."

"But I don't!" he answered, sullenly, opening the news-paper. "No, I desire to be alone."

"Havers, man, and are ye no' the vera loneliest body in a' this worrald, are ye no'?"

"Yes," he muttered, "yes I am, but only because I desire loneliness. So, Elspeth, pray go."

"No' me!" she snapped and, thrusting a chair close beside him, she seated herself with the utmost determination. "Ay," quoth she, meeting his scowl with fierce nod, "here's hersel' and here she'll bide to watch o'er ye, knit o'er ye and mebbe pray o'er ye as she did when ye were sic a wee helpless mither-less bairn." Here, taking the wherewithal from capacious reticule, she began to knit with furious speed, watching him the while beneath fierce-knit brows with those strangely gentle eyes.

"Rabbie man," said she at last, "thretty-six years twa months and five days syne I took ye tae this bosom—a wee thing at point o' death,—and kept the life in ye. Ye'll be aye minding this!"

"Yes, Elspeth," he replied, and less sullenly, "and in all this damned creation you are the one and only creature I care for,—the only one I have ever trusted—or ever shall!"

"Ay, I ken that fine, Rab, for ye're ever suspicious o' nature——"

"And with reason, Elspeth——"

"Aweel, when ye were tender babe I was your life; when motherless boy afeard o' your father—and sma' wonder—ye clung tae me, and well I protected ye, ay I did that! When ye were a youth ye confided in me and tookit my advice—eh but—when Sir Jamie our Laird died, God be thankit—and left ye sae unco' wealthy and sae young ah then ye gangit your ain gait regardless—and now see whaur it has brought ye——"

"To failure!" said he bitterly. "To defeat, mutilation—ay—and damnation!"

"Tae failure, ay!" she nodded. "Tae mutilation, vera true, wae's me for your bonny right hand! But tó damnation,—na, na, Robbie man, ye're no' precisely damned—yet! Ye're on the road but 'tis a lang road and I'm praying God forbid. But 'tis yoursel' maun decide, whateffer. Ay, your final damnation, Rabbie, is juist atwixt yoursel' and our Good Lord, and because He is God the Father He shall be mair mercifu' than your ain or any airthly father. Ah yes," she sighed, speaking now in a cultured English, "and as for the loss of your hand, that cruel wicked man-killing right hand, Robert, its loss brought you something infinitely better."

"Ha, and pray what was that, for God's sake?"

"Your old Elspeth, and for your own sake. And a poor, wild, grievous wretch she found you! Eh, my certie, without Elspeth to mother ye 'tis in your grave you'd be at this moment, Rob."

"Yes, that's the truth of it!" he muttered, glancing down at his stump with shrinking aversion. "And better so, perhaps. . . . And yet, since you have again saved my life, Elspeth, then by God I'll use it to good purpose."

"Robert, is your good purpose God's purpose òr that suggested by yon loathsome Viscount?"

"Just what do you mean, Elspeth?"

"Eh, what should I mean but murder? Did I no' hear him suggest it and mysel' wi' my lug tae the keyhole? Is it the murder o' your enemy, Rab?"

"Not so, Elspeth. Oh dear, no."

"His death, then?"

"No, again,—death would be too swift, too merciful. My method shall be more lingering, Elspeth, a—death in life!"

"Ha!" she nodded. "'Tis vengeance might shame Auld Hornie hissel'—and why for, Rob? Was it no' a fair fight ye had wi' yon Earl o' Wrybourne, man to man, face to face as is our auld Hielan' custom, was it no'?"

"Yes, Elspeth, but vengeance eye for eye and tooth for tooth is also a Highland custom."

"Mebbe so, but ye're no' a Hielander, Rab,—'tis myself, Elspeth McGregor, is so—one o' the lost 'children o' the mist' that maun see this waefu' worrald through mist o' their tears, —whiles yesel'—you, Robert, are just a mere Lowland body, and so vengeance is no' exactly natural to you by reason of your ancestry."

Now at this, Sir Robert scowled blackly,—then his lips were curved by such smile as none but this devoted nurse of his babyhood had ever seen as he answered and in the vernacular:

"Haud y' clack, ye besom, and this i' the lugs o' ye—a Lowland laird can avenge as cannily—ay and wi' mair grace than ony wild Hielan' cateran, y' ken! Ha, yes, woman, vengeance can be as dearly sweet to me as to any of your fierce ancestors."

"Then, Robert," she retorted, "if this be so, which I do not admit, you are the most perfect fool to confide the least hint of your bloody-minded intent to that mean-faced, shifty-eyed Viscount Twily,—a treacherous, ever-smiling, villainous rogue, if ever I saw one!"

"He is all you say, Elspeth, and of which I am sufficiently aware. But the sordid rascal is completely in my power and must obey me,—he is a tool very proper to my purpose."

"Then, Robert, take care this tool doesn't turn in your grasp and lop off your remaining hand; be heedful, that is all——"

"And enough, quite enough," fumed Sir Robert; "indeed it is quite too much! You become too officious, Elspeth, and so devilishly possessive that I—yes, damme,—I've been greatly minded of late to be rid of you——"

"Oh, my poor, fool man!" she sighed. "Such utter nonsense! You can never again be rid of me——"

"Ha!" he exclaimed, frowning up into this face of such serene assurance and ineffable calm. "Why the devil not, woman?"

"Woman, yes!" she nodded. "The woman that twice brought you back to life for good or ill, the woman who may have to save you yet again."

"From what?" he demanded.

"Yourself, to be sure!" she nodded. "Robert Chalmers is the worst enemy you ever had,—he was in the past, is now, and ever will be—unless——"

"Unless what, Elspeth,—damme—what?"

"Unless you have Elspeth to watch over you once more and are occasionally wise enough to follow her advice as you did in your past youth and late sickness. Why, y' gomeril, y' silly gowk, without me now you'd be utterly lost, you'd languish and die." Before her wide, steadfast gaze his fierce eyes gentled, wavered and fell, and in voice changed, as his look, he replied:

"Yes . . . come to think of it . . . I believe I should."

"Ye wad that," she nodded, rolling up her knitting, "forbye I am the only mither ye ever kenned, puir laddie."

"Exactly true, Elspeth,—and father, sisters and brothers also; I was a lonesome little wretch."

"Aweel, I'll awa' tae the kitchen; yon cook, Lisbeth, has no' a just regaird for that noble vegetable the onion. I'll awa', Rabbie, and leave ye tae your dreams o' bluidy vengeance."

II

Ralph, Lord Scrope, though a little more drunk than usual, was yet so well aware of it that, dreading to meet his lady's reproachful eyes, he reined his horse aside from the avenue of noble trees that led in gracious sweep to the front door and was such a splendid feature of this ancient Manor House and thus, by devious ways, reached the trim stable-yard, here to be met by his old head groom who shook grey head, sighing deeply, for his master was swaying in the saddle.

"T-Tom," he stammered thickly, straightening his powerful, shapely body with an effort, "Tom, ol' tulip, I'm shockin'ly d'sguised in liquor, so—question is"—here he glanced furtively about, very like a guilty schoolboy—"I'm ashkin' you—ish her la'ship anywhere 'bout, m'lady, eh, Tom?"

"No, m'lud, she ain't, I'm glad to say."

"Good . . . sho'm I—mustn't shee me jush yet . . . I'm trifle foxed . . . shlightly bottled, eh, Tom, m' ol' pippin, eh?"

"Master Ralph, my lord," replied the old groom severely, "you are most owdacious fuddled, too dis-gustin' drunk to go anigh my dearie leddy yet. Lord love and comfort her loveliness and too tender 'eart! And 'er that anxious along o' you; been 'ere twice, she 'ave, to see if you was safe 'ome, poor, bootiful, too-fond creeter! Geddown, Master Ralph, afore you tumble down, my lud, quick afore she comes again and ketches of ee—come ee into my cottage and sleep it off."

"Oh—no, T-Tom, 's water, pure, plain w-water I want. Help me d-down——"

With old Tom's not too gentle assistance, my lord dismounted and staggering to the pump nearby, bared his handsome head, stooped it beneath the spout, and cried: "Go!" whereat pump clanked, water gushed and his lordship gasped, spluttered, swore, and presently stood dripping and thus, a little sobered and refreshed, accepted the towel old Tom now proffered and began drying himself with a quite unnecessary violence until he checked suddenly, then, recoiling, crept on tiptoe, with elaborate caution, for the nearest hiding-place, and this being the pump, he crouched behind it in desperate though vain endeavour to screen his too-large person from the stately lady who stood regarding him with such very beautiful but woeful eyes,—this golden woman whose radiant loveliness seemed to shed a glory all about her,—and yet whose presence had sent her lord and master to cower thus in this quite inadequate shelter of the old pump; thus presently, with her sad gaze upon his abject form, she spoke in tone grievous as her look:

"Oh, Tom, he's very bad again! Please take you the towel and dry him properly for me."

"No—no, Cec'ly, m'dear," said her husband with exaggerated jauntiness. "No need o' Tom—do it m'self . . . though jus' at present I'm resting. Join you pres'nly indoors . . . home sweet home . . . dish o' tea . . . revelry 'n' joy."

"Oh, Tom," she sighed again, closing her eyes as if unable to bear the sight of her besotted husband, or because of the tears that blinded her, "oh, today he is . . . worse than usual! What am I to do with him? What can I do?"

"Go you indoors, my dearie leddy, and leave him to me!" replied the old groom very tenderly and blinking his keen old eyes that were moist for very sympathy. "Ar, leave him to me as have knowed and managed him ever since 'e were a squalling babby——"

"S'right, m' dear!" quoth his lordship brightly. " 'S perfeckly, abs-lootly right, y' know . . . ol' Tom . . . m' first pony . . . aha, and learned me t' box . . . s-s-straight left . . ." and clenching his powerful, quite terrible fists whereby he had won no little fame, his lordship began to box the pump, striking at it, ducking, weaving and side-stepping rather unsteadily but with the greatest spirit and gusto. Twice his wife called to him, but, finding her appeals unheard or quite unheeded, she sighed hopelessly and, with golden head bowed, went slowly and mournfully away. Meanwhile her lordly husband continued to dance, dodge and feint at the pump until a hard-driven fist tumbled him headlong.

"And there's for ye, m'lud, damn y'r eyes!" panted old Tom, scowling down on his thus prostrated master who made no attempt to rise. "I ought b'rights to tek a hoss-whip to ee. This be second time this week as you've filled them lovely eyes o' hern wi' tears o' grief and bitter shame! You'm breakin' 'er too-gentle 'eart; killin' 'er b'inches, I tell ee— ar, and because she du love ee too well, like as few men be ever loved! And though you ain't worth it, she'll go on lovin' ee till she sinks into her grave—and then p'r'aps you'll begin to larn and know what you've lost—and be lost too!"

"Hold your curst tongue, Tom, or you'll have me in tears next."

"Ar—crockydile's tears!" snorted the old groom fiercely. "Master Ralph, m'lord, you bean't nowise fit to tie her shoe, no, nor even touch it, never nowise and nohow."

"Well, damme, I know that," groaned his lordship. "I've always known it."

"She takes ye out o' prison. She pays y'r debts. She marrie: ye, and arl as you give her in return is misery and shame . . ."

Bowing curly head between clenched fists, his lordship rocked himself to and fro while this aged groom, who had fathered him more truly than his own lordly sire ever had, now reproached and berated him until, words and breath alike failing, the old man turned and, with sound that may have been a sob, trudged heavily away.

But Ralph continued to sit crouched thus miserably on the flagstones, nor moved until, roused by a light step, he beheld his lady standing before him,—this young wife who nineteen short months ago had been merely a farmer's daughter (and drudge), yet who now showed sweetly proud and dignified as any lady in England.

Mutely she stood, and he, knowing her for all loveliness from dainty, sandalled foot to the crowning glory of her corn-coloured hair, gazed up at her with a wistful adoration and she down on him with such pitying sadness as smote him to a remorse beyond his utterance, therefore he bowed his head again between clenched fists and so remained until:

"My lord, stand up!" said this lady of months, and this gentleman of so many generations humbly obeyed. "My poor Ralph," she murmured, tenderly, "your dear eyes look so heavy, so very tired—is your head aching you so much?"

"Yes," he groaned.

"Then come indoors and let me bathe it for you; come, my poor love, do now."

And so dumbly he followed her, keeping his head averted lest she saw the tears that now were blinding him.

III

Japhet Scrope, Earl of Wrybourne Feveril, known to his particular friends as Sam, sat alone in his spacious library scowling down at a newspaper outspread upon the great desk before him, and the longer he read the blacker he frowned until at last, uttering a sound only describable as a contemptuous snort, he crumpled up the news-sheet, threw himself back in his chair, and scowled up at the carved and gilded ceiling instead. And thus he remained until, roused by the door opening, he glanced thither and beheld his countess; gone was my lord's scowl in that instant, and as instantly he rose to greet her.

Andromeda closed the door, made three or four graceful paces, then, pausing, stood to survey this square-jowled, nearly handsome spouse of hers who, though now bearing himself like the nobleman he was, still had about him, and despite modish attire, a vague suggestion of ships and the sea; my lord, gazing upon his stately wife, was quick to heed, and despite the shade of her coquettish, plumed bonnet, that her cheeks were flushed and eyes very bright beneath their low-arching brows, these golden eyes in such vivid contrast to the glossy, night-black hair framing the oval beauty of her face. . . . Thus stood they at gaze, then in the same instant they moved—and she was in his arms.

"Andromeda!" said Sam, putting back her bonnet the better to come at her lips. "Oh, my Andromeda!" he murmured, and they kissed. Then, holding her away, "Madam," said my lord, "the sun has flushed you or your ladyship is angry, I perceive. So come and sit on your Sam and let's hear." Saying this, he led her to a cushioned settle nearby and, here seated, with her throned upon his knee, he watched her remove and lay aside her bonnet and draw off her long, silk mittens; which done:

"Well now?" he questioned.

"Yes—now, my lord——" she retorted, slender finger upraised to admonish, but, meeting his gaze, she faltered and, nestling to him, said murmurously:

"Hold me close, my Sam, for Japhet the Earl can still make me ridiculously self-conscious and absurdly—shy!"

"And rightly so, madam," the Earl replied. "Such delicious shyness mightily becomes my countess and enhances her beauty, these peerless charms, these——"

"Ah, no!" she whispered. "Be done with your lordly affectations and be my Sam, my dear, true-hearted, over-bearing gruff and grim man of the sea."

"Why then," said Sam, drawing her close, "kiss him, lass, this poor, proud, humble fellow who loves you more as his wife and mother than he did as a maid."

"Oh, Sam," she murmured, clinging to him, "I am so very, so—dreadfully happy that . . . sometimes I become afraid, yes . . . terrified!"

"Terrified?" he repeated. "Lord love you—why?"

"Because such perfect, such—unearthly happiness seems too wonderful to last. We are quite—too happy, my dearest."

"Well, now," growled Sam, yet gazing down very tenderly at this splendid woman of his, "whoever heard the like o' this! Are you going to make our happiness your misery, sweetheart?"

"No, silly man, of course not! Only it seems as though——" She caught her breath and he was amazed to feel her clinging loveliness shiver violently.

"Why, Andromeda," he exclaimed. "Oh, my dear, what is it?"

"I don't—know," she answered, staring at him wide-eyed, "only I feel, perhaps because I love you so terribly, that you are . . . threatened by . . . something vile and deadly . . . and through you, myself, and through me—our baby, our little Sam."

"Nonsense!" he laughed, giving her a loving shake and squeeze. "And as to our baby, you mean, of course, our little Edward for old Ned and Samuel for me——?"

"I mean our little blessed child, our Sam first and Edward after."

"But, my dearest, I promised Ned, my old messmate, d'ye see, and——"

"I know you did, but, d'ye see," she mocked, "'twas I bore him——"

"Ay, b'gad!" he exclaimed, clasping her tighter, "shall I ever forget it? That frightful waiting . . . the damnable suspense . . . not knowing if you were to live or die——"

"Dear love," she murmured, kissing his furrowed brow, "I had no thought of dying, silly man; I was too proud and happy to bear your child . . . praying for a son . . . to be your heir! So you see things happened very well; you need not have worried so terribly and, besides, you had our Grannyanne to comfort you."

"Ay, thank God!" said he, fervently. "Lord only knows what I should ha' done without her!"

"What a great comfort she is, Sam, and how wonderfully she manages this great house!"

"And brings me up with a round turn if I dare call it a rabbit-warren, which it certainly is."

"Yet a glory, Sam, and our dear home."

"Home, ay!" he nodded. "But only because you make it so."

"And you tell me," said she, smoothing his thick eyebrows with caressing finger, "you love your Andromeda more as a wife than you ever did when——"

"Ay, when she was the loveliest, saddest, gipsy-like 'fairy aunt' that hardly knew how to smile, and with her pretty feet and lovely legs in clumsy boots and worsted stockings,—so very different from these bewitchments——"

"Ah, no; wait, my lord, and listen to me, because I am going to ask Sam a very serious question."

"Pray speak, madam; your Sam is all attention."

"Well, then, you noticed when I came in that I was rather flushed and not because of the sun, but wifely indignation."

"Oho," exclaimed my lord, "then I presume the cause was, or is, your very awkward, clumsy Sam fellow."

"Is he, I wonder?" said she with a tone and look become suddenly grave. "The day before yesterday there were several ladies, all neighbours, here for tea as usual, but—things were not as usual, I sensed an odd awkwardness. Today I drove out to pay duty calls, and at once, wherever I went, there was the same vague uneasiness, queer looks; I knew then that something was wrong, but it was not until I was leaving the Fancourts and about to enter the carriage that Lady Lavinia, twitching her nostrils at me and speaking loud enough for all to hear,—we had been having tea on the lawn,—said 'my dear soul',—meaning me, Sam,—'we are all hoping you can prevail upon the Earl',—meaning you, Sam,—'not to be led astray by his new republican friends and associates.' So then, of course, not having the least idea what on earth she meant, I laughed gaily and said I would and that you should not, and drove home wondering—as I am at this moment, and therefore, sir, demand to know if you can inform me what it is all about and what in the world Lady Lavinia meant?" For answer Sam took up the newspaper, smoothed it out and, pointing to certain close-printed columns, said:

"There!"

So Andromeda took the paper, but had not read very far before she, in her turn, began to frown, and presently, letting fall the paper, looked at her husband with troubled eyes, saying:

"Oh, Sam, my dear, surely you never said such dreadful things?"

"Ay, but I did!" he nodded. "I said more, whole sentences that have been carefully left out, omissions which make what you read there very different to my actual speech. And that's the devilry of it, d'ye see; by omitting words and sentences here and there, the whole sense is altered and distorted to give an absolutely false meaning."

"Even so," sighed she, her look still troubled, "it is quite evident you were speaking to defend that—that dreadful Mr. Cobbett, such violent person, so rough——"

"Ay, he's rough, sweetheart, but he's right."

"Oh, surely not, Sam? And anyhow, this explains our neighbours' odd behaviour. Yes, I'm afraid this speech is going to make you very unpopular, my dear."

"Well," growled Sam, "who cares!"

"I do!" she retorted. "I care very much indeed! I desire my husband to be esteemed for the truly noble man he is."

"So long as you can believe me so, Andromeda, that's all I care about."

"But you should care, you must for my sake, and most especially for our child's sake. . . . Now I understand what that horrid old Mrs. Dene meant, though I hardly troubled to listen at the time because she is such a hateful rattle and gossip, and of course I don't and won't believe it now!"

"What did she say, sweetheart?"

"Well,—that she had heard you described as a Jacobin revolutionary and a traitor to your order."

"Ay, faith," growled Sam grimly, "so I shall and must be so long as my order, we the ruling class, persist in the infliction of such cruel, such iniquitous laws——"

"Oh, but, Sam, surely our laws, the laws of our England, are the grandest and most just in all the world!"

"Ay, true enough—for those of our order, we the landed gentry that ha' never lacked for bodily ease and comfort or known what hunger is! But, dear soul, d'ye know I can send a man to transportation for poaching a rabbit."

"But you never would, Sam."

"Not likely! But d'ye know that by our law a man may be hanged for picking a pocket, firing a rick, or cutting down an apple tree?"

"Ah, surely not, Sam?"

"Andromeda, it is most surely so! Yes, our laws are reducing the poorer people to slavery while we gentlefolk are buying and selling seats in Parliament and Government offices. While some folk are too miserable poor, others are too absurdly rich. Take me, for instance,—beside Wrybourne Feveril and the mansion in town, I have five or six other great houses here and there in England, houses I've never troubled to look at and probably never shall, while some poor fellows haven't a roof to shelter them. There's something wrong somewhere."

"And do you propose to set it right, Sam?"

"Oh no, this can be done only by the people themselves. . . . But as regards our neighbours here in Sussex, d'ye know these gentry compel men to labour for sevenpence a day?"

"But not our Wrybourne folk, Sam, not your tenantry!"

"Of course not. I incline so much t'other way that already some of our county folk have begun to murmur against me, and now this misrepresented, devilish misquoted speech o' mine, as you see, will—but enough o' this! Instead, let me tell you that I am going to rebuild half the cottages at Wrexford, buy the old mill, do away with that murderous pool and lay it out as a fair-ground for thatching, ploughing and scything matches, with such sports as tug-o'-war, village against village, quoits, sparring, wrestling and single-stick. And what d'you say to that, madam mine?"

"That it is splendidly Sam-like, my lord, and will mean health, happiness and——" At this juncture a sweet-toned clock chimed the hour, whereat, up sprang my lady to order her frills and furbelows, smooth and pat her raven hair, saying as she did so:

"I go now to feed and sustain your lordship's flourishing heir!"

"What—again, madam? It's becoming a habit, morning, noon and night! He would seem to be a remarkably hungry brat."

"Oh, he is—thank heaven! So loose me, Sam, I mustn't keep his bratship waiting."

"Which makes me wonder again, sweetheart. Why not a wet nurse and what not?"

"Certainly—not, Sam! No nurses and what nots,—whatever they may be,—for our baby."

"But other wives do, it seems, and——"

"Other wives may, but not your wife, Sam. Our little man shall be most completely ours! Yes, all that he is and will be,—must and shall be by us alone. Oh, Sam, my dear, silly man, don't you know what rapture it is for me that this baby who is of us both now draws his life and strength from me that love has made part of you, you of me and so all of us one—if you understand what I mean—which of course you cannot, because I hardly do myself and mustn't stop to explain because our lovely brat will be howling for me, bless him!"

"Then I hope he'll prove worthy such mother!"

"Of course he will if anything like his sire—and there is a very Sam-y look about his sweet little nose and mouth—occasionally! Now I must fly!" And away sped this glad young wife and mother; leaving her spouse to gaze after her precisely as a (young) husband should. Presently he rose and, having traversed divers lofty rooms, echoing hall with its array of aged banners, burnished weapons and effigies in gleaming armour, followed a deep-carpeted corridor and tapped upon a certain door which he opened, saying cheerily:

"It's only Sam, Grannyanne."

Mistress Anne Leet, a somewhat aged, very formidable-seeming person clad austerely in laced cap and voluminous bombazine skirts that rustled with her every stately movement, this my lord's Lady Housekeeper who ruled his many servants with firm suasion, rose from her high-backed chair, rustling of course, but with such smile as quite transfigured her; the great, shaggy dog at her feet, rose also to wag stumpy tail in greeting quite as affectionate, while the small person, busied with slate and pencil, dropping both, leapt at Sam with squeal of delight.

"Jane!" quoth her great-grandmother with commanding gesture. "Manners, child!"

"Yes, Granny, I know," sighed Jane, "only my Uncle Sam doesn't mind any manners, do you, Uncle Sam dear?"

"Hoity-toity!" exclaimed Mrs. Leet. "Make your reverence to his lordship the Earl—this moment, miss."

"Very well, Granny,—only besides being a nearl you're Uncle Sam too, aren't you, Uncle Sam?"

"Yes, my Jane," he answered, heartily, "always and ever, just as surely as I'm your Granny's adopted grandson."

"Then, when you've shook Esau's paw what he's offering you so p'litely, please watch while I do you my curtsey—now, like this!" And Sam watched as, with small finger gracefully crooked beneath pointed elfin chin, Jane sank before him in demure, though rather wobbly curtsey, and gravely my lord bowed in acknowledgment; then Sam laughed, reaching out his long arms, and with another squeal she leapt—to be caught up, kissed and throned upon his broad shoulder.

"Well, I'm sure!" exclaimed Grannyanne, reseating herself with prodigious rustle. "Pray what now, Sam?"

"Now, Granny, with your kind permission, I'll order

Jane's pony and my horse and we'll ride over to visit Ned and Kate."

"Ooh—Granny!" gasped Jane, ecstatic. "Do please let us —pleeeeze!"

"Eh, miss, but you haven't finished that sum I set you— and what you have done is quite wrong, I see."

"Yes, I was 'fraid so," Jane admitted ruefully, "but after you've 'llowed me to ride with my Uncle Sam I'll be able to do it much—oh, much better, so may we go?"

"Very well,—run and put on your habit."

"Oh, you lovely Granny!" cried Jane, and away she scampered, while Mrs. Leet, busied again, in stately manner, with the knitting that never seemed to end, nodded at my lord now perched upon corner of the table, swinging spurred foot, and said with lips beautified by their rare smile: "How that child adores you! And 'tis good to win the love of a child, and especially such as our Jane."

"Ay, I know," he replied, "and, b'George, I'm proud of it."

"Because, my lord, you are still—just Sam. . . . And this is the first real talk we've had since you returned from London."

"Ay, it is. That's why I'm here, to know what you think of—that speech o' mine. You read it, I suppose?"

"Of course, every word, Sam."

"Not in the lying *Gazette*, I hope."

"No, in *The Times*."

"Good! That report was pretty accurate. Well?"

"Well, Sam, I heartily endorse the matter of your speech, but you could and should have put your case for poor Mr. Cobbett—well—more diplomatically."

"Too true!" he nodded. "For Andromeda thinks badly of it, and Standish is on his beam-ends; ay, it took poor Harry all aback; he's afraid it may damn me socially, which nowise disturbs me, but he remained in town to bear up for Vanity Fair, ply off and on, the clubs and what not—to learn how it's been received. However, if I've stirred things up somewhat, so much the better! For, d'ye see, Grannyanne, I meant every word, and stand by my speech. I'm no quibbler, no juggler o' words; I say what I mean, blunt and to the point. So if my lords and fine folk generally take it amiss and sheer off—let 'em and welcome. I'll steer a straight course, blow high or low, Grannyanne!"

"Yes, I know that," said she, clashing her knitting pins rather louder than usual, "but—they stigmatize Mr. Cobbett as a revolutionary, yes—and rebel, Sam."

"They do indeed, Anne; they even threaten to jail him because he dare speak the truth—that's why I stood up for him."

"And that's why, Sam, they may use you the same!"

"True enough, Grannyanne!"

"And you—a Scrope! My gracious!"

"What of it, my dear,—why the ladylike oath?"

"Because no Scrope before you ever stood up for anything or anyone but themselves,—except the Admiral of course! He fought the then Government in his days, when Charles was King, for his poor, brave, hard-used, ill-paid sailors, God bless his soul,—and made himself so very unpopular with certain fine gentlemen that he had to fight three duels, Sam!"

"Well, Grannyanne, I've fought only one—as yet, but, if compelled, I shall be quite happy to——" He fell silent as came a rapping of discreet knuckles upon the door.

"En-ter!" Mrs. Leet commanded, whereat the door opened to disclose the portly form of Mr. Henry James Perkins, the butler,—but such butler indeed as never was or ever could be other described than as a personage; he bowed profoundly to my lord, a degree less so to Mrs. Leet, and presented a very small, rather dingy folded paper upon a large, embossed silver tray, much as if this poor little missive had been a kingly diadem upon embroidered cushion, saying as he did so:

"Learning, my lord, that your lordship was closeted with Mrs. Leet, I none the less venture to trouble your lordship, having due regard to your lordship's own expressed command."

"Thanks, Henry," said my lord, and, taking up this paper, unfolded it and saw these words:

"Dear lord humbly praying fayvour of a word sir."

These lines seemed very painfully written in both senses, for, though each pencilled letter was carefully formed, they showed blotched and smeared here and there as if by fast-dropping tears.

"Grannyanne," said my lord, rising, "I'll send for Jane when I'm ready—and pray let Andromeda know we have ridden across to Willowmead for an hour or so," and, with smiling nod, he followed his majestical butler from the room, saying, as he closed the door:

"Henry, who gave you this?"

"A young person, my lord, of gender feminine, comely of seeming, poor of habit and at present much disguised in tears, my lord. And minding your lordship's expressed commands regarding all cases of distress, I——"

"Did quite rightly, Henry. Where is she?"

"She awaits your lordship on the lower terrace."

"Then lay me our course, show me where."

Their course brought them (in time) to the great front door with its noble flights of marble steps leading down to wide terrace whence yet other steps descended (in more time) to a broad tree-shaded drive with park-land beyond, sweeping away to distant woods; and here they (at last) beheld the slender, very forlorn and desolate figure of this "feminine disguised in tears." Indeed she wept so bitterly, and was so utterly lost in grief, that she started violently and cowered as Mr. Perkins addressed her, speaking of course as only a personage possibly could:

"Woman, you behold my lord the Earl!"

"My lass," said the Earl, speaking as only Sam might, "what's your trouble?"

"Oh, gentleman . . . sir . . . lord," she gasped, by reason of her sobs, "I be come for . . . to plead mercy on my poor Si . . . my Simon, sir . . . we was married quite lawful just afore the press-gang dragged him from me and took him . . . to sea for to fight they French and got hurted. . . ."

Now here my lord said "Ah?", no more, and yet his timid suppliant opened her tear-swollen eyes wider and seemed to find more courage and something of hope, for, stifling her sobs, she continued:

"When he come back t'me with his prize-money we thought we was rich—oh, but . . . on our road we was set upon and robbed and Si got hurted again. . . . We've been sleeping out . . . woods and barns . . . hayricks . . . hedges . . . any shelter we could find . . . but no money, no food, so Si did snare rabbits for to keep us alive . . . but today we gets took b'your keepers and a . . . a gentleman as do say my dear husband must be . . . must be . . . persecuted!"

"She means 'pros' my lord, prosecuted!"

"She does, Henry, though it's much the same."

"And . . . oh, sir . . . m'lord, the gentleman do say as Si must be sent overseas . . . a convict . . . transplanted."

" 'Ported,' woman! 'Trans-ported!' "

"Easy, Henry; bring to; you overawe her. My lass, tell me your name."

"I be Mrs. Gray, sir—Ruth Gray."

"God love you, child," said my lord. " 'Ruth' was my—— Where is your Simon?"

"They've got him in stableyard, sir, along of the gentleman —ah—no, here he do come now!" she gasped, cowering again as, towards them up the long drive, cantered a plumpish, rubi-cund gentleman astride a plumply glossy steed, a gentleman obtrusively jovial from jaunty hat worn at rakish angle to the toes of his gleaming boots,—in voice, face, teeth, whiskers and buttons all was beaming, twinkling joviality, except for his eyes, which, being suspiciously watchful and keen, gave the lie to all,—or so thought Sam.

He saluted with hat jovially a-flourish as he cried in accents quite as jovial:

"Aha, Wrybourne, how de do? Been travelling, wife and I, year and more; should ha' dropped in on ya before this otherwise. Hope ya've not forgotten me, eh? Aha, those wild nights in Town when we were carefree bachelors, eh? Oho, those were the days—and nights! The Town, the 'Ton!' Dogs, sad dogs all of us, free to rove and flit before matrimony clipped our pinions. Aha, ya've not forgotten Jonas Fan-shawe, I hope?" My lord's bow was ceremonious as he re-plied:

"I remember you very well, Sir Jonas."

"Capital!" laughed Sir Jonas. "And after a year and more! Aha,—and today, my dear neighbour, I've been happily able to render ya neighbourly service in the matter of a rascally poacher. I chanced to see this rogue caught in the act b'your keepers, but—damme, Wrybourne, I almost believe they'd ha' let the fellow off with a warning but for me! Something wrong there, neighbour, devilish amiss! However, I insisted, and they've got him now fast enough in your stable-yard."

"That, Sir Jonas," said my lord with another stately bow, "is why I am on my way there."

"Good!" nodded Sir Jonas, reining his horse about. "Then I'll with ya."

"By all means!" said my lord, and set off with that long, rolling stride which soon brought him to an imposing range of buildings which might have stabled a squadron of cavalry and where everything from lofty clock-tower to smooth flag-stones showed the very perfection of order. And here, besides staring grooms, stood four stalwart, rather sheepish-looking gamekeepers with their solitary captive,—a rough-clad, power-fully-built young fellow, his arms roped behind him, just at present drooping feebly and in such utter dejection that he seemed the veriest figure of shame and hopelessness; but, hearing my lord's approach and all about him suddenly hushed, he straightened up and squared his shoulders, thus showing a comely young face though woefully haggard and pale.

"So!" exclaimed my lord, halting with a ring of spurred heels. At this word, so harshly uttered, the prisoner set himself the more resolutely to endure what he must; his girl-wife clasped her hands in mute appeal and, striving to speak, was dumb. Sir Jonas nodded and beamed more jovially than ever, only the four gamekeepers, gazing on their lord, stirred uneasily as in growing apprehension.

"So," repeated the Earl, "you have been a sailorman, Simon Gray, and fought the mounseers!"

"Yes, sir."

"You have shed your blood for this Old England of ours, have you, Simon?"

"Yes, sir."

"Then," said my lord in hushed though quite terrible voice as he turned upon his four dismayed gamekeepers, "what the devil d'ye mean by it? Why is an English sailorman used like a villain, seized up in a rope—and on my land—well? Daniel Ward, you are head keeper, answer me!"

"Why . . . my lord," replied Daniel unhappily, "none of we knowed as 'ow 'e were a seaman, though we did know 'e were a poacher, seein' as us ketches him in the hact—likewise this yer gentleman, Sir Jonas Fanshawe, your lordship's nighest neighbour, says as 'ow he must be took and made a hexample of and be brought to y'lordship,—and so we done, m'lord."

"True enough, Wrybourne!" said Sir Jonas, genial as ever. "I certainly did. And permit me to say, since he is proven guilty, this rascal should be——"

"No, Sir Jonas, this seaman shall!"

"Eh, shall, Wrybourne? Shall—what?"

"Show as every British sailorman should!" As he spoke, my lord took out his penknife, opened it, and therewith cut loose the prisoner, who, freed thus unexpectedly of his bonds, stood like one dazed and bereft of speech; even Sir Jonas was dumb, and his joviality seemed to suffer momentary eclipse, then he contrived to laugh, saying genially:

"Aha,—to be sure there is a rumour, probably false, that you were once a seaman of—eh—somewhat humble rank, though——"

"A.B.," said my lord, slipping knife back into pocket. "Rumour for once is perfectly true; I was a 'foremast tarry Jack, much the same as Simon Gray here."

"Oh? . . . Oh—ah? Indeed!" stammered Sir Jonas, joviality once more on the wane. "Ha—well, as regards this same rasc—hum—poaching mariner. You'll prosecute him, of course, and——"

"No, Sir Jonas."

"Eh—not? D'ya mean you'll loose him to prey upon ya neighbours' preserves,—most probably mine, eh?"

"No, sir."

"Then what shall ya do with the—him?"

"Feed him."

"Fee——" Sir Jonas rocked in his saddle, then, recovering poise but not joviality, demanded: "D'ya mean . . . actually . . . feed him?"

"Actually that, Sir Jonas. A good, hearty meal for him and his valiant little wife."

"Ho! Ha!" exclaimed Sir Jonas, explosively. "Well, now damn me if ever——"

"Oh, never, Sir Jonas, without just cause!" said my lord, shaking his head but with flash of white teeth so that Sir Jonas, in the act of frowning, chuckled instead and enquired:

"And after you've stuffed 'em, how then?"

"I shall offer them work on the estate."

"Work, hey? A thieving, poaching——"

"Sailorman, Sir Jonas."

"Well, well, here's devilish odd business! But then to be sure, begad, you're the most deucedly odd and original fellow, Wrybourne, as f'rinstance—that duel you fought with Chalmers! Ha, that was so devilish odd that he's been odd-handed ever since—eh? And, by the way, I won a cool thousand over that same odd business,—I was one o' the knowing ones that time, aha! As to your—eh—poaching seaman—well, time will show. Meanwhile, I'll bid ya a very good day, Wrybourne, with my humble duty to ya lady, the Countess."

And when Sir Jonas's plump steed had cantered away with him:

"Henry," said my lord, "you will take charge of Gray and his wife,—a good, square meal, you understand."

"Oh, perfectly, my lord!" bowed the personage. "And how thereafter, my lord, do I suffer their departure?"

"You do not, Henry, until I have talked with them. . . . And inform Miss Jane that I am awaiting her. You may go."

"At once, my lord!" quoth the personage, bowing deeply; then, turning to husband and wife who now stood side by side, he beckoned them with stately gesture, saying in commanding tones:

"Foll-ow me!" Mutely they obeyed,—then back sped this girl-wife to their deliverer; she stooped swiftly and for a

B

moment upon that right hand of his he felt the shy pressure of her lips, then she was away, leaving this hand wet with the tears of an unspeakable gratitude.

IV

It was as they walked their animals up a steep grassy ascent that Jane, a demurely quaint little figure in plumed cap and flowing habit, looked up at the Earl to shake her small head much as her stately "Granny" might have done and said:

"Uncle Sam, last time what I took my Auntie Ciss'ly for a walk to visit Mrs. Jennings she looked like she'd been crying."

"Who, Mrs. Jennings?"

"No, Auntie Ciss'ly."

"Did she, my dear?"

"Yes, an' then we met a gentleman what I don't like, no—not a bit."

"Why not, my Jane?"

"'Cause he des-gusted me an' frightened me too!"

"Eh,—what did he do?"

"Well, when he took my auntie's hand she couldn't get it away from him, he kept on kissing it so—like he was biting it."

"Ah, did he so, my dear?"

"Yes, he did, till I thought he was eating it."

"Who was he, what was this—gentleman like?"

"Oh, very nice-looking, Uncle Sam, in a lovely green coat with silvery buttons on to it and shining boots like yours, wiv spurs what jingled."

"Did you hear his name?"

"Yes, an' I forget it, and auntie asked him to leave us, only he wouldn't, so we turned an' went to her house an' he followed us all the way there, talking and talking how lovely and beautiful she was, till we came right up to the door."

"And where was Lord Ralph, her husband?"

"Oh, he'd gone to bed 'cause auntie said he wasn't feeling very well."

"Ha!" murmured Sam, scowling at his horse's ears.

"Now please why do you frown so an' say 'Ha,' Uncle Sam dear?"

"Thoughts, my Jane, only thoughts,—so away with 'em and let's smile and talk of other things,—no, first tell me what became of the gentleman."

"Oh, Auntie Ciss'ly said he must go, an' so he did at last, an' she wouldn't even say 'Goodbye' to him though he took off his nice hat to her an' bowed ever so p'litely."

"And, my dear, can't you remember his name?"

"No, Uncle Sam, I'm afraid I can't."

"Oh well, never mind. Tell me, have you seen Mrs. Jennings lately, my Jane?"

"Yes, I paid her a visit with Auntie Ciss'ly an' she played for us, Mrs. Jennings did, first on her big piano-fortey and then on the harp till she began to cry, so then auntie kissed her an' so did I till she was comfortable an' smiled again, though her smiles are always rather weepy ones, Uncle Sam, don't you think?"

"Yes, Jane, I'm afraid they are."

"Yes," nodded Jane, "because she had a lovely clever son what could make beautiful music an' got drownded quite dead in that nasty old mill-pool what tried to drown me too when I was a child, only Auntie Meda what you married came down to me in the water so dark as night and brought me up into the light."

"My word, Jane, you're making rhymes."

"Yes, I know, I'm making a pome all about it and my Granny has 'llowed me to write it in pen an' ink, 'stead of my slate, and says I ought to 'cite it to you, so I will now if you like."

"I should indeed, so let's hear it, my Jane."

"Very well, only I haven't quite finished it yet, 'cause I can't find any word what'll rhyme with 'baby.' "

"Eh—'baby?' " repeated Sam, turning to glance down very lovingly at the demure, little speaker. "Ay, to be sure, 'baby' is a very difficult word, sweetheart. However, please let me hear and I shall do it better if we stop, so let's pull up." Upon this green and sunny up-land they paused and, thus seated gracefully upon her glossy-coated dapple-grey pony, Jane recited in sweet, clear voice, this, her first attempt at verse:

> " 'When that old mill-pool tried to drownd me
>   My fairy aunt came down and found me
>   My lovely aunt what's An-dro-me-da
>   So now I always love an' need her.
>   But now she's married Uncle Sam
>   Sometimes I'm lonely, yes I am
>   'Cause now she's been an' got a baby
>   Instead of me——'

"An' that," sighed Jane, rather mournfully, "that's all I can do 'cause of the baby."

"Ah . . . yes," Sam replied, averting his head lest his quite uncontrollable smile should wound this youthful poetess, "I see——"

"Oh—Uncle Sam," she wailed, "I b'lieve you're laughing at me!"

With thick brows close-knit, big jaw squared and lips tight-drawn, Sam turned to face her scrutiny.

"Laughing?" he demanded. "Am I?"

"Well—no," she admitted, gazing up at him searchingly with her clear eyes wide. "But why are you looking at me so frighflee fierce?"

"No, no," said he, laughing now as he reached down to cuddle her.

"Then, please, do you like my pome—lots an' lots, do you?"

"Yes," he answered, as they rode on again, "I like it so very, very much that I'm hoping, yes, my Jane, I want you to recite it for me to the dear folks at Willowmead."

"Oh, but I made it for only you and Auntie Meda—so how can I?"

"Ah well, sweetheart, here we are at top of the hill at last! Look, away down there is Willowmead Farm, behind those trees!"

"Ooh yes! An' there in the lane is Granny's old cottage where we lived when I was a child 'til you took us to be with you at the Great House."

"And I hope that you're happy there, my Jane?"

"Yes, very, Uncle Sam, an' so's my Granny too, 'cause she never says she's a lone widow's body any more, 'cause she's too busy with all the servants an' me."

Being come within hailing distance of this cosy farmstead, Sam rose in his stirrups, hand to mouth, and saluted the house (as usual) with his seamanly roar:

"Willowmead ahoy! Oho, Ned,—coming aboard, stand by!"

And from spicy rick-yard came an answering bellow:

"Heave ahead, shipmate! Back y'r tops'ls, stand in and let go!" Even as these commands were issued, Sam and his small companion clattered into the sunny farmyard there to be greeted by Captain Edward Harlow, this erstwhile redoubtable seaman now turned farmer, and his handsome Kate who came hurrying to welcome them right joyfully and presently lead Jane into the house, leaving these two old shipmates together. And each today, especially, was the other's opposite, —my lord an imposing figure in his modish riding-coat with its crested, gold buttons, his skin-tight buckskins and gleaming boots,—the Captain, bare-armed, gaitered, rough-shod, yet apparently as happily suited here among his fragrant ricks and clucking hens as on the shot-riven deck of the *Fortune* privateer whose daring exploits under his able command and dashing leadership had brought fame and fortune indeed to all on board.

And Sam, now thinking of those desperate ventures, contrasting the smoke and uproar of close action with the peace and sweet, homely sounds of this sunny farmyard, enquired:

"Ned, are you as perfectly content as you look?" And glancing up and around him and lastly at the homestead itself, Captain Ned answered heartily:

"Yes! Yes, I am indeed, Sam. Are you?"

"Ay, that I am!" replied Sam, as heartily. "No man could possibly be any happier—though, d'ye see, there's so little ever happens to go amiss at Wrybourne; all things are so continually right, and as they should be, that sometimes I almost wish they weren't. Andromeda says we are too happy, and, b'George, she's perfectly right, as usual!"

"Sam, can anyone ever be too happy?"

"'Twould seem so, Ned."

"Shipmate," retorted the Captain, "old shipmate and right noble lord, what you need is—work!"

"But, damme, Ned, I'm never idle, or very seldom. I'm for ever planning and scheming how to better my estates and folk, if not here at Wrybourne, then t'other properties, d'ye see, and what with bailiffs, agents, surveyors and what not I'm pretty well occupied."

"Ay, perched upon your stern, shipmate, giving your orders, throned in cushioned chair,—what I mean is manual labour."

"That's an idea!" Sam agreed. "I might have another go with the scythe. . . ."

"Tell me," said the Captain, as they strolled arm in arm towards the shady orchard, "have you completed the purchase of Wrexford Mill?"

"Not yet, but there's no particular hurry. Why do you ask?"

"Because, from what I hear, Sam, you've every cause for hurry."

"Oh?" he murmured. "Ah! Why?"

"For the good reason, shipmate, that there is 'another Richmond in the field.' "

"Eh? You mean another purchaser? Who else could possibly want such dam' place—who?"

"I have no idea, but, according to old Toop, there's a stranger after it, some 'fine London gentleman,' according to him. It seems that old Gaffer, musing over his customary pint outside the 'Wrybourne Arms,' saw and heard your cousin, Lord Ralph, with this stranger, agree to sell——"

"Eh—Ralph did? But, damn the fellow, he knows I want it and why!"

"But old Toop says Lord Ralph was pretty far shot, half seas over, or, as Gaffer put it—'right fuddly-muddlesome 'e were.' "

"Ay, he would be,—poor, miserable devil!"

"Sam, wherefore the sympathy?"

"Because he's a Scrope, d'ye see, and the curse is on him."

"Curse be damned, Sam! I don't believe in such fool ideas, nor do you really."

"I'm none too sure o' that, Ned, for what's bred in the bone, d'ye see, comes out in the flesh——"

"And," quoth the Captain grimly, "should be fought down by the spirit."

"True enough, Ned, except the spirit be too weak to struggle or predisposed to evil. Ralph can never save himself from this—this curse of Scrope; 'twill all depend on that right splendid wife o' his—Cecily. A grand, strong soul, Ned! 'Twill be a fight to the death 'twixt the angel in her and the Scrope-devil in him."

"But the hell of a life for any woman, Sam!"

"Too true, Ned! But—what a crowning glory if she win— as I believe she may! For, d'ye see, there's good in the fellow; 'tis devilish hard to find, but there it certainly is."

"Ye-e-s," replied the Captain, dubiously, "I must confess I've found him a likely-seeming fellow, on the few occasions we've met."

"Likely, ay!" nodded Sam, with a sigh. "Cecily liked him well enough to marry him, God love her! The question is— will it be well for her in the end? She'll either die of him or— become the angel of his deliverance,—one or t'other, Ned. And this troubles me because, but for me, she could never have wed him, con-found him!"

By this time they had reached the orchard where leaves rustled, birds piped and butterflies hovered. Here, seated together on that rustic bench fashioned some years ago by Sam's capable hands, they filled and lighted their pipes to puff awhile in companionly silence like the old and tried friends they were; at last Sam enquired:

"Ned, how's your baby?"

And, emitting gush of smoke, Ned answered, eyes aglow:

"Grand, Sam, grand! How's yours?"

"Prime, Ned, prime!" Then, after a musing puff or so, "Such arms and legs to him, messmate! B'George and James, he's all a baby ever was or possibly could be,—perfect from trucks to keelson!"

"So is mine, Sam! He's everything he should be—alow and aloft!" Here ensued more puffing until, suddenly removing his pipe, Sam exclaimed:

"B'gad, I was forgetting to tell you,—my little fellow now tips the beam at twelve pounds,—d'ye hear? Twelve pounds and one ounce!"

"Aha!" cried the Captain. "Then mine's got yours by two!"

"Eh? Damme! Two what?"

"Ounces, Sam!"

"Ha—well, time'll show, Ned. However, they're as grand a brace of babies as ever howled, bless 'em!"

"Amen!" quoth the Captain, fervently. After this was another smokily thoughtful silence, broken at last by the Captain, who enquired:

"Sam, what have you been up to in London? What's all this I hear of you running foul of the House of Lords and upsetting the dignity of your fellow peers?"

"Just what did you hear and where, Ned?"

"Everywhere, but, to be precise, at Lewes market yesterday. It seemed the chief topic of conversation."

"What was said?"

"Well, folks were talking—against you, Sam."

"Oh?" he murmured. "Ah? Called me a republican and revolutionary perhaps?"

"They did, shipmate, and—more besides."

"Ha, they named me a rebel and traitor, maybe?"

"Which I made bold to deny, Sam, and pretty forcibly, you may be sure."

"These accusers would be some of the gentry, eh, Ned, and well-to-do farmers?"

"Precisely, old fellow."

"What surprises me," said Sam, running fingers through his short-cut hair, "is how rapidly this business has got around, it's as-tounding! Such dam' fuss and most of it false!"

"Yes," nodded the Captain, frowning rather anxiously, "it might suggest you had enemies at work."

"Likely enough, Ned. But I'm wondering who and—why?"

"Have you no idea, shipmate?"

"Why, d'ye see, old fellow, I ran athwart so many folk of all sorts in London and may have given offence all unknowing."

"But your duel, Sam, the fellow you out-fought, what was his name?"

"Chalmers," replied Sam, puffing thoughtfully at his pipe.

"Ah, yes, of course," sighed the Captain, "and a notorious killer! Well, what of him, shipmate? He is not likely to forgive your ruining him socially and as a duellist, not to mention hacking off that right hand of his! You were always the devil with a cutlass, Sam! What of this Chalmers?"

"He's not exactly a forgiving sort of customer, Ned—no! A vain, arrogant fellow who made terror his glory—he'll never forgive me, it stands to reason, d'ye see."

"But where is he, Sam; what became of him?"

"He vanished—Lord knows where."

"However, I'll lay any odds he's after you, Sam,—a hidden enemy biding his time."

"Ay, maybe—though it seems that speech o' mine has stirred things up in Town,—Vanity Fair and what not, quite surprisingly."

"But, Sam, why in heaven's name make such a speech, vilifying the Government, our laws, politics, institutions and Lord knows what?"

"You read it in the *Gazette*, I suppose?"

"I did—and was taken all aback, Sam."

"And no wonder! For d'ye see, my actual words were nothing like so brutally radical. To be sure I did attack the Government and the injustice of things generally, and demanded a full reform, especially of our penal laws,— eh, you don't agree?"

"Certainly—not, Sam. I stand by and for the laws of England as they are!"

"But I stood up for them as they should and ought to be, Ned."

"How would you have them, shipmate?"

"No privileges for wealth, Ned. Fairer treatment of the under dog. No rich fool should buy himself into Parliament. No poor wretch should ever starve, or be prisoned for debt, or hanged for theft. Reform is England's bitterest need, and reform I stand for. And what d'ye say to that, old messmate?"

The Captain puffed hard at his pipe, shook his always trim and comely head, sighed and answered:

"Sam, when you were a sailorman you loved a fight with fist or steel, and now that you are an aristocrat and one of our richest noblemen, it seems you have an equal passion for factious strife and trouble——"

"Not so, Ned, lord—no! When I had to fight as seaman, I made joy of it for fear I might do t'otherwise. And now as an earl with so many dam' responsibilities I take 'em all seriously and try to be a goodish sort of earl."

"That I believe, Sam, and so you are, but——"

"Ay, 'but' it is, Ned! For d'ye see, my idea of how a good earl should act seems quite the reverse of how most other earls and noble what nots actually do act and think, and that's the devil of it! Now the question is, how soon shall I bear away for London to face 'em all or leave 'em to it—whether or no?"

" 'No' is my advice, Sam. Steer full and by, shipmate, and keep trouble well in your lee—far astern of you—so long as may be."

"To be sure," replied Sam, musingly, "this would be the easy course, Ned. But, d'ye see, here in my own place, among my own good folk, life, as I said afore, is almost too easy."

"Then," retorted the Captain, "let's hope you don't make it too hard—for all our sakes and especially—your lady's."

"Ay," nodded Sam, "there's always Andromeda to be considered."

"Aha!" exclaimed the Captain, tapping out his pipe. "And yonder my Kate is hailing us,—tea, shipmate, tea!"

"With a will!" quoth Sam, rising.

CHAPTER II

WHICH TELLS OF A WARNING

THREE days have elapsed, and there is a cloud of dust upon the London road sweeping rapidly south; and in this rolling cloud, his habitual modish languor quite forgotten, rides Mr. Harry Standish, private secretary (and much beside) to my lord the Earl of Wrybourne Feveril.

The road becoming steep, Mr. Standish, like the horse-master and lover that he is, eases his willing animal to a gentler pace, and thus it is at leisured amble that he reaches the hill-top and here, where the ways divide, beholds another horseman gazing up pensively at a weather-beaten fingerpost; at the sound of his approach this horseman turns, stares, smiles and salutes him with an airy flourish, saying as he does so:

"Ah, Standish, well met! I rejoice to see you! You remember me, I'm sure—and behold me, my dear fellow, most humbly at your service."

The Viscount is cool, immaculate as to person and perfectly assured,—Mr. Standish, on the contrary, is hot, dusty and somewhat dishevelled with hard riding, which may possibly account for his entire lack of cordiality as he responds:

"Viscount Twily . . . is it?"

"Aha," rejoins that gentleman with smiling bow, "I rejoice that you should remember me, sir, considering I have not experienced the joy of your company since the Chalmers and Wrybourne affair, that quite preposterous business with—cutlasses! Perfectly absurd, you'll agree, I'm sure!"

"Ah, no!" murmurs Mr. Standish, becoming languid. "Don't 'gree,—can't! Your S'Robert didn't think so then, nor do I now. Oh no,—Chalmers fought to kill——"

"Oh, he did! Indeed yes!" replies the Viscount airily. "Robert assured me repeatedly he intended to lay the Earl

35

dead at his feet,—that nothing would satisfy him but his heart's blood."

"Well, well," sighed Mr. Standish, shortening his reins, "'twas dooced murd'rous 'ffair happily ended——"

"Is it?" enquires the Viscount, eyebrows raised.

"Isn't it?" demands Mr. Standish, eyebrows lowered. Thus for a space they smile and frown at one another until in widening smile is such veiled suggestion of gloating malice that the frown becomes darker as Mr. Standish at last, and as with an effort, contrives to shake languid head and murmurs:

"Venture t'quire what the devil y'mean?"

To which query the Viscount, drawling also, responds:

"My—dear—fellow, is it possible you—are not—aware?"

"Yes," sighs Mr. Standish, again preparing to ride on. "Oh yes, perfectly!"

The Viscount blinks, almost frowns, smiles instead, and enquires:

"Of what, pray?"

"That you're wastin' m'time damnably!"

The Viscount titters, nods and rejoins:

"My dear Standish, perhaps I do, yet if so—to good and friendly purpose, for I intend to—warn you!"

"Dev'lish kind 'f you! Accept gratitude and Goo'bye——"

"Though," continues the Viscount somewhat hastily and urging his horse a little nearer, "I must again express surprise at your continued ignorance of the fact that Sir Robert Chalmers has made himself your, or rather Lord Wrybourne's, neighbour!"

"Really?" murmurs Mr. Standish, drooping in his saddle with a languid grace. "And does this explain your presence— why you're so dooced far from Town?"

"Well," smiles the Viscount, "hardly. It does, and then again it does not. For—between you and me, my dear Standish, Beauty, as of course you are now perfectly aware, may be more devilish alluring here 'mid these rustical surroundings than in the fragrant glamour and artful voluptuousness of our dear, delightful Vanity Fair."

"In-deed?" murmurs Mr. Standish, slapping dust from

coatskirts with his riding whip as though half minded to use it upon the speaker.

"And this," continued the Viscount meaningly, "naturally reminds me to ask if you can tell me my most direct route to Lord Scrope's place, Wrexham Manor?"

In the act of urging his willing horse forward, Mr. Standish reins him in rather forcibly, though his voice sounds almost slumbrous as he enquires:

"So you're 'quainted with his lordship?"

"I have that honour, indeed, yes! I have also the extreme felicity of knowing his most charming lady—a mag-nificent creature! Ah, what a form! What voluptuous splendours! Venus personified! Indeed, my——" Mr. Standish's whip quivers in a grip anything but languid,—his horse rears suddenly, swerves and almost cannons into the Viscount's animal which, rearing in turn, leaps away down hill at furious gallop while Mr. Standish, having soothed his nervous steed, watches hopefully, but, seeing the Viscount contrives to remain unthrown, sighs plaintively and rides upon his way, but now at slower pace like one heavy with thought. . . .

Reaching the Great House, he summons divers grooms to take his horse and remove as much of the road from his dusty person as possible; which done, he goes in quest of the Earl and finds him in the library busied with plans for his new cottages.

"Well, Harry," said my lord, smiling a greeting, "I'm glad you're home. How are things in Town? Sit down and tell me, let's hear." Mr. Standish sank into the nearest chair, rose instantly as if it burnt him, shook his head and exclaimed:

"Ha, m'dear old lord—Sam, old f'lo', you've kicked up hell's delight in London! Fat's in the dooced fire! No end of to-do."

"Good!" nodded my lord. "I'm glad to know it."

"Eh—glad?"

"Heartily glad if I've made folks think."

"Ah, but they not only think but—talk!"

"So much the better."

"Yes, but—against you."

"Well, no matter."

"But, my lord—Sam—m'dear old Earl. I'm tryin' t' tell you . . . if you knew what they are saying——"

"I do! The word is that I'm a rebel and what not, which of course is dam' nonsense, so I repeat—no matter."

"But damme, Sam, it—it does matter most infernally—to me at least!" said Mr. Standish, who, being greatly moved, became quite articulate or nearly so: "I'm doing my best t' inform you that you have come the devil and all of a social cropper! Vanity Fair is 'bout to close its doors 'gainst you with reverberating, everlastingly dooced bang! There's even talk of—of—oh, egad—of barring you from the clubs! Your prestige is a minus quantity—popularity nowhere—gone to the dogs, damme! You're becoming the rankest of outsiders! Consequently I'm devilish low and sinkin' lower, plumbing the dooced, abysmal, awful deeps of woe and shame."

"Ha—so!" exclaimed my lord, becoming Sam at his grimmest. "Shame, d'ye say? Then say I—cast adrift and right handily. If you're wishful to be quit o' me, free o' my service and cast off from the sinking hulk, my answer is—ay ay and good luck t'you."

Mr. Standish fell back a step, and in this moment the last vestiges of his languor vanished, his shoulders squared themselves, hands clenched and eyes flashed as he answered, enunciating each word with indignant care:

"My lord, your implication is an insult, a very real affront! I hastened to you with this depressing news, spurred on by— by Friendship, to avow myself more than ever at your service. But now, my lord, since you can so readily doubt my loyalty, all I desire to say is——"

"Belay!" cried Sam, joyously; then, rising as the Earl, bowed ceremoniously, saying: "Mr. Standish, I crave your pardon. Harry, good friend, give me your hand. . . ."

Now after brief interlude, being seated again, Mr. Standish said:

"By the way, Sam, I met that Viscount f'ler Twily on the road, seemingly very full of oats, and, among other prattle and blithesome chit-chat, he took pleasure to inform me that

S'Robert Chalmers is living in our neighbourhood and hinted at the possibility of more trouble."

"Oh?" murmured Sam, pondering this. "Ah? Strangely enough Ned mentioned him the other day . . . yes . . . he seemed to think Chalmers meant some sort of mischief."

"Pre-cisely!" exclaimed Mr. Standish, with fervour. "Captain Ned's man o' ripe judgment, foresight and so forth, y'know, smart as he looks, and I b'lieve he's perfectly right."

"Did you learn Chalmers' present whereabouts, Harry?"

"No,—didn't trouble t'ask, but shall very soon find out— first thing tomorrow! And, Sam, it seems this Viscount f'ler knows your cousin Ralph and is on visiting terms!"

"Ah?" murmured Sam, again.

"Exactly! And what's more, this f'ler has met Lady Cecily —boasted of it. Slavered over her beauty! Oh, b'gad, he made the description of her charms s'dooced, dev'lish suggestive that I felt compelled to shut his mouth."

"How so, Harry?"

"Tried to give him a tumble, but—no go! His horse bolted and downhill, but—f'ler can ride, y'know. So next time must try other and more direct means."

"No!" said my lord, becoming Sam. "We want no more duelling or chance o' bloodshed! So, Harry, you'll promise on your honour, here and now, to steer clear of any such chance."

"Eh? Why then, how would you have me act—how?"

"No how at all! To put it plainly, you'll lie to with a spring on your cable and guns double-shotted and stand by for orders."

"Sam, if all that means I'm not t'act on my own judgment——"

"Ay, it does so!"

"Then, my lord, I must beg leave to inform you that I cannot, and——"

"Messmate, avast!" quoth Sam, becoming slightly grim. "Belay all that and stand by! Are ye listening?"

"Of course, my lord."

"Very good! Then here are your orders: you will ply off and on well to wind'ard, keeping a sharp lookout for the first sign of hostilities in any shape, having sighted which, you will instantly bear up, go about and——"

"Old f'lo', hold hard! You're getting too confounded nautical."

"Plainly then, Harry, should violence threaten, you will leave me to deal with it alone and in my own way. Is this understood?"

"It is, my lord, and so dooced well that I utterly and positively refuse to accept such orders."

"Well—damme!" exclaimed Sam. "This is plain insubordination!"

"It is! Ex-actly, my lord. And so it is going to be!" Saying which, Mr. Standish nodded and folded his arms with an air of the utmost determination. "And," he added, "I don't know how you can ask or expect such conduct of me."

"For two reasons, Harry. Firstly, because I alone am concerned, d'ye see,—and secondly, because of Rowena, that young wife of yours."

"But, Sam, she would be the first to bid me support you to the uttermost in any foul business that may happen, and scorn me if I shirked. But you know this."

"Ay, I do, God love her! All the same, her husband shall never risk his blood in quarrel o' mine—and that's final!"

"But Sam, old f'lo'——"

"I repeat—final, Harry! If Chalmers means to risk his other hand against me, well and good,—you, I hope, will second me. But should he try other methods as, for instance, to set this Viscount Twily and others to decry and defame me, you will let it pass,—take no action that may lead to your being drawn into a duel, d'ye see? This you must promise on your honour."

"And how if I don't?"

"Then, Harry, my dear fellow, I vow by God—we part company."

Once again Mr. Standish leapt from his chair and, striding to the window, stood there a while, frowning out upon the sunny prospect.

"Come," said my lord, at last, "give me your word, Harry,

for 'pon my life I should grieve to lose you. So now, will you promise?"

Mr. Standish turned, hesitated, then, striding forward, both hands outstretched, made answer:

"Yes, Sam, dear old lord, I'll dodge all chance of violence, speech or action, like the damnedest craven, if in return you promise to call on me the moment you find yourself outnumbered, in any sort of hole . . . back to the dooced wall, and so on,—then you'll give me the word and I'll jump to it with joy—though, damme, I should do that whether or no! However, let me hear you say so."

"I do, Harry, and I will."

"Good!" sighed Mr. Standish, sinking into his chair again. "This being happily settled, what now, Sam? Having regard to this undoubted menace, what are you going to do at present?"

And smiling into his faithful friend's anxious face, Sam answered:

"Mow."

"Eh—mow? Mow what—where—how?"

"In the usual way, Harry, with a scythe, while you look over these plans for the new cottages. You'll see I've made some alterations."

"But—a scythe?" repeated Mr. Standish. "D'you mean to say—actually—a scythe——?"

"Ay, I do," nodded Sam, rising. "Let me tell you I'm a pretty fair performer on the scythe, thanks to old Mr. Toop, and it's notable good exercise, so a-scything I will go."

CHAPTER III

DESCRIBES THE MAKING OF "A TOOL"

AND SO presently, with Jane beside him, bearing that somewhat battered yet still favourite doll Batilda, away went Sam,
hand in hand, saying as they set out across the sunny park:

"But, my dear, where's our Esau dog?"

"Oh, he's very busy," she replied, "'cause he's taking baby
and Auntie Meda for a walk."

"Oh? Ah—I see!"

"Yes, but you aren't seeing how nice I've made myself for
you, Uncle Sam."

"Because you're always so very nice, sweetheart."

"But today I've put on my very bestest bonnet for you
and——"

"Why, Jane—so you have! And very smart it looks,—my
word!"

"And look! I'm wearing the lovely necklace what my
Auntie Meda gave me for my last birfday!"

"Ay—b'George!" murmured Sam, eyeing this precious thing
somewhat askance. "Does your Grannyanne know?"

"Well—not quite. I did it while she was too busy and I
wanted to make me very nice for you to take out, Uncle Sam
dear, 'stead of my lessons what I don't like 'cause they never
seem to 'gree with me. Did you like sums and jogafree an'
histree an' pothooks an' hangers when you were a child, did
you?"

"No, Jane, I did not!"

"I'm glad! An' that's what makes me love you such lots!"

"Do you, my Jane? But then, d'ye see, we all have to do
our lessons the best we can, some time or other."

"Yes, I know, an' that's what makes the sunshine so hard
to bear when it watches me doing sums, and the wind in the
trees calling 'hush' an' whispering pomes to me like it was

doing today just before you came and took me this lovely walk."

"What sort of poems, sweetheart, tell me."

"Well, I was doing sub-straction, what I don't like, and trying to take seven from four, which you can't, and then the wind in the rose-bush outside the open window began to whisper to me."

"What did it say, Jane?"

"It whispered quite plain, like this:

'Four from seven, Jane, don't you know
Won't ever, never, ever go.
So listen to the tale I sing
'Bout fairies in a fairy ring
What you can't ever see 'cause they
Only in the moonlight play
What you can't ever see, you know,
'Cause, Jane, at night to sleep you go
And bofe your eyes so tight are shut
How can you 'spect to see——'

It didn't sing any more 'cause I s'pose that word 'shut' got in the way."

"And no wonder!" quoth Sam, stooping to kiss her. By this time they had reached the Home Farm where my lord was supplied with hone and scythe, and with this last borne safely upon his shoulder, on they went to the five-acre meadow that swept up in gentle slope to a dense and shady woodland.

Here, while Jane (and Batilda) sat to watch, Sam removed coat, waistcoat and ruffled shirt, set an edge to scythe-blade, thumbed it, nodded, and began to mow with wide, smooth sweeps of the long, keen blade.

How long he had wrought thus joying in his labour, he never knew, when—all of a sudden—he was roused and startled by a wail, a shrill scream of frantic terror from the wood. Down went scythe and thither he leapt—to behold Jane struggling feebly in the grasp of a powerful-looking man.

"Loose her!" snarled Sam. The man obeyed, dropping the necklace also that he might better defend himself against the oncoming fury. . . . Fist to fist they met, while Jane, catching up her beloved trinket, cowered away, watching with wide, horrified eyes such dreadful sight as no child should ever see— brutality out-brutalized. For this man, stung repeatedly by merciless blows, was so misguided as to try the murderous tactics of butting head, of fists that became claws to gouge, rend and tear,—feet, knees and elbows, weapons to maim and crush.

"S-s-s-o!" hissed Sam, and laughed, setting himself to out-match savagery with a brutality more experienced and far better skilled. Thus he now fought, using such ghastly methods (and quite joyously) until this child-aggressor roared in agony, whimpered with futility and whined for mercy—all quite vainly until Jane screamed again:

"Oh . . . Uncle Sam . . . don't . . . don't!"

Smitten by the note of horror in this so loved childish voice, Sam hurled his now helpless victim to earth, made to kick him, checked the impulse and panted instead:

"Crawl . . . beast! Creep . . . y'scum! Don't get afoot or . . . I'll . . . do for ye . . . !"

And when this half-murdered brute had writhed away into the undergrowth, Sam turned with arms outstretched, saying:

"Did he hurt you, my Jane?"

"No . . . no, he only frightened me, but . . . Oh, Uncle Sam, you . . . you hurted me . . . awful!"

"Hurt you, my precious? I did? How?"

" 'Cause you looked so frighflee awful . . . you hurted me inside me——"

"Oh, my dear!" he exclaimed penitently. "Come then and let me kiss you."

"Ah no—not yet! Not till I've wiped your poor face an' made it nice again. Please kneel down an' let me."

So before her upon the trampled grass he knelt obediently while little Jane, inspired by that sweet spirit of motherhood which glorifies all creatures feminine, proceeded, and very tenderly, to dab the ugly stains from his face with her small,

and somewhat grimy handkerchief, saying as she thus minis-
tered:

"The man kicked you, too!"

"No, sweetheart, he only tried. Now, have you made me
quite 'nice' again?"

"Yes!" she answered, and kissing, clung to him, saying
rather weepily, "Now will you take me safe home, Uncle Sam-
dear?"

"Ay, 'home' is the word!" said he, cheerily. "I've lost my
taste for mowing, at least for today."

"That . . . that man," said Jane with a catch in her voice,
"tried to take my necklace, but he didn't; here it is! So will
you please put it on me again, Uncle Sam."

"I can't, sweetheart; the clasp is broken, d'ye see,—but
never mind, we'll soon have it mended. Just for the present
I'll put it in my pocket for you. And now let's go home."
So when he had put the scythe out of harm's way and donned
his garments, he swung Jane up to his shoulder, and thus
together home they went.

Meanwhile, the man in question, having wormed himself
to safe distance, contrived to get afoot and, groaning with
pain, staggered on until he reached a little clearing in the
wood where stood a miserable, ill-used pony harnessed to a
rickety cart; here, stumbling to a halt, he sank upon the grass
and lay there whimpering like the beaten, pain-racked animal
he was, until, hearing a soft laugh, he glanced up, smearing
blood from his eyes the better to see. . . . Two persons were
gazing down at him, the one blond and slim, who lolled against
a tree and smiled,—the other tall, dark and masterful, who
scowled, grasping a whip in his left hand, his right hidden
in the breast of his close-fitting, silver-buttoned coat; now
instantly aware that these were gentlemen of the Quality, the
man cowered before them and groaned.

"Pah!" exclaimed the dark man, spitting disgustedly.
"Come away, Twily, the fellow's a sickening object!"

"He is indeed," murmured the Viscount. "Yes, a perfect
horror, Bob, and therefore may become useful—another tool,
eh, my Robert? Ha—you!" said he, addressing this grovel-

ling "horror" who instantly writhed and whimpered. "Tell me, Mr. Blood and Grief, do you know who gave you so much more than you expected, eh—do you know who he was?"

"Yessir, 'twere a labouring man, a reaper——"

"Oh no, my poor, bleeding fool! The man who has left his mark on you, yes, a good many in fact, the man who has turned you into a crawling misery, is the Earl of Wrybourne."

"Eh!" gasped the man, cowering again. "Were it the Earl as savaged me?"

"It was. And he savaged you with quite remarkable dexterity! You were never a beauty, of course, but now you are a crouching nightmare! And you are suffering, I see! The Earl has indeed made you a very painful mess! You are in pain,—eh?" Once again the man smeared his gory visage, writhed his agonized body and groaned.

"Quite so!" nodded the Viscount.

"Come!" growled Sir Robert, impatiently. "What the devil——"

"Patience, dear Bob, and perpend! Tell me, Mr. Bloody Bones, as the Earl has made that foul body of yours so very cursedly painful, you would probably enjoy the chance, a safe chance of course, to make him suffer more, eh?"

"Ar!" snarled the man, with look and gesture so murderous that his questioner nodded and smiled again. "Sir . . . sir," panted the man struggling up to his knees. "Gimme . . . only gimme . . . the chance!"

"You see, my dear Bob, you apprehend—a tool! Well, Mr. Gory Ghastliness, what is your name?"

"'Tis no matter, sir, but on the roads I'm called Mumping Jim."

"Aha, Jim, now I see your nose and mouth are torn, dear me,—and as I watched the Earl at work on you I thought his gouging thumbs would have burst your eyes out."

"Ar——!" cried Mumping Jim, wincing at the recollection. "That's wot I thought! That's why I give in——"

"And, given the chance, James, you would enjoy doing the same to him."

"Ar, by blood—I'd love it! Only gimme the chance—try me! Ay, I'd put 'is lights out—for good an' all, I would!"

"You hear, Robert? Tell us, Jim,—how do you live, what do you do?"

"Anythink, sir, but tinkerin' mostly."

"Ah, well, Mumping Jim, I think we might find you other and more profitable work—one of these fine days. . . . Easier work and, as I say, far better paid! Where could you be found?"

"Why, sir, at any o' the 'ouses o' call, inns and taverns, sir, on the road twixt 'ere and Guildford, that's me beat, and all the true padding-coves can get word of me or to me. And, sir, I ain't never a chap as frisks his chaffer,—mum's the word for me, sir, mum!"

"However, you'll know the Earl of Wrybourne again—if ever you should chance to see him——"

"Ar!" snarled Mumping Jim, with another wildly-threatening gesture. "Ar—I'll know 'im!"

"Yes, I'm sure you will! Meanwhile, here's a trifle to help you cherish his memory until—yes, until you are fit to earn more."

So saying, the Viscount tossed a coin at this vengeful "horror" and, nodding, sauntered away after Sir Robert who was waiting impatiently beside their tethered horses.

CHAPTER IV

WHICH IS A CHAPTER SUGGESTIVE

"WELL, DEAR fellow," said the Viscount as they walked their animals through this pleasant woodland, "yonder is a tool, very foul, of course, yet sufficiently deadly, properly used."

"Not for me!" Sir Robert retorted contemptuously. "What a fool you are, Twily,—after all these years to so misjudge me."

"Do I, Robert?"

"Hearkee and learn—if you can! My vengeance far transcends the sordid vulgarity of murder."

"That is, at least, a sounding phrase, Bob!"

"I'll thank you not to interrupt! Be silent and heed me well, for—here and now, where none can possibly overhear, I shall disclose to you—something—of what I have in mind. First, then, you will understand I purpose no bodily violence. Is this perfectly understood?"

"No! What then do you propose?"

Sir Robert drew forth his stump, glanced down at it, hid it again and answered:

"The penalty I shall exact will be more enduring, far-reaching and . . . persistent! Yes, it shall be a perpetual reckoning to be paid so long as life lasts. . . . Tell me, Viscount, what does a man hold most dear?"

"Why surely—life itself, Robert."

"Not all men, fool, and surely not—this man! The answer is: honour, reputation, wife and child,—and there shall he be assailed! His reputation is already shaken by his speech in the Lords,—well, I have written Bellenger how to use this against him in Town; soon the county hereabout shall be astir also. Then as to his wife,—you will begin at once to——"

"Eh, Robert—his wife? A glorious creature! Nothing would give me greater pleasure, but—my dear fellow—her husband!

After the exhibition of his methods with Mr. Bloody Bones I must beg leave to be excused any attempt——"

"Fool!" exclaimed Sir Robert, fiercely scornful. "She is above the attempt of any man, most especially such as you! No! If her body is his, yet her mind is her own, and always will be; so it is her mind shall be won to the absolute belief in his perfidy, and vice-versa,—they must each suspect the other."

"Per-fectly, my dear Bob! How glibly you say it! How simple and charmingly easy it all sounds!"

"Yes-s-s!" murmured Sir Robert, dwelling upon the word with a sibilant hiss. "And how easily it must and shall achieve —with proper manage! All the essentials are to hand, yes— all the factors and need but a resolute will to guide them. . . . And that will is mine!"

"As—how, Robert?"

And in the same hushed, rather dreadful voice, Sir Robert made reply:

"Ralph Scrope, becoming a confirmed sot, grieves his adoring wife more often with his ever more frequent drunkenness,—she seeks help and comfort more often of her dear friends at Wrybourne Feveril,—very well! Now, contrive that she sometime meets the Earl in some leafy remoteness; ensure his Countess shall hear whispers, vague rumours of this—better and better! Arrange that our guilty innocents meet so again and that in this charming seclusion his Countess surprises them together . . . then leave the potent leaven of doubt and suspicion to work . . . !"

After this they rode some distance in silence except for the jingle of bits, creak of saddle leather and muffled thud of hoofs, for they were now out upon the highroad; at last, and glancing very much askance at his silent companion, the Viscount enquired in husky whisper:

"And . . . his baby?"

And in the same utterly passionless murmur Sir Robert answered slowly:

"His . . . baby . . . shall be . . . the last blow,—perhaps! Yesss, the crowning glory of achievement . . . the grand finality. . . ."

By this time they had reached a place where the ways divided, and here the Viscount, drawing rein, turned to look at Sir Robert with an expression very like consternation.

"By God, Robert," said he in tone matching his look, "there's that in you . . . so unexpected . . . I—well, I'm devilish glad you are my—friend!"

"Your . . . friend?" repeated Sir Robert, slowly. "Am I?"

"Are you—not so, Robert?"

"This . . . depends!"

"On what, Robert?"

"Upon how long you prove of use to me,—faithful and zealous to serve my purposes."

"Can you possibly have the least reason to doubt this, Robert?"

And after an interval of silence Sir Robert, turning in his saddle, looked at his questioner, who met this scrutiny with his usual smile and the further enquiry:

"Well, my very dear fellow?"

Slowly Sir Robert nodded, saying in that emotionless voice of his:

"I permit Viscount Twily to find the answer of and for himself! Yes, and to further explain why the promised deeds of that Wrexford property are still not forthcoming?"

"The delay is entirely owing to fool Ralph's lady wife—this luscious though strangely resolute creature, a deliciously wilful beauty, my Robert! But today I am fairly confident we shall receive them. I am on my way to the Manor now. So here, for the nonce, we part. . . . Au revoir! And, my dear fellow, it occurs to me that our Mumping wretch, Mr. Blood and Bones, may prove a very, very useful tool—sometime or other."

Then, wheeling his mare down the adjacent side road, Viscount Twily cantered away; but presently he eased his mare to a walk and, caressing her glossy neck, spoke to her softly:

"So, my Lais, our beloved Robert ventures threats at last! Our Sir Arrogant permits us to exist—on sufferance and only so long as he will . . . ! Ah well, well—forewarned is forearmed, an adage very trite and yet how true! And now for fool Ralph —and his Cecily! His? And yet—for how long? I wonder!"

CHAPTER V

DESCRIBES ONE KIND OF POISON

CECILY, Lady Scrope, was burgling her own desk. Stealthily and with tremulous fingers she inserted key in lock; silently as any furtive, guilty wretch, she opened a certain drawer, took thence a bundle of folded papers—then, warned by some fearful sense, started and, glancing round, beheld the husband she had believed deep in drunken slumber, watching her from beyond the half-opened door.

"Thought I was asleep, eh, sweetheart?" he demanded, entering and closing the door with needless violence. "B'lieved I was drunk, but I'm not—much! Not enough to 'llow you t' cheat me——"

"Oh, Ralph," she sighed, distressfully, "how can you say or even think it of me, when you know——"

"Those are th' deeds o' the Wrexford property, ain't they?"

"Yes, Ralph, but——"

"Well, I want 'em, m'dearest."

"No!" she answered, clasping the papers instinctively to her bosom. "We mustn't . . . you cannot, shall not have them——"

"Ah! And why not, m'lady?"

"Because, as you know, we promised Sam——"

"Eh, Sam?" repeated his lordship, scornfully. "If you mean m'damned cousin, use his right name and call him Japhet."

"No, Ralph," said she, gently. "Oh no; I have always called him Sam and always shall. And I must not give you these deeds because we both promised him——"

"Ay, but you can, m'dear, and you will."

"No!" she repeated, in the same gentle way. "No, Ralph dear, I cannot and never shall——"

"Listen, Cecily! Am I your husband or not?"

"Yes, yes, of course you are."

"Then, do you belong to me or don't you?"

51

"Yes, Ralph, yes—now and ever, like I always have and always must."

"Very well then, m'dearest, by law—all of you and yours, yes, everything you are and own—is mine! So now, Sweetheart, give me those deeds of mine."

"Ah, Ralph, no!" she pleaded. "Ask me for anything else, yes—anything except these papers, for give them to you—— Oh, I can't and won't——"

"Ha, because of Japhet?"

"Yes, because of Sam."

"Then curse him——"

"No, Ralph, don't—don't, for shame! How can you after all he has done for us? But for Sam's goodness you would still be in that debtor's prison,—yes, at this very moment you would and I, with never a penny to help you, should be breaking my poor heart for you like I was till Sam made me rich——"

"Enough, enough—for God's sake!"

"Yes, for dear God's sake, Ralph, be always grateful to Sam for saving us from——"

"Oh damme, but I'm sick o' the fellow's name! So will you ha' done with it?"

"No—I will not!" she retorted, her blue eyes ablaze. "No, I won't be done along o' Sam—not never and nohow!"

"Well," he sneered, "at least mind your grammar."

"What's my grammar matter?" she demanded, her splendid form endued now with a native majesty. "'Tis your wicked ingratitude shames you and me too—when you know that everything we own, yes, and all that we are is owing to Sam. You know all this, of course you do, and you can't ha' forgot. And now Sam wants to buy old Wrexford Mill to do away with that—oh, that deadly, murderous pool as has been death to so many in its time—and so he shall! So this is why I can't and won't give you the deeds."

"Then, damme, I must take them!"

"No . . . Ralph dear, please don't try because . . . if you do . . . I'm afraid I might——" Her lips quivered and were mute.

"Well, what might you do?"

"Hurt you, Ralph."

"You?" he cried, scornfully. "Try!" And he leapt. . . .

And now in this spacious chamber yet haunted by memories of his evil sire, there befell a hateful scene to shame the day,—a struggle between calmly resolute wife and furiously determined husband; his grip was cruel, yet she endured unflinching and with no complaint until at last, finding him utterly remorseless, she uttered a broken, despairing cry and, using all her splendid strength, hurled him so violently that he reeled backward to the wall to lean there, breathless, shaken, but with the deeds in his clutch.

"Egad . . . Cecily," he panted, "you're grand . . . a right glorious . . . woman——"

"But—you," she gasped. "Oh Ralph . . . Ralph . . . what are you?" Then with such look in those great eyes of hers as he had never seen before, she turned and left him to the triumph that now shamed him almost beyond endurance. Rigid and motionless he stood gazing remorsefully upon the closed door until, becoming aware of the papers in his hand, he dashed them to the floor and set his foot upon them, and thus, stared at that closed door again like one quite horror-stricken. At last he turned and, coming to that ornate desk whereat his father had once talked so placidly concerning the necessity of murder,[1] he sank down there, miserable head between clenched fists, grieving for his wife, her broken cry, the strange look in her eyes ere the closing door shut her away from him. Small wonder now if she hated him . . . scorned him. And yet could such love as hers ever die? Could she ever come to hate him, his gentle, too-loving Cecily who was always so ready to forgive? Good God, suppose he lost her—how ever could he endure life without her—his Cecily? These and many other thoughts so tormented him that, after some while, unable to endure them any longer, he rose, minded to seek her and humbly plead forgiveness. His hand was upon the door-latch when, becoming aware of a gentle though pertinacious tapping on the window, he turned, scowling, to

[1] See *Heritage Perilous*.

see Viscount Twily smiling in at him through the open lattice
and, the casement being wide and low, in he came thereby,
saying as he did so:

"Is this permitted? However, my dear lord, here I am
and sincerely hopeful that I don't intrude."

"Eh, no,—oh no!" answered Ralph, shaking his woeful
head in such dazed, helpless manner that the Viscount's smile
widened and his voice became almost caressing as he enquired:

"My dear Scrope,—nothing wrong, I trust?"

"Wrong?" echoed Ralph. "Certainly not! Why d'you ask?"

"Simply that you appear a leetle—shall we say—agitated?
Perhaps I startled you?"

"No,—yes, you were dev'lish sudden, Viscount."

"Then behold me all humble apology. But I happened to be
in the vicinity and hoping I might be so fortunate as to find
you and your most gracious lady at home. Yes, I had hoped
for the pleasure of your lady's company if merely for the
extreme joy of kissing her hand,—but, alas, it seems I am not
to be so fortunate!"

"How d'ye mean, sir?"

"That she is at present in the enjoyment of perhaps more
agreeable company, more attractive perhaps than my poor
self."

"Viscount, what the devil d'you mean?"

"That your gracious lady is at this moment blessing a far
happier man——"

"Damme, sir, be plain! What are you tryin' to tell me?"

"Simply that Lady Scrope is riding with your noble cousin,
the Earl. And, 'pon my life, a splendid pair they make!
Indeed and indeed my Lady Scrope is a magnificent figure on
horseback—ah, happy, happy man!"

"Who is?"

"My dear Scrope, who but her thrice blessed husband, for,
as I say, your lady——"

"Is my wife, sir, so by your leave we'll change the subject."

"As you will, my dear fellow, though for my part,—but as
you will. Let us then from subject beauteous change to subject
quite the reverse,—business, Scrope, which I detest. Heigh-ho!

Well, can those be the deeds of that Wrexford property yonder on your desk, laid out for my perusal and acceptance?"

"No,—yes, yes, they are, but—on second thoughts, well—I don't think I'll part with the property."

"But—I say, my dear man, it was so agreed, and you can't go back on your word! Besides——" From the breast of his modish coat the Viscount drew a bulky wallet from which he extracted a sheaf of bank-notes which he laid before Ralph with graceful turn of wrist, saying:

"Three hundred pounds was the price agreed, my lord."

"Well, yes—but——"

"Three hundred for that dismal marsh is an excellent price, you must admit?"

"Yes,—yes it is, of course. And yet . . ." Slowly, almost unwillingly, Ralph touched these notes, took them up rather as if they might have stung him, and instinctively began to count them. Seeing which, the Viscount smiled and put away his wallet, saying, as he did so:

"And now, my lord Ralph, since I, or rather we, are denied the pleasure of your lady's company, I'll bid you 'Good day' —unless you care to ride with me so far as the Wrybourne Arms; the Burgundy, as you'll remember, is surprisingly good and the port eminently drinkable. Come, what do you say?"

"No, thanks—and yet—yes, I will," answered Ralph, and, thrusting the notes carelessly into pocket, he rang and ordered his horse. Thus in a while these ill-sorted companions mounted and rode away through the afternoon sunshine, and of course began to talk, or rather the Viscount did as thus:

"My dear lord, may I take it that you incline to share my sentiments and regard me in the light of friendship?"

And after keen side glance and momentary hesitation, Ralph answered:

"Oh yes, certainly!"

"Splendid, my dear Scrope! For between you and me and my Lais here, I find things damnably dull. Sir Robert Chalmers, as you may have noticed when I made you known, is scarcely a glad and joyous soul or cheerful company. So

much so indeed that until my return to Town I am residing at
the Wrybourne Arms. And the word 'Wrybourne' reminds me
naturally of your noble cousin—the Earl."

"What of him, Viscount?"

"Ah, no no, my dear fellow,—no! If we are to be the
friends I hope and desire, pray know me henceforth as your
friend Raymond. Agreed?"

"Yes—Raymond."

"Excellent! This emboldens me to enquire if it is the fact
that your noble cousin was once no better than a common
seaman?"

"Yes. But that's no disparagement, for he was a right good
seaman and rose to commanding rank—and besides, an English
seaman, being so, is—well—second to none."

"Nobly said, my dear Ralph, and admirably true! Yet
what stupendous change of fortune! How vastly romantic!
Just consider,—a tarry mariner with a pigtail one day, the
next—a powerful nobleman enormously wealthy and, of
course, extremely popular and—ah yes—adored by women—
the sex!"

"Oh? What women?"

"All women—or most. For rumour tells how no woman can
possibly resist him, that he has but to beckon the happy, chosen
one and—she is in his arms——"

"Eh? Cousin Japhet? Gammon! He's no lady's man, no
squire o' dames, not he!"

"Why should you so imagine?"

"Well, he don't look the part, nor act the part—no graces
of deportment or pretty tricks o' speech, nor he ain't handsome
o' face——"

"And therefore the more—dangerous!"

"How so? What the devil——"

"Precisely, dear fellow, he is, on good authority, the devil
and all of a fellow, being so infernally and supremely—male!
And, Ralph, with the sex, the fair—the frail, that is more
devilish alluring and irresistible than all your good looks and
pretty manners!"

"Ha, d'ye think so?"

"Ralph, I know it! And consequently rejoice that I am not married to a gloriously handsome wife—with my lord the Earl for neighbour!"

"What are you hinting at?"

"Nothing, dear fellow, nothing! I merely state a fact, or rather my certain belief that beauty may be cold as ice and chaste as snow and yet must melt before such masculine volcanoes as certain of our species—lucky dogs! Ah well, well, let us change the subject."

"Yes," muttered Ralph, "we'd better!"

"Then, dear fellow, this Wrybourne heritage, this vast wealth which, but for damnable trick o' fate, you would now be enjoying—eh?"

"True enough!" answered Ralph, frowning. "My father so expected and I was bred up to believe so."

"Ah, my poor, dear friend, then let me condole with you on so narrowly missing it, a mere question of inches, Ralph!"

"Eh, inches? What the devil d'ye mean?"

"Death of course, my dear fellow."

"Eh—eh—death——? Who—who has—what d'ye mean?" stammered Ralph and with such dreadful look that the Viscount, instantly suspicious, pressed him with further question —though very gently:

"What do you suspect I mean, Ralph?"

"How—damme, how should I know?" he retorted, sullenly.

"I—wonder!" murmured the Viscount, smiling. "However, to answer your question,—two or three inches either way, and Sir Robert's sword would have been through your cousin's heart instead of—merely his arm!"

"Ah, you mean that duel,—you saw it?"

"Of course! I was Sir Robert's chief second—'twas a ridiculous affair—cutlasses! Yet it was hell and fury while it lasted, I can assure you. We all thought Wrybourne was done for, the odds were all against him, but—fortune or chance decreed otherwise——"

"Yes, he cut Chalmers' hand off!"

"He did, my poor, dear fellow, and with that same blow— cut you out of your heritage! So, alas, your luck was com-

c

pletely out! Aha,—but yonder is our inn where noble cheer awaits us to warm our hearts and gladden our souls. So come, my dear fellow, let us pledge and cement our friendship in the best of all ways—come!"

And the wine was indeed so good that the Viscount sipped with a deliberate enjoyment while Ralph quaffed thirstily.

Thus the Viscount sipped and talked while Ralph, for the most part, drank and listened—to such effect that when at last these now boon companions parted, he rode homewards with his lithe, powerful body swaying in the saddle and comely head bowed as though very drowsy—but—in his consciousness the seeds of those evils that were to germinate to his own future misery and grief.

He had ridden thus some distance, plagued already by new suspicions that to his now befuddled mind became ever more vile and dreadfully real, when he was roused by a voice hailing him and, glancing up, beheld another horseman approaching.

"Eh?" he demanded, peering. "Mr. Standish—is it?"

"That same, my lord. Rode over with message from th' Countess——"

"Ha—yes! Japhet's wife. An—dromeda, to b'sure, yes. But what o' my wife—what?"

"Th' Countess sends compliments and so on, and bids m'inform you Lady Scrope will remain—sleep at Wrybourne t'night."

"Will remain, hey? Will? And whether I will or no, eh? Will remain! And sleep without any 'by y'r leave' o' my part! But then, of course, I'm only a husband . . . t'be laughed at like all the others. . . . Yes, damme, and I'll be first to laugh—ha ha! And so, very well, sir, very well, tell 'em I laughed too, with 'em and—at 'em! Good day, t'ye!"

Spurring his horse, Ralph galloped furiously away like the now haunted man he was, for beside him went those vicious demons whose names are Jealousy and Hate.

CHAPTER VI

DESCRIBES POISON OF ANOTHER SORT

"Poison?"

Having uttered this truly dreadful word in harsh whisper, Mistress Elspeth McGregor actually let fall her knitting to gaze at her informant with eyes widening in horror.

"Eh—poison?" she repeated. "Sae that was it?"

"Yes," nodded Sir Robert, "that was it,—or so I believe."

"Ye're no' juist pree-cisely sure then?"

"No, Elspeth. You see, I have not the slightest proof."

"And what," she demanded, leaning nearer and speaking in her precise English, "what first caused you to suspect such dreadful thing?"

"The fact that although my wound—this hideous stump of mine—was healed, or very nearly, I felt myself failing, becoming very sensibly weaker every day, which puzzled my doctors, damn them—and so troubled me that—well—at last I sent for you, Elspeth."

"And 'twas at death's door I found ye, Robert!"

"And 'twas back again to life you brought me, Elspeth."

"Ay, I did that—thanks to God and your own strong constitution! And yet here's all this time elapsed and not one word have you breathed to me of these ghastly suspicions until now—and why for no'?"

"Perhaps because they are indeed no more than suspicions and there may be nothing in them after all, who knows?"

"I know, Robert—ay, I ken this right weel, that you were ever a proud, dour, very quarrelsome body raising enemies against yourself, a solitary creature ganging your ain gait until today—see where it's brought ye!"

"Yes," he said, gloomily, "I am a man with no friends and a host of enemies."

"Of your own making, Robert!"

59

"Not so, Elspeth! No, damn it,—I was born without the gift of winning friendship! My genius has been the winning of enemies . . . many have wished me dead and done their best that way with steel and bullet but, thanks to myself, have always failed—so far! Lastly, there are two have, as I believe, attempted my life with poison and failed again, thanks to you."

"Who and why, Robert?"

"No matter for 'who', Elspeth, but as to 'why'—for the sufficing reason that I hold the future ruin of both—in this hand of mine!" And speaking, he closed that remaining hand to a powerful, quivering fist. Mistress Elspeth glanced at it, sniffed at it and retorted:

"Then for their sakes and your own ye'll be wise to unclose that fool-fistie and let them gang free, Rab."

"So I will, Elspeth. But not—ah no, not until they have done my will and served my turn—as they must and shall."

"And what is your will?"

"You may guess this, Elspeth—if you can."

"Of course I can, my poor Robert—fool! You will use these helpless wretches, will-they-nill-they, to harass and destroy your enemy the Earl! And why for are you his so merciless, inveterate enemy? Because in fair fight he cut off that wicked hand of yours. And why for was it wicked? Because with that hand you snatched life from other men—them to bleed and their kin to grieve,—blood o' victory and triumph for you, tears and sorrow for them——"

"Oh—damnation!" exclaimed Sir Robert, starting afoot, stung to sudden fury—and perhaps another more troublous emotion. "I never fought without proper cause! And whether or no—a gentleman must fight and—and—— Oh, the devil, you talk like—like an old doting woman."

"Ay, but a Hie'lan woman—a woman o' the McGregor, and my race is royal! Also there are times when I have 'the sight'! So now I'm warning you, man Robert,—free your wretched captives—forgo your vengeance or it shall prove your own destruction! Yes, Robert, I am telling how there are for you only two courses,—up to new effort and a better life, or—down to seek your lusted vengeance and find only your own woeful end! The choice now is yours, Robert, a new and better life and future or empty vengeance and death!"

"Then of course I choose vengeance!" he retorted. "But —not empty! Ah no, Elspeth, not empty but full—full to overflowing."

She bowed her head with hopeless gesture and clasped her bony hands as if in prayer.

"Aweel," she sighed mournfully, "ye maun dree ye' ain weird, Robbie . . . but here's mysel' shall weep o'er your grave, a lonely mourner, my dear, for there's none but mysel' wha kens the lovesome youth ye were and the grand man you might have been. . . ." Now as, blinded by tears, she groped for her fallen knitting, he stooped, gave it to her tremulous fingers and thus, seeing her tears, Sir Robert, acting on rare and sudden impulse, kissed her grey hair, her furrowed brow, saying as he did so and with strange gentleness:

"Elspeth, if anything in this world could stay me or win this miserable soul of mine to heaven, if there be such place, it is the sweet, bright, strong spirit of yours——" Then, even as her yearning arms came out to him he drew away, frowning as if ashamed, and began striding up and down the spacious chamber, his spurred heels jingling angrily. . . . And it was now that with lightsome tap the door opened and Viscount Twily entered; he glanced swiftly from scowling man to grievous woman and, smiling, bowed—but before he could speak, up rose Mistress Elspeth and, with head averted, stalked from the room.

"Well, my dear Bob," said the Viscount as the door closed, "I succeeded for you! Behold the Wrexford Deeds!" And he laid the papers upon adjacent table. Sir Robert merely glanced towards them, then looked at the Viscount who, disconcerted by this silent almost threatening scrutiny, raised his eyebrows and enquired:

"What now, Robert?"

"Sit down, Twily!" The Viscount did so with a languid grace, saying:

"The deeds, my dear fellow! I repeat, lo—the deeds duly signed and attested—to prove my undoubted zeal, yet not a word of thanks, dear Robert, not that I expect any——"

"Very well then," said Sir Robert, his keen gaze still fixed, "I will talk instead. Have I your complete attention?"

Stirred again by something in the speaker's cold and piercing regard, Viscount Twily ceasing to lounge, gradually stiffened in his chair and watching his watcher, answered between tight lips:

"I am listening."

"Very well again!" nodded Sir Robert, and, sinking back in easy chair, it was he who now lounged as he continued, gently:

"I have frequently looked close into the face of that dark angel called Death, Twily, and have often fought him off, but —never was I so near my grave as when he stole upon me in the guise of—Friendship." Sir Robert paused, watching how the Viscount's gaze, suddenly abased, stole sideways across the floor to the sunlit green of the trees beyond the open lattice and remained fixed there yearningly.

"Twily, are you listening?" And from those tight-drawn unwilling lips came the answer:

"Yes!"

"Then for the third time, very well! And now referring to my illness in London, so very deadly and mysterious, when you and—our friend—Bellenger were so assiduous in your visitations and, let us say, ministrations to a perfectly helpless invalid—Twily, are you still listening?" The Viscount's lips seemingly too stiff for any utterance, he nodded and remained chin on breast.

And now it was Sir Robert who smiled, and quite terribly, as he continued in the same impassive tone:

"For the fourth time, very well then,—this is my pronouncement . . ."

CHAPTER VII

GIVES SOME DESCRIPTION OF A BREAKFAST

MY LORD the Earl was at breakfast seated between the midnight beauty of his stately Countess and the radiant-morning loveliness of yellow-haired Cecily, Lady Scrope; but just at present his rapt gaze was fixed upon a—or rather—the—vast, pink ham throned between other notably English viands, a ham indeed whose succulent allurement no hungry man could possibly resist; therefore he rose and, coming to the well-laden sideboard, took up carving knife and fork, saying:

"Here we have ham, cold beef roast and boiled, ox-tongue and—ham!"

"I've been thinking," said Andromeda, pursuing her own ruminations as she poured fragrant coffee, "how it is all your own too kindly, foolish fault, Sam dear!"

"What is, sweetheart? Ham, Cecily?"

"That attack on our little Jane the other day, because, my lord, your lordship is still very much too much the free-and-easy sailor in some ways!"

"How so, m'dearest? Did you say 'ham', Cecily?"

"By permitting all kinds of vagrants to camp and trespass on your land, Sam."

"But then, dear lass, I have so much of it! Ham for you too?"

"Consequently, my lord, owing to my Sam's too good nature all kinds of horrid folk may rove where they will in spite of your lordship's keepers, yes, Sam, like that brute-beast who so terrified Jane! I dare not think what would have happened if you had not been there to fight him away! It really is quite wrong to be so blindly kind."

"B'George, how perfectly right you are, Andromeda, as usual!"

"Of course, Sam! Though you look and sound so extremely meek and surprisingly humble that I know you will do exactly as you will."

"Of course, Andromeda!" he answered, with his flashing grin. "For, d'ye see, my loveliness, these poor, homeless folk generally keep to the woods away from here, twenty-five odd miles and more."

"However, Sam, remembering little Jane and that brute, I feel and know you are wrong to—to harbour these outcasts. And what pray of that poacher Sir Jonas Fanshawe had caught for you?"

"A sailorman, yes—and I'll be shot if I hadn't forgot all about him and his pretty girl-wife! But how did you know, m'dearest?"

"The Fanshawes told me. They seem to think you encourage poaching and even hinted your conduct was unneighbourly and reprehensible—which I would not allow, of course!"

"Ha, they would! And how think you, Cecily?"

"Only," she replied in her slow, gentle manner, "that I don't like the Fanshawes, Sam."

"Neither do I," said Andromeda, "yet, between ourselves I'm afraid they are right as regards poachers, Sam."

"Of course they are," he nodded, "because, d'ye see, they have never known what it is to be really hungry—and I do and have. Besides, this case was exceptional, sweetheart,—my poachers were a seaman and his lass and both mighty hungry by their looks—and this reminds me!" So saying, he rang for the butler, Mr. Perkins,—which personage duly presented himself with profound obeisance thrice repeated, enquiring sonorously:

"My lord—ladies, how can I be happy to serve you?"

"Henry, stand up, old fellow, and tell me what became of the sailorman, Gray, and his young wife?"

"Ah, my lord, according to your lordship's desire I had them plenteously supplied with food and drink, after which, and so soon as my back was turned, they departed with what I can only describe, my lord, as a heinous stealth."

"And left no word?"

"None, my lord, the woman merely left a scribble, a missive fragmentary and very——"

"You mean a note, Henry. Where is it?"

"My lord, it was but a scrawl upon a small dingy scrap of paper too noxious for your lordship's acceptance."

"However, I'll have it. Where is it?"

"Alas, my lord, I threw it away among the waste paper——"

"Then go find it, Henry lad."

The personage started, blinked, bowed and departed, and no sooner had he closed himself out of the room than Andromeda laughed:

"Oh, Sam, how ridiculous,—to call our haughty Henry, our peerless Perkins, 'lad' and 'old fellow'! He almost gaped and positively jumped."

" 'Peerless Perkins!' " repeated Sam. "By James, how right you are again, for so he is—yes, almost too good to be true, too sublimely superb to be real! He's a treasure, eh, Cecily?"

"Yes," she answered, smiling rather wistfully. "Though in the old days, when I used to drive here from Uncle's farm with the milk and butter, he used to quite overawe me and made me feel so dreadfully inferior."

"Ay, I can well believe he'd do his best that way."

"But even now," sighed Cecily, "I often feel—a little afraid of trying to be a lady in my grand house—instead of just myself in a dairy. Because I'm not a real lady and I hate being an imitation. None of the grand folk visit us at the Manor now, and I'm afraid this worries my poor Ralph."

"More fool he!" growled Sam.

"But," said Andromeda, "you know you are our dear friend and always welcome. And I want you to teach me to make butter if you will, Cecily."

"Oh, I'd love to!"

"Then you shall give me my first lesson today at the home farm, if you will?"

"Yes, yes of course! Let's start after breakfast—and yet," she sighed, drooping golden head, "I ought to go back to my poor Ralph."

"No!" quoth Sam, busied at the sideboard again. "Not yet at all events, my dear. 'Twill do him a power o' good to miss and want you for a day or so. Besides, I intend to ride over for a word with him this morning, d'ye see."

"Oh!" exclaimed Cecily, rather breathlessly. "Why, Sam, please—what for?"

"Just to pass the time o' day, my dear." Now at this she glanced from Sam's unconscious back to Andromeda with expression of troublous anxiety that, returning this look, Andromeda laid finger on ruddy lips and shook her head, after which she pronounced:

"Then, Cecily, of course you will remain, my dear. After we have seen baby take his bath you shall give me my first lesson in butter-making." Here Andromeda nodded emphatically.

"Yes," replied Cecily, looking rather dazed. "Oh yes, I will."

"Talking of Ralph," said my lord, seated at the table once more, "I understand he has lately become intimate with a newcomer hereabouts, a Viscount Twily, eh, Cecily?"

"Yes," she answered, sighing deeply, "and this is what has been troubling me so,—because this gentleman is—oh—wicked!"

"Oh?" murmured Sam. "Ah? How so, m'dear?"

"In every way . . . but he's having such a bad effect on my poor Ralph . . . they are always together. I think he's trying to ruin my Ralph . . . and it was he bought Wrexford Mill like I told you, Sam . . . And then, besides——"

"Well?" enquired Sam, for she had stopped and averted her head though not before he had seen the wave of hot colour that flushed her lovely face. "What besides, my dear?"

"Me!" she answered, between set white teeth. "Yes, it's me too! He seems always on the watch for me! Whenever I go out and wherever I go—there he is—smiling and bowing at me!"

"Ah?" murmured Sam, coffee-cup arrested at lip. "Is he though?"

"Yes," she nodded, her blue eyes suddenly wide and fierce. "If I happened to be a timid person—which I'm not—he'd terrify me! This is why I carry one of Ralph's heaviest riding-whips when I ride here through the Home Wood."

"But the wood is mine," quoth Sam, between sips of coffee. "Yes, and that ride through it is a private thoroughfare."

"No, Sam dear," murmured Andromeda, "it was private, it should and would be but for your much too kindly free-and-easy ways!"

Sam emptied his cup and set it down, saying with a smile:

"I can only repeat, yet again, how perfectly right you are, sweetheart. The Home Wood shall be closed to trespassers from today. And now, by your gracious leaves, I'll go get into my boots." But as he made to rise, Andromeda stayed him with a gesture and question:

"Sam dear, pray what do you want with your cousin Ralph?"

"Oh, just to make him an offer, a—very friendly offer, d'ye see——" At this moment, with discreet tap, the personage reappeared bearing a vast silver tray whereon he tendered a small, crumpled, dingy paper, intoning, and with bow even more profound than usual:

"Having instituted a search of the utmost diligence, my lord, I am happy to gratify your lordship with—the result." Sam took up the paper, Mr. Perkins bowed himself out as, smoothing this sorry missive, Sam read aloud:

" 'Dear sir and lord, your ten guineas is our life and hope. Some day Si will come and pay back. Always we shall be grateful and ever I shall pray God bless you, sir. Ruth Gray.'

"Ha, well," exclaimed Sam, "this sounds as sincere and honest as they looked."

"And I pray God bless you also, my dearest," murmured Andromeda.

"And I also," said Cecily, "with all my heart!"

Sam blew them a kiss and fled.

Now scarcely had the door closed than she exclaimed: "Andromeda, oh my dear, what does he want with my Ralph? . . . I'm afraid!"

"So am I!" said Andromeda, setting that dimpled chin of hers. "He was looking at your poor, bruised wrists—and pretending not to!"

"Yes, yes, I know! I tried my best to hide them, but—— Oh, what's going to happen?"

"Anything, unless we act! There was a gleam in Sam's eye that means trouble!"

"Oh, my gracious! Bloodshed—a duel? What—Andromeda, what can we do?"

"Get into our habits, ride after him and—stop them,— come!" So, up the wide stair they sped together, like the adoring, and therefore anxious, young wives they were.

CHAPTER VIII

HOW SAM HAD WORD WITH HIS COUSIN RALPH

MEANWHILE Sam, very sailorly and at his grimmest, was riding hard and making heavy weather of it (despite the past, careful schooling of Mr. Standish) until, having reached the sun-dappled shadow of the Home Wood, he reined his horse to a walk, the better to listen and glance about him. Birds were in full song, filling these leafy aisles with their glad, morning anthem; a brook rippled amid the denser underbrush, but, save for these right pleasant sounds, a deep silence brooded, for the morning sun was warm and very still. Thus at a walk rode Sam, his scowling gaze questing here and there, his ears alert, but he saw and heard nothing of the prowler he had hoped to meet; so at last, coming out into the joyous sunlight, he banished his frown, urged his horse to faster gait and presently, reaching the Manor, cantered into the trim stableyard where the old head groom hastened to greet him.

"How are you, Tom?" said he, extending his hand to the old man who, having wiped his own quite needlessly on leg of his neat breeches, grasped this proffered hand, saying:

"Thankee, m'lord, I be purty spry and bobbish and mighty glad to see y'r lordship."

"Is my cousin about, Tom?"

"Ay, my lord, in stable yonder. I'll go fetch——" But at this moment Ralph came striding, a scowl on his handsome face, broad shoulders squared, menace in every line of his powerful, shapely figure, and who, quick to notice his old groom's smiling welcome, gestured him angrily aside, demanding as he did so:

"Well, my noble lord, virtuous damned cousin Japhet, what's for you? Ah, and where the devil's that wife of mine?"

"Ha!" exclaimed Sam, disgustedly. "Drunk as usual, and so early in the day!"

"Damn that for an insult! Answer my question, where's Cecily? She is my wife, you know!"

"Too true!" nodded Sam. "She is so, the poor, sweet, too-patient soul,—'tis this that grieves me."

"Eh, grieves you, does it—you!"

"Ay, it does indeed! For d'ye see, I helped her to the curse of you and that's my grief."

"Well, you can go and do your damned grieving somewhere else. Yes, you can ride back and bid her come home and instantly! Do you hear me?"

"Of course."

"Well, are you going?"

"Certainly not."

"Then, b'God, I'll fetch her myself!"

"Nor that either."

"What the devil d'you mean?"

"That I won't have you at Wrybourne, for, d'you see, I don't like your company."

"Nor I yours. So why are you here?"

"To make you an offer."

"If it's for Wrexford old Mill you're too late, I'm glad to say—I've sold it!"

"So I understand——"

"Ah yes, Cecily told you, of course."

"Ay, she did——"

"And poured out for you her tale of woe, her—her misunderstanding with me——"

"Never a word! Cecily is too grand a woman——"

"I don't need you to tell me that, curse you!"

"However," continued Sam, imperturbably, "Cecily is too nobly loyal to you, Lord help her! She did her best to seem the happy wife she is not and ought to be. Ah—but she couldn't hide those bruised and swollen wrists of hers, damn you! What a cursed Scrope you are! But, Ralph, it is because of your splendid, unhappy wife's bruised wrists that I am here, and why do you suppose?"

"I can guess!" hissed Ralph, clenching ready fists.

"Oh no!" Sam retorted, shaking his head. "I have come

to offer you enough money to drink yourself dead and free Cecily of the grief and shame of you speedily as possible, so name the figure and——"

Uttering an inarticulate cry, Ralph fell back a step, for the moment incapable of speech, then, with face convulsed and whole body quivering, he stammered harshly:

"I . . . now, I . . . I . . . b'God, for this I'll hammer the cursed life out of you!"

"Avast!" growled Sam, in sudden, fierce mockery. "You're in no fit state! Keep sober till you're at your best."

"Now——!" gasped Ralph, tearing off his coat and flinging it away. "It shall be now, damn you!"

"Don't tempt me!" Sam retorted. "Don't! For d'ye see, I'm yearning to thrash the brutish scoundrel who could so misuse any woman—especially—Cecily, for she is and always will be very dear to me——" He avoided the furious, expected blow, laughed savagely and clenched his fists,—but as they fronted each other, old Tom stepped between them like the aged hero and fighting man he was and had been.

"Gentlemen—oh, gentlemen!" he cried. "Not here—not on these yere cobblestones, 'twould be bloody murder! If ye must have a go, as I think you should ought for to do, come ye along o' me to the paddock and go to it like English sportsmen should! Come ye now, gen'lemen."

"A happy thought!" nodded Sam. "Lead the way, Tom my hearty."

And now, as side by side they followed the old fellow, Sam regarded his cousin's stalwart form and handsome face and said:

"'Tis great pity you're such a damned Scrope, Ralph!"

To the which Ralph made instant, passionate retort:

"So are you, curse and be damned t'you!"

"Too true, I am!" mourned Sam. "Ay, I'm a Scrope also, but, d'ye see, with this difference,—I'm doing my best to trample the curse of it down into the mud where it should be, while you are grovelling down to it."

"Here y'are, m'lords!" said old Tom, as he led them into the paddock. "Turf nice and smooth and a sight easier to fall 'pon than they murderous cobbles! Can I help y'r lordship off wi' your coat?"

"Thankee, no, Tom, I'll do as I am."

"Then, gen'lemen," quoth the old man, bright of eye as he eased a large, silver watch from his fob, "wi' your permission I'll keep time and——"

"No!" cried Ralph. "Out o' the way, Tom! We'll fight as long as we can stand,—yes, damme,—and when we can't stand we'll fight lying down! Here shall be no respite!"

"As you will!" nodded Sam, buttoning up his coat.

"Eh, but, my lord," cried old Tom, anxiously, "what o' your 'at, my lord? Won't you tek it off and——"

"No, Tom. Cousin Ralph shall do that for me—if he can." Here, settling his hat more firmly, Sam raised his fists and the cousins fronted each other, and one smiled grimly, and one as grimly scowled, yet both equally remorseless and determined. . . . Slowly they approached each other—then was a cry, the flutter of draperies, and Cecily rushed between them; forgetting her long habit, she reached protecting arms towards her Ralph, tripped, but as she fell, Sam caught her in his arms and reeled back from her husband's vengeful fist.

"Coward!" exclaimed another voice, and, lowering his clenched hands, Ralph stood mute and abashed before Andromeda's scornful regard. "My lord Scrope," said she, bitterly contemptuous, "that was a dastard stroke unworthy any man, but then, of course, I remember and know you for the base, dis-honourable——"

"No!" cried Cecily. "Ah—no!" And in that moment was beside her husband to cherish him, comfort and plead for him.

"Oh, Andromeda, my dear, my dear,—don't! Please, please believe he didn't mean to . . . he struck before he knew! So I beg you'll pray forgive him! Tell them, dear Ralph, tell them how sorry you are—do now, do!" And humble in his shame, obedient to her love, Ralph bowed his head and muttered:

"Yes. . . . I ask pardon . . . pray forgive me!"

Then, yielding to her gentle suasion, he turned and followed whither she led.

And now Andromeda surveyed her own husband, knitting her black brows at him, but with betraying dimple at the corner of her sensitive, ruddy mouth.

"Sam!" she exclaimed, chidingly. "Sam, you great, naughty child,—so this is how you 'have a word' with your hateful cousin! Unclose that brutal fist,—now give me your hand and come with me, this moment, sir!"

So, and despite bruised cheek, Sam flashed her his smile and mutely, with the utmost meekness, obeyed his dominant lady. . . . But when they had mounted their horses —these wise animals who knew each other and also the ways and manners of their riders—Andromeda enquired very tenderly:

"Did that wild, that drunken brute hurt you, my Sam?"

"Nothing to matter, sweetheart," he answered, feeling his jaw solicitously. "And he wasn't drunk."

"Marvellous!" she scoffed.

"And I'm pretty sure he struck me before he was aware."

"Why make excuses for the brute, Sam dear? Though to be sure you were cuddling his wife!"

"Ay, so I was."

"And quite—possessively, Sam!"

"Surely not, sweetheart."

"Most surely so, my Sam!"

"However, but for his dam' Scropishness I could like the fellow."

"Nonsense, Sam! I hope not indeed! Ralph is a mere beast, he always was and always will be! Even now I hate the idea of leaving poor, gentle Cecily to his tender mercies."

"My dear lass," chuckled Sam, "you may be very sure that Cecily has him as securely under her thumb as you have your meek and humble Sam."

"Have I, my dear one?" she enquired, murmurously, leaning nearer.

"Ay, most truly!" he answered, reaching to clasp her ready hand. "Indeed, and well you know it, my Andromeda!"

"Yes," she sighed, with smiling glance. "Yes, I do know this, Sam dearest, and I glory in it! Ah, but—only when you are my own, beloved, simple sailorman, for when you are the Earl,—how then?"

"Then, madam," he replied, lifting her hand to his lips, "from the sole of each pretty foot to the topmost curl of your lovely, midnight hair, you are of course all and entirely his! Yes, madam, you are my lordship's property hide and hair——"

"Fie, my lord!" she cried, laughing, but with heightened colour. "I protest—your lordship speaks like—oh—like a very common sailorman indeed!"

"No, madam, such truly vulgar fellow would have phrased it quite differently."

"Oh?" she murmured, and, after briefest of pauses, "How, pray?"

"Your common, fore-mast, tarry Jack, would say—'You're mine, dear lass, from trucks to keelson, fore and aft,—ay, from stem to stern——'"

"Sam——!" she exclaimed, glancing up at him shyly askance. "That sounds,—I don't know why,—but it does sound very coarsely suggestive!"

"However, it's perfectly true—isn't it?" he demanded, and reached out a long, wooing arm, whereat their horses, being (as hath been writ) such exceeding wise and knowing animals, drew so close to each other that this same arm became happily filled, and, nestling in its firm embrace, the Countess raised her head; the Earl bowed his; their wise horses stopped that Sam might kiss Andromeda, until . . .

"Oh, Sam," she whispered, gently freeing herself, "what—idiots we must look!"

"Ah, my Andromeda," he replied, "but how truly wise we are!"

And so they rode on together by leafy ways, through sunshine and shadow, pausing often to gaze happy-eyed upon their world and each other (of course). And thus at last, as the sunlight mellowed about them, home they came. Then while Andromeda went upstairs to be rid of her riding-habit, and visit her baby, Sam, seated in his library, indited the following innocent yet very fateful letter:

"My Dear Cecily,

Meet me in the wood this evening at six o'clock, alone
of course. Come riding and you need not bring a whip.
Yours as ever.
Sam."

This missive he despatched forthwith by one of his grooms
and thereafter sought and found Mr. Standish in that chamber
wherein this his zealous man of business and trusty friend
transacted all affairs connected with the estate.

"Well, Harry," he enquired, perching himself on corner of
the littered desk, "did you learn where Chalmers has gone
to earth?"

"Old f'lo, I did. He's bought place called Priors Dene,
ancient, smallish but bang-up, quite an establishment. Just
off London road, ten odd miles from here. And, m'dear old
lord, question is—why?"

"And to which question," murmured Sam, "as friend Shrig
would say: 'Ekker alone responds!' However, d'you know
if Viscount Twily is with him?"

"Well, it seems he was for a time, Sam, but has lately
shifted his quarters to—'The Wrybourne Arms' which, as
y'know, is scarce two miles away. So again, the question
is—why?"

"And as before, Harry, ekker alone can reply—unless he
desires to be near cousin Ralph—and his wife!"

"Aha!" exclaimed Mr. Standish, frowning. "So that's how
the wind blows, damn him!"

"Ay, so, Harry, but 'tis a wind shall take him all aback,
d'ye see?"

"But, Sam, what's he want with Ralph?"

"Wrexford Mill, Harry."

"And what with—Cecily?"

"Herself!"

"Sam, are you sure?"

"Ay, I am!"

"Then what d'you propose t'do 'bout it?"

"Bring him to and lay him aboard, Harry."

"Oh, certainly, old f'lo'. But if y'lordship could be a trifle less nautical . . ."

Instead of replying the Earl drew a smallish, leather-bound volume from his pocket, saying:

"I found this tucked away in the library,—listen, Harry!" And opening this book at the title page he read aloud therefrom:

"'A Memorial of Charteris, lord and earl of Wrybourne in Virginia. Together with divers incidents of the late war herein briefly recorded by Anthony Falconbridge. New York. Seventeen hundred and seventy-nine!'[1] Now what on earth does this mean? Can there possibly be another Wrybourne?"

"Oh yes," nodded Mr. Standish, "according to the old records there are two—one is an ancient ruin in the north of England, another in America,—but there is only one Wrybourne Feveril. It seems that in the reign of that rather unpleasant sportsman, King John—Magna Charta, mailed barons and so on, a Lady Johan Scrope being sole heiress, fled from the nunnery where her doting kinsman, a Reginald Scrope, had 'prisoned her and wed a Border lord named Anthony Charteris. Meanwhile Kinsman Reginald seized her domains, garrisoned this place which was a castle then, sheltered King John here against barons aforesaid, and so made it his own, whereupon Johan and her lord built themselves another castle in the North and called it Wrybourne. In the sixteenth century or thereabouts some of their descendants emigrated to Virginia and there built yet another Wrybourne. So say the old records, Sam. But now——"

"Lord love me!" he exclaimed. "What a hell-fire crew of piratical villains we Scropes are!"

"Were, Sam! Past tense, m'dear old lord! But for the present—now, what d'you mean t'do in regard to that villain Twily?"

"Well," replied Sam, with flash of white teeth, "if luck serves, I shall bear up, stand athwart his hawse and rake him fore and aft!" Then, closing the book, away he went, leaving Harry Standish, this faithful friend, gazing after him very wistfully.

[1] See *The Pageant of Victory*.

CHAPTER IX

IN WHICH IS BRIEF MENTION OF A WHIP

At precisely a quarter to six on this same afternoon, Cecily, a splendid figure in her close-fitting habit, mounted her favourite horse with Tom's eager assistance and, smiling down on the old fellow, said in her soft, sweet voice:

"Bless you, Tom dear! Oh, whatever should I do without you?"

"And the good Lord love and bless 'ee, m'deary leddy!" he replied, clasping his once-powerful hands as if the words had indeed been a prayer.

"Tom," said she, suddenly troubled, "you remember the letter came for me this afternoon, don't you?"

"Ay, for sure, m'leddy, Will Fisher brought it from the Great House and I give it to 'ee."

"Yes, Tom, yes and—I've lost it! I must have dropped it somewhere hereabout, for 'tis nowhere in the house. I've sought high and low, so will you have it looked for—hunted for?"

"Ay ay, m'leddy, I will so! Me and m'lads shall find it for 'ee—ef 'tis here for to be found. But wheer be Master Ralph,—his ludship, aren't he a'goin' with 'ee now?" At this, she shook her head and turned to glance sorrowfully at the house, saying in tone woeful as her look:

"No, Tom, I—I don't think he's very well."

"Then dang him!" exclaimed the old man fiercely. "Dannel him for a——"

"Hush, Tom!" she murmured. "He doesn't mean to be unkind. . . . If he should come asking for me, please tell him I have only ridden to Wrybourne and shall be back soon. . . . And do, ah, pray try to find my lost letter."

"I will, m'deary leddy, me and my lads shall seek in every corner, every nook and cranny, that us shall."

"Thank you, Tom. I know you will."

Then she cantered away, leaving old Tom the memory of a smile sadder than any tears.

By leafy bridle path and sunny upland she rode, vigorous with youth, in prime of beauty, yet with sorrow in every lovely line of her,—a forlorn and grieving goddess, or so thought the man who had waited so patiently and now watched her approach with such trembling eagerness; this man so torn by fiercely conflicting passions that he viewed her now with the gloating eyes of a merciless satyr because of her glowing beauty, and now with look of humble suppliant by reason of her sweetly simple goodness and the innate purity that cloaked her like a garment.

Thus, unconscious alike of her loveliness or the eyes that viewed it so avidly, she rode into the wood whose soft green shadow was pierced here and there by the level rays of a glowing sunset. . . . Here and now beholding at last this patient watcher, his passion-ravaged face, she checked her horse instinctively and turned to avoid him; but the Viscount's sleek mare turned also, barring her way, and the Viscount, hat in hand, was bowing to her and, for once, without a smile. Checked thus, Cecily gazed upon him with eyes so piteously mournful that he, well knowing for whom and why she grieved, hated Ralph and scorned him the more for her sake and yet was so wildly glad for his own sake that his usually glib tongue quite failed him awhile; at last:

"Oh, Cecily," he murmured, "how wonderful you are with your sad, sweet eyes . . . a gentle saint for reverent worship . . . a glorious woman to bless a lover's yearning——"

"No!" she cried, and with this word "grieving goddess" became a woman indeed whose fierce disgust roused all the worst in him, transforming humble suppliant to remorseless satyr. "No," she repeated, "I'll not hear you!"

"Ah, but you must!" he smiled. "You must and shall hear me confess my deathless love . . . my adoration . . . you are become my one desire and object in life——"

"Oh, my lord—hush! How can you, how dare you——"

"Cecily, there is nothing I will not dare for the glory of

you—you that are at once so virginally pure and lusciously provoking——"

"I'm not!" she exclaimed. "And you—you shouldn't speak me so—nor look at me so, 'tis shameful in you and dis—gusts me——"

"Because," he answered, leaning nearer, "I have the power to make you so sweetly aware of your womanhood, ah yes, so shyly conscious of beauties you cannot hide from my all-seeing, all-sensing adoration——"

"Viscount Twily, you look and talk such wickedness—I will not listen—let me pass——"

"Cecily, with that Venus shape you are so deliciously modest and, though a wife, so bewitchingly innocent that I vow on my immortal soul——" Here she made to turn her horse, but he seized the rein, saying, and with sudden passionate sincerity:

"Cecily, I'm not a religious man, but now before God I swear it is not only your beauty I adore but the sweet soul of you that would hold me aloof while your glorious body bids me——"

"Oh!" she cried, distressfully. "If I only had a whip——"

"But, my adored one, you have not——"

"Ah, but . . . I have!" panted a voice, breathless with haste. "A trifle late perhaps, still . . . here it is!" The Viscount's restraining hand was smitten from Cecily's rein to dangle helplessly; gasping with pain of this sudden blow, he reached instinctively towards the pistols always holstered at his saddle, then paused—for all about him were men in velveteen, armed with guns.

And now, having regained breath, the Earl spoke again:

"Viscount Twily, my lord, I now permit you the choice of two alternatives: either you crave this lady's pardon and thereafter give yourself in charge of my keepers, or remain silent and be horse-whipped in her presence. Choose, sir, and instantly!"

For a moment the Viscount sat dumb and motionless . . . then, since his right hand was still useless, he took off his hat gracefully with his left and, smiling into Cecily's wide eyes, bowed deeply, saying as he did so:

"Madam, most gracious, lovely lady, if these my poor lips have anyway offended, I, and from a sincere heart and soul, do most humbly crave your ladyship's pardon and forgiveness."

Then, putting on his hat slightly askew, he turned and, looking down at the Earl beneath drooping lids, nodded.

"My lord," said he, between upcurling lips, "right noble Earl, enjoy your present triumph, but—my lord, though not usually a prayerful person . . . yet now . . . I am most earnestly imploring Almighty God that there may come a time——" He nodded once more, and then his eyes, widening to sudden glare, he nodded for the third time and suffered the keepers to lead him away.

"Oh!" gasped Cecily, when both sight and sound of him were gone. "Oh, Sam," she whispered, wringing her hands, "there was . . . murder . . . in his look! Yes, a threat of . . . death . . . for you——!"

"Why then, my dear," quoth Sam, "come along home to Andromeda and tea—but, Cecily, mum's the word, sweet lass!"

CHAPTER X

DESCRIBES THE TORMENT OF DEMON JEALOUSY

LONG AND faithfully old Tom sought his lady's vanished letter and all in vain since even then his master, seated within-doors, was crouching, head in hands, scowling down at this same letter, reading it over and over again, each time contriving to find in it more cause for a jealousy long dormant—until now; for this vile Demon was awake and up at last—plaguing him with unworthy doubts—whispering obscenities—jibing, goading him until Suspicion became hateful Certainty and riotous Imagination a Torment. . . . Thus harassed, bemused and agonized, with fevered head between clenched fists, Ralph stared down at this fateful letter, quite unaware of the eyes that watched him with such keen speculation from beyond the open lattice until he started violently and glanced up, roused by Viscount Twily's pleasant voice:

"Aha, Ralph, are you alone? May I share your solitude?" And in through the casement, with nimble grace, came the Viscount, repeating, as he did so: "Alone, eh, dear fellow,—as usual!"

"Yes!" muttered Ralph. "Alone—and as usual! You're right—'as usual' my wife's out and away—and only God knows where by now——"

"Ah no, Ralph, this is a knowledge I share with the Almighty——"

"Eh? You know——?"

"Certainly, dear fellow!"

"Well . . . well, let's hear—speak, can't you?"

Glancing from the speaker's haggard face to his own bruised and swollen wrist, the Viscount smiled and answered, gently:

"Where would she be, dear friend, but safe in the care and —protection of your so estimable cousin the noble Earl—as usual."

"With Japhet—hey? With—him! And, ha yes—of course, as—usual! They met in the Home Wood, but—where have they got to—by this time? Oh, I know—and here's why! Look at this,—read it!" and, snatching up that much-read letter, he crumpled it into the Viscount's ready fingers. "Well —well, what d'you think o' that?"

The Viscount perused it deliberately, shook his head at it regretfully, sighed over it distressfully and replied murmurously:

"I think now as I have always thought."

"Well—let's hear—what?"

"That your Cecily, dearest fellow, is an extremely beautiful woman . . . yes, such alluring creature as few mortal men could possibly resist——"

"What the—the devil are you suggesting?"

"Nothing, Ralph! I should not—dare!"

"But you saw them—in the wood?"

"I did."

"Well, what—tell me what—were they doing?"

The Viscount glanced at his quivering, distraught questioner, glanced away, shook his head and was mute.

"Speak! Speak, man—speak!" gasped Ralph, with wild, imploring gesture. "Ha, can't you say . . . daren't you tell me? Were they . . . kissing . . . in each other's arms . . . were they——?"

"No, Ralph, dear fellow—no!"

"What were they . . . doing then—what?"

Again the Viscount was dumb—then started and recoiled as, with hoarse, inarticulate cry, Ralph leapt where lay a horse-whip, snatched it up and strode to and fro thrashing at table and chairs as he panted:

"If she's false . . . I'll lash the truth out of her . . . and b'God I'll kill him . . . for the vile hypocrite he is . . . curse and damn him! Yes . . . I'll choke . . . the life out of him. . . ." Thus he raved in blind frenzy while the Viscount, taking up the now forgotten letter, as if to re-read it, folded it deliberately instead and thrust it into his pocket, which done, he exclaimed like one utterly amazed:

"Ralph! Ralph, my dear fellow, why this wild and quite wasted fury? Why such eagerness to meet your trouble half-way? Why rave and rant and do violence to the furniture because your too-beauteous lady rides with your noble kinsman in a wood——?"

"Eh, rides—rides, d'ye say?"

"Yes, to be sure I do. They were riding together, side by side, towards Wrybourne as I informed you and——"

"But you didn't—you did not say that, damn you! No, you told me—you hinted——" Here Ralph, becoming aware of the whip in his quivering fist, stared as if wondering how it got there; from this he scowled at the Viscount, saying between shut teeth:

"Twily, curse you, why—why did you suggest such ha, such abominable——"

"Nothing of the kind, Ralph, dear fellow, 'twas your own too perfervid imagination. So calm yourself do, for what I truly suggest is dinner with me and a bottle or so at the 'Wrybourne Arms' and——"

"Damn your suggestions—no!" snarled Ralph, crossing to the door.

"Ah? Then what shall you do, dear fellow?"

"Ride!" said Ralph fiercely. "Ride till I find them."

"Find them? But, my poor Ralph, what perfectly hopeless quest; the woods stretch for miles——"

"Then I'll—ride!" quoth Ralph, and away he strode, followed more slowly by the Viscount who once again was smiling down at that bruised wrist of his.

CHAPTER XI

INTRODUCES MR. ALFRED BELLENGER

In the best and most private room of the "Wrybourne Arms", Viscount Twily, having fed himself adequately, lounged in the leisured enjoyment of his wine though, despite this show of easeful languor, his thin nostrils quivered suggestively. Also his bandaged wrist seemed to irk him, while his twitching fingers were restless as the eyes that watched his companion with such keen though furtive calculation, yet his voice seemed drowsily content as, glass at lip, he enquired:

"None so bad—for the country, eh, Bellenger?"

An extremely modish person, Mr. Bellenger, youngish, stoutish, dandified, inclined to swagger and flourish, whose hair, whiskers, cravat, waistcoat and affectations of speech and manner were as entirely up-to-date as they possibly could be and who now, having performed elegantly with a toothpick, made answer in full, throaty voice:

"Agad, most sa—prising good fodder, Twily! But, m'good Raymond, ya didn't hale a fellah into these dem leafy solitoods merely to feed and wine a fellah, eh—what say?"

"Well, no, Alfred, no." Here the Viscount paused to sip and savour his wine. "In point of fact I summoned you hither that I might utter, and very very softly, a—word of warning." Mr. Bellenger, in the act of drinking, checked and set down his wine untasted.

"Warning? To—me? You mean——?" he enquired in voice suddenly hushed.

"To both of us, my dear Alfred, but most—ah, yes, most especially—to you!"

"Ah-h! Chalmers?" The questioner's ruddy visage had paled and his voice sunk to awed whisper. "Is it—Robert?"

"Himself, of course."

"Well—what? How——?"

"He threatens us again!"

"Why?" Even the whispering lips were pale now.

"Pure devilry . . . to remind us of his complete mastery . . . to exercise his whip-hand . . . to make us dance and squirm, my dear Alfred."

"His—hand!" said Mr. Bellenger in whisper that was now a venomous hiss. "Ha, if only Wrybourne had sliced off his damned head!"

"As you say, my Alfred, if only! But since he did not, we must continue to . . . squirm and dance obediently so long as it please our Robert, or until he elects to put his threat into—execution!"

"Execu——" Mr. Bellenger, choked and cowering, seemed actually to shrink in size, both hands upon his throat as if he felt there something much less comfortable than his ornate cravat.

"Ah yes," sighed the Viscount, nodding at him mournfully, "I see you apprehend our very desperate situation—and your own more dismal, most horrible plight, my poor Alfred. By reason of past, let us say, indiscretions, our Robert may use us how he will,—for me ruin and exile; but for you, Alfred, for you, alas—the ghastly horror of——"

"Don't . . . don't . . . say it. . . ."

This breathless speaker, transformed now to shuddering, pallid wretch, gazed wild-eyed upon the empty air,—a long and very dreadful look that crept up fearfully—up and up from floor to ceiling as if at some thing of horror, some shape of ghastly doom, while the quivering lips still whispered:

"No . . . no . . . for God's sake . . . don't. . . ."

The Viscount, watching, sipped his wine, savoured it, swallowed and murmured:

"Alfred, my dear soul, don't babble. Drink, man, drink, then let us take counsel how best to checkmate our threatening Bob, thwart destiny and avert certain disaster. And you need not whisper in such ghostly manner; we are quite private here; I've taken good care to be, you may be sure. So up with our glasses and drink, old friend and fellow slave, to our speedy, final and happy deliverance."

"Yes . . . yes!" gasped Mr. Bellenger, fiercely. "And to the eternal damnation of our tyrant, rot him!" With ferocious gulps he emptied his glass and made to refill it, but the Viscount stayed him, gently though firmly, saying:

"Not yet, Alfred! Our heads must be clear to think and contrive how quickest and safest to make Sir Tyranny his own destruction. Have you any ideas?"

"Certainly! We must ensure that his forthcoming duel with Wrybourne shall be fatal this time!"

The Viscount shook his head mournfully, saying:

"Alas, my Alfred, there will be no duel."

"Then what of his declared revenge? He vowed, boasted of it in London."

"And, Alfred, he talks of it still,—but——"

"Then why—why the devil did he follow the Earl down here into Sussex?"

"To fulfil his vow and exact vengeance, but——"

"Well and good, there lies our chance, Raymond! So soon as he acts, we must do likewise and——"

"Alfred, I am convinced he never will act."

"Not? D'ya mean to say he——"

"Consequently will exact no vengeance, dear fellow, as you and I understand the word."

"Raymond, what the devil d'ya mean? I know, and you know, how Robert lives only for revenge upon the Earl."

"Exactly true, Alfred! Yes indeed, our Robert lives for it, dreams of it, gloats upon it, and is so perfectly content to dream and gloat that he will do nothing actually. Do you comprehend?"

"No, I don't!" said Mr. Bellenger, pettishly. "No, damme if I do! Why shouldn't he, why won't he?"

"Because," answered the Viscount with a patient weariness, "because this vengeance, once achieved, and his enemy utterly ruined or dead, our Robert will have nothing left to make life endurable. Now do you begin to have some vague inkling, my very dear Alfred?"

"Yes, I—suppose so. Yet I can't believe it—no, it seems such utter damned nonsense! If dreams and so on can ever content such cold, remorseless demon as Chalmers, then he must be altogether different, yes, curse him, most confoundedly altered from the vicious devil he was."

"Right again, Alfred! Since his late illness he is indeed very oddly changed and——"

"Ah—his illness!" repeated Mr. Bellenger, in tone ugly as his look. "That was damnably bungled,—we should have been freed then but for——"

"Mistress Elspeth McGregor!" said the Viscount.

"A mere woman, Twily, an old harridan——"

"True, dearest fellow, and yet how very much beside,— bold as a lion, wise as a serpent, furtive as a lynx—with all his servants under her thumb, and himself most of all——"

"Yes, yes, but what now?" demanded Mr. Bellenger impatiently. "Having regard to his threat of exposure, how are we to prevent him—as we must—at any hazard, yes, by all and any means. . . . To be rid of him for good and all—how, Raymond, tell me how?"

"By so ordering matters that, as I suggested before, our Robert shall be made to destroy—himself."

"Yes, but how, man, how? You talk so—so infernal vaguely! Be plain and explain how."

"By the skilful use of tools—various! As, for instance— and pray leave the bottle alone,—I have troubled to make conquest of a rustic nymph pretty, utterly brainless but adoring, and therefore perfectly devoted and—chiefest nurse to my lord of Wrybourne's son and heir! I have demeaned myself to consort with a disgusting, murderous ruffian thirsting for Wrybourne's blood! I constantly weary myself with a drunken, gentlemanly fool who hates——"

"Yes yes!" exclaimed Mr. Bellenger, again and even more pettishly. "But how the devil does this concern Chalmers and me—eh?"

"Refrain from interrupting and you shall learn, I hope! Are you listening, my Alfred?"

"Of course I am!"

"Very well then. These tools we shall use for and against our Robert,—by them he shall appear to act and seem to

attempt Wrybourne's life; if successfully—there shall be an
end to both; if not—then Wrybourne shall seem to attempt
his and—ah yes, quite triumphantly, be sure. 'Quod erat
demonstrandum,' old fellow."

"That," said Mr. Bellenger, nodding puzzled head, "yes,
that sounds more promising though dooced involved, ya know.
Agad, Raymond, y'are too subtle for me; ya must be plainer
yet, ya know. F'rinstance, where and when do I come into
it? What part do I play?"

"You, dearest Alfred, having most to lose and therefore,
paradoxically, most to gain, will consequently play a most
important part, yet one suited to your quite unique capabilities.
And you will begin, if possible, tomorrow—and—from the
shelter of such hedge or tree as may offer."

"Eh? Hedge? Tree? Twily, what in hell are you driving
at?"

"Among divers other gifts, Alfred, you are blessed with an
amazingly accurate eye and have acquired a very dexterous
trigger-finger——"

"No!" gasped Mr. Bellenger, recoiling as from a blow, and
once again he cowered and shrank, pallid, abject and whispering. "Not—that! I'm deep enough already! No—I say
no——"

"Fool!" The Viscount's smile and softly modulate tone
served only to make his contempt more viciously apparent.
"Miserable fool, will you then permit our remorseless tyrant to
give you up to disgrace and the worst of deaths? Will you
wait to be dragged whining to the han——" He checked
suddenly and Mr. Bellenger uttered a bleating cry and glared
dreadfully at the door whereon a hand was rapping.

"Damn you—sit up!" said the Viscount, hushed though
imperiously. "Commend yourself—so! Now fill your glass
and drink—drink, I say!" Then, while Mr. Bellenger did his
best to obey, the Viscount lolled back in his chair and called,
mellifluously:

"Enter!"

The door opened forthwith to disclose a waiter, who, with
a bow for each fine gentleman, announced:

"M'lord Viscount, I beg to announce my lord Scrope below for you. I told him you was engaged, but——" Even as he spoke, the waiter was drawn aside to make way for Ralph, dusty and dishevelled with hard riding and already somewhat drunk.

"Ha, Twily!" he exclaimed, swaying uncertainly. "There y'are—merry as a—confounded grig—friend and bottle. . . . But here's me—alone—as usual . . . poor, deserted soul, so I've come t'you——"

"And you're very welcome, Ralph. This is my friend, Mr. Bellenger. Alfred—Lord Scrope. Now we'll have up more wine and make a night of it."

"Night of it—yes!" nodded Ralph and so fiercely that he staggered. "A hell of a night, but no more drinking, no—not yet. 'Stead o' bottles—these!" And from the deep side-pockets of his riding-coat he dragged a brace of duelling pistols.

"Eh—what the devil?" exclaimed the Viscount rising very nimbly.

"Yes," nodded Ralph, "the devil—Cousin Japhet—mean t'kill him presently. Ride over t' the Great House and shoot it out with m' damned cousin Japhet—here's one for him and t'other for me—man t' man—'cross the supper-table! So get y'r hat, Twily, and let's ride." The Viscount surveyed Ralph's swaying body, blinking eyes and unsteady hands—then, edging from the peril of these weapons they grasped and flourished so carelessly (and so ineptly), he sighed, frowned, smiled and said, lightly:

"Not tonight, old fellow; any other time. So give me those things and let's crack a bottle instead."

"D-Damn y'r b-bottle!" stammered Ralph. "Get y'r hat —must have you along for second and—t'witness 'twill be fair duel and no—murder—man t'man—'cross the table— can't miss him then. So let's t'horse."

"No no, Ralph, this is madness——"

"On the c-cont'ry this is p-perfect sense—all gentlemanly and—proper—so let's t'horse."

"But my dear fellow, this is no way to settle the affair——"

"This is—my way, sir. So—le's ride." The Viscount glanced

D

from Ralph's flushed though terribly determined face and shrugged resignedly, saying:

"As you will, Ralph,—but first a bumper for the road. Come now, I insist!" And he filled and tendered a brimming glass; Ralph blinked at it, hesitated then, laying those threatening weapons on the table, accepted the wine with mutter of thanks, gulped thirstily and, before he could set down the empty glass, Viscount Twily refilled it, crying jovially:

"Drink, dear boy, drink while I get into my riding boots. By the way, what sort of night is it?"

"F-Fine!" stammered Ralph, thickly.

"Let us take a look, old fellow." So to the window they went, Ralph on stumbling feet, the Viscount with swift backward glance and gesture at Mr. Bellenger ere he peered forth of the open casement into a fragrant dusk, exclaiming:

"Ah, you were right, my dear Ralph, it is fine; lean out and breathe the fragrant air—steady, old fellow, steady!"

"I'm—perfeck-ly all righ'!" retorted Ralph, leaning half out of the casement, whereupon Mr. Bellenger snatched up the pistols, hid them under the table and in their place set another glass of wine.

"Yes, a fine night!" repeated the Viscount at the window. "And there'll be a moon——"

"Ha!" exclaimed Ralph, drawing in his head. "Damn th' moon an' curse Japhet—lemme go and kill him—'t once— man t' man—'cross table—le's ride!" And turning from the window, he lurched to the table, tried to set down his empty glass, dropped it, spied the full one, took it instinctively, emptied it at a gulp and, sinking heavily into the nearest chair, blinked around slumberously and muttered:

"Kill m' dam' cousin—like a dog——" Then, sinking forward across the table, began to snore.

"Well, he's safe for tonight at least," said the Viscount, and to prove it shook this helpless sleeper viciously. "Yes, he will do no killing—yet awhile!"

Mr. Bellenger, thus reassured, assumed a posture of lofty scorn; he folded his arms, wagged his head and spat disgustedly towards the fireplace:

"Pah!" he exclaimed. "If this is one of your 'tools,' Raymond, that's what I think of him!"

"So?" murmured the Viscount, sinking into his chair again. "But then you are merely Alfred Bellenger, who, if left to think for himself, and without my guidance, would inevitably end his inglorious career very shamefully upon the——"

"Hush!" gasped his hearer, recoiling behind outflung arms. "Damn you—ah, no no,—Raymond—old friend, don't—I beg—implore——"

"Then, dearest Alfred, let me inform you how this particular tool can and shall be perhaps particularly deadly though double-edged and apt to cut his employer unless skilfully handled—as he shall be, of course. Now have the goodness to pull the bell and we'll have his lordship hauled off to bed."

So waiters were summoned and poor, helpless Ralph was borne away.

Then Viscount Twily, beckoning his companion near, they took counsel together, like the fear-driven, utterly desperate men they were.

CHAPTER XII

CONCERNING A SHOT FROM THE LEAFAGE

LIFE, THIS great highway that all of us each one must travel, had brought Sam thus far by rough ways of hardship afloat and ashore, through peril of battle and tempest, to a happiness beyond his dreams, a haven of such eventless calm and joyous plenty as almost confounded him by the effortless ease of his present existence and which had also caused his Andromeda a foreboding dread lest such very perfect felicity be too unearthly for this mundane world; which fear was to be realized soon and quite dreadfully—for, this road they had journeyed together so blissfully, making a sharp bend, was to lead them, by such toilsome steps, through such gulfs of awful darkness, such storms of doubt and fear, as would test and prove the strength of their love and faith to the uttermost.

And this dire change began with the sudden shot from whispering leafage that killed his horse and flung Sam headlong to lie inert, dazed by the shock and the lightning rapidity of it all. . . . But arms raised him at last, hands cherished him, a voice cried his name, calling him so insistently that, perforce and unwillingly, he opened dazzled eyes and thus beheld the lovely, anxious face of Cecily bent down to him . . . he did his best to smile reassuringly, then closed his eyes again at sound of another voice, harsh and strident:

"Loose him, Cecily, d'ye hear? Let the fellow alone, will you?"

"No, Ralph, of course I won't! It's Sam and he's hurt——"

"That's no reason for you to cling and cuddle him so lovingly, damn him!"

"For shame, Ralph, for shame! Ride for Doctor Finch and, oh—ride fast. Go, Ralph, go—now!"

"Ha, and leave you to kiss and cosset my dam' cousin? Not likely—unless you vow and swear——"

"Hush, Ralph—someone's coming, thank God! Listen!"
Thud of hoofs approaching at furious gallop . . . a warning
shout and over the hedge nearby leapt a horseman who had
reined up his rearing animal, leapt to earth and was beside
Sam all in as many moments:

"Oh God! . . . Feared so! . . . Heard the shot!" gasped
Mr. Standish in wildest distress. "God, Cecily . . . did they
get him? What happened?"

"Someone shot at him and killed his horse. . . . 'Twas so
I found him once before."

"Sam . . . Sam . . . dear old f'lo'. . . . Oh, Cecily, is he
—dead?"

"Far . . . from it . . . messmate!" replied Sam, haltingly,
but opening his eyes again. "Took a . . . bit of a toss . . .
that's all. Soon be . . . shipshape."

"Thank God!" exclaimed Mr. Standish with fervour. "Can
you sit up, m'dear old lord, eh?"

"Ay . . . watch me!" answered Sam, and did so with an
effort, and thus beholding Ralph nearby, nodded, saying
in stronger voice: "Thankee, cousin, for your very Scrope-
like sympathy and kindness . . . now I'll be glad of your
absence, for, d'ye see, you spoil the scenery, so bear up
and stand away." Then turning to Cecily, still upon her
knees beside him, he said gently: "God love you, lass,
you are my good angel again!" Taking her hand, he raised
it to his lips, whereat Ralph leapt from saddle and advanced so threateningly that up started Mr. Standish to front
him.

"Hold hard, m'lord!" said he, with menace in every slender
line of him. Ralph clenched his fists, Mr. Standish did likewise; then, rising with swift, effortless ease, Cecily was between them, quiet though very dominating.

"Oh, Ralph, Ralph!" she murmured, seizing his passionate
fist in those strong, shapely hands of hers. "Come you now,
—go home with me—come!" Now though her voice was
gentle as ever, her clasp was so compelling that Ralph suffered
her to lead him where stood their horses; so together they
mounted, and side by side, away they rode.

"Lord help her!" exclaimed Sam, gazing after them. "What a very cursed Scrope he is!"

"Agreed!" said Mr. Standish, heartily. "But no matter for him,—look, Sam, look at this!" And from the breast of his coat—this exquisite garment—he drew a silver-mounted pistol. "Here, old f'lo, is the weapon of your would-be murderer,— must have heard me coming, dropped it and fled, the dastard! I found it still warm from the discharge. A duelling-pistol, Sam, and one of a pair o' course. Take it, old lord, look at it!" Sam did so and, having duly inspected this splendid weapon, sat shaking his head at it as though greatly puzzled.

"You see whose it is, old f'lo',—the name engraved upon it?"

"Chalmers of course, Harry. It even bears his monogram as well! Which makes me wonder all the more."

"Eh? But wha' the dooce is there t'wonder at?"

"First I wonder why such a betraying weapon should be used? And next, I wonder even more why such betraying weapon should be left to bear such damning evidence."

"Because, as I tell you, the dastard was startled,—dropped it in his haste and made off, and before I could even glimpse him, damn him."

"Also," continued Sam, still intent upon the pistol, "to shoot from a hedge is not and never would be the method of such fellow as Chalmers."

"Probably not—when normal. But, Sam, I believe, yes, I'm convinced, he is beside himself and raving mad for your blood!"

"Likely enough, Harry, indeed I think he is, but this would not be his way——"

"Sam, I believe the dev'lish fellow would take any way to sate his vengeance,—hating you as he does! And, demme, we know he has killed before now."

"Too true, Harry. But always man to man, d'ye see, on the cursed 'field of honour'! Sir Robert is, or was, a merciless duellist, and yet—never a cold-blooded, hole-and-corner murderer."

"So far as we know, Sam! But how little we do know of the fellow—except that all these months, ever since you bested him, he has been nursing his hate, scheming revenge on you, and now—well, yonder lies your dead horse and here is his pistol!"

"Ay, but not the hand that fired it, Harry."

"Oh, dammit, Sam,—with such evidence so plain and manifest, why boggle?"

"Because it is too plain and manifest!"

"Well—dooce take everything! My dear old Sam lord, who but this your inveterate enemy would attempt your life and run such infernal risk,—who?"

"I can think of one or two, Harry, more or less likely."

"So can I, Sam, hordes of 'em in town and here in this seeming peaceful rurality—as for instance your loving cousin Ralph! He doesn't love you, old f'lo', and he was here on the spot!"

"Ay, but with Cecily!"

"Oh no! I saw him galloping this way and alone, Sam, alone! He arrived here only a few minutes before me. So if you want him—there's your suspect number two."

"And the Scropes," nodded Sam, "were and are regular bloodthirsty murderous crew!"

"With—some exceptions, old f'lo'!"

"Few enough, Harry, very very few!"

"However," quoth Mr. Standish, with the utmost finality, "the perfectly damning evidence of Sir Robert's pistol is proof conclusive to my mind. I am convinced he is our man and that we should act accordingly—Bow Street officers, law and order and so on—we should be up and doing."

"Ay, so I will."

"What will you, Sam?"

"Be up and doing."

"Oh? Ah? But how?"

"I'll ask him."

"Him? Who? Eh, you never mean Chalmers?"

"Of course. I think you told me his house is called Priors Dene, and on the London road?"

"Yes, but d'you mean you'll actually question him and believe his word?"

"And," said Sam, getting to his feet rather awkwardly, "I'll go at once."

"Then by heavens—I'll go with you, Sam."

"Ay, so you shall, Harry, so get another horse; I'm riding yours."

"Oh, but, my dear f'lo, this will take me twenty minutes at least——"

"More," answered Sam with his flashing grin as he crammed the pistol into his pocket, "I should say a good half-hour."

"But are you fit to ride—and alone?"

"As a trivet!" answered Sam, though it was with such visible effort he got himself into the saddle that Mr. Standish cried anxiously:

"Oh demme, I doubt it! Are you quite sure?"

"Yes, Lord love you! And Harry—no word o' this ugly business to Andromeda. I must tell her myself—remember!" Then, nodding down cheerily at his friend's anxious face, Sam jogged away.

CHAPTER XIII

TELLS HOW SAM QUESTIONED HIS ENEMY

SAM HAD reined up his horse that he might better survey the stately old house before him, when a woman appeared to whom he touched his hat, saying:

"Good day, marm. Is this Priors Dene?" And instantly as she had confronted him she replied:

"Ay, it is that. And ye'sel' will be the Earrrl o' Wrybourne, I'm thinkin'!" Now at this, he turned from the house to regard the speaker,—tall, bony, dignified, whose harsh features were relieved and gentled by a generous mouth, wide though shapely and eyes large, black-lashed and beautiful.

"You are the lord of Wrybourne, are you not?" she enquired again and in her very perfect English; and it was Japhet the Earl who now saluted her, hat in hand to bow as he answered:

"Indeed, madam, at your service."

"And pray, my lord, to what do we owe this honour?"

"I am hoping for a brief interview with Sir Robert Chalmers."

"My certie!" she exclaimed, gesturing with the garden-trowel she held. "Ye'll no' be chopping off his other hand, whateffer?"

"Eh?" quoth the Earl, becoming Sam. "Lord love ye— no——"

"Aweel, his one should content ye, forby he is an unco' helpless body for lack o't. And 'tis mysel', Elspeth McGregor, tellin' ye so, and being a McGregor, I'm bold tae demand o' ye why for ye wad speak wi' Sir Robert?"

"To return certain property of his which——"

"Ah," she exclaimed, "that will not be his hand, of course, my lord——"

"Mistress McGregor," quoth Sam, looking down into the eyes that gazed up at him so very shrewdly, "were it in my power, I would indeed!"

97

"Oh man," she demanded, drawing a slow pace nearer, "d'ye mean that?"

"Ay, I do, with all my heart!" Here for a space they surveyed each other speechlessly, eye to eye, until at last she nodded, saying less harshly:

"Yes, indeed—I believe you would."

"Marm," quoth Sam, now his most sailorly self, "for your belief I give you my most grateful thanks and my hand with 'em—if ye care to take it and so honour me . . . will you, Mistress McGregor?" For a moment ensued another pregnant silence, then, tossing aside her trowel, she grasped Sam's proffered hand, shook it vigorously, loosed it and nodded, her wide mouth curving to somewhat grim smile as she said:

"Weel, my lord, ye're no' exactly the ferocious bluidy-minded, duelling body they tell o' ye. So now I'm bidding ye light doon and welcome."

"And," answered Sam, as he dismounted, "I'm to thank you again."

"Come then," said she, beckoning. "Go with me, and I'll show you a poor, tormented soul, ah yes,—a man who might have been good and maybe great but for—himself! For Robert has aye been his own worst enemy, the bitterest, most merciless! So today he's in yon summer-house learning himself to write left-handed. Hist now, let me speak him first!" Thus, presently, Sam beheld this one-time enemy of his, this sore-stricken man, seated, quill in awkward fingers, at a small writing-table littered with past smudged and blotted efforts, yet persistently inscribing and with painful care those first necessary characters which little Jane called "pot-hooks and hangers", but doing them so badly that he frowned and muttered plaintive imprecations upon his own clumsiness.

Sam instinctively made to retreat unseen, whereupon Mistress Elspeth instantly clutched him by the sleeve and, holding him thus captive, spoke:

"Rabbie man, I've brought ye a veesitor——" Sir Robert glanced up swiftly, uttered furious exclamation and, dashing pen to ground, stamped on it and rose.

"Elspeth," he cried harshly, "woman, how dared you? Ha

—and you, Wrybourne—what means this very damnable intrusion? I desire neither sight nor sound of you——"

"However," said the Earl, advancing, "I fear you must endure both for a few moments." Sir Robert clenched his only hand, made instinctively to hide his stump, but brandished it fiercely instead as if meditating an assault, then, with gesture of wild despair at his futility, sank down again at the table, chin on breast, and said in strangled voice:

"Elspeth—leave us."

"Ay," she answered, "I will that, but I'll no' be vera far awa', so behave—the baith o' ye!" And with a nod to each, away she strode, leaving Sir Robert to glare up at his visitor beneath lowering brows.

"Well, my lord," he demanded, "why must I endure this affliction—why are you here?"

"First, Sir Robert, I notice your riding-boots are dusty; may I assume you have been abroad today?"

"You may. I returned scarcely an hour ago. And again I demand—why do you intrude upon me?"

"To return your property, sir,—this!" And my lord laid the pistol before Sir Robert, who merely glanced at it and enquired:

"Well?"

"Hardly an hour ago, Sir Robert, a ball from this weapon killed my horse. Not far away the pistol was found—still warm from the discharge. I am here to enquire if this ball was intended for my unoffending animal or myself?"

"Wrybourne, you affront me!"

"Sir Robert, I await your answer."

And after a moment of frowning silence, Sir Robert replied:

"Since the weapon is mine, I hold your question admissible and will answer by informing you—firstly, that I have no idea; secondly, that I am not ambidextrous; and thirdly, to assure you that were this awkward left hand as dextrous as my vanished right, I should not foul it by murder. Furthermore, I have neither seen nor touched this weapon for a year or more. There is the truth, my lord, believe it or not as you will. Your opinion is of no least interest to me."

"However, I do believe you."

"Then, my lord, pray believe this also,—under no circumstances should I ever—shoot you! Oh no, such death is altogether too swift and merciful."

The Earl merely bowed and crossed to the door, but paused there to enquire:

"It would be of interest to know whose hand levelled your pistol and if at me or my horse—and why? You may perhaps have some suspicion?" Sir Robert shook his head, saying, and with a strange intensity:

"I can only, and most earnestly, beg you to be careful, Wrybourne! Avoid riding or walking alone,—be warned for my sake!"

"Eh? Your sake? Ah, I see,—you mean——?"

"I mean that your life, my lord, is so very precious to me that I beg you will not risk it needlessly."

The Earl laughed, and becoming Sam, clapped hand to thigh exclaiming:

"Sink me if you aren't an original hater, Chalmers, ay— the one and only! So, b'George, I'll do my best to stay alive if only for your revenge, d'ye see, and that's a promise." Then away went Sam with his rolling, seaman's stride to find Mistress McGregor feeding an apple to his horse.

"Well," she said with her grim smile, "ye hae your orders, my lord,—oh, I was listening, of course,—he issued his commands how you are to cherish and take every care of yourself that he may be avenged on ye later on!"

"Which," quoth Sam, shaking his head, "is quite preposterous!"

"Ay, and juist Robert."

"But, Mistress Elspeth, it's fantastic."

"Ay, but so is Robert! Howandever, ye believe his denial o' yon shooting?"

"Of course!"

"And why of course?"

"Because, whatever else he is, Sir Robert is neither coward nor murderer."

"And that's gospel-true, my lord. But what do you know of this shooting business?"

"Merely that someone shot from the woods, my horse reared and was killed, and Sir Robert's pistol was found nearby."

"Oomph-humph!" exclaimed Miss Elspeth, pondering this.

"Have you any idea, marm?"

"Mebbe!" she nodded. "But hae ye ony enemies besides my puir Rabbie?"

"Maybe!" Sam echoed. "Indeed, 'twould appear so."

"Ay, and a man without an enemy is either vera nigh the angels or nae better than a weathercock! But, oh man, Robert was mightily concerned and upset for that you took his word and believed so readily, forby he was hoping you'd give him the lie. Then too, ye let him see you pitied him and that he couldna bear,—especially from you, his enemy."

"But, d'ye see, I'm not his enemy."

"Eh—not? And why for no'?"

"Because my hostility ended with our duel."

"Because you won!"

"Ay, maybe. Though, win or lose, a good fight breeds respect—or should do. And he fought so very well that I respected him accordingly and could now—ay, and like him too, if he'd let me. I'll confess I had some vague hopes until today. But now, his mad hatred of me——"

"Ah no, not mad!" said she, impressively. "For think, my lord, think! Is not such hate reasonable—under the circumstances? If so, he cannot be mad. And these are the circumstances,—hating you, he abominates himself more, despising himself as a failure. That handless stump of his has become his insistent shame and reminder—he can scarce bear sight of it. Ah yes, so much his shame that . . . the last time he handled yon pistol 'twas to end his torment . . . but I leapt and pushed it aside just in time and was deafened and nigh blinded by the dreadful thing. . . . Then I clung to him and cried to God . . . praying for him as I have so often done when he was a child, until he promised never to take his own life . . . and though nowise a good man, Robert never breaks his word. . . . So now, my lord, believe this,—though he cries vengeance on you—yet 'tis himself he most truly hates,—believe this and pity him—if you can."

"I do!" nodded Sam. "I do indeed and heartily. . . . But still I'm wondering what form his revenge will take and how best to guard against it."

"And would to God I could tell you!" said she, fervently. "For I would keep him guiltless of your blood for his own sake."

"And," said Sam, with somewhat wry smile, "and my sake, I hope, Mistress Elspeth?"

"Yes, yes, and yours, my lord! For, though ye were his ruin, you are such man that I'm hoping . . . praying you may become his salvation."

"A good thought," nodded Sam, "but hopelessly impossible, I'm afraid."

"Sir, is there aught in heaven or airth impossible to God Almighty?"

"Well, no," answered Sam, rather dubiously.

"Vera weel then! I shall implore God our Almighty Father for the baith o' ye——"

"Elspeth!" cried a distant though very fretful voice. "Elspeth!"

"And yon's my puir Rabbie wailing and wearying for me as he did years syne when onyways hairted or frighted,—I maun awa'! But first, this in the lug o' ye—beware o' yon Viscount body! And now, goodbye, my lord; I'm praying God will ever have you in his love and care, amen!" So, with gesture of farewell, she hurried away towards that insistent, so querulous voice, leaving Sam to gaze after her very wistfully until she was out of sight; then he mounted his horse and ambled away, but had not gone far when he beheld Mr. Standish approaching at furious gallop.

"Well, Sam?" he cried, reining up and wheeling his animal with a dexterity Sam admired and envied. "Well, thank heaven you're safe, m'dear old lord! Did y'see Chalmers and question him?"

"Yes, Harry."

"What did the dam' f'lo' say of his murderous attempt?"

"Denied all knowledge of it."

"He would! You didn't believe him, I hope?"

"Ay, but I did. Chalmers is no liar."

"How can you be so sure o' that, Sam? How did the cursed f'lo' receive you? What happened?" Reining his horse to a walk, Sam told briefly of Sir Robert, of Mistress McGregor, and the conclusions he had drawn, while Mr. Standish listened in frowning disapproval, saying, when the tale ended:

"Ha, Sam, as I suspected, the dooced villain is stark, staring mad, and the woman little better."

"However," Sam rejoined, urging his horse to faster pace, "mad or no, Robert Chalmers is the woefullest, most pitiable fellow in Sussex, ay, or anywhere else!"

CHAPTER XIV

TELLS OF A STEALTHY EVIL

MEANWHILE:

Andromeda, armed with scissors, gauntlets and basket, was on her way to the rose-garden when, in turning sharp corner of a tall yew hedge, she came upon Lucy Jay, her lordly infant's chief day-nurse, who, starting back as in sudden dread, contrived a tremulous curtsey and burst into breathless speech:

"Oh, if you please, my lady, I . . . I was but looking for your ladyship . . . 'tis why I'm here. . . . Baby being now asleep and Mary Sims willing to take my place . . . will your ladyship be pleased to allow me the afternoon?"

"But, Lucy, you have had several afternoons lately. Heavens, girl, how flustered you show! What ails you?"

"Nought, my lady,—only a headache and—and my poor aunt."

"What of her?"

"Twisted her back, my lady, and now a-bed wi' nobody to do for her."

"Then of course you may go, yes, and take her a few bunches of grapes. . . . My little Viscount is asleep, you say?"

"Oh yes, my lady, and Mary and Jemima a-watching over him this minute."

"Very well, child, you may go and remain with your aunt until she is better."

"Thank you, my lady, I . . . I . . . Oh, my lady, thank you . . ." gasped Lucy, and fled, leaving her mistress to gaze after her curiously ere she continued her way.

So Andromeda came to her rose-garden and began filling the basket with many-hued fragrance, snipping joyously until, spiked securely upon the thorns of a certain bush, she beheld a crumpled paper bearing in great, scrawling characters the words:

"To Countess Wrybourne"

For a moment she remained utterly still, gazing at this as if warned by some fearful premonition that made her dread to touch it; then, setting that dimpled, resolute chin of hers, she snatched it, unfolded it and read these ill-written, misspelt lines:

"Madame and Lady Countess annonymouse letters being trubbelsome dont read this onless you love yore husband earl to worn same agin meeting the beautiful golden lady so secret becase such is apt to lead to shootings and bludshed from your ladyships well wisher."

Having scanned this, once hastily and again very deliberately, she set down her basket the better to rend this evil thing across and across; tearing it small and crumpling the fragments, then tossing them away, she went on culling her roses, yet ever and anon her busy scissors were arrested, and more than once she turned to frown where lay those scattered pieces of paper.

She had filled her basket and turned housewards when she heard the jingle of spurs and the deliberate footsteps so dearly familiar,—then Sam's loved voice sounding to her keen, wifely ears rather more cheery than usual:

"Andromeda—ahoy! Bear up and stand by——" Then, basket, scissors and all, she was in his arms.

"Lord!" he exclaimed. "How fragrant the roses are today, and yet best of all I love the smell of your hair!" And he kissed it. And now because of past dread, she clung to him, whereupon he kissed her again so that, for the moment, she forgot all save this vigorous, cheery sailorman of hers.

"Where have you been, Sam dear?"

"I rode towards Wrexham meaning to have word with Cecily, as I told you."

"Oh—why?"

"To know about her Scropish Ralph; he's been drinking harder than ever, I hear."

"Cecily!" she repeated, glancing almost furtively towards those distant scraps of paper. "Did you see her, Sam?"

"Well—no, sweetheart."

"And why not?"

"Because my horse, I was on Ranger, happened to fall with me——"

"Oh, my dearest, were you hurt?"

"No, but—Ranger was."

"But Ranger is such a dear, steady old horse."

"Yes, he—was."

"Was, Sam—do you mean——"

"Dead, yes, sweetheart."

"Did the—fall kill him, Sam? Ah, was it the fall?"

"Well, no—not exactly. Oh no, it wasn't the fall, dearest, for, d'ye see, by some unlucky chance a bullet happened to strike the poor old fellow and——"

"A—bullet?" she gasped, and once again glanced towards those fragments of paper, but now with eyes of horror.

"Yes, my dear, a stray bullet out of the wood,—some rascally poacher, of course."

"The wood!" she repeated. "And you were going . . . to meet . . . Cecily!"

"Yes, I was, as I told you——"

"Where did it happen? Where were you?"

"Passing Fallowdene Thicket; the bushes are very dense thereabout, just the place for poachers, d'ye see, and——"

"No, Sam! Ah no—no!" she gasped in horrified whisper. "You were shot at deliberately—murderously, and you—— Oh, you know it and are trying to deceive me!"

"Eh? Deceive you? I? Well, now all I can say is—damme if ever——"

"Now God help us!" she exclaimed, dropping basket and scissors to clasp and wring her hands. "The dreadful thing I feared has come upon us—this is the beginning! And, oh, my Sam, now I am quite sure you believe, as I do, that someone meant to—kill you!"

"But, Andromeda! I'm trying to tell you it was just a chance shot—some poacher——"

"Sam," she murmured, looking up at him now with eyes of tearful reproach, "how can you think to deceive me, I who know you so well because I love you so truly. . . . Oh, how can you?" Then, not waiting his answer to this agonized question, she turned and sped away, nor did he attempt to stay or follow her. Instead he remained looking down gloomily at her fallen scissors and the basket that had spilled its fragrant burden at his feet. And it was thus he was found by Harry Standish who, taking in all this at a glance, enquired, somewhat apprehensively:

"Old f'lo', what's to do?"

Whereto Sam replied, dejectedly:

"She won't swallow my poacher, Harry—what I mean is, she believes, ay and says, I'm deceiving her!"

"And no wonder, Sam! Such dooced tale of confounded cock and bull! Simply beggin' and pleadin' f' trouble, demme! Why on earth not tell her the truth 'n' shame the devil?"

"Ay, but what is the truth?"

"The devil,—Chalmers of course."

"Never in this world, Harry!"

"So sure as I'm standing here, Sam! And I'm hoping to God you won't give him another and better chance at you! However, horsed or afoot, I don't let you out o' my sight from now on, demme no!"

"Which," growled Sam, "is merest dam' nonsense!"

"Nevertheless, m'dear old Earl, I'm your dooced devotedly pertinacious shadow henceforth, according to promise."

"What promise?"

"To Andromeda, o' course! She nailed me on my way here t'you, with tears in her eyes, Sam! Told me your perfectly dem preposterous account of chance poachers—stray shots— ha, and also that she knew your murder was intended—and by whom!"

"Ah? Did she mention a name?"

"No, but suggested it."

"Who?"

"Chalmers, of course, devil take him!" At this juncture a smart young footman presented himself to bow and announce:

"Tea awaits you, gentlemen, in 'Queen Elizabeth's chamber.'"

"Tell her ladyship we are coming. . . . Look, Harry, the dear sweet soul dropped all her flowers; let's pick 'em up for her; stand by now and bear a hand."

Thus presently, Sam bearing the refilled basket and Mr. Standish the scissors, tea-wards they went together.

CHAPTER XV

TELLS OF A DEEPENING SHADOW

IN SPITE of these halcyon days of a glorious summer, a shadow was gathering about the great house of Wrybourne Feveril, an ominous, ever deepening gloom that even old Sol could not dissipate; thus Sam was gloomy likewise as he trudged heavily stablewards, though the morning was so radiant.

Thus presently he was met by Mr. Standish, immaculate as ever, from hat-crown to soles of his polished riding-boots and himself joyous as the day, who flourished whip airily and cried gaily:

"Greetings, dear old Earl, with yoicks, tally-ho, not forgettin' tantivvy, hark forrard and away! The question being—where?"

"Ha!" exclaimed Sam, frowning and sardonic. "What's for you, Harry?"

"Duty, old f'lo'! You behold your faithful, trusty, one and only Standish all dooced devotion, loyalty and zeal, up and about to be your escort."

"Ay," nodded Sam, with disparaging gesture, "and heavily armed, I see."

"Not heavily, old f'lo', merely a brace of pocket pops," Mr. Standish explained, glancing down at the slight bulges that marred his elegant outline. "Are they so dem conspicuous?"

"As a couple of thirty-six pounder cannonades! Why carry 'em, Harry?"

"Well, why not?" he retorted, with some heat. "If any other dam' villain tries a shot at you I'll try two at him."

"If he should, Harry, you'd never see him."

"Then I'll shoot at his flash, and if no flash, I'll fire at the sound and smoke, and give chase. So if you're going to ride, let's up and away, the question still being—where, Sam?"

"First to the 'Wrybourne Arms' and then Lewes Market to meet Ned and possibly buy cattle." So presently they mounted and set forth together, but scarcely had they reached the open road than Mr. Standish, glancing somewhat anxiously at Sam's lowering visage, enquired:

"Viscount Twily is lodging at the 'Wrybourne Arms' . . . you're not looking for trouble with him, are you, old f'lo'?"

"No, I merely want a word or so with John Bascomb, the landlord, about that Scropish cousin o' mine."

After this, they rode in silence some while until, reining his horse to a walk, Sam turned to his companion so suddenly and with such look that Mr. Standish enquired and more anxiously than ever:

"Eh—why, what's the matter, old f'lo'?"

"God only knows!" replied Sam miserably, shaking his troubled head. "But, Harry, there's something very wrong with Andromeda!"

"Wrong, Sam?"

"Oh, she's well enough in health, thank God! But there's something the matter . . . she won't tell me, and I can't think what!"

"How so, Sam?"

"Well, she'll sit motionless and silent . . . and often I catch her watching, looking at me very oddly . . . almost furtively. Sometimes she seems about to speak, yet never does! She's changed, Harry, yes and—changing! She's never been the same since poor old Ranger was shot. . . . Consequently, I'm all out o' my reckoning, d'ye see, in the cursed doldrums, damme, with no steerage way and all adrift! She's changed, I tell you."

"Not she, Sam, no, no! It's merely her anxiety,—wifely anxiety, old f'lo', fostering affection and what not, Sam. All wives that are wives, mother their husbands, y'know,—my own Rowena does,—mothers me with the most absolute, dooced confounded pertinacity, and b'gad, Sam, I like it no end."

"Sink me!" exclaimed Sam, clapping hand to thigh. "Ay, sink and damme, but you've said it, Harry,—that's it!"

"What's it, old Earl, what?"

"Andromeda has—stopped mothering me!"

"Nonsense, Sam! She couldn't and wouldn't and never will! Goo' Lord—no! You're the dooced apple of her lovely eye! The absolute one and only! She can scarce bear you out of her sight! Never knew of such confounded absolute perfection o' devotion—except my own Rowena, o' course! We're most infernally lucky in our spouses, Sam!"

"Yes," he agreed, with gloomy nod, "though mine's changed, for some reason or other, d'ye see, and I mean to know why."

"She thinks your life's in danger, old f'lo'—all manner o' perils, dangers and what not, yes, and all b' reason of Chalmers, curse him! Ah well, yonder's the inn—where ale shall foam in beakers, strong ale ripe and nappy, eh, old lord?"

"Ay, ay," answered Sam, but in tone so dismal and with such deep-fetched sigh that Mr. Standish eyed him more anxiously than ever.

Scarcely had they dismounted than forth came landlord John to welcome them, but even he, this usually cheerful man, seemed unwontedly grave, or so thought Mr. Standish, and therefore became extremely watchful and alert as they followed stalwart John Bascomb into his spacious inn, to a remote and cosy chamber where to greet them stood two frothing tankards, the which landlord John introduced with wide-armed gesture, saying:

"The ale—as usual, gentlemen! Ripe and right old October! Good health, Sirs!"

Now as they drank, Mr. Standish, watchful as ever, beheld the door opening furtively, espied the oval of a whiskered face that seemed to peer and listen as Sam, addressing the landlord, said:

"I'm on my way to Lewes Market, John, but first—what's your news . . . ?" Stealthily as the door had opened, it closed; whereupon, tankard in hand, Mr. Standish crossed to this door, opened it silently and went out, shutting it carefully behind him while Sam repeated his question:

"Well, John, here I am; why did you send for me? Sit down and let's hear." With murmur of thanks, landlord

John sank into a chair and, leaning across the table, said in hoarse whisper:

"My lord, I made so bold for that I must speak you a word o' warning along o' your cousin, Lord Ralph!"

"Ah? What of him, John?"

"Sir, he come here t'other night—threatening your life!"

"So?" murmured Sam. "Then, of course, he was drunk, eh, John?"

"He was so, my lord, yet sober enough to mean it! Ah, turble fierce he was and likewise—armed! A brace o' pistols, my lord, and him for riding to the Great House for to shoot ye—forcing of you to fight him a dooel! Thank God the Vi-count was here."

"Eh, d'you mean Viscount Twily?"

"Himself, my lord! Ah, but for the Vi-count 'tis sartin sure you'd ha' been shot, my lord."

"D'you tell me that Viscount Twily actually stopped him?"

"Ah, that he did, sir!"

"Tell me how, John, and be particular."

"Well, sir, here's your cousin flourishing his pistols and swearing to be the death o' you, and says he: 'Come, Vi-count,' he says, 'you must be along o' me as my second and to witness as 'tis fair dooel across the table, so let's ride,' says he. 'No,' says the Vi-count, 'not till you've drank a glass,' he says. So he tricks Lord Ralph to drinking one glass arter another till he's fair helpless and so we puts him to bed—and there he bides all night and half the next day! So here's you, my lord, safe and sound in consequence—and all owing to Vi-count Twily."

"Oh?" murmured Sam. "Ah? Now damme, but you surprise me, John."

"Ah, but there's summat more, my lord. All that happened last week, but—this here very morning and precious early, afore the house was astir, I hears hoss-hoofs coming at a gallop till they stops in the yard—and there's my Lady Scrope all wild-like! 'Oh, John,' says she, 'Oh, John, please let me in for I must write a letter,' says she. So in she comes—and then, my lord, I sees as she's marvellous troubled, her poor, lovely face all wet wi' tears! So I brings her pens and ink and down she sets and writes her letter and, my lord, the sweet soul was a-weeping as she writ. Then she gives me the letter and bids me give it to you, begs and pleads as I'll give it to you unbeknown and secret-like, to you and nobody else! So, my lord, here it be!"

Sam noticed this letter bore no superscription and was sealed with a great smear of wax; and these were the hastily-written words he now read:

"Oh Sam dear do please to meet me in the wood at about five o'clock because I have something to tell you that no-one but you must ever hear, not even Andromeda. So dear Sam for your sake and mine do not fail me. At five this evening I shall wait until you come to me.

CECILY."

Refolding this letter, Sam thrust it into pocket and glanced across at solemn John with the question:

"You have known Lady Scrope a long time, I think?"

"All her days, my lord. A sweet, happy child till her parents died so sudden, then a good, lovely maid none too well used by her aunt and uncle, today beautiful creeter and grand lady and—woeful! Ah, 'tis a marvellous great pity as she ever wed—who she did, my lord!"

"Too true, John, too damnably true! Yet it was a love match, d'ye see, a boy-and-girl affair, eh, John?"

"Yes, my lord, the Master Ralph were a fine youngster in them days. 'Twere his father, Lord Julian, as larned him to drink! My cousin were butler at the Manor and used for to tell how Lord Julian would make Master Ralph drink him glass and glass till the poor lad were helpless! Ah, if only Lord Julian had got hisself murdered a bit earlier, why then, p'r'aps Master Ralph might ha' growed up a bit different like —maybe."

"Yes, John, I'm pretty sure he would. He never had much of a chance with such a father."

"Which be gospel-true, my lord."

At this moment, Mr. Standish reappeared to set down his empty tankard and enquire, casually:

"John, who is the ornate being, the very dashing sportsman in black whiskers and a bottle-green coat?"

"Why, sir, that will be Mr. Bellenger, a London gen'leman and friend o' the Vi-count."

"Ah, to be sure—the Viscount!" nodded Mr. Standish. "Birds of a confoundedly dooced feather! Well now, dear old lord, my beaker is empty, so if you're ready, shall we go?"

CHAPTER XVI

TELLS OF MISCHIEF, DAN'L AND MR. SHRIG

"Oh Sam," moaned Mr. Standish after they had ridden a goodish distance in silence and at a funeral pace. "Ah, m'dear old f'lo'," he groaned, reining back his eager horse beside Sam's slow, plodding animal, "why on earth are y' so dooced, dismally speechless, and why do we ride like two confounded snails?"

"I was thinking!" answered Sam gloomily.

"Well, so am I, old f'lo'; yes, I'm thinking dev'lish hard, —first that if you intend reaching Lewes today we'd better venture a trot or even a gentle canter! And secondly, I'm thinking and am pretty sure there's some new mischief afoot!"

"Oh?" murmured Sam. "Ah? What?"

"Well, that whiskery sportsman Bellenger overheard you saying we were on our way to Lewes, whereupon—away he steals, mounts a bob-tailed, fleabitten grey and is off like the devil. A dem sly and downy customer—and—a friend of Twily, remember!"

"Ah, the Viscount, yes!" nodded Sam. "He becomes my astonishment, Harry, for he has lately troubled himself to save my life!" And forthwith Sam repeated landlord John's story; which done, he demanded: "Now what d'you say to that?"

"Spots, old f'lo'! I say spots and leopards! Never change! Can't! 'Gainst nature! Also stripes and tigers! Moreover, beg t'remind you ' all's not gold that glitters!' A burnt child shuns the fire and—Twily is always Twily—Q.E.D., and so forth. Th' question is—what's he up to?"

"No!" growled Sam. "The question is—what's got into Ralph that he should want to shoot me?"

"Drink, m'dear old Earl, drink! It gets into him mornin', noon and night. Drink's your answer."

"Ay, maybe, Harry. Yes, 'tis like enough—the poor fool can't help it, I suppose."

"Old f'lo', 'strong drink is a mocker' and raging, says the scribe, 'it stinketh like an 'addick and biteth like a servant' —why—what the dooce——?" He broke off, for up the hill towards them a horseman was coming at reckless, breakneck speed, urging his animal with flailing whip and goading spurs, a very desperate rider who, swerving his horse in full career, set him at the hedge, burst through it and galloped away across country at the same wild and headlong speed.

"Demme!" exclaimed Mr. Standish. "Man must be mad!"

"Ay, or drunk!" growled Sam.

"Rides as if the very devil were after him."

"Probably is!" quoth Sam.

"Did you notice his horse?"

"No."

"Can't be sure at this distance, but looked uncommonly like a fleabitten grey . . . I wonder! Well, he's gone now, whoever he was . . . but, I wonder . . . !"

After this they rode in silence, for now it seemed that even Mr. Standish's usually high spirits had ebbed, leaving him thoughtful and gloomy, almost, as his brooding companion. . . . And it is to be noted that Sam made no mention of Cecily's tear-blotched, imploring letter or the fact that he had determined to meet her, of course, and alone, come what might.

Thus it was they rode at last into Lewes town where, it being market-day, all was stir and bustle. But this afternoon, amid all this cheery clamour, was an ominous undertone, or so thought Mr. Standish as, with much ado, they made their way into the very spacious stable-yard of the "White Hart" Inn.

"Seem to be a dooced lot o' people about today!" said Mr. Standish uneasily, as they dismounted.

"Too true!" nodded Sam. "And devilish ugly-looking customers, see yonder—those are no honest country folk!" And he gestured where beneath shadowy arch, leading in from the busy High Street, a crowd was gathering.

"Those f'lo's, eh?" enquired Mr. Standish, languid of gesture but keenly alert of glance. "Well, well!" he murmured. "What's it mean, Sam?"

"The mischief you foretold, Harry."

"Yes, 'fraid so, m'dear old lord, for I b'lieve they mean business."

"So much the better!" growled Sam. "Violent exercise is precisely what I need. But where the devil are all the stable-lads and ostlers?"

"Gone to earth, old f'lo', and left us, like two dem, devoted foxes, to the hounds yonder. Yes, b'gad, they're stirring— the hunt is up! And what now, do we cheer 'em on with a yoicks, tantivvy and tally-ho; what now, Sam?"

"Wait!"

So these two fronted the many, a motley concourse that now, and very slowly, began to advance against them, and urged on from behind by such cries as:

"Yon's the rebel lord! Down with the Jacobin! Send him back to France and his bloody giller-teen!"

And now the mob began to hoot and jeer:

"Ya—boo! Rebel! Traitor!"

"At him, boys! Duck him! Pitch him into the river!"

"Yes!" nodded Sam, clenching his fists. "Stand back, Harry; it's me they're after, d'ye see——"

"Which, m'dear old lord, means me as well, naturally and of course!" replied Mr. Standish, coiling the lash of his whip to make it a more effective weapon. "Though I venture t'suggest a strategic, though dignified retreat within doors— siege 'stead o' slaughter——"

"NO!" replied Sam, smiling his grimmest. "Oh no. Since they want me, then damm'em they shall have me—stand away and leave 'em to me! Ay, you'll keep out of it, Harry, and that's an order!"

"Tush, Sam, likewise bah, not forgettin' pshaw, tut-tut and a fiddlestick!" sighed Mr. Standish, very mournfully though bright of eye. "If you will have blood and bruises, so must your dooced devoted Standish, and the sooner the better. Let's meet 'em under the arch before they can spread and outflank us. So now—yoicks, old f'lo', tally-ho, hark forrard and away!"

Shouting these words and with whip a-flourish, Harry Standish leapt to battle,—then Sam was beside him and thus, shoulder to shoulder, they assailed their would-be assailants where the way was narrowest. So furiously sudden and unexpected was their attack that the many, crowded thus together and hampered by their very number, reeled back before the shattering impact of Sam's potent fists and the vicious blows of Mr. Standish's flailing whip.

Thus, in the shadow of that narrow archway, the battle raged furiously, and for a while the two held the many at bay until an unseen missile dashed away Sam's hat and, a moment later, another smote him to his knees; but there sprang Harry Standish to defend that now helpless, drooping head in very fury of desperation and gasping as he fought:

"Up . . . old f'lo' . . . up for . . . y'life . . . backs t'the . . . dooced wall now——" And heartened by this so familiar voice, Sam panted in answer:

"Ay, ay . . . messmate, the . . . wall it is!" And speaking, was afoot and grasping a cudgel he had found: feet kicked at him, sticks and fists struck at him, hands clutched and dragged at him, but, smiting now with fist and bludgeon, he won to the wall. And here, shoulder to shoulder again, the devoted two made their last stand, fighting now with the grim desperation of despair. Then, suddenly, above the din and tumult, a hoarse voice bellowed encouragement, the surging mob was riven asunder and their immediate assailants, attacked thus from behind, were hurled aside by the whirlwind onset of a man whose grim visage was rendered the fiercer by a halo of pale whisker that bristled with the utmost ferocity, an exceedingly nimble man whose hatless head, crowned with tow-like hair, became a battering-ram driving all before it, and whose fists, elbows, knees and feet played their several parts with devastating effect.

"B'gad!" panted Mr. Standish in the respite thus afforded. "A perfect . . . dooced paladin!"

"Yes," gasped Sam, watching this whiskered ferocity in joyous wonder, "and, damme, I . . . believe——" His words were cut short by the echoing report of a firearm that seemed to stun all to a silence wherein the hoarse voice bellowed again and very imperiously:

"In the King's name! Give over, ha' done, and—diss-perse afore I blood some on ye and jail more on ye!" Awed by this deafening shot and fiercely commanding voice, the mob swayed, surged backward, hooted, cheered, broke and was gone, leaving in its stead a squatly powerful individual chiefly remarkable for hat, eyes, top-boots and a formidable, very knobbly stick, not to mention the still smoking pistol that he now flourished as in friendly salutation.

"Shrig!" exclaimed Sam, striding forward. "Aha, Jasper old friend, it seems you are again 'my guardian angel in top-boots!'"

"Now blow my dicky!" quoth Mr. Shrig with his rare, throaty chuckle as their hands met and gripped. "My lord and Sam pal, you can burn my neck if them ain't his werry i-dentical vords, spoke and likewise wrote—ar, dog bite me if they ain't!"

"What words and whose, Jasper?"

"Pal Sam, your lordship shall be dooly and fully in-formed thereof so soon as us can be private and no peepers and pryers to look nor yet spy;" and he pointed where divers inquisitive persons adventuring into the yard now stood at gaze; he had gestured with his pistol-hand, whereat these gapers and starers flinched and recoiled, yet paused to stare again though from safer distance. Mr. Shrig sighed, beckoned and said:

"Shush 'em off, Dan'l!"

"Eh? Daniel? Of course!" exclaimed Sam, turning to salute their rescuer. "Daniel my hearty," quoth he, hand outstretched, "you bore down to our help in right gallant style, ay, damme, you broke their line and laid 'em close aboard like Nelson at Trafalgar,—give me that fist o' yours and accept my gratitude!"

And lo! in this moment, even as his hand was gripped, Daniel became his usual self, a mild-eyed, meek-seeming

creature whose hay-like whiskers, ferocious no longer but
instantly tamed, now languished, drooping in their wonted
abject humility as he murmured, feebly:

"Glad t' sarve y'r ludship."

"Ay, but not only me, Daniel, but my friend and messmate,
Mr. Standish. Harry, you behold Daniel and Mr. Jasper Shrig
of Bow Street, old and proved friends of mine, yet never more
so than today. So now follow me and we'll pledge such friendship with a bottle o' the best, Jasper. Put away your pistol
and come."

"Pistol!" repeated Mr. Standish, ruefully. "Now dooce
take me if I didn't forget my own!"

CHAPTER XVII

IN WHICH "THINGS ARE ON THE MOVE"

MOST VISIBLE signs of the recent conflict having been removed, —washed, brushed, refreshed (and refreshing), they sat in a private room of this goodly inn of the "White Hart," partaking together of "the best." And it was now, that is to say, as Sam refilled all glasses for the third time, that Mr. Shrig unbuttoned his trim, blue coat, drew thence a much worn, bulbous pocket-book, saying as he did so:

"Pal and sir, my lord, though your noble tibby or, as you might say, mazzard or nob has took a tidy knock, according to the bump above your right listener, said bump don't obtrood itself upon the general public b'reason of your thick and curly thatch—but—the wiciousness as aimed aforesaid knock or vallop, may have another go! Agreed?"

"Well—possibly," answered Sam, with his flashing smile, "though not very likely, Jasper."

"Contrairiwise, pal and m'lord, there's them as thinks different, seeing as how."

"As how what, Jasper?"

"As how your misfort'nate hoss, chancing to rear, took the ball aimed at y'lordship and died instead o' you."

"Eh, my horse?" repeated Sam, wine glass arrested at lip. "But how on earth should you know of this?"

"Information received, m'lord."

"But who from?"

"Sir and pal—ekker alone responds!"

"Aha," nodded Sam, "mysterious as ever, Jasper!"

"Cautious, my lord, 'cautious' is the vord. But noos of this same willainous attempt agin your lordly person and life has took vings and flew to them as has your velfare at heart, pal, at heart—as this here shall here and now dooly ex-plain."

And from his pocket-book Mr. Shrig drew a letter which he tendered to Sam who, breaking the seal, read this:

> "London (as before),
> July 29, '18.

Right noble lord, this being more than mere business letter, I venture to address you also in hearty friendship as:

My Dear Sam, learning from an unimpeachable source of the late murderous attempt against your person (more precious now than heretofore for obvious reasons) and fearing this dastardly attack may be renewed and with graver consequences to you and yours, I have (maugre your possible displeasure) placed you once again in the protecting care of that same top-booted guardian angel Jasper Shrig, to whose oft-proven sagacity, courage and devotion we (and especially you, my dear Sam), have owed so very much in the past. To know he is again in your vicinity unobtrusively watchful, greatly relieves the newly awakened anxiety of

> Your truly devoted and obedient servant and friend,
> EBENEZER (BEN) JOLIFFE."

"Do you know what's written here, Jasper?"

"Ar, every vord, sir."

"Why then," groaned Sam, with rueful smile, "since you are to haunt me again, you'd best take up your quarters, you and Daniel, at Wrybourne Feveril."

"M'lord, as a pal I thankee, but as a nofficer o' the Law I beg to inform y'r lordship as dooty, vith a werry large Dee, forbids."

"Oh? Ah? Why, Jasper?"

"Sir, since you ax me so p'inted I up and answers you bold and free, because dooty is—dooty!" Sam laughed and, turning to Mr. Standish, enquired:

"Harry, did you ever hear such a fellow?"

"Never, Sam! But now that I do, I regret I didn't and hope I shall—and often. Indeed, Mr. Shrig, I trust you will favour me with your regard and that our acquaintance may ripen to something better, not forgetting Daniel, this paladin and doughty man at arms."

"Honoured sir," answered Mr. Shrig, bowing. "How says you, Dan'l?" This meek-seeming person touched pale eye-brow with sinewy finger, glanced shyly at Mr. Standish and murmured:

"Same here, Jarsper!" At this moment was a tapping on the door which opened to disclose a neatly-clad, snub-nosed boy, who, bobbing uncapped head to the company, came smartly to "attention," regarding the room and apparently everything in it, with very sharp, bright eyes.

"Gimblet," enquired Mr. Shrig, "how's the cows?"

"Bolted, guv!"

"Oh ar?"

"Yus, guv, they've went, 'ooked it they 'ave, one arter t'other."

"Werry good,—though you dropped a couple o' them h-aiches!"

"Well, I h-axes your parding, guv."

"Now yo' got vun o' them too many! And don't call me 'guv'!"

"I axes parding again, guv'nor, and I wishes as they weren't no aitches."

"Hows'ever, gen'lemen," said Mr. Shrig, rising, "since things is on the move, it be-hoves me to do ditter. So, for the present, sirs, the vord is a-doo!"

CHAPTER XVIII

TELLS HOW AND WHY MY LORD RID HIMSELF OF HIS FRIEND

THE HANDS of Sam's watch were close upon the numeral V when he reined up his horse, saying as he did so:

"Ride on, Harry; I'll meet you at the cross-roads yonder, say—in half an hour."

"Eh?" exclaimed Mr. Standish, in sudden anxiety. "Ride on and leave you—here and alone—in almost the exact demmed and dooced spot where your horse was murdered? No no, Sam! Can't leave you—mustn't and won't!"

"At the cross-roads, in half an hour or thereabout," Sam repeated.

"But what the dooce? Why here of all demmed places? And how the devil can I break my word to Andromeda? I cannot and will not——"

"What word, let's hear?"

"Sam, I told you, but I'll tell you again how she made me promise, yes, most solemnly and on my word of honour, that whenever you ventured abroad I must venture too—nor let you out of sight and never alone, that's to say, by yourself. So for her sake and yours, I swore I never would,—which promise I mean to keep, yes, in spite of you, old f'lo'—and dem the confounded consequences! Now, d'you understand?"

"Ay," growled Sam at his grimmest. "Yes, I believe I do! So—that's it, is it?"

"That's what, pray?" demanded Mr. Standish, very stiff in the back.

"You are set on to watch me, eh?"

"No, to watch over you."

"It's pretty much the same."

"On the contrary, it's different as dooced chalk from confounded cheese! One may be the act of a spy, the other the duty of a friend."

"However, I refuse to be spied upon or watched over! Is that plain?"

"It is!" retorted Mr. Standish, chin aloft. "Oh yes, so dev'lish plain that I must tell you as plainly that no dam' thing or body shall make me break my promise to Andromeda."

"Such promise ought never to have been demanded of you——"

"Nevertheless, it was! And, I repeat, it is a promise I am determined to honour—at all hazards!"

"Ha!" growled Sam, in growing fury of bafflement. "D'ye tell me so?"

"Repeatedly!" nodded Mr. Standish, with the utmost resolution. "I shall watch over you with the most dem absolute and unremittingly dooced pertinacity! I don't know why you wish to be alone and risk your life again, and don't wish to know, but if you will, then—so must I!"

Sam began to curse and swear like the rough sailorman he had been, but, checking himself, spoke now like the aristocrat he was:

"Then, sir, you compel me to rid myself of this too-persistent annoyance calling itself Standish."

"Eh, what—what——" stammered that astonished person. "What th' dooce, I say now—wait a bit——" Here Mr. Standish also checked himself and, sitting very erect, continued like the high-bred gentleman he was: "My lord, am I to understand that you are—er—giving me notice, discharging me? Your lordship has been pleased to show devilish bad temper all day,—is this merely a further exhibition of ill-humour to be passed over and dutifully unheeded, or a considered and final order to be obeyed? Your lordship will pray inform me."

"Sir," answered my lord, in tone and with look utterly unlike Sam, "you may be perfectly assured here and now that you are no longer in my service. You will therefore pay yourself a year's salary and relieve me of your officiousness soon as may be. Is this understood?"

"Oh, quite, my lord, quite! Though I must beg to refuse your lordship's proffered bounty and shall accept no more

than is legally due. And now, my lord, since you so desired,
I . . . I'll go . . . but . . . I . . . Oh, dooce take everything—
goodbye!"

Even as he uttered this word of finality, he turned his back
very suddenly and, spurring his horse, galloped away, leaving
Sam to gaze after him more gloomily than ever until all sight
and sound of this his too-devoted friend were lost: then, scowling up at cloudless sky and round about upon this sunny
peaceful landscape, Sam turned from dusty highway and rode
slowly into the shady woodland.

Birds chirped and piped from stately tree and mazy thicket,
Old Sol shot arrowy beams athwart his way, checkering these
leafy solitudes with radiant glory, but Sam rode on, head
adroop, broad shoulders bowed,—all unheeding.

CHAPTER XIX

A CHAPTER SHORT BUT TO THE POINT

MR. STANDISH, meanwhile riding dejectedly homewards, was pondering this sudden, quite ruinous alteration in his circumstances; this unbelievably cruel blow dealt him, and so casually, by the one man he had loved and admired.

How, he asked himself, for perhaps the hundredth time, how on earth was he to break this shattering news to his Rowena? . . . And their baby not yet born! By God, the shock at such time might kill her! . . . Oh, curse Sam . . . damn his soul to hell fire! However could he speak this blasting news to Rowena, as tell her he must. Would she sink and swoon . . . and then? Oh God help them both! . . . Well, if it killed her . . . if she died of it, he would have Sam's blood. Yet Rowena would be dead and the baby too . . . their innocent child. . . . Two in one grave! Merciful God, what was he to do?

Thus, agonizing, poor Harry Standish suffered his horse to wander all unheeded until a thorny bramble clawed him, and, lifting woeful head, he beheld trees, mazy thickets—and—that which suddenly and for the time banished all thoughts of his despairing self; for at no great distance a horseman was standing in his stirrups to peer over a bush, evidently watching someone or something with eyes that glared beneath drawn brows while his lips, backdrawn in wolfish snarl, showed the gleam of fierce-set teeth. . . . Slowly this furtive watcher sank down into his saddle and as slowly, almost as if against his will, drew a long-barrelled pistol from its holster, stared down at it, rammed it fiercely back again and, lifting tremulous fists, bowed his contorted face between them. . . . And it was now that Mr. Standish drew from coat-pocket one of his own pistols, small, elegant, yet sufficiently deadly, and with this levelled against the bowed form of the horseman, rode forward, saying pleasantly:

"Good afternoon, my lord. I'll trouble you for the loan of your barkers." Ralph started erect, and turning, glared speechlessly, wherefore Mr. Standish repeated, gently though firmly: "Your pistols, my lord! And do pray take care how you give them, for," and here he cocked his own weapon, "for, believe me, your lordship inspires me with such feelings that I should be glad to see you a bleeding corpse, I should indeed! So, my lord, be careful!"

Uttering no word, Ralph surrendered his weapons which Mr. Standish, having shaken and blown away their primings, contrived to get into the already weighted pockets of his riding coat, watching Ralph the while who sat motionless, chin on breast, glaring sightlessly earthwards.

Thus they remained, neither speaking until—borne to them on the warm, still air came the sound of distant voices and, though no more than vaguest murmur, their effect upon Ralph was so terrible that Harry Standish, once again forgetting his own grievous trouble, levelled his pistol; but still mute, and without even a glance, Ralph turned his horse and began to ride,—then breaking the silence at last with quite dreadful laugh, he said, over his shoulder:

"Come on, Standish . . . follow close and I'll show you . . . what I've waited to see. . . ."

CHAPTER XX

IN WHICH SAM IS WARNED AND MISJUDGED

ON RODE Sam through sunshine and shadow, yet heedless of both until Old Sol roused him at last by making a glory of Cecily's hair, for she had taken off her plumed hat and now waved it in eager welcome as she rode to meet him.

"Oh, but Sam—my dear!" she exclaimed, as they met. "Whatever is the matter, you look so—so very——"

"Bad-tempered, eh, Cecily?"

"I was going to say 'mournful,' Sam, and so you are."

"However, the sight of you, dear lass, has done me a power o' good."

"But something is grieving you, so won't you tell me, please, and let me try—— Oh my gracious—that dreadful bruise above your temple! And your coat torn! Did—ah, did Ralph meet you—have you been—fighting him——?"

"No, my dear, no! Just a trifling unpleasantness at Lewes, no more. But, Cecily, why did you appoint to meet me here so —well—secretly; why not at Wrybourne as you used to do?"

"Because I durstn't any longer, for fear Ralph should follow me and—harm you. For, oh, Sam, he is so bitterly fierce against you lately that if—if it wasn't for Viscount Twily, I don't know what would happen——"

"Eh, the Viscount? Does he still trouble you?"

"No, Sam, ah no! He is quite—quite changed, so very kind and gentle, Sam! Indeed he is most wonderfully altered since that day here in the wood when you—checked him."

"Ay, with my whip! And you, I remember, told me he looked murderous."

"So he did, Sam, yes and no wonder, for you hit him so very hard!"

"Have you seen him often o' late, Cecily?"

"Yes," she sighed, drooping that very beautiful head of hers, "ah, yes! For when my poor Ralph isn't—very well, the Viscount always brings him safe home to me."

"Ha!" murmured Sam. "So—that's the way of it!"

"What way, Sam, please?"

Sam answered her question with another:

"Ralph has become very friendly with the Viscount lately, hasn't he?"

"Yes," she answered, "yes, he has."

"And Ralph has been drinking harder than ever lately, hasn't he?"

"Yes," she replied with troubled look. "Oh, Sam, what are you suggesting?"

"More than I can prove, Cecily. But I can think, d'ye see, so—what think you?"

"I think," she answered, clasping her hands and wringing them with that gesture of distress he remembered, "I think, ah no,—I'm sure that surely as the Viscount has changed for the better, my poor Ralph has changed and—oh God help us both—is changing for the worse! And this is what I am here to tell you, Sam dear. He raves against you continually and threatens to be the death of you and—himself! Twice lately he has taken his pistols to ride over and shoot you, and each time 'twas only the Viscount could stay him. Last night when they came home he was so—so terrible that—oh, Sam, for the first time I . . . who used to fear nothing . . . last night was afraid of my own husband, though of course I didn't show it. So at last I quieted him. Then the Viscount drew me aside, and made me see how very necessary it was I should write asking you to meet me—not at the Great House as usual, lest Ralph, knowing how often I am there, should surprise us, but here in the wood and—oh, Sam, to warn you of this terrible danger that is—my own husband! So now, Sam dear, now you know what it grieves and shames me to tell and what terrifies me to even think upon. . . . For I be all adread lest some time when I cannot watch, for sleep I must now and then, my poor Ralph may steal away and kill 'ee, Sam, and then—himself! Oh now—what can I, what must I do?"

"Come home with me to Andromeda, my dear."

"No—no, I dare not! He would guess I was there and follow me and maybe—shoot you dead. No, I must surely keep away from the Great House lest I bring death."

"And it was the Viscount suggested you should meet me here in the wood, Cecily?"

"Yes, the wood or anywhere away from the Great House."

"Where is Ralph now?"

"I left him at home asleep—I think. But he may have been only pretending! He may have followed me, he may even be . . . watching us at this moment, which I pray God forbid!"

"Amen!" quoth Sam, with fervour, glancing round about them instinctively. "Now, Cecily, before we go, can you explain Ralph's devilish, murderous hatred of me?"

"Yes," she murmured, with shy, lovely side-glance, "but . . . oh, Sam . . . can't you guess?"

"No, damme if I can!"

"Why then," she answered, speaking like the country girl she had been, " 'tis because he be so . . . mad jealous of 'ee!"

"Eh?" gasped Sam. "Jealous? Of me? The curst, blind fool! I have never given him the least cause——"

"Oh, but Sam—yes!" sighed she, and with another shy, quite adorable side-glance. "Yes . . . indeed you have . . . the very greatest cause!"

"Well, now sink and damme!" exclaimed Sam, in blank and breathless amazement. "I'm all aback! On my beam-ends! Cause? What cause? How, Cecily, how? Good great Lord love us! What have I ever done to cause the fool any least jealousy? Come, let's hear?"

"Dear Sam," she murmured, leaning nearer, "don't look so wildly astonished or so dreadfully troubled; you've no need to because the only reason for Ralph's jealousy is that you are just yourself and that self always so kindly gentle to poor me, besides giving me all that money and making me so very rich."

"The money?" cried Sam. "So—that's it?"

"Yes, that is it," she answered, gently. "And your dear, generous self."

"Well now, bilge me! Whoever heard the like o' this? So

fool Ralph believes that money was to buy you, does he? Ha, what a cursed Scrope he is!"

"There are others do believe the same!" she murmured, long lashes adroop.

"Who, damn 'em, who?"

"They don't matter, Sam. Only I want you to know 'tis my poor Ralph's cruel jealousy makes him drink to forget it."

"More fool he!" growled Sam.

"And then, besides, I want you to know——" The words ended in a startled gasp as from somewhere nearby rose sudden clamour of fierce voices:

"Curse you—stop! Back, d'ye hear?"

"Not I! The devil himself shan't stay me! Shoot and be damned!" Quick thudding of horsehoofs, a crash and rustle in the undergrowth and thence leapt a horseman at furious gallop.

"So ho!" cried Ralph, reining up in full career. "I've caught ye, hey, damned Japhet! So sweetly private—and with your fellow yonder to keep watch and be cursed t'you! Yes, b'God, as cursed as we are now and shall be hereafter—all three of us, you and I and—she, this woman, this too-beautiful wife o' mine that shall be the death and damnation of each of us! I had meant to end you, damned Japhet, and my utterly accursed self too, but, thanks t'your watchdog, this must wait—yet not for long, I promise you——"

"Listen!" cried Sam, fiercely, breaking in upon this wild, breathless tirade. "Listen to me, Ralph, y'fool——"

"Not I, Japhet, y'cursed hypocrite, not a dam' word! I'm snatching this woman away from you, d'ye hear? I'm taking this—this wife of mine home where she ought to be! So, my love, my Cecily, sweet wife, go with your adoring husband,—ha, ride, Beauty, ride!" Then, lashing Cecily's horse and spurring his own, away they went at such reckless speed as very soon bore them out of sight.

"And for once," quoth Sam, addressing his sleek and sleepy mare, "for once, Jennifer lass, our cousin Ralph was deadly sober!"

"Deadly is right!" said a harsh, quite unfamiliar voice, and so unexpectedly near that Sam actually started and, glancing swiftly round, beheld Mr. Standish, tense and motionless in saddle, wide of eye, unwontedly pale and a long-barrelled pistol in each fist. Now motionless also was Sam, for the rigid form seemed poised and strung for desperate action; in this haggard young face, glowing eye, quivering nostril and tight-drawn lip was such a menace that to bring matters to a head and dare all, Sam now spoke with the chill aloofness of his most earl-like self.

"Mr. Standish, I believed myself relieved of your services. Why do I find you trespassing on my land?"

"Right noble lord," answered Mr. Standish with faint though disdainful smile, "first as regards your so lordly cousin. I surprised him peeping over a bush and fondling these very businesslike tools, so, having relieved him of them, deemed it advisable to keep him in sight. This explains my unwelcome presence—and now—take these dem unwelcome things!" and he thrust the weapons upon Sam, who made to throw them away, pocketed them instead, and inquired:

"Well, Harry, what now?"

"Now, my lord, I shall rid myself of your lordship right speedily."

Sam blinked, frowned, laughed and held out his hand, saying:

"Harry, if I so hurt your feelings I ask your forgiveness, for, as you know, I'm damnably troubled and perplexed and —need you. So come, shake hands and—I'll double your salary."

"My lord," answered Mr. Standish, bowing with extreme of languid irony, "be damned to you and your offer!"

"Eh . . . what . . . what?" stuttered Sam. "Why . . . what the devil——"

"I mean, my lord, that any man with such lady as your Andromeda, who can dally in a wood with another man's wife, is totally unfitted for my society! So permit me to repeat, and very earnestly, be damned to you!"

Sam, being quite beyond adequate retort, clenched his fists, whereat Mr. Standish smiled more disdainfully than before, shook his head contemptuously, and galloped away, leaving Sam in such fury as even he had never known.

CHAPTER XXI

HOW THE DOLL BATILDA DELIVERED AN EVIL MESSAGE

CLOCKS were chiming to tell the hour was six as Andromeda, returning from certain duty calls, dismissed the carriage and turned to enter the Great House, this vast relic of so many differing ages; this glory of richly-carved timbering, white plaster, ruddy brick and mellow stone—though all overshadowed by the grey, embattled walls and soaring, mighty keep of the castle that from time far beyond memory had been called Feveril.

Now, as Andromeda stood to gaze up at this hoary structure, its shadow seemed to deepen about her with such ominous and deadly chill that instinctively she recoiled, until kindly Old Sol took her in his warm embrace, blessing her with his life-giving radiance.

And now she was further comforted and gladdened by the deep, joyous barking of a dog (her one-time shaggy champion and defender), and therewith the sweet, clear voice of Jane calling to her rather breathlessly by reason of her quick, light-scampering feet:

"Ooh . . . Auntie . . . Meeda . . . dear Auntie Mee . . . don't go in . . . yet . . . 'cause here's Esau an' me coming to . . . tell you such a . . . wonnerful, magic——"

"Darling!" said Andromeda, stooping very joyfully to kiss the small, eager face and fondle the great dog's shaggy head. "Tell me, dear, what is so wonderful?"

"Well," Jane explained, "I do b'lieve there's magic an' witches all about us, because my Batilda, that cheevious child of mine, has gone and climbed herself up into a tree. So I'm 'fraid she's got herself frighflee magicanwitched!"

"Goodness me, Jane, how?"

"That's what I want you to find out for me, please, Auntie Meedear. You see, I left my Batilda sitting on the lawn so good as gold with my slate an' pencil to do the sum what I'd set her—two and two make four—while I took Esau to the stables for some water because he was thirsty an' so was I. Well—when we came back—there was my Batilda up into a tree, out of reach like a bird—only she's got something in her arms. So will you please to come and get her for me?"

"Of course, my precious! Come along."

Thus presently Andromeda beheld this greatly-loved, much-pampered, oft-chastised doll perched securely in the fork of a branch—but—clasping in its small arms something at mere sight of which Andromeda, suddenly arrested, stood rigid and felt again that dreadful, icy chill.

"Ooh, Auntie Mee, whyever do you stare so? It's only my Batilda an' she won't hurt you. So won't you please to help her down for me?" Dumb with a sickening premonition, Andromeda hesitated, then, setting her chin, she took down the doll and, fingers atwitch with a horrified repugnance, drew from its clasping arms a folded paper. . . . Then Jane spoke, hushed and whimpering:

"Oh, Auntie Meeda—don't—please don't, you—frighten me! Your eyes look so big an' norful! An' why do you shiver like you felt very cold?"

"Because," answered Andromeda, with lips almost too stiff for utterance, "Jane dear . . . I . . . am cold——"

"But, Auntie Meedear, the sun's so nice an' warm."

"Yes, Jane . . . yes, it is . . . but . . . Oh, take your Batilda, my dearest."

"Thank you! An' now—what was it she gave you, please, Auntie?"

"Only this . . . nasty piece of . . . paper. A very nasty . . . dirty thing—see!" And speaking, Andromeda crumpled this so hateful thing in the daintily-gloved hand that shook so pitiably "There! Now, Jane dear, go and tell Grannyanne I am home and should like a . . . cup of tea, will you, my precious?"

"Yes, dear Auntie Mee—wiv the greatest of pleasures!" answered Jane, with a bright nod; then, clutching Batilda under her arm, away she sped, the great dog bounding joyously beside her. . . . Not until this sweet innocence was out of sight did Andromeda unclose that tremulous hand, then un-folding the paper, she read these ill-spelt, badly-written words:

"Onnered lady if you was to go into the wood this after-noon att five you might see dooings to shame and brake yore hart your own lord as shud no better and his golden beauty I say no moor only tis crewel as you shud be so abyoused."

Again this paper was crumpled up angrily and then thrown away disgustedly, only to be snatched up, smoothed out and re-perused, this time more carefully—and now hidden swiftly at sound of approaching horsehoofs; glancing thitherward, she beheld Mr. Standish who, thinking himself unobserved, was riding slowly like the utterly dejected, bitterly disillusioned young fellow he was.

"Harry!" she cried, whereat he started erect, wheeled his horse adroitly, and instantly seemed his most gaily debonair self who smiled, bowed gracefully, hat aflourish, and dis-mounted, all in as many moments.

"Well?" she demanded, and with no answering smile. "Why are you alone?" Mr. Standish fumbled with his hat, put it on, took it off again and answered:

"Force of dooced circumstance, Andromeda! For, my dear, you must know—and it grieves me no end to tell you, as I must, though, 'pon my soul, I don't know how——"

"Is it about—Sam?"

"Well, yes—yes, of course, but——"

"Oh—is he hurt?"

"No! Oh Lord no,—boot's on t'other leg—contrariwise, Andromeda, for as I tell you——"

"But you don't! You aren't telling me anything, Harry."

"I'm doing my poor, confounded best," he sighed, "for confounded I am and most doocedly——"

"Oh," she cried, rather wildly, "why have you broken your word to me? What are you doing here—alone? Why are you not with Sam? How could you have left him—and after your sacred promise to me?—Oh, Harry!"

"Ex-actly!" he groaned. "My promise! I—I did my absolute best to keep it, my dear, with the result that I have lost—lost all, yes—every dooced thing and——"

"Harry, what do you—mean?"

"That I'm the sufferer, and my Rowena, not Sam! I'm the poor, confoundedly injured innocent, though I may not look it, but it's the fact—and such fact that I'm wondering how on earth to break such news to Rowena!"

"What are you trying to tell me, Harry?"

"Well, plainly, that I have received notice, that's the proper phrase, I believe; I have been—discharged, dismissed, turned away—all in a moment! Though I can scarcely believe it—yet."

"Nor can I!" said Andromeda, her golden eyes very bright. "Nor will I believe such perfect nonsense!"

"Would to heaven it were nonsense!" he sighed. "But the word has been spoken, the fiat has gone forth, and I, we,—Rowena and I,—leave Wrybourne tonight or as soon as possible."

"No!" said Andromeda, setting that dimpled, resolute chin of hers. "Oh no! I will not allow it! I will never permit such cruel, such base injustice! This I utterly forbid!"

"Dear Andromeda!" he sighed, and with rueful smile, "You are always your gracious self, but—Sam is lord and master here, a very dominating lord and occasionally, at present, very much so, and a bad man to cross at all times."

"Yes, he is very determined, but—so am I! Now tell me where you and he parted company?"

"On our way home."

"Ah, so you rode from Lewes together? Where did he leave you?"

"About a mile from here."

"A mile?" she murmured. "That would be near Fallowdene Thicket. And why did he leave you?"

"Well . . . I suppose to . . . be rid of my company."

"Had you quarrelled?"

"Oh no, but he had been low-spirited all day, very gloomily thoughtful——"

"Yes? Now tell me—why did he desire to be left alone, and in—such place?"

"And I'm fairly sure," continued Mr. Standish, avoiding this awkward question, "that you were responsible, Andromeda."

"For what?"

"His persistent gloom and depression."

"Did he tell you that?"

"Not exactly; all he said was that he felt you were 'changed and changing'. Those were his precise words."

"Well, if that was all, now answer my question, Harry, and tell me,—why did you leave him?"

"Because I—I rather gathered that he suspected—I mean to say, he suggested——"

"What did he suspect?"

"Oh well—that I was—actually—spying on him——"

"As you were, of course, Harry."

"Who? I? Spying? Good lord—no! Should scorn such odious business!"

"And he suspected you, Harry, because—guilt is always suspicious. So now, answer me unreservedly—why did he so desire to be alone, meaning, of course—out of your sight?"

"But . . . Andromeda . . . good heavens! Oh, I say, now . . . how can I tell you that?"

"You could, Harry, but you won't, because you are a man and he is a man and I am his wife! He was . . . expecting . . . hoping to . . . meet . . . somebody in Fallowdene Wood, of course! Wasn't he?"

"Not that I knew."

"But . . . he did . . . didn't he?"

"Oh, the . . . the dooce . . ." stammered Mr. Standish, not daring to meet her searching gaze. "I say, you know . . . what I mean is, I . . . I can't . . . cannot answer."

"My poor Harry!" she murmured, with soft, quite terrible laugh. "Really, it is quite ridiculous and no use your prevaricating, because . . . God help me . . . I know!"

"Eh . . . oh . . . do you . . . then . . . egad——" And when he had thus stuttered to dismayed silence, Andromeda continued:

"Yes, I know when and where and . . . whom he met . . . and has met before with such . . . hateful stealth and in such . . . abominable secrecy! I know because this . . . this vile, sordid thing tells the shameful truth! Take it, read it, and say of it what you can, Harry!" And speaking thus breathlessly, she thrust the anonymous letter into his unwilling grasp and unwillingly he read.

"Well?" she demanded, taking back the letter. "What have you to tell me—now?"

"That this . . . this devilish, quite damnable message suggests more, far more than the actual truth."

"Oh, but what—what is the truth?" she cried, with despairing gesture. "What am I to believe?"

"That they met and talked, no more!"

"Then you . . . saw them together . . . in the wood?"

"Yes, I saw them upon their horses, talking together—and I know that vile letter for very foul, scandalous lie!"

"How can you be . . . sure?"

"I am sure!"

"But . . . how is it possible? Could you see them, hear them . . . all the time they were . . . together?"

"No, but sure I am!"

"But why, Harry, why?"

"Because I know them, especially Sam."

"And do you think I don't? Do you?"

"Why, no, I . . . b'gad, I don't know what to think! But, Andromeda, oh my dear, have patience and don't, ah, don't judge hastily! To doubt Sam is to do him cruel injustice; to show him your doubt would hurt him so deeply that—well, God alone knows what would happen! So, for your own sake and his, I beg you to have faith in him, believe only the best of him, and when he comes home to you give him glad welcome. So now,—do pray tear up that cursed letter, my dear, let me see you tear up the foul thing——"

But instead of so doing, she folded it very carefully and slipped it into her glove, saying:

"Harry, you're a very true, a wonderfully loyal friend, yet— only a man, judging as a man will and must, I suppose. But, being a woman, I naturally see all things from a totally opposite viewpoint and must act accordingly. And my present act is to right a cruel wrong and countermand my . . . husband's most unjust order. You will, therefore, remain at Wrybourne!"

"Oh, but . . . Andromeda, I . . . I'm eternally grateful t'you, but . . . well . . . how can I?"

"If you cannot and will not, Harry, then—neither will I! If you leave Wrybourne, dragging your poor Rowena with you—and she in no fit state for travel or worry,—if you do, then, Harry, in that same hour I shall go too and with my precious baby, of course. Yes, we will all go to my god-mother in London!"

"Aha, the Duchess!" exclaimed Mr. Standish, laughing for the first time during this scene. "B'ged, she could set matters right, I'll warrant!"

"Well, Harry, do I order the carriage? Yes or no."

"No, my dear, no,—at least not for the present, but . . . if needs must . . . b'Jingo, there's nobody like Her Grace of Camberhurst! So small, so dooced great, so quick-witted, so altogether potent!"

"Yes, she is all that, thank God! If needful, her strength shall be our refuge. Now, I must to my precious beloved infant. I haven't seen or heard him for hours. . . . Oh, Harry, what a joy and comfort a baby can be—but you'll know soon, I hope! Now, home with you to your beautiful Rowena, give her my love, but—not a word to trouble her!"

"Not a single word!" he repeated fervently. "And . . . b'ged, Andromeda, you're rather wonderful, y'know,—but then you always were and you've comforted me no end, new hope, and . . . and . . . so on! I'm more grateful than I can ever say and—all I do say is—thank you!" Raising her hand to his lips he kissed it with an ardour tempered with deepest reverence. Then lightly he swung to saddle and gaily away he rode towards the Dower House, a young husband speeding to those best of all earthly joys, home and wife, while this other wife watched through sudden mist of painful tears ere she turned towards her own more stately home where that ominous shadow was deepening even now, for kindly Old Sol was gone.

CHAPTER XXII

TELLS OF A LOCKED DOOR

Clocks again are chiming news that the hour is eight, when Sam (or rather the Earl) tosses his horse's reins to the waiting groom, scowling so malevolently that the poor fellow, mistakenly thinking himself the cause therefor, shrinks and touches his hat repeatedly and is so doing when my lord enters the Great House,—where footmen and servants, instantly aware that something is amiss, melt seemingly into thin air as their lord and master strides, spurs jingling, from room to room—seeking, perhaps, his once too-devoted Standish, but certainly his wife, and, finding neither, tugs bell-rope so violently that the bell is still ringing when a footman appears, breathless with haste and apprehension.

"Her ladyship—is she in?" The writhing footman believes so, but is not sure.

"Send Perkins here, at once!"

The footman bows and vanishes, glad to flee that scowling presence. A knock, and the butler, his usual stateliness somewhat mitigated, bows upon the threshold.

"Is my lady home yet?"

"Yes, my lord. Oh, indeed—yes! Her ladyship returned some hours ago——"

"Then where is she?"

"My lord, I can but venture to opine that her ladyship may be in the nursery or peradventure secluded in her boodwar——"

"Go and say I desire speech with her."

"Yes, my lord. Oh yes, I will at once so inform——"

"Then go! And hurry, d'ye hear?"

"Indeed, yes, my lord!" And, for once at least, Mr. Perkins makes such haste that very soon he is back again, his pomposity quite, quite gone,—indeed he might be almost said to wilt as, wheezing and breathless, he reports:

"The Countess, my lord, has retired, and I—ahem!—am to inform your lordship that—hem—her gracious ladyship—ahem—desires, that is, my lord, I—ahum——"

"Desires what, fool? What does she desire?"

"No—n-no—disturbance, my lord."

"Ha!" exclaims the Earl, with such look and gesture that Mr. Perkins retreats backward to the door, but there pauses heroically, to inquire:

"Is there—anything more, my lord?"

"No, damme, this will suffice!"

"Then, my lord, pray will your lordship be pleased to suffer me to—to go?"

"Ay, to the devil and be damned!"

"I th-thank your lordship." Mr. Perkins closes himself from the presence with shaking hand, mops perspiring brow and totters to the haven of his pantry, there to hearten and solace himself with something potent in a glass; thus comforted and strengthened, he seeks Mrs. Leet, this never-failing standby, and lays the nerve-shattering case before her: my lord's shocking humour and her ladyship's so dreadfully rash defiance. Grannyanne listens serenely, asks a question or so, bids him check all gossip in the servants' hall and rises with her usual placid dignity and prodigious rustling of voluminous bombazeen skirts; then, in leisured manner, rustles across vast, echoing hall and up wide stairway, and thus at last to a certain richly-carved and gilded door whereon she taps softly, though with decision, until:

"Who is it?" a muffled voice inquires.

"Only Grannyanne."

A key turns, bolts are withdrawn, the door opens and, almost in that moment, Andromeda, uttering a heartbroken cry, is in those cherishing arms, her tear-wet face hidden in the warm, strong comfort of Grannyanne's embrace, while a sobbing voice gasps breathlessly:

"I . . . loved him! Oh, Grannyanne, I . . . loved him . . . too much . . . too much, and now he . . . is killing it and I am . . . praying for death . . . to end this anguish." The wise old eyes, so quick to see and heed, look deep; the bony old hand smoothes pain-wrinkled brow; the placid, gentle voice has in its every tone an infinity of consolation:

"My love, my dear, tell me all about it."

"Yes . . . yes, I will. Oh, Grannyanne, how glad I am to have you! Now, hold me close and listen——" The door closes, key turns, and bolts are shot . . . a splendid, strong and very forbidding door!

The hours pass; my lord sups in lonely state, eating little but, for once, drinking deep,—rises with a suddenness that causes a waiting footman to drop a dish and Mr. Perkins to emit a faint inarticulate croak, and strides away to wander disconsolate in a silence broken only by his own solitary going . . .

Slowly the laggard hours pass until, once again, the clocks are telling all who are yet awake that it is now eleven . . . and my lord stands, candle in hand, the Great House all hushed and grimly silent as a tomb. . . .

Very slowly my lord ascends the stair . . . he reaches that gilded door, attempts to open it, finds it resists him and, falling back a step, scowls at this forbidding obstacle whose gilded panels seem to mock him; he raises clenched fist to strike, yet does not; draws breath for angry speech, but is dumb,— for here and in his own house my lord stands utterly confounded. . . . Turning at last, he goes silently away, back down the stair, across dim, lofty old hall where the flickering light of his candle wakes the gleam of shapes in polished armour that seem to start out upon him from the surrounding gloom as if endued with sudden life to menace him; but on he goes and, entering his library, takes paper and quill that squeaks and scratches as he writes:

"To Andromeda, Countess of Wrybourne:

Madam: Your will, now as ever, shall be my law. But my law shall compel you to plead with all humility and sue my forgiveness before I consent to cross your ladyship's threshold again.

Wrybourne."

"To my wife Andromeda: So be it, lass, though what 'tis all about, damme if I can fathom, nor shall I trouble. But you are on a foul course and with breakers hard in your lee and no anchorhold. Yet carry on till the wind shifts or you are aground, bilged and helpless. Then give me a hail and I'll haul you clear, like the faithful,

Sore puzzled,
devilish angry sailorman
and confounded husband I am,
SAM.

Now I'll to bed and as far from you as may be."

So the clocks, ticking life away, told the passing hours that lengthened to days, while with each hour and day the shadow on Wrybourne Feveril grew ever blacker.

CHAPTER XXIII

TELLS HOW JANE TRANSFORMED SIR ROBERT HER "FAIRY UNCLE", ROBIN GOODFELLOW

SIR ROBERT CHALMERS having laboured at his "pot-hooks and hangers" with very ill success, tossed aside his quill, crumpled up his inky efforts and, the afternoon being glad with sunshine, rang for his horse.

"So?" demanded Mistress Elspeth, appearing from nowhere as he mounted. "And whaur awa' the noo, Rabbie man?"

"Out!" said he, pettishly. "For if I can't write left-handed, I can at least ride."

"And I am asking you—where?"

"Anywhere!" he answered, carefully hiding his stump in breast of the riding coat that moulded his powerful form.

"Aweel, tak heed o' the shaws, woods and siccan murdersome places."

"Ay, I will that!" he nodded. "Though life is none so joyous, I should cherish it, or dread the losing of it, Elspeth. If a murderer's bullet chances to end me, 'twould be no great matter; there'd be none to grieve or miss me, save yourself, Elspeth."

"True enough, Robin, and more's the pity! 'Tis a vera loveless, friendless body y'are, and all by reason o' your own proud self, Robin!"

"Well, I want no friends, not I! And . . . as for love, the only woman I ever could and did love, eloped with the fellow I ought to have shot to death instead of only to wound."

"Howandever, fool Robin, that was no way to win any true woman's love! Oh, Robert, you that might have been such a man o' men, are yet no more and no better than a bit fool boy. Ay and spoilt at that; a pampered, pettish child."

"And you are a shrew, Elspeth, and with right curst tongue! Devil take me if I know how or why I endure you——"

"Because ye must, my mannie! And because, spite all your
tom-fool arrogance, your silly, futile furies and flummeries,
you love me like a son! Now, deny it if ye can, puir, lonesome wean that y'are! Go on, deny it if ye can—and dare!"
Sir Robert frowned, took firm grip of the reins with his one
hand, then, looking down into the keen eyes that gazed up
at him so defiantly and yet with a patient wistfulness, smiled
suddenly and nodded ere he cantered away.

"And," sighed Mistress Elspeth, thin hands tight-clasped,
"may the kind Lord God and Father of us all go with him
and guide him, amen!"

Sir Robert, always too conscious of that ghastly stump of
his, avoiding all main roads as usual, went by sequestered
lanes and bridle-paths and thus it befell that, as he followed
a certain leafy track, there reached him a childish voice, very
clearly sweet, upraised in song; the tune was "Barbara Allen",
but the words were very different, being these:

> " 'When I have growed myself quite big
>   I know what I shall do—hoo.
> I'll have a cow an' a nice, fat pig,
>   An' lots of babies too—hoo.
> An' if my babies aren't quite good
>   Then they shall have no——' "

This song was interrupted by the sudden fierce barking of a
dog until:

"Be quiet, Esau!" cried the child-voice. "Hush an' lie down
like a nice, p'lite, 'bedient gentleman dog!" The deep barking sank to a whine, a snuffle and silence; Sir Robert drew his
horse to a walk and, slowly approaching thus, beheld a small
feminine person seated demurely between a somewhat bedraggled doll and a very large, powerful dog who, watchful
of eye, had bowed shaggy head submissively beneath the small
hand of his mistress, while she gazed up at this tall horseman
who, pulling up his animal, looked down at her; and so for
a while was silence. At last, as if reassured, Jane nodded,
saying:

"Good afternoon! I'm writing another pome into my copy-book—this one, so please can you tell me what rhymes wiv 'pudding'?" Sir Robert's sombre eyes were lit by a sudden, quite unwonted gleam as he answered, and in tone that matched his dawning smile:

"Why no, I'm afraid not. 'Pudding' is such an awkward word, at least in a poem, but would 'pie' do instead?"

"Oh—yes, yes it will, puffeckly! How frightflee clever of you! D'you make pomes, too?"

"No, I don't . . . but then, I have never tried."

"Why haven't you?"

"Because I'm afraid writing poems is quite beyond me. . . . I mean, I'm not clever enough."

"Well, would you like me to read you mine?"

"Very much."

"Then I will, 'cause you're so clever with 'pie' an' so nice an' big, an' I like you."

"Like—me?" he repeated, almost as if finding this difficult to believe. "Do you—really?"

"Yes, reely an' trooly! I like all men what are nice an' big an' strong like my Uncle Sam, an' kind, like you."

"Do you think I am kind?"

"Oh yes—yes I do, so now I'll read you my pome if you'll get off your horse and sit here by me and my Batilda. An' you needn't be 'fraid of Esau. I'll take care of you, an', besides, he only bites nasty people. Come!"

Obediently, Sir Robert alighted and, having tethered his horse, sat down beside Jane, who instantly gave him Batilda to nurse, which he did rather awkwardly, cuddling her in his left arm and to his own profound amazement.

"Now," said Jane, taking up her copy-book, "if you'll give me your 'tention like my Granny says to me when she reads to me, I'll read to you. In this book," said she, opening it, "I have wrote three pomes, one 'bout a little, lonely star, and two 'bout the moon, so which shall I read first, please?"

"About the star."

"Very well, only please don't hold my Batilda so upside downy, 'cause she's quite a dellycate child an' so easily upset

—yes, that's much better. Now I'll read you of the star what peeped at me froo the lattice window one night when I couldn't go to sleep." And forthwith, in her peculiarly clear voice, Jane read:

> " 'Sometimes when I'm in bed, I see
> A little star peep down at me.
> An' all alone, alone is he,
> As lonely, lonely as can be——'

Please do you think that's too many lonely's?"

"Oh no. Please go on." And Jane continued:

> " 'As lonely, lonely as can be
> An' so I said—poor, little star,
> If you so lonely, lonely are,
> Wivout a sister or a brother,
> Or any father, any mother,
> Then you're like me and I'm like you,
> For sometimes I get lonely too,
> 'Cause I've no sister an' no brother,
> Nor any father, any mother,
> To kiss an' tuck me up in bed,
> 'Cause long ago they both went dead,
> So I've got Granny now instead.
> So little star, I hope that you
> Have got yourself a Granny too.'

That's the end of that one; did you—do you like it?" she inquired, with the harrowing anxiety of authorship.

"Yes," he answered gravely. "Yes, indeed I do."

"Well, now here's the two 'bout the moon an' they're quite short:

> 'The man what in the moon I see,
> I think so very tired must be,
> For always, always on his back
> He carries such a great, big sack.'

An' here's the last what I made today—it reely belongs to the other, only I've made it two to look more:

'But when the moon goes small an' pale
An' looks just like a big thumbnail,
Then 'stead of the old man, I see
A lady looking down at me.'

And that," said Jane, closing her book, "that's all I've got
with me, 'cept one more 'bout a fairy, an' this is my very
lastest last." And forthwith she read aloud:

" 'Robin is a fairy who
Loves all nice kind things to do,
Robin Goodfellow his name is,
An' so Robin just the same is——'

Oh!" she gasped, in quick distress, "why d'you smile . . .
is it 'cause you think my pome is silly?"

"No, no!" he replied with almost passionate fervour. "No,
I only smiled because—well—my name is Robin, too."

"Is it?" she cried, shrill with joy. "Is it—reely an' truly?"

"Yes, that really is my name. Will you tell me yours?"

"I'm Jane an' you are Robin Goodfellow, so you shall be
my fairy uncle! So give me your hands and say the magic
what my Auntie Meeda learned me when she made herself
my fairy auntie—and this is the magic what we must say:

'Hands in hands I promise thee
Thy fairy uncle I will be——'

So now,—take hands."

He gave her his left.

"Oh, but," said she, "I must have your other one too!"

"No!" he replied, smile instantly banished from quivering
lip. "No, not—the other."

"Oh, why? Have you hurted it?"

"Yes!" he muttered, avoiding her eager gaze.

"Then I'll bind it up in my hankchief an' make it better
for you."

"No, you couldn't!"

"But my Granny says you never know till you try. So here's

my hankchief; it's not very dirty,—then I'll kiss the place to make it well like my Auntie Mee does when things hurt me."

"Kiss it?" he repeated, rather bitterly. "Would you? I wonder!"

"What d'you wonder, please?"

"If it wouldn't disgust you—make you afraid."

"Oh no, I'm never 'fraid of anything—'cept wild bears and nasty men in woods an' things what squeak at me in the dark,—so let me 'tend to your poor hand, like a good 'bedient uncle."

"I can't . . . my dear."

"Are you 'fraid I'd hurt it again?"

"No. . . . Oh no," he replied, his deep voice faltering. "You wouldn't . . . cannot, because . . . ah, Jane . . . you must know . . . yes, I must tell you . . . this right arm of mine . . . has no hand——"

"Ooh!" she exclaimed, in a kind of ecstasy. "How frightflee wonnerful you are, Uncle Robin!"

"Wonderful?" he repeated, marvellously surprised. "But how, Jane, why?"

"'Cause you must be so very, very clever to ride your horse an' do everything with only one hand! D'you s'pose if you showed me the place an' I kissed it prop'ly, oh, do you s'pose we could grow you another, a fairy an' magic one?"

"Jane," said he, leaning nearer, "would you . . . actually actually try?"

"O' course," she nodded, "with greatest of pleasure! That's what Mr. Perkins always says an' he's very p'lite always. . . . And now, 'cause you're my fairy uncle there must be lots of magic all 'bout us, so—show me where your poor hand used to be——"

"But," said he, hesitating, "I'm afraid it may shock you . . . will it, Jane?"

"Oh no!" she answered serenely. "No, it won't, not a bit, for when my Batilda's arm came off, her whole arm, it didn't shock me a bit. So then James came an' stuck it on again. James is frightflee clever like you."

"Who is James?"

"Our second footman. Now show me your poor arm, an' I'll do my bestest best for you, come 'long!" And so, from its hiding-place, slowly, almost fearfully, Sir Robert withdrew his mutilated arm and, expectant of her shrinking horror, watched her with a quite painful intensity. . . . Jane surveyed this silk-clad stump, touched it very tenderly with one small, gentle finger, clasped it in cherishing hands and, drawing it to her breast, stooped and touched it with her lips. . . . Then his other arm was about her, and she looked up into eyes bright and gentle, almost, as her own.

"Oh," she whispered, "I do b'leeve you're going to cry! Did I hurt you again?"

"No!" he murmured, rather brokenly. "God love you . . . no! Ah, Jane . . . little Jane, you have given me something . . . better than my hand . . . something I have been missing all my life, though never knew it—until now." And stooping suddenly, he kissed her bright hair and this smooth, childish brow unmarked as yet by care or sorrow.

"Dear Uncle Robin," said she, nestling closer within his arm, "I like you such lots an' lots that I'll write you into a pome. Would you like me to?"

"Yes, I should!" he answered fervently. "Yes, indeed I should."

"Well then, tonight, before my Granny makes me go to bed, I'll——" A distant clock chimed the hour and Jane, having counted the strokes, sighed: "Five! That means tea-time, so I must go or Granny'll send everybody to look for me like she always does when I'm the teeniest bit late. So, Goodbye, Uncle Robin Goodfellow, till I find you again."

"Tomorrow, and here, Jane?"

"Yes, t'morrow!" she nodded. "So now please stoop an' let me kiss you goodbye." And, almost shyly, he obeyed. . . . Then clutching Batilda and copy-book with one arm and Esau's shaggy neck with the other, away she went, the afternoon mellow sunshine all about her, while Sir Robert stood to watch her, and in his eyes now a light not of the sun. Presently he mounted and rode his solitary way, but, thinking of Jane, he forgot all else and felt a gladness never known until now.

CHAPTER XXIV

TELLS OF A REMORSEFUL DAWN

IN THE light of guttering candles, Ralph, Lord Scrope, sat perfectly sober, unutterably woeful and completely despairing, for he had, at last, committed the unforgivable crime. Head in hands, he thought of and grieved for what had befallen a few hours ago—his furious, raving jealousy and Cecily's pitying gentleness, which of itself had maddened him the more . . . and he had demanded answer to that question which shamed him to utter and which, after one passionate denial, had rendered her dumb until, fury rising to frenzy, he had struck. . . .

He glanced now with horror from his torn knuckle to that corner where she had fallen. . . . He heard again her voice, gentle then as ever, saying—and, oh, God forgive him—with bleeding lips, those words he was never to forget . . . "Oh, Ralph, I'm afraid my teeth have cut your hand; go and bathe it. . . ." And he had gone, not to tend his broken knuckle, but because her very gentleness had shamed him from her presence; when he ventured to return she had gone upstairs to that room he now dared not profane. Thus all night long he had sat here in misery of shame and remorse, knowing himself beyond all forgiveness, even hers. So now, as he crouched, head in hands, he saw there was but one course open, either somehow or other to win back her love and his own self-respect or end his wretched existence.

The candles flickered, the curtains before the open lattice rustled with faint and ghostly sound, as in from the garden stole a cool breath, sweet with the fragrance of flowers—her flowers; and, lifting heavy head, he saw that between these curtains day was beginning to peep; haggardly he watched this growing brightness until, like promise of new life, into this dim chamber shot a beam of sunlight. Then he arose and,

sweeping back the curtains, looked out into a radiant dawn. . . .
Yes, surely hope was there, a new beginning, a better life—perhaps even the way back to Cecily's love—and happiness, could
he but find that way. Yes, out yonder it must be sought, this
way to fit and prove himself worthy, if only to kneel and
crave her pity. Some way . . . any way, could he only find
it . . . as find it he must, or die. . . . Stirred by this determination, he crossed to the table and began to write desperately,
heedless alike of spelling or grammar, setting down all that his
bitterly remorseful grief prompted:

"Most deer and ever beloved Cecily, because I am no
longer worthy, nor ever was, of your angellic gentle goodness, nor ever shall be, I am going away in the hope that
someday and somehow I may win back your deer love and
my self respeckt. God only knows how truly and deeply I
regret the past and hait and despyse myself. So beloved
Cecily dearest have mercy to think the best of me you can,
pray for me and know that I have always loved you and
allways shall, but never moor than now that I am

Your grieving remorssfull
adoring husband
and most miserabble
RALPH.

P.S. If ever I can think myself a littel more worthy I shall
speed back to kiss your dear, beloved feet, but till then
God bless and keep you."

This ill-spelt, rather boyish, very manly letter, he folded,
sealed and superscribed, then, moving silently as possible, he
took hat, cloak and pistols, glanced once more towards that
one particular corner, sighed deeply, and went forth into this
new day to seek his better self.

F

CHAPTER XXV

HOW RALPH SOUGHT HIS BETTER SELF

RALPH had travelled hardly a mile when his horse cast a shoe. Ralph thereupon drew a deep breath to curse, but—sighed instead and, dismounting, led his animal by field paths and woodland tracks long familiar, until he came where, bowered in trees and close beside an exceeding neat white-washed cottage, stood a particularly grim and grimy forge, this village smithy where Jem Lacey plied his ancient craft and whose smoke-blackened roof and walls had so often been Ralph's secure haven and refuge in the days of his motherless boyhood, against and from that stately, soft-spoken terror—his lordly sire.

Just at present the place was silent and deserted, for the clock of Wrybourne Church had not yet struck five; nevertheless, on ordinary occasions Ralph would have bellowed and roared the smith to wakefulness and service, but this morning, having tied his horse, he entered the smithy, took a battered three-legged stool from its usual corner, and sat down to wait.

Elbow on knee, chin in hand, he gazed out from this place of gloom to the glory outside where the young sun's level beams were lighting small fires in dewy grass and leafage, while birds, newly waked, sang together their joyous anthem of the dawn, filling the fragrant air with a very ecstasy of gladness. . . . But Ralph, crouched in the shadow of smoke-blackened, silent forge, stared before him with haggard eyes, beneath brows knit in mental anguish; for, instead of this sunny prospect, he saw again that candle-lit room . . . and Cecily lying, felled by his dastard blow; above the rapturous chorus of these carolling birds he heard again her voice, gentle as ever . . . her softly uttered words: "Oh Ralph, I'm afraid my teeth have cut your hand. . . ." Ralph closed his eyes but the haunting vision persisted—he covered his ears, but those heartbreaking words seemed only the clearer. And knowing this was in some part the penalty exacted by his remorse-ful and better self, he bowed his head and folded long arms submissively, to suffer and endure how best he might.

Motionless he sat, living that dreadful scene over and over again,—his furious blow, her sobbing cry as she fell, her words of tender care for the brutal fist that had disfigured and struck her down. . . .

Thus, crouched upon this same old stool wherefrom he had often dangled his short legs as a small boy, Ralph the man now suffered all the agonies of a remorse inflicted by his better self with no mercy for his old and evil self. . . .

"Lor' love us all!"

Roused by these words, he started, glanced up and beheld Jem Lacey, this middle-aged, bearded Hercules who in his day had been a "man of his hands", later on a champion wrestler, and always young Ralph's boyish defender and hero, who now gazed down on him with reproachful blue eyes and shake of grey head as he enquired:

"Mas'r Ralph, m'lord, you'm oncommon early, or are ye late? Be this for you the end o' last night or the beginning of today?"

"A beginning—I hope!" answered Ralph, hoarsely. "A new beginning, Jem, or it shall be the end, the final end, by God it shall!"

"B'goles!" exclaimed the smith, giving his beard a sharp tug. "You'm uncommon low this time, my lord, that y'are. I've seen ee pretty much so afore now arter a night of it, many's the time, and more's the pity! But this mornin' you'm sunk complete, almost! So I rackon your need is a hair from the tail o' the dog as bit ee last night, ay I rackon!" And away he strode to return very soon with bottle and glass, which latter he filled generously, saying:

"The right stuff, m'lord! Ar, primest o' the prime, too good to drink, almost, and as I only sip occasional, me being, as you know, a chap as treats his innards wi' proper respect so far as sperrits is consarned. But you, Mas'r Ralph, 'aving played fast and loose wi' yourn till they can't nowise do wi'out it, well—there y'are, sir!" So saying, he handed the glass to

Ralph who took it eagerly, snuffed at it with quivering nostril, raised it to twitching lips—then, with fierce, wide-armed gesture, dashed the precious liquor to sooty floor and gave back the empty glass, saying, and in unexpectedly calm tone:

"Never again, Jem!"

Jem Lacey took back the glass, up-ended it as if to prove its emptiness, glanced from it to the splash on the floor, from this to Ralph's pale, set face and enquired, anxiously:

"Lor' m'lord! Eh, Mas'r Ralph, you bean't took sick, be ee now?"

"Yes, yes I am—by God I am! Ha, Jem, I'm sick of myself, sick to death!"

"'Ow so? What's got ee?"

"Truth, Jem, it's got me in a stranglehold nothing can ever break!"

"Lord love us, Master Ralph! I've never see or heered ee like this afore, never, and here's me has knowed ee arl your days——"

"All my days, yes. And you'll mind, Jem, that on the whole I was quite a decent little fellow, as a boy. You'll remember that?"

"As a b'y and on the 'ole, you was sure-ly! Many's the time as you've perched on this yere stool and watched me make the sparks fly! Good as gold you was in them days, as a little lad——"

"But as a man," Ralph continued, in the same toneless voice, "as a grown man I'm no better than a cursed blight, a useless, drunken sot, as you know. Ah, but what you don't know is that I am also a brute, a beast and—worse! And here's what proves it!" And he showed his lacerated knuckles. "Yes, Jem, old friend, here's my undying shame and bitter remorse! The Bible tells how Cain was marked upon the brow—though he only murdered his brother. I am only marked on the hand, yet I have murdered my own happiness and peace of mind—yes, and something far better, purer, sweeter, God help and forgive me!" Down went bottle and glass and down upon knees went the smith, to clasp brawny arm about this bowed, disconsolate speaker, saying:

"Master Ralph, when you was a little motherless lad afeard o' that feythur o' yourn, and no wonder,—you'd come creepin' into my forge here for to tell me arl your troubles and I'd cuddle ee up, so—and precious sooty I'd mek ee! But I'd dry your tears and comfort ee wi' a bullseye or so, or mebbe a lollipop if they chanced handy—which they gen'rally allus was, for I worked better them days when suckin' of a sweet. So now, tell me arl about your trouble and mebbe I can comfort 'ee again." And so, holding the smith at arm's-length the better to read the expression of his honest features, Ralph's better self told of his worse self, sparing no shameful detail.

"Well, Jem, old friend and comforter, what have you to say, —can you comfort me now?" The smith looked down at sooty floor, up at blackened roof, round about upon grimy walls, made to speak, gulped, and was dumb.

"Oh, Jem, can't you—even—look at me?"

The smith did so, showing a face grievous now as Ralph's own. So youth and middle age gazed on each other, neither speaking, the young man haggard and wistful, the elder sad-eyed and troubled beyond expression. . . . But, upon this tense silence, in this most tragical moment, stole the fragrance of—frying bacon. Then the smith, drawing deep breath, spoke at last.

"Mas'r Ralph, I rackon no man can't never nohow and nowhen think proper nor yet speak or act proper on a empty stomach! So, my lord, go along o' me to my cottage and Mary where is summat sure-ly to comfort your inner man and Mary to welcome your outer man as ever and always have been, ar, since you was not so tall as my old sledge hammer,—so, come along o' your old Jem."

Then together they rose and went forth of that gloom—out into the radiance of this new day,—to the whitewashed cottage where Ralph found breakfast, Mary and a right glad and hearty welcome.

CHAPTER XXVI

INTRODUCES A ROMANY RYE

AT A PLACE where four roads met, commonly known in Sussex as a "four-wents", Ralph pulled up his horse, for, since all roads were familiar hereabout and each and every could only bring him to the abomination of desolation, here was for him no choice, so he took out a coin and was in the act of spinning it to let chance decide, when he was arrested by a voice at no great distance:

"I believe I address Lord Scrope; if so, I'm in luck; if not, I ask pardon." Glancing round, Ralph beheld the speaker peering up at him from a hedge nearby. At ordinary times he would instantly have scowled upon and damned such impertinence; today he approached and surveyed this fellow without the shadow of a frown; a slender, shapely man, and well dressed, though his garments showed somewhat rumpled and dusty with travel; a man whose face, darkly handsome, was marred by the white line of an old wound.

"No," said Ralph, "I don't recollect you, though your face seems vaguely familiar, but no matter. What's your trouble?"

"This ankle, sir. I've twisted it, sprained it so badly that I can neither stand nor go, and go I must."

"Where?"

"'Tis no matter for that either, my lord, so long as it be away from this road, the further the better!"

"Why? But no, I'll not ask, so no matter again. Instead, tell me how you happen to know my name."

"Sir, I won fifty guineas on you that day you conquered the Bermondsey Butcher on Chaily Common."

"Oh?" exclaimed Ralph, sitting more upright. "Did you though? That was a pretty good fight."

"Never a better, my lord, and I've seen a many."

"You show like a fighting man yourself," said Ralph.

"Yes, b'George, and a pretty fancy article with those shoulders and good, clean legs, eh?"

"Yet, my lord, you lost on me and heavily, I fear, the time I was beaten in the ninety-seventh round by Jessamy Todd at——"

"Jessamy . . . Todd?" gasped Ralph, with such gesture that his saddle creaked. "You . . . actually lasted ninety-seven rounds . . . and against . . . Jessamy Todd? Then who —who under heaven are you?"

"I was known as 'The Fibbing Gipsy' then, and am now Tawno Lovel, at your lordship's service——"

"Tawno Lovel—eh?" repeated Ralph, bright of eye. "Yes, b'Jingo, I remember you now, of course! Tawno the Non-pareil, the unbeatable Romany!"

"But, my lord, I was beaten at last!"

"Yes, but only by Jessamy, the only one man on two legs that could have done it! No wonder your phiz was familiar, though you're greatly altered!"

"True, my lord, for much can happen in six years! But now, if you could manage to get me away from this road, if only far as the wood yonder, I should be vastly grateful."

"Could you mount my horse?"

"With your help I can and surely will."

"Then," said Ralph, dismounting, "up with you." This, with some difficulty, having been accomplished, Ralph took the bridle, enquiring:

"Where now?"

"The wood yonder, sir." Thus presently they turned from the road into a leafy ride that wound through this wood between dense thickets.

"Egad, yes!" exclaimed Ralph, somewhat ruefully. "I lost a 'monkey' on you that day Jessamy beat you!"

"Which I regret, my lord, though I did my best."

"That you did, Tawno—and for ninety-seven rounds and a bit! Yes, indeed, it was a noble fight, a battle royal and worth the money. Jessamy's victory set him at the very top, a true-blue champion, and there he's been ever since, and likely to remain."

"Yes, my lord, there isn't a man today can beat Jessamy Todd, as I'm hoping to tell him fairly soon."

"Tell him?" enquired Ralph, glancing up at his companion. "No, are you though, b'Jingo! When and where?"

"With the Lovels, when I find them."

"But he's no Romany."

"True, sir, but he and his friend, Jarvis the Tinker, are well beknown among my folk and always welcome, especially among the Lovels when in their neighbourhood, and, this being July, there they'll be."

"The wonder is," said Ralph, after a while, "the great wonder is that I failed to recognize you instantly,—though, to be sure, your looks are—altered rather."

"Yes, I was six years younger and without—this!" and he touched the scar upon his cheek.

"Well, but what became of you, Tawno Lovel? We never heard of you after that day. Did you quit the game?"

"Yes, sir. One of my wealthiest backers, Sir Peregrine Beverley, set me up in the book trade."

"Eh? Book trade? My eye!" exclaimed Ralph in shocked accents. "But what for? Why books? And you such a bang-up fighting cove! Good Gad, why on earth—books?"

"Because, though a fighting cove, I have always loved books, second to music, especially old books. I like 'em outside and in, the feel of them, the smell of 'em! And among them I should be yet—but for an accident that was my ruin and made me a homeless fugitive and wanderer."

"Well now," exclaimed Ralph, "that's pretty odd! Yes, that's devilish odd because . . . in a way . . . so am I. It seems we are companions in—in misfortune, Tawno, and, if you feel so inclined, I should be mighty glad of your company."

"My lord," answered Lovel, even more gravely than usual, "I feel so greatly inclined that I must now inform you that I am a felon, an escaped convict returned from transportation and with the Bow Street runners on my track."

"Oh? Are they? The devil!"

"If they take me it means the noose, a hempen collar and the Tyburn Jig."

"Why then," said Ralph, glancing about instinctively, "they mustn't take you, damn 'em!"

"You don't ask of my crime, sir, or whether I'm guilty——"

"Not I, no!" said Ralph, glancing up at this man who spoke and moved with such quiet dignity. "I remember you six years ago as a straight, clean fighting man, and today I see you such fellow as I should be glad to company with! And you show so far from my idea of guilt that I'm laying long odds on your innocence."

"My lord," said Lovel, after they had gone some way, "as you know, they called me 'The Fibbing Gipsy', for I was born and bred a Romany chal, one of this now despised race, yet one never forgetful of any kindness and holding friendship very precious and sacred. So now as Lovel of the Romany I ask you to accept my deep gratitude for your faith in me, and as Tawno the fighting gipsy cove I will tell you my story and very briefly, if you will allow."

"Pray do."

" 'Twas a street brawl, a woman screamed by reason of a man, so I hit him—once—and down he went but never got up again, for that blow killed him because he was rotten with evil-living. But they tried me for murder, transported me for manslaughter—a life sentence! Five years I endured before escaping, and the mark of my freedom is—this!" And again he touched the scar upon his cheek.

"But, Lovel, free you are!"

"Yet for how long, I wonder? Because by ill chance one of the officers who first apprehended me saw and recognized me four days ago, followed me down here and all but had me last night. But I downed him and ran, twisted my ankle and —here am I astride your horse and everlasting grateful to you."

"Well, and now," enquired Ralph, "where are we going?"

"We, my lord? Do you really mean——"

"Of course! Being companions together in—misfortune, together we'll go, but where?"

"To the camp of the Lovels, though first to a place where, if need be, I—we can be secure and never possibly be found,

no not by all the officers in London or anywhere else. I found
it quite by accident years ago when a youngster with my tribe,
a place perfectly impossible to find except by accident."

"And known only to yourself, Tawno?"

"And one other, my lord, and I showed him because he was
hurt and running from the plastramengros—officers, my lord,
and because, being so young, I was a fool! For this fellow,
Mumper Jim, was or is the sort of animal better dead and likely
as not hanged ere now."

"Tell me, Lovel, was this officer who first took you a
man named Shrig, because if so he's the very devil of a
fellow!"

"No, my lord, my officer is named Smally, Jabez Smally,
a stoutish, hairless man very unpleasant to sight and hearing."

By this time they had reached the very heart of these dense
woodlands and now, guided by Tawno, followed a devious
course through a maze of thickets until, some distance before
them, rose a bush-girt steep, very precipitous and crowned by
lofty trees, a green barrier forbidding all further progress.

"This," said Lovel, glancing up and around, "this is a
camping-ground known only to the Lovels! Hark now, d'you
hear it, my lord?"

"Yes, a sound of rushing water."

"And 'tis calling us, my lord; yonder lies our refuge if need
arise." Following this sound, they came to a brook, its hurrying water making great to-do as it bubbled, splashed and
gurgled around and over mossy boulders and gnarled roots
of willows that grew very thickly hereabout, which clamorous
stream presently led them to a waterfall, a small torrent down-
plunging from the greeny height above to where, through
long ages, it had formed for itself a deep hollow or basin;
here Lovel reined to a halt at last, saying:

"Now, my lord, pray help me down and you shall see a
wonder." Thus presently, hopping awkwardly and limping
very painfully, Tawno Lovel approached this waterfall from
the side until he stood upon the very brink of the basin, then,
beckoning Ralph to follow, he bowed his head, stepped forward and vanished, apparently into the very midst of this

gushing torrent. . . . But now, as Ralph stood bewildered by this seemingly impossible disappearance, Lovel called to him above and through this watery tumult:

"Come on, my lord,—one quick stride and you'll be scarcely damped." Ralph hunched his shoulders, closed his eyes, drew a deep breath and plunged under and through this watery downrush to be caught and steadied in Lovel's powerful arms and find they were standing upon a small, grassy, roughly-semi-circular plateau shut in by an opalescent screen of tumbling water, an ever-changing, never-failing curtain that seemed as it were hung from a great jut of rock above them over which the torrent gushed and beneath which yawned a roomy cavern.

"Yes, b'gad, Tawno, you are right, here is a wonder indeed!"

"One of nature's marvels, my lord, and even more wonderful than you think, for this hill is quite honeycombed with caves which I've reason to believe were once the village or haven of the Forgotten Folk, the People of the Chalk and Flint, for I've lately found a number of their workings, with scrapers and borers both neo and paleolithic."

"Oh?" murmured Ralph. "Have you though? Not that I've the vaguest notion of what you mean."

Lovel smiled and, sitting down, did his pain-sweating best to draw the long Hessian boot from his injured foot until Ralph, seeing how vain and agonizing were his efforts, knelt to help him, saying:

"Let me have a go."

"Thanks!" gasped Lovel. "Don't mind if I howl, for off it must come even if I have to cut it."

"Ready, old fellow?" Lovel nodded . . . Then for a long minute Ralph pulled and lifted while Lovel writhed, groaning and hissing between teeth clenched in such anguish that, when at last the boot was off, he lay so utterly helpless that it was Ralph who bared that bruised and swollen ankle,—it was Ralph who, instantly taking off his own modish hat, would have filled it with water from the fall had not Lovel, uttering a sound between groan and laugh, checked him, saying:

"No need to ruin your hat for me, sir; the water yonder shall do the business." Slowly he thrust naked foot and ankle towards the fall, first where the water dripped and then very cautiously further out that the torrent might beat upon it; he groaned, sighed, but persisted until presently, the pain abating, he began to describe these caves and their wonders while Ralph, seated nearby, thought of and grieved for his Cecily, until Lovel, finding him thus gloomily speechless, gave all his attention to his sprained ankle which it seemed he was now able to move with less pain. At last, glancing at Ralph's haggard face and drooping, disconsolate figure, he spoke:

"You're very silent, my lord."

"Silent?" echoed Ralph, rousing with a start. "Yes, I was —thinking! And, among other things, that you are as strange as this place. I mean, it's perfectly evident you are no ordinary gipsy."

"Indeed," answered Lovel, with his slow, grave smile, "I am a true Romany rye whose ancestors ruled long ago in ancient Egypt,—if you can believe that?"

"I can and do!" nodded Ralph, eyeing his companion's stately form and serene dignity of bearing. "This I can readily believe, for, b'gad, you—look it, though you were a 'fibbing cove.'"

"And, my lord, I became the 'Fibbing Gipsy,' not to win fame, but education."

"More books, eh? Could never stomach 'em myself, wouldn't learn at school, played the fool at college, was gated, rusticated and finally sent down. Consequence is today I'm the devil and all of a dunce—and—only just beginning to find it out, along with a—lot of other things. A boy who refuses to learn at school should be trounced. The youth who at college scorns learning for sport and so on is a headstrong young colt and should be ridden close and hard, on a curb and with sharp spurs. The grown man who fancies he knows all about the world, the flesh and the devil, and yet is stone blind, deaf and totally ignorant of his own damned nature, is a plague to others and finally a cursed misery to his own rightly-damned self and should be forced to mend or end his ways, preferably end 'em, for good and all for the good of all!"

Having thus delivered himself and at such very unusual length, Ralph drooped lower and eyed that down-rushing, luminous curtain more haggardly than ever,—which Lovel was quick to notice, so that after another interval he ventured to enquire:

"Are you as distressed as you look, my lord?" And Ralph, groaning, answered:

"Tawno, I'm the most miserably distressed, soul-shattered dog that ever howled! The saddest wretch in all England, or anywhere else!"

"Then, my lord, it is at such times a man most needs a friend . . . a cheering voice . . . a hand in the dark. So, if you can so regard and trust me, here is the hand of a friend!"

With a strangely pathetic eagerness Ralph leaned swiftly forward to grasp this proffered hand, then as suddenly drew back; yet this hand remained outstretched as Lovel enquired:

"Won't you honour me, my lord?"

"Honour—you?" gasped Ralph. "Tawno, I can't, for, damme, the boot's on t'other leg! Question is—can you honour me? For, hearksee, Tawno! Have you . . . ever felt like . . . cutting your own damned throat, have you?"

"Very frequently, my lord," answered Lovel placidly.

"Eh . . . you have?"

"Yes, often. First when they put me in the chaingang with poor rogues that past evil and present brutal usage had debased to worse than beasts. . . . I tried to kill myself then, but was prevented. Again there were times I grow sick to think on even yet . . . when they dragged me to Solitary . . . the Black Hole . . . utter darkness and never a sound except my own screams! An unending night filled with terror and the growing horror of madness . . . ! So, your lordship will agree I had some little cause for suicide?"

"Yes,—yes, by God you had! The wonder is you never did."

"A wonder, yes, my lord! For when at last I found my

chance—death and freedom mine for a gesture, I was stayed by the notes of a fiddle."

"Fiddle?" echoed Ralph. "How . . . whose? Tell me!"

"A fiddle played very ill by the small daughter of one of the prison warders. I contrived to gain her friendship; she allowed me to play—I've fiddled from boyhood and do yet,—the Guvernor chanced to hear, he sent for me. I used to play for him and his lady at fêtes and receptions. I was made a 'trusty,' found my opportunity to escape and, to cut long tale short, here I am. A fiddle saved me, fiddling freed me to live out my life how best I may."

"And," sighed Ralph, "Lord love us, Tawno, life has used you devilish hard, while I . . . Oh, damme! I've misused life, and there's the difference between us! You are the victim, the sufferer, while I have made others suffer,—especially one! And she the dearest!—Oh hell! You have never loathed and hated yourself, of course?"

"No, thank God!"

"Well, I do! I am my own cursed abomination!" Here both men were silent, gazing steadfastly at that never-failing, ever-changing barrier which shut them from the familiar world in such close intimacy that Ralph demanded:

"Tawno Lovel, why don't you ask me why?"

"Because, my lord, until you have taken my hand I shall not presume or—dare."

"And I dare not take your hand till you know."

"Then, my lord, I——"

"And do stop calling me 'my lord!' "

"Then what shall I call you?"

"Any dam' thing you please."

"How would 'brother' suit?"

"Better than I deserve."

"Then, brother, speak your trouble." So once again Ralph told his lamentable story. ". . . and that," he ended, "that's the kind of brute and drunken fool I am! Well?"

"Yes, brother, well it surely will be—if you are sincere as you look and sound, and 'tis plain you need a friend, so here am I to do all friend may—if you will have me——" Ralph grasped the proffered hand this time, shook it heartily but without a word, whereafter they sat, shoulder to shoulder, gazing speechlessly at the tumbling water again.

"Question is," said Ralph suddenly, "what am I to do, Tawno, old fellow? Those words of hers torment me! Yet I can't go back, though I'm pretty sure she'd welcome me. I ought, somehow or other, to prove myself first, and first—to myself and then to her."

"Brother, you've said it! You must first make and feel yourself worthy of forgiveness. . . . In my old books of romance, writ when this world was younger and simpler,— when a man had committed some crime against others and therefore against himself,—for the evil we do always affects ourselves soon or late,—he took horse and arms and went in quest of his better self, I mean, to right the wrong at hazard of his life, to perform some worthy deed, making hardship and peril a ladder of penance to climb from the pit of his self-hatred, suffering much and doing greatly, not for the glory of achievement, but that this glory might blind him to his past misdoing and that the reproachful voice of his conscience might be stilled at last. How think you of this?"

"B'gad, I only wish I had lived in those simpler times,— horse, armour and so on would have suited me no end. But as it is——!" Ralph sighed mournfully and shook his head.

"My ankle," said Lovel, flexing it, "begins to be pretty well again, so, boot or no, we'll be off when you are ready."

"Good!" nodded Ralph. "At once! Where to? Though it doesn't matter if we go together."

"Yes, brother, for as long as need be."

"The longer the better, Tawno. Now let me get you into your boot, old fellow." So on went stocking, but the boot, proving too painful, Ralph tucked it under one arm, set his other about Lovel, and thus clinging together like brothers, or rather the friends they now were, forth they went by that one place where the volume of the fall was least, and so together they came into the sunlit world again.

"Tell me, friend," said Ralph as he helped him to the saddle, "this name of yours—Tawno, what's it mean?"

"In the Romany it stands for 'tiny,' brother."

"But, good gad, you're a big fellow and tall as myself, almost."

"Maybe that's the reason, brother, or the fact that I was a very 'tawno' infant."

All day long they travelled by forest tracks and leafy ways until, as evening fell, they espied a red spark amid the deepening shadows, a spark that winked, went out, winked again, growing larger, towards which Tawno nodded, saying:

"Yonder are the Lovels." Even as he spoke, dogs began to bark, and then from leafy shadows into the twilight glow stepped a woman, or rather girl, for she was young, though tall and nobly formed; she glanced at Ralph, she gazed at his companion great-eyed and utterly motionless, then:

"Tawno?" she whispered, reaching out her shapely arms, and now Ralph saw the gleam of gold on slim wrists, round throat and in the braided coils of her blue-black hair; and now she spoke again but in the Romany dialect in which he made answer; then, gesturing towards Ralph, said:

"Lord Ralph, behold Nerilla, a Romany rawni of the black Lovels! Nerilla, speak this gentleman greeting, for he is my brother."

Ralph bared his head and bowed. Nerilla curtseyed and advancing with lithe, free step, gave him her hands saying:

"Lord Lovel's brother shall be welcome to me and the Folk. We thought Tawno dead, but he tells me by your kindness he is here. You come now, my gorgio rye, to the Lovel; he shall be grateful." She brought them to a wide clearing lit by fires whose flickering glow showed dingy tents and booths of different shapes and sizes backed by carts, wagons and horses; dogs barked, children peeped, men and women stared, till recognizing Tawno, they hastened to give him glad and hearty welcome; then all were hushed as into the firelight strode a very tall man, old he was, for long hair and flowing beard were snow white, but the eyes beneath hoary peak of brow showed bright and youthful and he bore himself as one long used to command.

Beholding Tawno, he raised both thin hands in strange gesture and burst into a torrent of speech; and thus awhile in their own speech they talked, eager question and deliberate answer.

"Yes," said Tawno at last in English, "back from the grave come I; the dead is alive again; wherefore give welcome to this gentleman that is my brother, by whose kindness I am here, to fiddle for you all once more as of old and to abide among you as long as I may, so now give welcome to this Ralph that is my brother."

CHAPTER XXVII

HOW AND WHY SAM WAS SAVED BY HIS ENEMY

So THESE days, freed of the too watchful care and devotion of Mr. Standish, unnoticed by his stately Countess who became ever more proudly remote, my lord the Earl now rode abroad, how, when and where he would. Heedless of Jasper Shrig's warning, he chose for his excursions the most sequestered places; a grim man within-doors, feared and avoided by his servants, a silent man out of doors who, when traversing any of his villages, rode fast, speaking with none of his folk whose respect and affection he had won by his one-time heartiness; a foolhardy man who in places where murder might be supposed to lurk, reined his horse to a walk as if proffering himself to bullet or steel.

Thus upon a certain extremely hot, windless afternoon, finding himself in the vicinity of Wrexford Old Mill, this dreary place where death had struck more than once, he turned thither and, coming in sight of that dark, tree-shaded, sinister pool, dismounted, tethered his horse and, advancing, paused on the brink to stare down into those watery deeps. Down here the heat seemed more oppressive than ever, so my lord took off his hat and stood for awhile bare-headed, still gazing down into this dark pool which had always seemed to menace him—even as it was doing at this moment; a faint breeze stirred his hair, rustling the bushes behind him. . . . Then my lord put on his hat, turned to go, and thereby saved his life, for thus stealthy murder smote amiss—and yet to such effect that, stumbling blindly forward, my lord plunged down—and down into the dark watery horror of this ever hungry pool . . . . down and ever deeper where death reached out for him with clammy, sinuous arms that clutched and held. Weakened by the blow, he strove desperately against these slimy growths that clung only the closer . . . that fettered and choked him. Death glared

upon him exultingly. . . . His feeble efforts ceased . . . life
was a weariness, let it go, what matter. . . .

But in that dire moment, when he knew all effort vain and
himself past caring, powerful fingers clutched his hair, a strong
hand dragged and bore him up . . . and up . . . to light
that blinded. . . . But here was air to breathe again and returning life and the will to live in each painful gasp . . . thus
instinctively he strove for life. . . . Ensued a confused struggling,
helped and guided by this same strong hand, so that at last
he won free of those deathly waters and sank outstretched upon
the kindly mother earth, weary head pillowed on her bosom.
So thus he lay, groaning . . . panting . . . glad of the sun's
blessed heat, until life and strength were renewed within him.
And now, with an effort, he turned to see and thank his
deliverer . . . a pallid face framed in a clinging draggle of
black hair . . . yet a face there was no mistaking; then Sam
uttered a wheezing, shaky laugh:

"Ch-Chalmers!" he gasped.

"My-self!" gasped Sir Robert. "And I want . . . none of
your . . . damned gratitude or . . . thanks!"

"Very . . . well!" panted Sam, contriving to sit up. "Then
I'll . . . think 'em, instead. For, d'e see, I . . . thought it
was my . . . finish."

"For that . . . matter," panted Sir Robert, "I thought 'twas
. . . mine. A devilish business I had with you . . . tangled
down there in those . . . damned weeds . . . especially as I
have only . . . one hand to help us both, as . . . you may
have noticed,—this, damn you!"

"Ay, ay!" nodded Sam, blinking at the stump out-thrust
at him in such menacing fashion. "Which makes me the more
curious to know why you troubled to run such risk and
get dam' damp on my account. Was it a sudden change of
mind?"

"What the devil d'you mean by that?"

"Since you hove me in, why haul me out?"

"Fool! So you think 'twas I tried to murder you do you,
damn you?"

"Who else?"

"With my one hand?"

"It's pretty strong and has just served us well enough, and to my wonder."

"Is it any good my utterly denying your vile accusation?"

"Maybe, if——"

"Look there! What do you see?"

"Why—damme, a bludgeon!" exclaimed Sam, scowling at the ugly thing where it lay close by.

"Wrybourne, that was cut and trimmed to be your death! I have only one hand, yet had I meant to murder you, it is just such weapon I should have chosen, or you or any other of our class, since no gentleman could be readily suspected of using such vulgar, clumsy thing,—and yet, one did, my lord! And I can tell you the—person, if you care to be informed."

"Naturally I do. So tell me the villain's name and—— No! On second thoughts, never mind! Whatever is to be known I prefer to discover for myself." And speaking, Sam turned his back upon that murderous thing which now filled him with a dreadful apprehension.

"Now, can it be," enquired Sir Robert, showing his big, white teeth in that cruel smile of his, "am I to believe you do not wish to know?"

"Believe what you will, sir."

"Of course, Wrybourne, of course! And yet your quite unnatural lack of curiosity amuses me, yes indeed, because it is so very obvious that you—dare not ask!"

"And why the devil not, sir?"

"Lest your own suspicions be verified! And that you should so suspect—whom you do suspect is not to be wondered at— considering!"

"Considering what, pray?"

"Past events, Wrybourne, bygone happenings!"

"Sir," quoth Sam, becoming the Earl, "may I ask precisely to what—and whom, you refer?"

"Oh yes, you may ask, my lord, but until you dare enquire of me whose murderous hand wielded that bludgeon yonder you will ask all other questions in vain."

"Very well, Chalmers. Let us instead talk of ourselves."

"A quite repulsive suggestion! No, Wrybourne, I'll return home and rid myself of these unpleasantly wet clothes and advise you to do the same."

"Nonsense man! Sit still and let this good, hot sun dry us, and while it does so, do you talk to me like the very original enemy who has just risked his life to save mine! Give me your reason for such extremely illogical, most friendly act."

"Can you be so obtuse, Wrybourne, so grossly dense as to be in doubt still?"

"Let us suppose so!" nodded my lord.

"As you will, Wrybourne,—here briefly is my reason. Had I permitted you to drown, you would now be at peace down there in the mud, instead of sitting here in the sun,—grieving for the—trouble in your home." The Earl sat motionless, only his eyes narrowed beneath thick brows that slowly knit themselves while his shapely mouth tightened and thinned to down-trending line; then, drawing a deep breath, he reached out very deliberately and, taking up that murderous bludgeon, balanced it in powerful grasp while Sir Robert, seated within easy striking distance, watched very much askance yet seeming otherwise wholly unperturbed, and when at last he spoke it was in tone almost casual:

"By the way, Wrybourne, if you mean to use that thing on me, pray do so and get it over. I find the suspense a little trying!" And seeing the Earl took not the slightest notice, he enquired, sneeringly:

"Bloodshed and murder run in your family, I believe?"

"Too true!" nodded Sam, twirling the bludgeon lightly. "We Scropes have always been damnably Scropish,—two eyes for one, and for a tooth—a whole mouthful. But," and here he tossed the bludgeon far out into the pool, "today, Sir Robert, here sits a Scrope who so hates all strife and bloodshed that, here and now, he humbles himself to ask—to beg your friendship. For your sake and mine, forget the past and let us live neighbourly in growing good fellowship. Come, Robert Chalmers, be now the man I believe you truly are,—great enough to be done with hate and to live for better thing than revenge.

You saved my life; will you let me use it to our better understanding?"

Sir Robert made no response for a while, and when he did, it was in strange, halting manner as if compelled by some power other than his own:

"So . . . because I . . . dragged your carcase from death to life . . . will you presume therefore to . . . thrust your friendship upon me? Will you dare . . . bid me forget, with this ghastly reminder always beside me? This useless . . . stump of horror! . . . Give you my friendship? Yes, that will I when . . . you give me back my hand! When you can restore my peace of mind and self-respect! But, until you do, my lord, know me for your persistent . . . your very determined and . . . quite remorseless enemy!"

Breathing quickly and distressfully, Sir Robert got him slowly to his feet, mounted his horse very awkwardly and rode away, leaving the Earl to gaze wistfully at this dread pool where now the bludgeon floated,— a man very lonely and sick at heart since he was almost, and dreadfully, sure whose hand it was had used it to such purpose.

Homewards he rode, pondering Sir Robert's sneering words, and home came he, where bowing servants flinched from the eyes that saw them not; for, as he traversed this great, silent house, as he stripped off damp clothes, his harassed mind was still obsessed by these too-veracious words:

"Bloodshed and murder run in your family."

CHAPTER XXVIII

HOW GRANNYANNE ARGUED AND PLEADED IN VAIN

THIS PHRASE haunted him later as he sat alone in the silence of his spacious library until he was roused by a knock on the door which, opening to his call, disclosed the stately form of Mrs. Leet who, having closed the door with a certain decisiveness of manner, advanced against him resolutely, her voluminous petticoats rustling rather more portentously than usual, or so thought Sam, for her set features wore no smile and those keen eyes of hers seemed very sharp indeed as, folding mittened hands, she said:

"If you please, my lord, I desire a word with you."

"Ah!" he sighed, wearily, sinking back in his chair. "Even you, Grannyanne! You, like all the rest of 'em, have drawn away from me,—become so damnably remote that I'm a stranger in my own house that is no longer 'home'! What the devil ails you all?"

"My lord, if by 'all' you mean her ladyship——"

"Not particularly, though she began it. But you have avoided me lately, so now that you are visible at last, I ask you again, what has so changed you all, what is this dismal shadow that seems deepening all about us?"

"Since you refuse to know or be aware, my lord, I am not the person to inform your lordship."

"Nonsense, Grannyanne! Sink me, but I shall be calling you 'Mrs. Leet' if this goes on,—you that have been my kind, good friend and wise counsellor since the day when, as merely Sam, a grandmotherless grandson, you allowed me to adopt you as my very own, Grannyanne. Lord love us,— what's this blight that's come upon us all? Sit down, Granny, here in this armchair, and let's hear. Sit down, I say, or, b'Jingo, I'll pick you up and sit you on my knee!" At this dire threat, Grannyanne obeyed, though her petticoats rustled in furious protest.

"Now!" Sam commanded, setting his long arm about her with hearty squeeze. "Grannyanne—explain."

"Very well, my lord."

"No! Begin again."

"If your lordship won't allow me——"

"My lordship won't! So begin once more, and rightly this time."

Grannyanne turned in his embrace to look up at him with eyes that had lost nothing of their sharpness, eyes that, having questioned his every feature, became suddenly very gentle, as was her voice when next she spoke:

"Oh, Sam, can it be? Yes, it must be, for looking at you now, I do—I must believe that you actually—don't know."

"Grannyanne, I have not the vaguest notion what I'm supposed to know."

"That you are carrying on an intrigue!"

"Oh?" murmured Sam, pondering this. "Ah? What kind of intrigue?"

"With another man's wife! And," continued Grannyanne, remorselessly, "that you are consequently a perjured and faithless husband!" The arm about her fell away and, rising to his feet, Sam gazed down at her with expression of such stark amazement that Grannyanne very nearly smiled.

"Faithless?" he repeated, in strange, hushed tone.

"And perjured!" she nodded. "What have you to say about all that?"

"Say?" he gasped. "Well now—damme——"

"Don't swear, but answer me. Do you—can you deny it?"

"Utterly and absolutely!"

"And Sam dear, I believe you."

"So you should!" he growled. "For whoever heard such preposterous, damned nonsense and——"

"Don't swear, Sam dear, but sit down again." Mutely he obeyed. "And I should like your arm again too."

"And you believe me, Grannyanne?"

"Of course I do. You can't lie, never could and never will; it isn't in you, and I should never have doubted you but for——"

"Ha!" he exclaimed, leaping from his chair again. "Andromeda, of course! Sink and curse me,—that explains it——"

"Do not swear, Sam! Sit down and listen to me."

"Grannyanne, how the devil can I sit—knowing she believes it? My own wife to believe such a damnable thing of me!"

"Sam, if you continue to curse and swear, I shall leave you to do it alone——"

"Alone?" he repeated bitterly. "I'm getting pretty used to it, these days!"

"Your own foolish fault, my dear! Why not have gone to Andromeda, why not go now and tell her——"

"Not a dam' word, no! How could she credit—how dared she believe such a thing of me?"

"For quite a number of very good reasons, Sam, all of which, added together, carried conviction—yes, even to me!"

"For God's sake, what reasons? Let's hear!"

"Then sit down again and compose yourself!" He did so, frowning blackly. "Now, are you quite composed, my dear?"

"No, how the dev—on earth can you expect it?"

"Then I'll wait till you are. For you must be perfectly calm when I explain, and show you why we believed such odious thing of you, my dear."

"But that—Andromeda should—believe me guilty!"

"And I, too, Sam, so did I."

"Why?" he demanded.

"First because you are a man, and all men are so persistently male, even the few best of them, that they are too readily prone to fall to the lure of a lovely woman! For as Mr. Pope writes: 'Beauty draws 'em by a single hair'—especially if it be long and—golden!"

"Eh?" gasped Sam. "Now what the——"

"Hush, my dear! As I was saying, all manly men are lovers and rovers by nature and by nature all women know it and expect it! Indeed, Dame Nature has much to answer for, the wanton witch and slyly furtive hag that she is! And you, Sam, being so extremely manly and male, we—Andromeda and I—for this very reason could not help but suspect——"

"Then," cried Sam, "all I can say is——"

"Don't say 'damme', Sam!"

"I was about to say 'unjust', cruelly, wickedly—yes, by heavens, abominably unjust to suspect me so readily——"

"Not readily, my dear, at least—not very! But, and tell me this. Since all male men are prone to follow Beauty when she beckons, why should you be the one sole exception, the second Joseph, whom all women reckon a fool, poor youth! Why should you be the one and only?"

"Perhaps because I am only myself! And I don't agree with your sweeping assertions about all men and all women, and as to sex——"

"It's a—no, it is the—curse, Sam, it always was and ever will be, so the less said of it the better! Instead, look at this!" And from her capacious reticule she drew that anonymous letter and thrust it into his hand. . . . Sam glanced through it, tossed it on the desk, scowled at it and said, very softly though between clenched teeth:

"So this is the reason for Andromeda doubting me! This poor trash the cause of her belief in my unfaithfulness,—the cause of her right damnable treatment of me, eh? Well, Granny, this has done it,—for I'm done too!"

"Sam, what do you mean? Done indeed!"

"Yes—and indeed!" said he, still gently and still between hard-shut teeth. "I'm done with her! These last weeks have been a long-drawn agony and I've had enough! You can take this cursed thing back to her and say I will never forgive her."

"Nonsense, Sam! Don't be so absurd—so—so unreasonable —so cruel——"

"Take it now and tell her so, or I will!" Grannyanne rose in sudden, trembling dismay, shocked and aghast by his look and tone.

"Sam. . . . Oh, Sam . . . my dear," she faltered. "You cannot . . . no, you don't mean it! You must not . . . you shall not——" Striding to the door he opened it and, becoming the Earl, bowed, saying:

"Mrs. Leet, favour me by giving her ladyship my message." Grannyanne drew herself up, threw back her head, parted her lips to speak, but, meeting the Earl's coldly polite yet compelling gaze, bowed her head, caught back a sob and mutely obeyed.

CHAPTER XXIX

HOW THE GLOOMING SHADOW DEEPENED

IN LOFTY watch-tower above the mighty embattled keep of Wrybourne Feveril, amid cobwebs and the dust of centuries, hung the great alarm bell whose harsh, brazen clamour had been the summons to battle or foray in those far-distant, lawless bad old times when life was cheap, might was right and the sword paramount.

This old bell, in its dusty eyrie, so long motionless and silent, waiting patiently through the scurrying years,—was suddenly in motion once more, pealing wild alarm upon the sunny air of this drowsy afternoon, sending forth its dread summons once again, near and far, to the folk of Wrybourne and beyond.

And from near and far they came speeding to the summons; from hamlet and village, from cottage, farmstead and mansion came they, horsed on wheels and afoot, neighbours one and all hastening to afford such aid and comfort as true neighbours should. Hastily they marshalled themselves before the Great House where, astride his horse at the head of his mounted grooms and stable-lads, his footmen and servants, the Earl awaited them, grim-lipped, fierce-eyed, pale and haggard, yet whose voice rang out commandingly as, rising in his stirrups, he addressed them:

"Men of Wrybourne, good neighbours and friends, aloft there the old bell is crying on you, one and all, to help to find my little son . . . our baby, Viscount Feveril, who scarcely an hour ago was snatched from his nurse's arms by a wild gypsy-looking fellow and three or four others——"

Here, from the ever-growing assemblage, rose sudden, angry hubbub above which voice cried:

"Lead us, my lord! Ay, show us the way!"

"Good friends," he continued, speaking more rapidly, "well I know there is no need to offer to pay for your help, yet because he is my little son and heir, so very young and helpless, to whomsoever finds or gives news shall lead to his rescue, I give a thousand guineas. Now, let us all line out on a wide front to beat the woods, every bush, thicket and hedge, every barn, hut and steading 'twixt here and the coast,— come!"

So away they went, a great and very purposeful company, growing constantly more numerous,—men who searched fiercely, beating all coverts, wood, copse and spinney, bursting through underbrush and thicket like a vengeful storm. . . . But afternoon faded to evening, evening to glimmering dusk, and still this passionate search proved unavailing.

Night fell, very still, very dark and never a star: my lord the Earl called for lanterns; thus presently, one after another, lights appeared until across this wide countryside of forest, down-land and valley, lights twinkled far as eye could see, flickering beams that swung, bobbed and danced, yet all moving slowly uphill and down towards a far, dim expanse that was the sea.

"Ha, damme!" groaned Sam to the vague forms about him. "Of course there would be no moon!"

Scarcely had he spoken than a tall horseman loomed beside him and a voice said:

"Wrybourne, if I may advise——"

"Eh, is it you, Chalmers? Are you here to help or mock at my distress?"

"I am here for sake of—a child. And to say that I fear we have overshot the mark. . . . I think you should seek nearer home——"

"But I have news that the villains were seen making towards the coast!"

"But," said Sir Robert, leaning nearer and speaking in voice low and hesitant: "I have . . . every reason to believe . . . the rogue who stole your little son is . . . he that attempted your life the other day."

"Chalmers, what . . . who are you suggesting?"

"Not the man you suspect, my lord, but . . . that same brute-beast you once thrashed so unmercifully in your woods."

"So!" exclaimed Sam, 'twixt shut teeth. "Are you sure, Sir Robert, certain o' this?"

"I am sure 'twas he tried to murder you, for I sighted him as he made off and . . . I think it quite possible that he now . . . has your baby son."

"Then, God help my little innocent! Ay, and may the Lord help me too!" Now it was at this precise moment of his heart-breaking misery and despairing supplication that, as if in answer, a distant voice hailed him through the blinding darkness:

"Sam ho! Shipmate—ahoy!" Up went Sam's drooping head, back went his shoulders, and, rising in his stirrups, he cried, hoarsely:

"Ned—ahoy! Oh, Ned—whereaway, old shipmate. Bring to! Stand by and let me come alongside!" Thus alternately hailing one another, in the darkness they met.

"Any luck yet, Sam?"

"None!"

"Ah well, in a little we shall have the moon and that shall help, and before she's down 'twill be dawn. Ben Toop is with me somewhere about and his old father mounted on one of the plough horses."

So the search went on, close and persistent as ever, until up rose the moon in a splendour that dimmed the myriad lanterns that winked far and wide on grassy upland and shadowy vale, in sombre wood and forest glade, upon dusty high-road and shady lane, all to no purpose.

Dawn came at last and, as the sun rose making a path of glory on the sea below them, Sam, riding between his life-long friend and inveterate enemy, reined up his horse to gaze dejectedly where, far and near, men still sought his little son, or lay outstretched upon dewy turf to rest their wearied limbs.

"Well," enquired Ned, blinking in the sun's level beam, "shipmate, what now?"

"Home for you, Ned; go sleep and take my gratitude along with you."

"But, Sam, how of yourself?"

"Oh, I shall carry on, of course, ply off and on in hopes.

Though first we ought to eat, I suppose; there's a good inn down in the village yonder."

"And you, sir?" enquired Ned of the silent man who kept one arm half hidden in the breast of his riding-coat.

"I shall collect my men, feed them, and then beat the coverts around Wrybourne."

"Then," said Sam, "for your neighbourly efforts on my behalf, Chalmers, I——"

"Not yours, my lord, but on behalf of . . . all children, for the sake of . . . one, a child I met of late who gave me a . . . new interest in life. So because of her sweet innocence I shall continue my search for . . . your innocent with the utmost determination, and should I . . . take this miscreant he shall never harm innocence again!" Then wheeling his horse abruptly, Sir Robert rode away.

"Soho!" murmured Captain Ned, gazing after him. "And that is the man who threatens your life, eh, Sam?"

"Not my life, Ned, my happiness . . . and it seems that one way and another, he's done it, damn him!"

All through the heat of this long summer day, the desperate search went on, sweeping back towards Wrybourne and far beyond in all directions, and still without result. . . .

Came night again, and my lord, sick and worn for lack of sleep, despondent and well-nigh hopeless, returned to his Great House—there to be met by a distraught creature who, breaking from Grannyanne's restraining arms, leapt at him to demand her child; a mother wild-eyed and tearless, crying for her baby in one breath, in the next denouncing him as the cause of all her past bitter grief and present heart-breaking suspense; a wife who, receiving no reply, became so frantic that my lord, grasping the slender fists that struck at him so wildly, said with look and tone bitterly contemptuous:

"Madam, I beg you'll remember you are Countess of Wrybourne; bear yourself accordingly!" Then, thrusting her into Grannyanne's ready arms, he strode away and upstairs to that room he had made his own and there shut himself in with loneliness and a grief such as he had never known till now.

CHAPTER XXX

HOW AND WHY RALPH CHANGED HIS MIND

SEATED in place of honour beside a blazing fire Ralph was enjoying a new experience, a pleasure scarcely known until now, for there had been little music in his careless existence hitherto, but now—Tawno was fiddling to the accompaniment of a harp plucked by Nerilla's skilled hands, while all about them, hushed and still, were the men, women and children of the Lovels, this tribe called the "Black but Comely", as indeed they seemed, more especially this Romany rawni, Nerilla. So they listened one and all as though spellbound, for it seemed Tawno was famous in all the tribes, not only as fighting man and leader but as violinist also.

And verily it seemed to Ralph there was a heart-searching magic in Tawno's playing that touched to eager wakefulness all that was best in him. Thus he knew at last how and why the best and holiest place in this world is "home", and that for him, always and ever, home could be only where Cecily hallowed and blest it with her love and gentle presence. Cecily, his wife, whose innate purity reproached his shameful doubt. . . . Yet, being himself, he doubted still, though yearning to forgive, since whatever had been was but the outcome of his own drunkenness and folly. . . . How often she had pleaded! How often he had promised . . . until he had exhausted even her patience at last . . . killed her love and was today a hopeless misery, a lonely wanderer longing for home. . . . His young mother, who had died too soon for him to really know, had taught him to say prayers he still remembered. . . . Well, if he had a go now, would God, if there truly was a God of Justice and mercy,—trouble for a fellow who only troubled to pray when tortured by doubts of his wife, hate for his cousin and shame for his own wasted life? Would God listen to such useless, miserable failure as Ralph Scrope? Perhaps . . . The

Music, this glory of sound that had inspired these reflections, ended very suddenly, and, glancing up, he saw all faces were turned in the one direction whither Tawno was pointing with his bow.

And now in the sudden hush voices whispered and muttered.

"The plastramengros!"

"Ah, the cursed muskerros!"

Now was uneasy stir, children whimpered, dogs whined and both were fiercely silenced.

"What is it?" cried Ralph, leaping afoot. "What the devil's to-do, Tawno?"

"Horsemen they comes!" answered Nerilla, clasping her hands and gazing at Tawno with eyes that held more than anxiety.

"One!" said he. "Only one. But if it be a constable or Bow Street runner, I must not be found. Heark, one cries yonder!" A distant shout growing louder; horsehoofs coming rapidly nearer.

"'Tis Sam!" said Nerilla. "Here rides Sam Wardomescro!" Almost as she spoke, into the glade galloped a young gipsy, who reining up, burst into a very torrent of excited speech, answered by fiercely excited voices.

"Tawno, what's the fellow saying?"

"An evil thing, brother," sighed Tawno, giving his violin to Nerilla's ready hands, "truly a very evil thing and bad for we Romanys that are always blamed for every roguery! It seems the lord of Wrybourne's little son has been stolen, kidnapped, and all his tenantry are up and searching, aye, all Sussex is afoot, beating the country far and wide, every covert. Soon they will be here and 'twill go badly with us, for the guilty man has been known to consort with us Lovels, more's our shame!"

"The guilty man? Then you know who he is?"

"Brother, the folk know all things, good and bad, that chance in the wilderness. This child-stealer is that same fellow I told you of—Mumper Jim. Thus because of him shall be grievous trouble for these poor Lovels."

"Not while I am here, old fellow. For it so happens the Earl is my damned cousin."

G

"Yes, I guessed so, brother. He is a great gentleman, truly a noble man and greatly liked by the Romanys and all poor folk."

"Is he! Well, I hate the fellow, every damned hair of him! Why the devil should your people like him?"

"For that he is so kind never to prosecute for the stealing of his game, a rabbit or—even a pheasant or partridge. Also there are parts of his land where they may tarry in peace, no fear of keepers to drive them away."

"Well, he's got enough land,—too much, curse him."

"Then his trouble shall no-wise grieve or trouble you?"

"Devil a bit! I'm glad! It's about time he suffered,— learned the meaning of grief."

"May I know your reason for such ill-will?"

"Because he is—himself and I am—myself and—aha, what now?" enquired Ralph; for indeed all about them was a vague hubbub growing louder and more ominous,—a ceaseless rustling of leaves and thrashing amid the undergrowth with clamour of many voices,—a sound of terror that seemed to be closing in upon them.

"Yes!" nodded Tawno. "They are upon us! So now, brother, speak them fair and do what you may on behalf of my poor folk who, though great rascals by force of circumstance, are today innocent of this or any evil as you know and can bear witness to these that come——"

"Leave them to me!" nodded Ralph. "I'll talk to 'em and, if need be, use my whip on 'em,—where is it, by the way?"

"Here, good friend!" answered Nerilla, thrusting it into his ready hand. So, thus armed, Ralph turned to meet this approaching terror that now, above the rustle and crash of smitten thickets, had found innumerable voices that talked, shouted and then swelled to ferocious roar as these questing, multitudinous eyes espied the encampment.

Now foremost of this great company rode Sir Jonas Fanshaw, this jovial, smiling gentleman who flourished his whip, crying:

"Here we are, m'lads,—another damned hell-brood! The

kidnapping villain has probably taken refuge among these vile gipsies——"

"He has not!" shouted Ralph, indignantly.

"Silence!" cried Sir Jonas, scarcely deigning to glance towards him. "No insolence! Hold your tongue, rascal, or——"

"'Rascal' in your damned teeth!" cried Ralph, advancing. "Yes, and down your cursed throat! B'God, I'll make you swallow that 'rascal' with the butt-end of my whip."

"Eh—what?" exclaimed Sir Jonas, reining up abruptly and forgetting to be jovial. "Is it—can it be—Lord Ralph Scrope? No . . . impossible!"

"However, it is!" cried Ralph, still advancing. "I'm Ralph Scrope as certainly as you are your confounded self, damn you!"

"But—here, my lord, here? Consorting with these dirty ragamuffins?"

"Ragamuffin yourself, sir! These good folk are friends of mine and I'll see they are so treated! So what now, Fanshaw?"

"Now," smiled Sir Jonas, becoming his jovial self again, "now, my lord, I and my good fellows intend searching every tent, every nook and corner for the villain who has abducted——"

"Enough, sir!" said Ralph, coiling up the lash of his whip. "Let any man try to molest my friends and, by heavens, I'll ram that 'rascal' down your infernal throat!"

Sir Jonas smiled but—hesitated, well knowing Ralph's aptitude to bodily violence; then, turning to his followers, cried in tone anything but jovial:

"Some of you go find Wrybourne . . . the Earl!"

"Good!" exclaimed Ralph, caressing the heavy butt of his whip. "I shall be happy to deal with him too!"

"But, my lord," said Sir Jonas, "as your neighbour and, I hope friend, may I remark that your astounding choice of associates—well—astounds me, perfectly astonishes me, and, considering your cousin's dire misfortune, his little son, his only child and heir to such vast possessions—ah, here comes the Earl himself!" Ralph glanced round and beheld—a man so dreadfully worn by ceaseless anxiety and lack of sleep that his words of insult were unuttered and he could but gaze dumbly on that so greatly altered face, while Sir Jonas chattered:

"My dear Wrybourne, here among this rag-tag and bob-tail of roguery I find your cousin, Lord Ralph, who defies and refuses us search!"

"Why?"

"He says the particular rogue we're after—is not here."

"Then why waste time here?"

"But, m'dear Wrybourne, we have only his word, and——"

"Good enough, sir. My cousin Ralph, though a Scrope, has the one virtue of speaking truth. Come, every minute is precious—and an agony! Come, I say!" And away rode this weary man and now despairing father, without one backward glance. So my lord, with his great company, passed on, leaving this camp unmolested and Ralph to stand motionless, staring at the whip in his fist but seeing instead the face of a stricken father whose heart was breaking as he rode, and dying within him; and thus stood Ralph until, feeling a touch, he started and found Tawno beside him, who enquired:

"Well, brother, what now?"

"My horse, Tawno, my horse! I'll ride this very instant! For I must help, yes, b'gad, I must search and go on searching till I find this poor infant—dead or alive or—may the devil take me, as I suppose he will in the end, anyhow."

Smiling that grave smile of his, Tawno slipped his hand within Ralph's arm and led him where the horses were picketed, saying in his gentle voice:

"Brother, the devil shall not take you."

"Eh, why not, old fellow? What d'you mean, Tawno?"

"Because, brother, you shall find this stolen babe."

"Would to God I could!"

"And I say you shall find this child. Also I can tell you he is alive and well!"

"How d'you know this? Good God—how?"

"Brother, the folk know everything, good and bad, here in the wild. Thus 'tis known the child is well and unharmed, being held for ransom."

"Where, Tawno, do they know—where?"

"No, brother! Only you and I know that."

"Do we? Oh, b'gad, I'll be shot if I do!"

"Think, brother, how these four days and nights so many hundreds of men have sought high and low throughout all Sussex, and beyond! Such a seeking as surely never was and may never be again, and all without success because Villainy's hiding-place has been passed and re-passed and shall never be found except by you and me——"

"Ah,—the cave!" exclaimed Ralph in hushed tone. "The cave beyond the torrent! Tawno, old fellow, my dear old lad, you've hit it! Yes, yes, of course! I'll ride at once."

"Can you find it, brother?"

"To be sure I can. Ah, there's my horse, and—ready saddled!"

"Yes, brother. But think, now,—there will be three men, very desperate, and—a woman!"

"Thank my stars they're so few!"

"Also they will be armed."

"Well, so am I, a brace o' pistols."

"Then," said Tawno, gently as ever though with compelling look and gesture, "I must ask you to leave them behind."

"Good great heavens, man, why? The odds are fairly steep already!"

"Because you might kill and this would be judged murder, and I want no more of such. No, instead we shall go armed with weapons less deadly yet very sufficing——"

" 'We', Tawno? Meaning you'll along with me?"

"Surely! Are you not my brother?"

"Old fellow," said Ralph, fervently, "now were I a frog— a mounseer, damme if I wouldn't kiss you! As it is . . . well . . . give me that fist o' yours that conquered every fibbing cove—except Jessamy Todd, of course!" So, and very solemnly, they shook hands. Then, from his tent nearby, Tawno brought two cudgels cut to a size of good length and very neatly trimmed, bidding Ralph choose.

"You'll find they balance well and shall play very sweetly."

"They shall indeed!" nodded Ralph, taking one and twirling it lightly. "Nothing could be better, old fellow!"

So they swung to saddle, but, as they turned to go, Nerilla was between them, speaking to Tawno in their sonorous tongue. Then, turning to Ralph, she glanced up at him with one of her too-rare smiles, saying:

"Lord Ralph that I've oft hears tell on and sees, though you nowise sees me, now, as you are Tawno's brother, I greets you well and tells you shall ever be glad welcome to the Lovels. Now show me your hand and I shall dukker drey thy vast." Smiling, Ralph obeyed, and she, looking upon the palm of his large though shapely hand, presently spoke in quite altered voice:

"Here is blood lost in good cause! Here he bears a golden woman as steals away to hide her sorrer with her as grieves a son . . . as dies by the water . . . time ago, yet a son as greets her in the music. Here is a home now empty . . . where soon shall be two as shall be three . . . and over these three . . . the Hand o' Glory . . . and where that is . . . there bides happiness. . . ." With this last word she glanced up, nodded, smiled, and went from them with her long-limbed, graceful stride.

CHAPTER XXXI

DESCRIBES A RESCUE

"Slower, brother, slower! No need for any haste, for I would be there precisely at sunset, so we have a good hour and more."

"But why wait till sunset, Tawno?"

"That the sun himself, Old Sol aloft there, may fight for us."

"Tawno, I've no head for riddles,—and little else, I fear, so take pity on my poor wits and explain."

"Brother, 'tis only that you failed to notice how the cave faces due west, so that anyone coming out at sundown shall be dazzled and blinded by Sol's level rays; and when a man is so blinded he will shoot wide o' the mark or not at all,—thus Sol shall give us the vantage and initiative."

"Yes, b'gad, the vital moment!" said Ralph, admiringly. "Your wits are sharp enough, Tawno! 'Twas lucky for me when I met you——"

"And took pity on me! And later withstood Sir Jonas, that smiling, pitiless arrogance, on behalf of my poor folk, otherwise 'tis fairly certain their tents would now be ashes and themselves in sorry plight,—but for you, brother."

"Old fellow," said Ralph, after brief silence, "tell me, true and brotherly, of this fortune-telling, what is it precisely?"

"Mostly trickery, brother. Yet sometimes among my people, as among yours, those are born with a gift of second sight, a fore-knowledge of what is to be."

"Well . . . is Nerilla one such?"

"Brother, I . . . can't say. Nerilla is truly only known to —Nerilla."

"She's a very beautiful girl, Tawno."

"She is."

"Yes, old fellow, though dark as night. For myself I prefer . . . golden hair."

"And very rightly, brother."

"Why rightly, Tawno?"

"Considering your own lady is all gold! Yes, a golden woman sweetly pure as the day-spring."

"Old fellow," said Ralph, again after a pause, "how do you know this?"

"Through the years, brother, I have watched her grow, as I watched you, for we are the Lovels of Sussex. When you were a boy, so was I,—but you were a lord of creation and I a raggletail gipsy lad——"

"And today, Tawno, in education, and all that really matters, you are the better man! Yes, so much so that I am proud you should name me 'brother'. And what's more, we must never let this comradeship die, no, damme, never!"

"But a lord of this proud, great England and a Romany chal or even 'rye'—which means gentleman, such are no fit associates, oil and water cannot mix."

"To the devil with that! I'm a man and so are you, and such man that I can respect. Also, come to think of it, I haven't a real friend and never did have, so, I repeat, our fellowship must endure! How say you, Tawno?"

"Brother," he replied wistfully, "I can only say—what is to be must be. For we that think ourselves free agents to choose our course are ruled, I believe, by a remorseless destiny that pre-ordains our journey through life."

"Here is a thought, Tawno, that has in it some comfort for the poor devil who is a failure,—or worse, a murderer, or this rogue Mumper Jim. Who is to blame them if they are pre-destined to evil?"

"We do, brother, we prison and hang them."

"Seems devilish hard on 'em, old fellow."

"Maybe. But my books tell me nothing can ever be wasted or destroyed but only suffers a change. Thus I dare believe that after death all men shall be changed and go back to the Infinite pure again and innocent."

"Then you believe in an after living, Tawno?"

"Yes, brother, I do! Otherwise, life would be a meaningless injustice and cruel futility."

"Wish to heavens I could so believe!"

"You will, brother, soon or late. And here I think we had best leave our horses."

"Eh?" exclaimed Ralph, glancing around. "Here already? So soon!"

"Talk is a rare shortener of distances, prala."

"Now what d'you mean by 'prala'?"

"In the Romany it stands for something far more than 'brother'. See, Old Sol yonder will be ready to help us in ten minutes or so." Here Tawno halted, then, having dismounted and tethered their horses, flourished his long cudgel in strong, well-practised hands, saying:

"This is the forester's weapon that in olden times was called a quarterstaff, and its best play is this." And with dexterous shift of hands and wrists he dealt the air two such blows as might have felled a giant. "Come now, let us go and no need for stealth; the water-rush shall cover our approach."

Shoulder to shoulder they went until before them was the little cataract, that ever moving curtain of water now flaming and flashing in the sun's level beams. Leaning on his quarterstaff, Tawno watched and waited, placid as ever, while Ralph, poised and quivering for action, watched him; suddenly Tawno raised his staff and cried harshly in the Romany tongue, thus what he said Ralph never knew, but it had such effect that—forth of the torrent, like a raging bull, leaped Mumper Jim, closely followed by two other burly ruffians who, one and all, blinded by the sunglare, halted to rub dazzled eyes,—in which moment the pistol was smitten from Joe's unwary grasp and himself beaten to his knees. . . . And so the battle began.

But knives and bludgeons were no match for these long cudgels wielded by such arms and backed by fists so well-skilled and powerful; thus very soon the combat ended with the victors standing above the completely vanquished who now lay asprawl, peacefully at rest and snoring, all three.

"Grand!" panted Ralph. "Hurrah for the old quarterstaff! And now for the infant."

"Beware the woman!" cried Tawno; but even as he uttered this warning, Ralph was through the fall and in the cave where, above a squirming bundle, the woman crouched; Ralph stooped for this bundle; the woman struck viciously, made to strike again, but the knife was caught, wrested from her and she, beholding Tawno, fled away into the cavern's remoter shadow. Then with his friend's powerful arm about him, Ralph staggered out into the sunshine.

"Hurt, prala?"

"No!" gasped Ralph. "But I'm . . . wondering if . . . I've got this infant . . . right end up? Wrong, evidently!" For here the bundle emitted a squeal. "Lend me a hand with his lordship, old fellow."

"Brother, you bleed fast!"

"Eh—so I do! And damme, all over the infant! Nothing wrong with him, however, judging by the sound of him, eh? And, b'gad, Tawno, here's the blood Nerilla foretold! Quite amazing!"

"Off with your coat, brother, and let me see."

"What of the infant?"

"Lay him here on the turf. Now let me get your coat off—so!"

"How is it, Tawno?"

"Bad, yet not too bad. Kneel and I'll bathe it. . . . Pains you, does it, prala?"

"Pretty so so, old fellow."

"Now your handkerchief for a pad . . . my neckcloth to hold it. . . . Set your teeth, prala, for it must be fairly tight——"

"Ha, look out, Tawno! Behind you—the Mumper's up . . . on his knees, quick——" Turning from his surgery, Tawno smote Jim scientifically to peace again, and so back to his patient, who gasped with fervour:

"Beautiful . . . Tawno! So exact . . . to the mark! That fist o' yours is . . . still a wonder! And you're pretty good as . . . a surgeon!"

"Brother, this is by no means the first knife-thrust I've tended. . . . There! 'Twill serve till you can be properly treated."

Thus, his hurt neatly bound up and coat draped and buttoned across his shoulders, Ralph turned where lay the baby, this very small nobleman and cause of so much trouble, who was kicking and striving against the dingy shawls that swathed him, and again filling the air with his indignant protests.

"G'lord!" exclaimed Ralph in some dismay. "Why d'you suppose he squeals so, Tawno? For such a small oddment, he makes the devil and all of a to-do! Question is, does anything ail him?"

"Probably hunger, brother."

"Then we'd better try him. I spied a bottle affair, a sucking-arrangement, in the cave."

"I'll get it."

"Then look out for that woman, old lad!"

"Brother, she's a Lovel and won't dare me."

Very presently, Tawno was back with the feeding-bottle which his small lordship received with a crow of joy, followed by sound of perfervid suction.

"And to think," exclaimed Ralph, gazing down on this sucking nobleman, "to think we were all like this once, Tawno! Shakes a man, b'gad! Now tuck him under my arm for me, old fellow."

"Better wait till you're set in the saddle, prala. Come!"

So they left that place of strife where lay the fallen, who took care not to stir until these two extremely hard-hitting gentlemen were safely out of sight.

Reaching their horses, Ralph contrived to mount unaided, despite the pain that racked him, to hide which, he laughed, though rather shakily, and held out his good arm, saying:

"Now pass me that blue-blooded and bloody atom of gentility—so! And now—hey for Wrybourne, the 'Great House'."

"Then I'll with you, brother, so far as need be."

"Thanks, Tawno! And . . . should we part . . . 'twill only be to meet again, old lad!"

Thus closely, side by side, rode these two good friends, while at no great distance three other men were on their way to Wrybourne, three very weary, utterly despondent men.

"Four days!" Sam groaned. "Four mortal days, Ned!"

"And nights!" sighed Captain Ned.

"Seems like four years, a cursed lifetime! We've searched the whole county now!"

"And beyond, Sam."

"So . . . I'm in despair!"

"No no!" sighed Captain Ned, laying hand on his old friend's bowed shoulder. "Not you, Sam; never you. Remember your own old adage, 'Never say die!' I still believe your child is being held for ransom—alive and well!"

"Oh, Ned, Ned . . . if the kidnapper is the man we believe . . . I once half killed him for frightening little Jane . . . thrashed him without mercy, longshore fashion . . . and took joy in doing it! And this may be his revenge on me! The thought drives me nigh frantic. . . . And I'm afraid now for Andromeda! She won't eat and can't sleep! If this suspense don't end soon . . . one way or t'other, d'ye see, 'twill surely be the death of her!" Coming in sight of the Great House, Sam reined up to look at it with such dread that Ned inquired with sudden, new anxiety:

"What now, shipmate?"

"Andromeda, Ned! She's there . . . hoping and praying . . . waiting for news . . . and we have none! Now God help me, I'm afraid to face her! I don't know how she——" He paused suddenly to turn and stare at Captain Ned, who was staring back at him. "Oh . . . Ned," he whispered, harshly, "either I'm mad or . . . did you hear it too?"

"Yes, Sam—yes, by God—I do! The cry of a baby, somewhere. Now it's hushed!"

"Ay, it's gone! . . . Did we . . . really hear it . . . did we, Ned, or was it only a fancy of what we hope and pray for? Because I——"

" 'Twas no fancy, Sam! Look—look yonder, old shipmate —look!" And he pointed where a horseman came at leisured amble, a seemingly very weary man whose head drooped, hiding his face, a man who swayed oddly and bore, tucked in one arm, a lumpish bundle which, as they stared, squealed again.

"God!" whispered Sam.

" 'Bout-ship, messmate!" cried the Captain, wheeling his horse.

"Here . . . we are!" gasped Ralph as they pulled up beside him. "Pretty bloody, but . . . it's all only mine. . . . So, cousin . . . damned Japhet . . . take your son . . . before I drop him. . . ."

CHAPTER XXXII

HOW RALPH RODE BECAUSE OF A PROPHECY

"No . . . and no!" cried Ralph, sitting up with an effort. "I'll not accept your hospitality, Japhet! And do not afflict me with your thanks; I don't want 'em and won't have 'em, so—don't!"

"As you will!" sighed Sam. "You're the second to refuse 'em——"

"And I don't want your Andromeda's gratitude either! Instead, you'll oblige me with a horse, mine's about done, and I'll 'shake the dust' and so on and be away."

"Are you able, with that gash in your shoulder?"

"Certainly! And if I were at my last infernal gasp I wouldn't remain under your roof, no, b'gad, I'd crawl and creep to the nearest ditch! As it is, I'll ride, so pray ring for a horse."

"Doctor Little, what do you say?"

"Stuff!" retorted this practitioner, who was the perfect opposite of his name, being particularly large and ponderous. "I say stuff and nonsense! Your cousin, my lord, should instantly to bed, there to abide until I deem him fit to travel. And in bed he would be were he any other than his confounded, asinine, rebellious self! I have, my lord, tended this headstrong cousin o' yours since he was breeched—and before! 'Twas I, in fact, brought him into the world—more's the pity—and a devilish business he made of it even then,—a thwartwise presentation!"

"So I'll . . . ride," gasped Ralph, though the doctor's busy hands were very gentle, "so soon as . . . Old Sawbones has . . . done mauling me."

"And when," continued the doctor as if Ralph hadn't uttered a word, "when he was an urchinly imp I was usually compelled to half throttle him before I could urge or persuade a pill into him. But today"—here the doctor, having finished with his patient, addressed him for the first time—"today, Lord Ralph, you are your own misfortune and my present nuisance! So if you will ride, ride and ride to Gehenna for all I care!"

"That will I, right speedily," Ralph nodded. "And I'll beg Old Nick to stoke up specially for you, Tom Little! So, Japhet, have the civility to ring for my horse."

"At least," said Sam, hand on bell-rope, "drink a glass of wine before you go, for I——"

"Wine?" snarled Ralph. "I don't touch the cursed stuff! To hell with every dam' bottle!" At this staggering assertion, Sam let go the bell-rope and turned to stare, dumb with amazement. Not so Doctor Little, who exclaimed: "Eh— what's this?" then leaned down to examine his patient with instant professional anxiety; he felt his brow, which was jerked indignantly aside, seized his wrist in powerful grip, felt his pulse, demanded sight of his tongue and was sworn at, and, freeing his furious patient, pronounced judgment:

"Not delirious—no! I discover no trace, no symptom! Certainly not delirious! Statement must then be a stark-staring, downright lie! Yet, imp though you were, you were never a liar. Then if no lie, it must be fact, and if fact, then, by all the Faculty, 'tis a miracle! But miracles find no credence with me, no—all such being no more than subtle reflexes of nature! Therefore we shall forthwith attempt proof. Young Ralph—my lord, when summoned here I found you in a syncope—in deliquium, *vox et proeterea nihil*,—induced by copious effusion of the life element owing to severance of tissue by some sharp implement. You follow me, I hope?"

"No, I don't, and——"

"Excellent, my lord! Very good, young Ralph,—and I must beg or compel you to sit still and hear me pronounce that port wine, being a blood-maker, I here and now prescribe a glass or so of the Earl's noble vintage, than which I have never tasted an equal! Now, my lord Ralph, how say you to a glass of this richly succulent wine?"

"I say," quoth Ralph, "Tom Little, you boy-bullying old Sawbones, you can take the Earl's dam' wines and drown yourself in 'em and Japhet too and, b'gad, I'll dance with joy

on your infernal coffins! Now, cursed cousin, do you lend me
a horse or do I walk?"

Sam rang and gave such order to the bowing footman that
very soon he reappeared to say the horse was at the door.

"Well," said Sam gloomily, "if you will go, all I can say
is——"

"Spare me!" Ralph retorted. "But let me assure you,
damned Japhet, that, just as soon as my shoulder permits,
I shall certainly make occasion to finish the pleasure denied
me, some weeks ago, by female interruption. You understand, I think?"

"Certainly! And, as I was going to inform you——"

"Don't! The sight of you is bad enough; spare me the
sound of you until I'm strong enough to endure both together.
As for you, old Tom Sawbones, thanks for making me so comfortable; and let me advise you—give up tippling and forgo
the bottle! Remember your Bible: 'Strong drink is the devil
and rages, 'twill also bite you like a serpent and sting you
like any adder', so—beware!" Then Ralph got to his feet,
steadied himself, strode vigorously to the door and went forth,
leaving Doctor Little larger than ever by reason of the righ-
teous indignation that swelled within him.

But, as Ralph crossed the great old hall, his stride faltered
and, sinking upon a roomy settle, he leaned back wearily and
closed his eyes, opened them to sound of prodigious rustling,
and beheld Grannyanne, looking down on him.

"Eh—oh, Mrs. Leet, isn't it?" he murmured. "Years ago
. . . used to give me cakes . . . I remember."

"Yes, my lord Ralph, you were a lonely child then, sometimes pampered, oftener neglected by your father—now 'tis
you are neglectful of yourself for that self is in no fit state to
travel."

"Mrs. Leet, pray believe . . . I am a trivet . . . I mean,
right as one! If you'll be so good . . . help me so far as my
horse, all will be . . . joy and jollity."

"And," continued Grannyanne, concerned to feel how
heavily he leaned to her support, "her ladyship the Countess
bade me say——"

"Don't say anything! Pray don't, there's a good soul——"

"—that until she is well enough to see you, her love and gratitude go with you. Also, from today you will always be in her prayers that God may bless and keep you in His love."

"Oh?" murmured Ralph. "Well, I suppose that should help a fellow—even me! And . . . just at present I need help rather."

"Yes, Lord Ralph."

"I don't mean—bodily."

"I know what you mean, my lord."

"Yes, you generally did . . . in the old days, wherefore the joy and comfort of cakes, eh, Mrs. Leet?"

"And now, Lord Ralph, for sake of those old days, I tell you that if you go to the Manor you will find it is—only a house!"

"Ah!" he exclaimed, halting suddenly and with a stagger. "I see! You mean . . . she is not there to . . . make it 'home'!"

"She is not there, my lord."

"Oh . . . well, I'm . . . not surprised. . . . And do please call me Ralph again, as you did when I was a . . . not so very bad little boy . . . will you?"

"Yes, Ralph, for to me you are still a not so very bad little boy, especially just now. So I ask you, bid you, not to go riding to a desolate house—and with that dreadful wound! Bide here until——"

"Can't, dear soul, and—won't! Not beneath this cur—this roof, anywhere but here! Besides, I ride to learn if a gipsy prophecy be true. . . . How did it go? 'She flies to a mother who grieves a son that died of the water and returns in the music.' Well, who should this be but poor Mrs. Jennings, always such a gentle creature—and Eustace died by drowning —and made pretty good music. . . . What say you, dear soul?"

"Yes, Ralph, the prophecy is true, for she you seek is there, hoping, waiting——"

"Eh? For me? Hoping—for me?"

"Go you and find out, Ralph, and I pray God bless you— both!"

CHAPTER XXXIII

HOW RALPH PROVED THE PROPHECY TRUE

BESIDE the open kitchen window, with the sun bright in her lustrous hair, Cecily, Lady Scrope, was making pastry, and giving her whole mind to it, as every cook should; while, seated close at hand, Mrs. Jennings, this sad-eyed, gentle lady, was preparing the apples destined to fill this pie; out in the fragrant garden birds were in full song, for the day was young. Thus they wrought awhile in a companionly silence like the old and tried friends they were.

At last, pausing in her apple-peeling, Mrs. Jennings spoke in that soft, caressing voice of hers:

"I think you are quite wonderful, dear child!"

"Me?" exclaimed Cecily, opening her blue eyes in unaffected amazement. "Oh! Why, dearest?"

"Because you are so brave and lion-hearted, never to show your hurt—even to me, and never to weep over your grief for pity of yourself."

"Oh, but, dearest, I do! I often weep and pity myself in the lonely night, only I—pity him more."

"And I used to pity him,—when he was a boy, because he was so very lonesome, and didn't know it, then as a young man because he was so blindly reckless, and now because—without you he will certainly be——"

"Oh, what, dearest, what will he be?"

"Either completely lost, or—will find and know himself at last."

"I suppose," said Cecily, busied with rolling-pin again. "Yes, I've been thinking lately that I never ought to have let him marry me!"

"And why not, pray?"

"Because I'm not a real lady, and never shall be. I'm too

202

big and strong. And I like things no real lady ought to like, for instance, a pitchfork——"

"Goodness gracious—why?"

"Because I can use one better than most men, fork a bigger load and toss sheaves higher. And then, besides—instead of polite perfumes in bottles, I love the smell of cows, and stables, and new-mown hay, and honeysuckle and all such common things! Of course, I love silk stockings, the glidy feel of them, but they still make me feel self-conscious, like I do in my own house with too many servants to wait on me and do things I could do so much better. And I like baking and brewing, and love a dairy! No, I'm not a lady and know I never shall be, though I've tried so hard—for his sake. But I was born only a farmer's daughter and everybody knows it,—the county folk, I mean; that's why they never call at the Manor now, and that's why I shouldn't have . . . married him! And, oh, I'm dreadful afraid——" Here the busy rolling-pin faltered and stopped, that she might wipe tears with the back of her large, though shapely, hand. "Yes, I be sick with fear that he thinks so too—knows he's made a great mistake and that I'm the mistake. And, oh . . . how I do wish I was a lady!"

"My dear, you are best—just, exactly as you are!"

"But if he wants me a lady . . ."

"Cecily dear, a lady is merely a woman disguised—and sometimes very badly! As for your Ralph, he is your problem and a very difficult one because of his father! That hateful, wicked father who set himself wilfully—to corrupt and pervert his own little, motherless son, transforming a mischievous boy into a wildly reckless youth, and this poor youth into a drunken, lawless reprobate who may become evil—almost—as his dreadful father, unless——"

"Oh, unless—what, dearest, what?"

"Unless your patient love and sweet purity can shame the demon in him and the evil out of him! And this I believe you can and will, just because you are—as you are!"

"But, dearest"—here the rolling-pin fell to the floor and lay unheeded—"he believes I'm—not pure."

"You, Cecily, you? Then he is an even greater fool than I believed!"

"Oh, he is!" sighed Cecily. "Sometimes he's very, very silly, to think I could ever love anyone else, though, of course, he has every reason to be jealous of Sam, as I told him, Sam I mean, though when he, now I mean Ralph, threatened to kill Sam, I got frightened at last."

"Great—merciful—heaven!" gasped Mrs. Jennings, dropping the apple she had been peeling. "Whatever . . . whyever didn't you mention all this before? For your sake and theirs, tell me all about it, everything!" And when Cecily had done so, Mrs. Jennings smoothed back her abundant, snow-white hair, exclaiming:

"Oh, Cecily! Oh, my poor dear, how utterly foolish and silly it all is, and yet—how very dreadful it may be. Something must be done, and at once. It must all be explained, cleared up and—we will do it together, for put an end to, it must and shall be!"

"Yes, dearest, we must, and we will—but how?"

"We must see the Countess, of course! Yes, we must explain everything to Andromeda."

"That's what I thought—at first, dearest. But then I thought again, for, you see, though I love her and believe she likes me, yet I know—I've always known she's a bit jealous of me too, deep, deep down in her heart, even before Sam married her. And she has reason for it too, because Sam has always been so very kind to me! Yes, long before he gave me all that fortune of money so that I could free Ralph from that debtor's prison, as you'll mind, and marry him, like Sam promised I should when he pretended to tell my fortune by that awful pool where I'd meant to drown myself and wasn't brave enough."

"Yes . . . yes!" sighed Mrs. Jennings, now rubbing her smooth chin absent-mindedly with the handle of her apple-knife. "That money is the great stumbling-block, for it was such a terribly large amount, nearly one . . . million . . . pounds!"

"No, quite a million, dearest! That's what made his lawyer, Mr. Joliffe, so upset!"

"And no wonder!" nodded Mrs. Jennings. "Sam is always so—so wholesale! However, there is a way and we must find it!"

"Yes," sighed Cecily, clasping her hands, "yes, we must—only, as you know, dearest, because Andromeda is a real lady, she's so dreadfully, terribly, awfully—proud!"

"She is indeed——"

"And because she may believe Sam loves me, 'tis only Sam who can make her know how very silly it all is!"

"Very true, Cecily! Then perhaps we had better talk to him first? And yet—no, quite impossible, this trouble of their lost child forbids. Oh, good gracious me, what a coil! I must think, yes, and pray——"

"Goo' marnin' me leddies!" piped a voice beyond the open lattice and so near that both ladies started violently, and, turning, beheld old Mr. Toop, this lively ancient who, among many other feats, had taught Sam the subtleties of a scythe; though bowed with years, Mr. Toop was still hearty, and this morning extremely trim as to smockfrock, gaiters and boots, and he now saluted them with hat gallantly a-flourish, saying:

"Mistus Jennin's ma'm, I see as your cabbages be comin' along proper, though your turmuts need an 'oe and your radishers is fair cryin' for to be et. 'Ows'ever, 'tidn't 'bout they as I've looked in on ee, ma'm, but ta give ee a piece o' famious noos, it be. So now, ma'm, ax me wot."

"Pray what have you to tell us, Toop?"

"Leddies both, I'm yere to tell ee as 'ow the Earl's babby be found, so it be!"

"Oh now, thank God——"

"Ar!" nodded Mr. Toop. "And so says arl o' we—though the 'and, or fist-es as done it b'longs to your nobel, gallient lord and 'usband, me leddy Scrope! Ar, 'twere 'im as went and gone and done it wi' 'is two good fist-es, like a roaring lion an' tiger! Ar, like Lord Nelson at Trafalgar, bold, 'eeroic and likewise wounded in the arm! And—there's noos for ee!"

"Tell us more!" cried Cecily, leaning out through the lattice. "Oh, Toop, dear old William, tell us all about him, everything!"

"Well, so I be, me leddyship, so fast as I be able. For, lookee, arter the Earl wi' 'is 'undreds and thousands o' right men 'as looked and sarched and sought arl over and through Sussex, your noble 'eerio-'usband, Lord Ralph, ups and says, says 'e ef arl o' you can't nowise and no'ow find one li'l' bit of a babby, I'd better do it for ee. So—off 'e rides, finds they rask-ells, fights an' flattens 'em like an 'eerio should and brings the blessed babby, bloody and bleedin', safe 'ome 'e do! And there's for ee again!"

"Oh, William, was the poor, sweet mite hurt badly?"

"Not 'im, no—sound as a li'l' bell 'e were."

"But you said he was bleeding."

"Sa'e were, me leddy, ar—b'all accounts the babby were fair drippin' and droppin' wi' blood,—splishin' an' splashin' arl over everywheer, soakin' an' soppin' were the babby and yet—never so much as a scrat, nary one! For this yere blood b'longs to an' comes out of your 'eeroic 'usband, Lord Ralph, like I'm tellin' ee and——"

"Oh . . . my God! Is he much hurt?"

"Well, me leddyship, 'e arn't dead—yet! No, not quite. Theer still be life in 'im, so they do tell, but——"

"Where . . . where is he now?"

"Ar! Theer be question as naun can't go for ta answer, seein' as nobody don't know—nary soul! But arter 'e brings the babby safe t'the Great 'Ouse, 'e gives a gurt sigh like 'is pore 'eart were breakin' an' sinks off'n 'is 'orse in a swound. So the Earl hisself picks 'im up an' carries 'im indoors. Doctor Little patches of 'im up and away 'e goes again, nobody don't know wheer. But I spex as, bein' sich a fightin' 'eerio, 'e's off for to see ef theer be any more babbies as needs rescooin'. So theer's arl me noos, leddies! An' right praper noos it be, though—dry in the tellin', Mrs. Jennin's, ma'm."

"Of course, Mr. Toop. If you will step into the parlour, my Caroline shall bring you ale."

"Hurt!" said Cecily, when Mr. Toop had gone to refresh himself. "Hurt, and perhaps badly."

"No, my dear, it cannot be so very bad if he is able to mount his horse. But, oh, Cecily, how noble! How splendid!"

"Yes, he was always splendid. But now . . . suppose he has . . . fallen again and is lying somewhere now . . . at death's door——"

"I don't suppose any such thing, no—not for a single instant! And—even if he were, how could we help him?"

"No way!" sighed Cecily. "Except by praying for him." So this, forthwith, they did, silently to be sure, yet none the less fervently. Then since there was no more she could do for him, Cecily picked up the rolling-pin and went on with her pie-making like the very sensible person she was.

Meanwhile Mr. Toop, now plenteously refreshed, tottered forth, his old legs bearing him rather more spryly than usual, until, being come into the tree-shaded lane, he halted suddenly to lean on his stick and peer at a horseman who was approaching slowly and silently upon the grass that bordered the dusty road.

"Gorramity!" he exclaimed. "Mast' Ralph, be this you, me lord?"

"None other!" answered Ralph, drawing rein. "Tell me, William, is—is my—is Lady Scrope hereabouts?"

"Ar, that she be, me lord, and so blooming as a lovely flower, she be——"

"Good! Then back with you and—let her know I'm on my way. But tell her gently, mind! Don't be too sudden,—lead up to it cautiously, bit by bit. D'you understand?"

"Ar, that I du! Trust me, Mast' Ralph, leave it arl tu I!" And thus presently:

"Leddies," he piped, reappearing at the lattice, "I got more noos for ee! 'Tidn't a lot but 'tis summat, and ef you axes wot, I answers as 'ow Mast' Ralph. my leddyship's 'eerio-'usband, don't bleed no more! No! His blood be now a-flowin' jest 'ow and wheer it should ought for to flow. An' ef you axes me 'ow I know, I ups an' answers ee as 'ow me eyes du tell me so. Ef you then axes me 'when', I says to ee, says I, 'bout five minutes ago. And then ef you axes me 'wheer', then I says to ee, I says right promp' and j'yful—out yon in the road and——"

Cecily was out and away, running with the lithe grace of

Atalanta, though to far better purpose, for she sped to lift a man from the hell of his own making, to the heaven of that pure and steadfast love which was part of her lovely self.

"Ralph!" she cried. And, hearing the glad ring of this so yearned-for voice, Ralph leapt to meet her so eagerly that he staggered and fell, nor did he attempt rising to greet her but, being extreme in all things, he clasped and kissed her shapely feet until, sinking upon her knees, she lifted him with her splendid strength, holding him close, yet saying no word; therefore he did his best to speak instead, saying, and very brokenly:

"Will you . . . can you ever . . . forgive, and . . . try to love me again . . . a little?" And now indeed she spoke and with no hesitation whatever:

"I shall always love you, Ralph, because I must. And I have never loved any man but you and never shall, because I couldn't!"

Then, because truth shone out upon him from her beautiful, honest eyes, and sang to him in the deep, sweet tones of her voice, Ralph at last ventured to kiss her,—in which glad moment the tormenting demon, named Doubt, writhing in agony of frustration, fled and was gone—as if he had never been.

CHAPTER XXXIV

HOW JANE SAVED HER "FAIRY UNCLE"

In that leafy nook Jane now called Fairydell, Sir Robert Chalmers dismounted, tethered his horse and glanced around expectantly, but either he was early or Jane was late, for she was nowhere to be seen; therefore he sat down with his back against a convenient tree to wait the coming of her small ladyship.

Now as he sat thus waiting with a patience that surprised himself, there stole over him a feeling of peaceful content, quite new in his hitherto restless, turbulent life; here in this leafy seclusion, so remote from the world of men and action, this one-time notorious duellist and cynical man of the world found such comfort for his proud, wounded spirit that he wondered how and why this should be so. How was it that he who had lived so desperately and loved the glitter and adulation of great Vanity Fair could now find in this remoteness more true joy than he had ever known? What was it? How was it? Why and why?

Here at this moment, as if eager to answer this vexed question, a bird lighted on the bough directly above him, a blackbird, very sleek, very glossy and trim in every feather; this bold fellow having peered down first with one bright eye and then the other at this speechless questioner, this tall, wondering human, proceeded to answer these unspoken questions as only a blackbird might, for, giving an extra polish to his yellow beak, he opened it in melodious reply.

Blackbirds have sung in ages past and will do in years to come (thank God!), but surely never to better effect than this particular bird-fellow who now tuned his pipe to a very glory of song, a rippling, soaring ecstasy that sank ever and anon to long-drawn, plaintive notes richly sweet, ineffably tender . . . waking forgotten dreams and memories of other days, recalling voices long hushed and loved faces seen and lost awhile in a mist of tears. . . .

So piped this particular blackbird to the silent man below, who listened as never before while this same feathered advocate of nature proclaimed how, in this brief span of life, all the best, the noblest and most enduring joys are free and very simple, the birthright of us all, that can never be bought or sold since they are the gifts of the Almighty Creator. . . .

The blackbird, ending his song in the middle of a note, flew away and Sir Robert, glancing round for the cause, saw the leafage part and two faces gazing at him, the one pallid and smiling, the other flushed, with thick black brows close-knit above eyes that glared,—faces though utterly dissimilar in every feature, yet so dreadfully alike in expression that Sir Robert know he had never been nearer death than at this moment, though he seemed wholly unaware of this when he spoke:

"Well, Twily, what do you with that arch scoundrel, and why bring him here to foul and poison the air?"

"Why, my dear Bob," replied the Viscount, advancing with airy gesture of greeting, "'tis quite the contrary. Bellenger brought me and——"

"Yes, begod!" quoth Mr. Bellenger, with stamp of spurred heels. "I take charge today! And I mean business, d'ye hear, Chalmers? I'm here to give you my—our—final ultimatum and b'damned—once and for all, d'ye hear? And hear me you shall and answer me you shall, yes or no . . . or it shall be you for hell-fire! D'ye hear me?"

"I perceive," said Sir Robert, crossing his long legs, "yes, it is quite evident the scoundrel has been drinking."

"Yes, Bob, a little, I'll admit, but with reason. For, my dear Robert, our poor friend here has lately experienced a shock, yes, and one of no little magnitude, Bob! To alleviate which any man is apt to—well—take a glass or so as a nerve-steadier, a bracer, as I'm sure you agree when I inform you that this particular shock wears a red waistcoat and is known as Shrig, Jasper Shrig of Bow——"

"Yes—yes," panted Mr. Bellenger, "and you, Chalmers, you have informed and brought him down on me—us! You have betrayed me, damn you! And for this I'll have your blood or your evidence to acquit me,—which? Tell me which now and be quick about it! Now—speak!"

Sir Robert, having crossed his legs, now crossed his arms and, surveying Mr. Bellenger with the utmost contempt, spoke to the Viscount.

"Your friend here, Twily, is not only a villain but a fool and extremely unpleasant altogether; pray remove him."

"Dear Robert," sighed the Viscount, "how I admire you! So crippled! Yet indomitable, yes, perfectly unshakable as ever. We simply desire you to inform us——"

"Damnation—no! No, we don't!" panted Mr. Bellenger, trying to shake off the Viscount's restraining clutch. "Curse you, Sir Robert,—we demand an explanation, and you are going to tell why you set the runners on me—us, for Twily's in as deep——"

"Arthur!" The word was not loud, but the Viscount's white hand was so compelling that Mr. Bellenger uttered a gasp and writhed in its powerful clutch.

"And now," said the Viscount, smiling pleasantly, "now, my very dear Arthur, pray hush and permit me a few sane words!"

"Yes, yes . . . but I don't go without his word for my safety or—his blood for mine! Yes, and then there are my papers . . . my papers that he stole, damn him! I must have them! I will have them, and today, I tell you, today, or, begod, he shall never live to——"

"Of course, Arthur, of course! This is all quite understood! Now do I go on or leave you to it?"

"Oh, go on, put it to him and let's know one way or the other and be done with him at last, living or dead."

"Very well, then, be silent! Briefly, Robert, matters have indeed come to a crisis for all three of us. Poor Arthur here, distracted by the positive knowledge that such bloodhound as Shrig is nosing in his vicinity and suspecting—and I must say not without reason—that you are the *deus ex machina*, the god in the car, the compelling force,—in a word, that by means of Shrig you have decided to—end poor Arthur's earthly activities and in such highly unpleasant fashion, he, very naturally desiring to live, insists you shall call off this blood-hound and, furthermore—restore to Arthur certain papers which——"

"Twily," said Sir Robert, wearily, "your brevity is quite too prolix, so now—hear me! Nothing is bad enough, no death shameful enough for your friend Bellenger, this black-mailer whose chief victim was an unhappy woman he drove to suicide——"

"Liar . . . liar!" gasped Mr. Bellenger in choking voice.

"I do not," pursued Sir Robert, "mention that other death or the one later attempted—by poison! As to those papers you refer to,—I employed an expert cracksman to recover them, with others, from this blackmailer's possession and thus secured evidence sufficient to check his villainies there and then and—to hang him when so I will for the disgusting scoundrel he is——"

Uttering a wild, inarticulate cry, Mr. Bellenger thrust hand into breast for the weapon concealed there, but in that moment the Viscount had seized the wrist of this murderous hand, grip-ping it painfully, yet saying in that indolent voice of his:

"Don't . . . don't be such fool, Arthur!"

"Let me go, damn you!"

"Oh no——" Fiercely now they strove and wrestled while Sir Robert, lolling against his tree, watched this struggle for his life contemptuously and as if perfectly unconcerned by its final outcome, nor did he move or speak when at last Mr. Bel-lenger's hand reappeared unarmed.

"You see . . . my dear Bob," said the Viscount, rather breathlessly, "what it is to . . . sponsor a fool and . . . dastardly craven!"

"Begod . . . Twily!" panted Mr. Bellenger. "I begin to think . . . you are with him . . . against me! Let me only be . . . sure o' this and you shall never . . . betray another friend!"

"And, Viscount," said Sir Robert, "before you rid me, and I suggest yourself also, of your dastard, I trouble myself to assure you that I certainly did not, to use your phrase, 'set this law-hound' to work, preferring rather to inflict such black-mailer with the torture of suspense—as he so tormented his miserable victims before I checked him. But if now he is to be taken and hanged, well and good, so much the better——"

Once again Mr. Bellenger leapt and once again the Viscount seized him, but then—both stood, suddenly arrested, gazing motionless in the one direction whence, high and sweetly clear, a voice was singing:

> " 'In Scarlit Town where I was borned
> There was a fair maid dwellin'——'."

And so came Jane. . . .

CHAPTER XXXV

TELLS OF SAM, THE SOLITARY

CAPTAIN NED was busied with his stalwart man of all work, Tom, in the farmyard while old Mr. Toop perched nearby on upturned bucket, watched with the eye of former long experience and therefore an eye of cold disparagement.

"No!" he screeched, sudden and loud.

"No what, Gaffer?" demanded his son Tom, this one-time sailor and Trafalgar man. "What are you a-'no'-ing about now?"

"I sez no, Tom me lad, and I mean no, for I never no-how and no-when see no pitchfork mis'andled so cruel in arl me born days, never! We knowed better 'ow in my young days."

"Old 'un," retorted his son, forking a mountain of fragrant hay. "Your young days is so long ago you've forgot all about 'em."

"'Owsoever, me lad, I minds right well the day as I took ee 'crost this yere very knee and laid into ee wi' me belt for puttin' they twoads into your poor mother's bed and nigh frighten 'er into hestrix. Ar, I laid into ee, 'ole-'earted, I did!"

"And sarve me right too!" nodded Tom. "Though they toads were meant only for you, Dad,—me an' Will thinking as Mother were away that night. But—as for a pitchfork, 'twere you as larned me 'ow."

"So I did tu! But off you goes to sea for to fight they Frenchies and forgets arl as I did larn ee—and comes back the on-handiest chap as ever mis-druv a plough, so ee did. Th' gurt wonder is as Cap'n Ned do keep ee on. Ee, Cap'n, wot do ee think o' this gurt, numpish son o' mine?"

"That he does you credit, William."

"Du ee now? Well, 'e aren't nought to compare wi' his poor

brother Williyam as got hisself took up to glory along o' Lord Nelson by a cannon-ball aboard the *Victory*, no!"

"'Tweren't a cannon-ball, Gaffer, as I've telled ee before, 'twere a musket-ball fired from the mizzen-top o' the *Temeraire* arter she fell aboard us——"

"Eh—my whiskers!" exclaimed the ancient one. "Look oo be a-comin' yonder!" The two workers, master and man, glanced round and beheld a horseman approaching at funereal pace.

"And," quoth the old one, "'e don't 'ail so 'earty as wot 'e used for to du."

"No," answered the Captain, "he wants rousing." Then, leaning on his pitchfork, he sent forth a bellowing roar as if hailing the main top-gallant in a tempest:

"Sam—ahoy!" The horseman mended his pace, lifted a hand in greeting, but with no cheery answering hail.

"Still making heavy weather of it, Captain!" said Tom, shaking comely head.

"Ay, Tom, such mental suffering as he endured leaves its mark on a man. I'll bear away and meet him." And, setting aside pitchfork, off he went and, despite heavy boots and leggings, striding like a sailorman.

"Well, Sam," he enquired, as their hands gripped, "how goes it?" And, grasping his friend's hand rather harder than usual, Sam answered:

"She's gone, Ned, and with never a word! Andromeda . . . she's left me . . . she and the child . . . all gone! . . . and her women! The place is empty now . . . except for Grannyanne. A very hell of a place, Ned, all too big for me . . . it always was! Not a soul to talk with except Grannyanne, yes and, damme, even she seems aloof and afraid o' me, these days! So, shipmate, I've come aboard again, ay, back to Willowmead, d'ye see . . . my old gable room again . . . if you'll have me?"

"Have you?" repeated the Captain, joyously. "Can you doubt it, messmate? 'Twill be like old times before you were the Earl and merely my old shipmate—first officer aboard the *Fortune*. Kate will be right glad, not to mention Aunt

Deborah and all the rest of us. So heave ahead and bring to, for you're in harbour again." Thus, with the Captain leading his horse, Sam rode into the fragrant rickyard, there to be saluted smartly and greeted heartily by Tom and welcomed shrilly by his aged sire.

Now as, arm in arm, these old friends approached the farm-house so dearly familiar, from open door and latticed window issued sounds that arrested Sam so suddenly that the Captain enquired:

"What now, shipmate?"

"Cups and saucers, Ned—a woman's voice! There are no better sounds in all the world, for these help to make home . . . rattle of crockery, a woman singing at her work."

"Why then, old friend, come home."

And so, in that spacious chamber that was at once kitchen and parlour, a gladly-surprised Kate, beautified by mother-hood, welcomed him—first with both hands and then ruddy lips, saying thereafter:

"You're just in time for tea; help me lay the table while Ned cuts the ham—not too thick, Ned,—for Aunt Deborah's out with—the baby, Sam,—and Nancy and the maid's in the hayfield and—oh, Ned, go pull some lettuce and wash them, there's a dear!"

"Ay ay, Commodore!" laughed her husband. "And, Kate, Sam means to stay with us again, for a while. Tell her, Sam, while I obey her commands like the wife-broken spouse I am!" Thus while Kate cut the bread and butter, Sam told of the shadow that seemingly had quite engulfed the Great House and of his sudden loneliness; and though he made it a plain, matter-of-fact statement, Kate's eyes were moist as she said:

"Oh, Sam! My dear, what a great silly you are!"

"Am I?" he enquired meekly. "Pray how and why?"

"Because you're a man, nice and manly with nothing feminine about you, and consequently quite idiotically silly where women are concerned and always say and do the wrong thing, just as my Ned does! He sometimes drives me nearly frantic with his silliness, but then instead of showing pride like your poor, misunderstood Andromeda, I show my teeth, and instead of being coldly dignified I pull his hair, yes I do—bless him! And then—well, it all ends in smacks and kisses."

"But," Sam enquired, "suppose you had showed proud and coldly dignified, how then, Kate?"

"Then, Sam, I should have expected Ned to take and—compel me! Sam, the prouder a woman is, the more she needs —yes and loves—to be compelled. Though of course it must be done—properly—at the right time, by—the right man! So all you need do is—ride after her, pick her up in your arms, hold her nice and tight until she either sighs, weeps or laughs, then—kiss her and keep on till she kisses you back and—oh, here comes my baby with Aunt Deb!" So saying, up and away sped this young mother, to return bearing her first-born and Sam's diminutive namesake, a rosy gurgling personage seemingly all chubby arms and legs whom she thrust upon his godfather, saying:

"There! Feel how he's grown! The size and weight of him! And what is perfectly wonderful, Sam, he's beginning to talk already! The other day, Thursday it was, he said 'earwig' quite distinctly—didn't he, Aunt Deb?"

"Indeed he did distinctly, the darling——"

"Probably a hiccough," said Captain Ned entering with the lettuce, "or wind——"

"Ned, how can you, for shame!" cried the proud mother. "How can you?"

"Because," explained Aunt Deborah, removing her bonnet the better to kiss Sam, "though such a proud parent, he's still merely a male man, my child, and knows no better! Wind indeed! Now, Kate, while you take and tend his offspring I'll brew tea and finish cutting the bread and butter."

"No, I will!" said Sam, and began doing so with sailorly deftness.

"And," quoth the Captain, busied at vast, cold ham, "don't spare the butter, messmate, we're not aboardship now."

"Aboardship!" Sam repeated, knife suddenly arrested, and sat thus in profound thought until Aunt Deborah, teapot in hand, elbowed him into activity again.

H

Thus presently down they sat to eat and drink, talk and laugh like the old and well-tried friends they were, until:

"Hush and hark!" exclaimed Aunt Deborah, one small finger upraised. "I do believe——" Upon the flagstones of the garden path beyond wide-open door a heavy stick was thudding nearer with rustle of voluminous petticoats, and then upon the threshold Grannyanne halted to smile in upon them, saying:

"Wait, bide still and let me look at ye, it renews my faith and hope. Tea, a plenteous table, loving friendship, health and happiness! 'Tis picture of our good, clean England that I hope and pray shall never fade! Now I'll join ye."

This joyous meal ending at last, Grannyanne demanded and took Sam's ready arm and led him out to the shady orchard where stood that rustic seat and table his skilful hands had fashioned in other and perhaps happier days; here seated, she drew him beside her, saying:

"Now, Sam, I'm going to talk to you as a loving Grandmother (though by adoption) should, and, as my own sailor father might have said, 'plain as a jack-staff or main topgallant!' Ay, I'm going to let fly at you with every tier, and rake ye fore and aft, so beat to quarters and stand by! And first,—'tis your proudly arrogant self, my lord, is responsible for my poor Sam's present unhappiness——"

"Oh no!" retorted Sam, at his lordliest. "This I cannot and will not admit." Grannyanne shook her head at him, shook her finger against him and continued:

"Sam, I followed you to Willowmead because here, among these dear folk, this sweetly rustic simplicity, you cannot be the too-proud, cold-hearted aristocrat, for the Earl of Wrybourne has no place here in such home as this where England's true strength and greatness is, has been and ever will be—oh no! Here you are just Sam, simply a man, and at present a very foolish one——"

"Grannyanne, when was I ever arrogant or cold-hearted?"

"Never, except to your wife."

"She locked her door against me!" Sam retorted, scowling. "Ay, and before that, her heart! 'Twas she who changed!"

"And 'twas you did nothing about it!"

"Well, but . . . damme, what could I have done?"

"Well, Sam, damme, what are your arms for?"

"Ha, like Kate, you mean——"

"Of course I mean—everything you think, all you desire and long for. Andromeda is your wife, and, beneath the icy armour of her pride, the woman who loves you passionately as wife should."

"Ay, but then, d'ye see, ice begets ice——"

"Only with such chilly creature as my lord Arrogance, not with her hearty sailorman who with kiss or so could have melted the ice to such purpose she would have stripped off her armour, and then, ah—then!"

"Ay, and then . . . Grannyanne?"

"Leapt to his arms, Sam, his very heart!" Up rose Sam, took a quarter-deck walk, five long paces each way, and halted to declare:

"Well, I wrote to her!"

"You did, Sam, two in one, and better you'd writ neither."

"She let you read 'em?"

"Of course! I love her and she knows it."

"She never troubled to pen me a line!"

"Oh, but she did! Yes, quite a number, but she was wise enough to destroy them."

"She made no—no advances——"

"Of course not, being a woman she could only wait, as woman must——"

"Not a wife, surely?"

"Your wife did, night after night! Tremulous with hope and expectation."

"That is devilish hard to believe!"

"And you are devilish hard not to believe, Sam! Night after night she waited, listening for your step, a tap upon that closed door, but they never came. She took her babe to sleep with her at last—and now—she is gone——"

"And left me no written word of farewell, not one!"

"Oh yes, she did, but tore them up like the others, 'for,' said she to me, 'oh, Grannyanne——' But maybe in your present mood you don't wish to hear?"

"I do. Pray tell me."

"Not till you sit down again." Sam did so very stiffly, and she, viewing him askance, his outthrust chin and close-knit brows, remarked, sighing:

"You're looking damnably like the Earl, Sam."

"Grannyanne, that's twice you've sworn at me!"

"I wonder at my restraint, seeing the way you look!"

"Well, how d'you want me to look?"

"Like Sam, Sam!" His scowling brows relaxed, his tight-drawn lips quivered to something so nearly a smile, that she nodded:

"That's better, 'twill do to go on with and so will I: Andromeda said to me, and that pretty foot of hers on the carriage step, the great, four-horsed chariot it was, Sam, 'Oh, Grannyanne, 'tis a fateful course I'm taking, and though I'm leaving him'—meaning you, Sam—'with you,'—meaning me, Sam, —'I leave you both in this dreadful shadow of Wrybourne Feveril that has made this great place and everything in it so hateful lately,—see how dark it falls about us, chilling the very sun!' And I said to her: 'Lord bless you, my love, 'tis but the shadow of the old keep and part of this Old England of ours!' 'Yes,' said she, fetching a great sigh, 'but to me it is like the shadow of doom!' Then she kissed me and they drove away."

"And was this all, Grannyanne, no word for me?"

"No, Sam, not one!"

"Then," said he, leaping afoot again, "damme, that's done it!"

"Ho!" exclaimed Grannyanne, with emphatic gesture. "Then, if it has,—damned you will surely be!"

"I'll take my chance o' that!" he retorted, 'quarter-decking' again.

"Nonsense, Sam! 'Tis time you gave up such reckless fooleries; you're not at sea now and——"

"No!" he exclaimed, halting and clapping hand to brawny thigh. "But what's to stay me? Nothing now! And the Froggies yearning for blood! B'Jove, Granny, you've reminded me! To fit out a privateer of my own and sail against the mounseers again! To hear the piping o' wind in rigging! To feel the forward leap and roll of a stout ship! To feel her lurch and quiver to each broadside—then 'boarders away' and the hell-fire joy of close action!'"

"Sam, you are talking like selfish fool!"

"Grannyanne, England needs every fighting man she can muster!"

"And they're mustering, God bless them!"

"Ay, or being 'pressed!' But I, and such as I am, need no press-gangs, volunteers all to England's need."

"And what of your wife's need of you?"

"It's so vastly overwhelming that she's left me . . . alone in this shadow! Instead, she has her baby, her godmother, her servants, money, yes—everything a woman can need——"

"Except her husband, Sam!"

"Then let her come back to him! Ay, and pretty soon, d'ye see, or she'll be too late."

"Why, my poor Sam, why?"

"A stout ship, Grannyanne, a fighting crew, and hey for the mounseers! I wonder if Ned would join me?"

"Never! Edward Harlow is no such fool!"

"Ay, more's the pity! However, I'll put it to him, at once! So up with you, Granny, let's go find him. Come!"

"Not I, Sam, no! Sit you down again, for I haven't done."

"But, d'ye see, I have! So, come, or, b'Jingo, I'll pick you up and carry you."

"You wouldn't; besides, you couldn't——" His long arms were about her when she rose, freed herself (with a rustle), whereupon he kissed her, drew her arm within his and walked her out of the orchard.

They found the Captain with Tom hard at it again with pitchforks, whereon they both paused to lean while Sam, briefly, though with ardour, made known his great idea. And when the Captain had heard him out, he shook his head, saying:

"Messmate, while there are men to fight our ships our properest work is ashore, our best weapon the plough. For to fight well men must eat well. Should our fleets, these walls

of England, let in the damned invader then will be our time
for steel and musket. But until then, I am very sure our
duty is on the land, you, with your vast resources and influence
among your folk, are far more useful here than at sea, one
fighter among so many, ay, even though in command of your
own ship. Think it over, Sam, and know how true and right
this is. Here among your tenantry you are all powerful, at
sea you would be but one among the many."

"Oh, well," mourned Sam, turning from master to man,
"Tom, what say you? My bo'sun aboard a tight ship, well-
found, rightly armed and manned! How say you, old *Victory*
man?"

"Why . . . m'lord, sir," answered Tom, leaning on his pitchfork and glancing towards the farmhouse, "there be dooty at
sea and dooty ashore. There be likewise my Nancy as be expecting! So, having listened to his honour the Captain, I
agrees 'ole-'earted that till needful and the Frenchies ashore
and aboard of us, for me 'stead o' pike or cutlass—this here
pitchfork."

"Ay ay," nodded Sam gloomily. " 'Tis but as I expected.
So, Ned, I'll get aboard my horse and see how things are at
Wrybourne . . . there may be . . . news."

"I hope so, with all my heart, Sam. If not, we shall expect
you back; your old gable room will be ready and waiting you."

"Thanks, Ned, for I'm pretty sure it won't wait in vain."

CHAPTER XXXVI

TELLS HOW SAM CHERISHED HIS ENEMY

IT WAS as Sam passed a certain part of his woods, a lonely stretch now strictly forbidden to all trespassers and patrolled by his keepers, that the drowsy, late-afternoon hush was shattered by a sound he knew was not the discharge of a gun but the sharper report of a pistol fired at no great distance. . . . For a breathless moment he remained perfectly still, listening intently, but all was hushed again. So, turning from the road, he entered the shadowy wood, pausing frequently the better to use eyes and ears, and thus presently was aware of a vague disturbance amid the undergrowth, and, advancing the more cautiously, beheld a riderless horse grazing busily. Dismounting, he tethered this animal and his own and went on again, every sense alert . . . heard an agonized groaning and, guided by this, beheld Sir Robert Chalmers sprawled in an awkward huddle yet striving feebly with his one hand to staunch the blood that was staining him so horribly at throat and breast.

"Wait . . . lie still!" cried Sam, hurrying forward. "Let me!" And off came his coat and waistcoat.

"No good . . . Wrybourne!" gasped Sir Robert. "They've got me . . . this time . . . I'm done for!"

"Never think it!" growled Sam, pulling off his shirt and ripping it into bandages. "I've handled worse at sea. . . . Lie still now!" And with sailorly deftness he began such rough surgery as he had learned and practised aboard crowded fighting ships.

"Wrybourne . . . stop!"

"Lie still, damn you! And don't speak!"

"I must before . . . accepting your . . . help! Must tell you . . . 'twas I planned . . . stealing your child!" Sam's busy hands faltered in their ministry; Sir Robert's pallid lips curled in twisted smile as he gasped:

"Now go . . . dog's death for . . . your enemy———"
Scowling his grimmest, Sam gnashed his teeth but—bent
again to his surgery.

"Ah———" whispered Sir Robert. " 'Coals of fire' worse
than . . . death!" And he strove feebly against these too-
merciful hands.

"Curse you, lie still!" snarled Sam.

Groaning in his helplessness, Sir Robert gazed up at the
scowling but intent face above him and, striving desperately
to speak, mumbled incoherently and sank into unconscious-
ness.

Thus Sam, working now more speedily, contrived with pad
and bandages to check the blood-flow that was carrying life
with it, and, sitting back on his heels the better to survey his
handiwork, heard the gurgle of a rill at no great distance, and,
taking Sir Robert's hat, came to this brook, soaked it, filled it
and, returning, dashed this life-giving water into the haggard
face whose pallor was rendered the more ghastly by contrast
with the jet-black hair and neatly-trimmed whiskers that
framed it. Sir Robert sighed, shuddered, opened swimming
eyes and presently said, and in stronger voice:

"Can you get me . . . to my house?"

"No, I shall have to take you with me."

"Where?"

"Home," answered Sam, and then, very bitterly, "No, I
can't; I have no home; it's only Wrybourne Feveril, but it's
pretty near."

"Why no home . . . Wrybourne?"

"Because some devilry has destroyed it."

"Wrybourne, that devilry . . . was mine!"

"Ay, damme, I might have known it!"

"Yes, indeed, you . . . should have known. I . . . struck at
you . . . through your affections."

Sam scowled down on the speaker, who, gazing up at him
with eyes aglow in pain-racked face, continued:

"Those . . . anonymous letters . . . were . . . my suggestion. To breed distrust . . . between husband and wife and
. . . successfully it seems!"

Sam ground his teeth and glared up at the leafage overhead, while the faint, mocking voice persisted:

"Break your heart, not . . . your body."

Sam glared down at his two quivering fists, in a fury that well-nigh choked him.

"Wrybourne, why . . . why don't you . . . rip off these bandages and leave me . . . to die, as I . . . should have done . . . but for you! So . . . why not let me die?"

"Nothing I should like better, blast you!" growled Sam. "But I'm keeping the cursed life in you merely to please myself, d'ye see, and, yes, to thwart your will."

"Ah!" gasped Sir Robert with a note in his feeble utterance almost like triumph. "How you . . . must hate me . . . Wrybourne!"

"Well—no!" replied Sam. "I find it impossible to hate anything so contemptible as Robert Chalmers. If you live, as you probably will, for your sort are cursed hard to kill, you'll continue to be your own torment and most indefatigable torturer. Now stop talking or maybe you'll shift my bandages and restart your dam' bleeding and die in spite o' my cursed brotherly care! And now the question is, how get your infernal carcase to Wrybourne? I must haul you—no, b'George, someone's coming at last! One o' my keepers, it should be. Ahoy there!" he roared. "This way, whoever you are! Ahoy!" The hail was answered and thereafter two keepers came, running.

"A gate or hurdle!" Sam commanded. "And sharp about it, my lads, tumble to it now!" So a gate was brought and thereon the stricken man was laid, a man who spoke no more, perhaps because further speech was beyond his strength, for again he seemed unconscious and very near death when at last he was borne into the Great House, this home he had so very successfully destroyed.

CHAPTER XXXVII

HOW AND WHY MY LORD WAS SUSPECTED OF MURDER

EVENING had fallen, and Sam just risen from his solitary meal, when Mr. Perkins bowed himself into the presence saying:

"My lord, two . . . persons desire the favour of speech with your lordship."

"Then send them away. I'll see no one!"

"My lord, I did my endeavour so to do, but to none effect, for these, my lord, are no ordinary . . . persons!"

"Why?"

"My lord, they are—ahem—law officers, especially one—in a red waistcoat, my lord!"

"Good! This should be Mr. Jasper Shrig. Show him into the library and let there be wine." But, entering this spacious chamber, Sam was unpleasantly surprised to behold two strangers, the one a round, placid man, the other tall, sharp of nose, keen of eye and confident of air, who, making the most of his scarlet waistcoat, this badge of authority, tapped himself thereon with the little, brass-crowned staff he carried, this other sign of officialdom, saying in tone that matched eyes and nose:

"I'm Jacob Smalley of the Bow Street Office, London, and this," here he tapped his companion, "is John Figg, constable of Lewes; and you, I take it, are the Earl of Wrybourne?"

Sam glanced at each in turn and, misliking both, became his lordliest self and bowed.

"Ho no, no!" said Mr. Smalley, fingering his sharp nose. "This, being a very serious case, and myself officer in charge, and very zealous as you will find,—we can't have any nodding —if you please! So when we ask a question we'll have an answer vivvy-voochy, if you please! So now, sir, try again! Are you the Earl of Wrybourne, yes or no?"

"I am."

"Ex-cellent, my lord! Having thus established your lord-ship's identity, we must now, as officers authorized by law, trouble you, my lord, with a question or so. First——"

"Then, officer of the law, you may do it seated."

"Thanks, my lord, but we'd rather stand." My lord nodded and, sitting down, leaned back in his chair and regarded his questioner with calm though very evident disapproval.

"First, my lord, I believe you are acquainted with a certain Sir Robert Chalmers—am I right?" This last question de-manded with ferocious, sharp-nosed pounce.

"Yes."

"Secondly, it is in evidence as you and said Sir Robert Chalmers fought a desperate duel, some years or so ago—am I right?"

"Perfectly."

"Thirdly, it's in evidence as you and Sir Robert Chalmers have been and still are on very bad terms, in fact, deadly enemies,—am I right again?"

"More or less."

"Fourthly, from evidence lately received, we know as you were riding in the vicinity of Chedham coppice this afternoon at six-fifteen approximately,—is this admitted?"

"Yes."

"Now, my lord! At six-fifteen this afternoon in Chedham coppice, Sir Robert Chalmers was murderously shot."

"Were you a witness, officer?"

"I, my lord? Cer-tainly not."

"Then how do you know?"

"By information received."

"From whom?"

"Oh no, my lord! 'Tis I do the asking; you have only to reply. So now, my lord, I ask you." Here Officer Smalley reached out a hand to his silent companion who gave him something wrapped in a faded neckerchief. "Now," continued Mr. Smalley, approaching in almost threatening manner, "now I will ask you . . . to . . . look—at—this!" And, snatching away the neckerchief, showed the handsome riding-whip it had covered. "Look on this, my lord; gaze at it!"

"I am."

"Is it yours? Yes or no!"

"Possibly. I have many whips."

"This bears an earl's coronet and your initials on a gold mount, my lord."

"Then it is mine."

"Ha! You admit it?"

"Oh no, I inform you of its ownership."

"My lord, now look at it—just a bit closer,—these stains,— here and here again! You see 'em?"

"I do. They look like blood."

"They are blood, my lord."

"Yes, they would be."

"And," continued Officer Smalley, impressively, and coming a slow pace nearer, "this same whip as you admit is yours, was found—on the scene o' the crime!"

"Of course!" nodded my lord. "It would be!"

"Now what might you mean, my lord?"

"That somebody lacks imagination."

"Sir, I do not understand you."

"You wouldn't! But no matter."

"Ha! Well now, what say you to this evidence of your bloodstained whip?"

"Nothing!"

"Which don't surprise me. Because, my lord, from latest evidence I know as you, ah—you yourself were seen at the scene o' the crime!"

"Yes, I was there."

"Ha, then you admit it?"

"No, again I inform you."

"You were seen—bending over the body!"

"Yes."

"You were observed—actually—dragging the body——"

"No, lifting it."

"Then, my lord, I ask you, and you can answer or not, as you please, where have you hidden or deposited that body?"

"Upstairs in bed." Now though these words were gently uttered, Officer Smalley recoiled and dropped the whip which John Figg of Lewes took up, speaking for the first time:

"Muster Smalley, sir, I warned ee as 'ow ee couldn't no'ow get no change out o' the Earl." Officer Smalley drew himself up, expanded the red waistcoat and gestured towards the door with his little staff of authority, saying in tone to match it:

"In the King's name, my lord, I demand to be shown the body and shall, as a zealous officer, then act as my duty so dictates——"

"Vich nobody couldn't say fairer!" said a familiar voice, and in at the wide lattice, open to the fragrant rose garden, came a remarkably shaggy-napped hat and beneath it the beaming visage of Mr. Jasper Shrig, who, saluting my lord, continued addressing the officer: "Jacob, my pippin, your zeal is so terri-mendious it's took you in charge and run you in— up the wrong street! Here's you, Jake, chivvying the wrong party and leaving me to nab the right—as is the real wrong 'un, seeing as he's the real guilty 'un? Hows'ever——"

"Shrig, what's all this confounded gabble?"

"Jacob, my chickaleery cove, I'm telling you as how at this i-dentical minute the guilty party is kicking his heels, or, as you might say, vulgarly speaking, frisking his stampers under lock and key!"

"Eh—now dannel me!" exclaimed the silent Figg,—"axing y'r lordship's pardon! But—eh, Mr. Shrig, you've done it again, hey? As usual! Might I be so bold to ax ee—oo, when and wheer?"

"Ah yes," said Officer Smalley, bitterly. "If you're so in-fallible—name us the guilty man and——"

"In-fallible!" repeated Mr. Shrig, mouthing the word. "This is a new 'un to me, Jake, in-fallible! I've been called 'as-toot' afore now, ar, and other names, but——"

"Shrig, as a fellow officer, I ask, no—I demand of you the name of the guilty man and all particulars of his capture."

"Smalley, my lad o' zeal, since as a nofficer you ax and likewise demand so bold and official, I am bound to answer werry plain, full and free—ekker alone responds—for the present. Hows'ever, I thankee for that theer 'in-falluable'. I'll

note it down later on, but for the present, Jake and John Figg,
I'm bidding ye 'good evening' and many on 'em—unless you,
my lord, are hankering for more o' their company?"

"Thank you, no!"

"Nevertheless," said Officer Smalley, once more expanding
the waistcoat, "I shall impound your whip, my lord, holding it
as Exhibit Number One, just in case Shrig has been just a bit
too clever. Meantime,—Goodday!"

"Pal," said Mr. Shrig, as soon as they were alone, "if you'll
be so o-bleeging as to give me a heave I'll come in through
the winder and set down if I may, for my legs is feeling werry
like pipe-stems! And pray doo care for my damaged flipper."

Wondering, Sam arose and, leaning out, hauled Mr. Shrig in
through the wide lattice, sat him in the nearest easy chair and
filled two wine glasses, saying:

"So, Jasper old friend, you know all about this attempted
murder of Sir Robert Chalmers?"

"Eh?" exclaimed Mr. Shrig, wine-glass arrested at lips.
"Attempted? He ain't dead then?"

"He may be by this time. I'm waiting news from the
doctors; they're with him now. But he was alive when we
brought him in."

"Pal, if he don't die, he'll sp'ile my case!" Here Mr. Shrig
sipped his wine with melancholy relish.

"But, Jasper, how did you know of it so soon?"

"Because, sir and pal, I've been ex-pecting it ever since I
come into Sussex, ar—and long afore. So, I've been keeping
my right peeper on you and my left blinker on—wiciousness,
and in consequence werry nigh got myself murdered too!"

"Well, go on, man, let's hear all that happened."

Mr. Shrig gazed down at his left arm which he bore in a
sling, shook his head at it reproachfully, sighed profoundly
and answered:

"Pal, afore now I have took my chance agin windictiveness
in the shape o' boots, bludgeons, knives, firearms and a occasional
chimbly-pot, but have allus been spry enough to dodge
'em—except here in Sussex! For this here lovely county seems
per-werse to me, leading me on all smiling and serene till it

can ketch me off my guard and then—it ups and takes me in the rear, sudden as flash o' lightening. I like the looks of it and the folks in it, but—Sussex don't like me. You'll remember how, in the case o' your murdered uncle, I precious nigh got my dewoted tibby shot off, you'll mind that?"

"Yes of course! But what of your arm?"

"Same like as it nigh happened to you, my lord, a shot from the leafage. Here's me harking to the birds chirping so pretty one minute and flat as a flounder the next, b'reason o' windictiveness in the form of a pistol ball as spins me like a tee-to-tum and drops me into the dust——"

"Where did it happen, Jasper?"

"There's me, pal, having said goodbye to your bee-utiful lady-spouse and——"

"Eh? Oh! Where, Jasper?"

"The London road, my lord. I sees her, she ditto me, stops the carriage and 'Oh, dear Mr. Shrig', says she, 'take care of him while I'm in London, dear Mr. Shrig'."

"So—she said—that, did she, Jasper?"

"Ar, said it double, she did."

"Said what double?"

"'Dear Mr. Shrig.' She said it twice, and twice is double, ain't it?"

"Yes, yes of course. Did she say anything more?"

"She did, my lord."

"Well, what man—what?"

"'Goodbye, dear Jasper Shrig.' And that was three times! Also she used my baptismal monnicker—'Jasper'! Likewise she gives me her hand, ar, glove and all, vich I should likely have kissed, but for your young Standish gen'leman staring so uncommon hard."

"So,—he was there, was he?"

"Ar! And later on there's me—in bed and a fever as keeps me on my back for five long days, though Dan'l and the Gimblet keeps me informed and——"

"So you know the villain who shot Sir Robert, do you, Jasper?"

"Ar! But you tell me as Sir Robert ain't dead yet?"

"No. And so you captured his assailant——"

"Safe and sound, my lord! And you're pretty sure as this here ass-ailant didn't shoot in wain and that his wictim, Sir R.C.'ll be stiff and cold afore morning?"

"Most probably. But tell me——"

"And certainly a corpse afore tomorrow night?"

"I think it very likely. But tell——"

"Then," quoth Mr. Shrig, sipping his wine with gusto, "things might be worse."

"How so?"

"Considering as his ass-ailant is a werry extra-special Capital Cove, a slippery customer and downy bird suspected of another Capital Act three years ago, but—no proof! So if Sir R. don't die, this here Capital only serves a term for assault and then goes free to commit the Act again when so inclined thereto. Hence, pal, if Sir R. don't die he'll be cheating Justice, in a manner o' speaking."

"A highly original thought, Jasper. But who is this murderous scoundrel you've arrested? Let's hear."

"Pal and lord, I'd reether you made a guess."

"But, damme, Jasper, why so secret?"

"Cautious, my lord."

"Well then, my guess is—ha, what the devil?" he exclaimed, starting to his feet, for nearby was sound of excited voices, a thunderous knock and the door swung wide to disclose the man Daniel who wore a bloodstained bandage instead of hat and whose whiskers drooped in abject woe:

"Jarsper," he moaned, smiting himself on the breast, "he's away! You-know-oo has broke out and gone!"

"Sussex!" exclaimed Mr. Shrig, with hopeless gesture. "It's at it again!"

"Lookee, Jarsper, I should ought to ha' known better! He lays for me behind the door when I took in his fodder; he downs me with a stool and made off and—wi' them pops, them barkers of his!"

"Armed again is he, Dan'l?"

"Ay, Jarsper. Ye see that theer stool laid me out and——"

"Sussex," sighed Mr. Shrig, rising wearily, "Sussex is playing it werry low down on me! Our bird has flew the coop, hopped the perch and is now out arter more blood! So 'tis for me and you, Dan'l, to be out arter his'n. Is the gig handy?"

"Outside, Jarsper, with the Gimblet."

"Then it's goodbye, m'lord and pal, for this here Capital Cove has to be took alive or dead, ar—Sussex or no Sussex."

"But," said Sam, rising with certain eagerness, "remember your arm! So if you need a volunteer I should be right glad of the chance."

"Thankee, pal, but 'tis just sich chances as is my dooty to prewent, and dooty being so, your kind offer is refused with doo gratitood——"

"Then will you tell me this scoundrel's name?"

"Ar, that I will just so soon as I've got him—alive or dead."

CHAPTER XXXVIII

TELLS HOW THE VISCOUNT DEPARTED

WITH SHAKING hand Mr. Bellenger fumbled in the mildewed hay, then raised flask to unshaven lips while his haggard eyes darted fearful glances all about, like the hunted animal he was. For indeed these last few days had transformed this once dandified, swaggering adventurer into a dusty, sweat-streaked, half-frantic creature starting guiltily at every sound; a miserable wretch so appalled by menace of the fearful doom long merited and now so direly imminent, that to save his neck he was ready and prepared to slay again and yet again, even as now! For, in the very act of drinking, he dropped the flask, snatched up pistol instead and crouched with this levelled at the jagged opening that had once been a door. Thus he waited, finger on trigger, ready and eager to give death or take it; a creature dehumanized by terror of noose and gallows, he was now fearless of all else; breath in check, he waited, rigid and motionless, his wide gaze on the dense leafage beyond this yawning doorway. At last, as if reassured, he laid by the weapon and, taking up the flask, cursed bitterly, though in harsh whisper, to find it had spilt so much of the precious contents; but his whisper ended in fearful gasp and, clutching the weapon again, he started to his knees as, from somewhere nearby, somebody whistled softly and he groaned with relief. The bushes rustled, parted, and in through the jagged doorway slunk Mumper Jim who, like Mr. Bellenger, was altered for the worse; moreover, beneath tight-stretched fur cap was a dingy bandage.

"Well," demanded Mr. Bellenger, lowering the pistol and speaking with rapid, feverish utterance. "well, man, well— what news? Is it good . . . is it bad . . . what is it?"

"M'lud, I dunno, sir. For, y'see, that cursed robin redbreast Shrig has took arter us."

"I know . . . I know all that . . . too much! But the others . . . two other constables, are they informed? Have they the whip? Tell me!"

"Ar, my woman lays a information agin the Earl, a friend takes 'em the w'ip and they acts according."

"Ha, is he in custody, arrested . . . jailed . . . is he?"

"No, sir, he ain't."

"Not? Why . . . why the devil not?"

"All along o' that 'ere Shrig! So the sooner I'm quit o' Sussex, the better."

"Well then, why . . . why are you here? What d'you want, damn you?"

"The rest o' my money on account o' that kidnappin' lay——"

"I haven't your cursed money."

"No, sir, but the Vi-count has an' 'e says for me to meet 'im yere, so I——"

"Yes, yes . . . I'm expecting him too! He should have been here hours ago . . . hours! What's keeping him, curse it, what?"

"That 'ere Shrig, mebbe, sir. Now if—somebody 'ad shot a bit straighter, ar, if only—somebody,—'ad took 'im through the 'ead, 'stead of arm, 'e'd be cold meat now, screwed down in 'is coffin 'stead o' plaguin' the likes o' me—and you, sir!"

"Hush and listen! Damn you—listen!" hissed Mr. Bellenger, pistol levelled again as from without rose a rustle, growing louder, coming nearer,— and then, beyond the screen of dense leafage, a lazy voice enquired:

"Are you still there, safe and sound, my Alfred?"

"Yes, Raymond, yes! You've kept me the hell of a time! Come in, man, come in!" Again the leaves parted and in strolled the Viscount as smilingly serene of face and elegant of person as usual, despite the leather wallet he carried.

"You're hours past the time you named, hours, damn it! Why are you so devilish late?"

Viscount Twily eyed the speaker's wild expression and bedraggled appearance with a lively interest, shook his own trim head and sighed:

"My poor, dear fellow, you sound a trifle peevish, and look it, egad."

"So would you be," cried Mr. Bellenger, "or any other man . . . all day and all night in this cursed dismal hole!"

"Wrexham Old Mill, Alfred—a place of death, dear fellow! Here murder has struck more than once, suicides have wailed and died. Wherefore it is reputed to be haunted and consequently generally avoided by day and night. Thus, dear Alfred, what place better adapted to shelter murder? Surely none. Aha,—and here also is our child-snatcher, our bold baby-stealer, waiting his guerdon. Well, here it is, my valiant ruffian, take it and go!" Saying which, the Viscount took out a small well-filled net purse and tossed it at the Mumper, who caught it dexterously, counted its contents heedfully, nodded and slunk out upon his furtive way.

"You brought me food and drink, Raymond, I hope?"

"All here, Alfred! So take—'eat, drink and be merry, for tomorrow'—who knows—'we die!'"

"Curse you, Twily! What are you saying?"

"Merely quoting, my Alfred,—words, idle words—perhaps! However, eat, dear fellow, drink——"

"Don't! Don't say it, curse you! How the devil can I eat when you talk such hellish——"

"Cold chicken!" nodded the Viscount. "Bread, butter, cheese—and a bottle of John's best. So, eat, drink——"

"So I will, for, begod, I'm famished!"

"My poor, dear Alfred! But couldn't you feed yourself better without that pistol across your knees?"

"Oh no! I shall do well enough. So now, while I eat, give me all the news."

"To be sure. Well, item one,—the man Shrig is on his legs again and using them to some purpose, indeed very much so——"

"Ha, you've seen him then, have you? He's up and about again already, is he, damn him?"

"Oh yes, and already so hale and well, so extremely active that it seems—your hand has lost its cunning . . . a mere flesh wound and in the arm! Tut, tut, my Alfred! To be sure you did a little better with our Robert, for they tell me he is dying. . . . Only dying, Alfred, with a chance of recovery and life. Here was another bungle which forces me to the conclusion that you are not such successful murderer as you were. And in your attempt on Robert, why, my very dearest fellow, why did you, Alfred, use pistol of mine, to be particular,— this!" As he uttered the word the Viscount drew and levelled the pistol in question and with amazing speed for such languid person. "Why, Alfred?" he continued in the same lazy tone. "Why leave it on the scene of your crime to bear false witness against me, as you did once before? How inept to so repeat yourself as I expected you would. And how like your dastard self to betray your only friend! No, don't move or, by my soul, I'll kill you now. Instead——" With another incredibly swift movement the Viscount snatched up Mr. Bellenger's weapon and tossed it into a corner. "Now," he continued, "I might shoot you and claim it self-defence, but I, like Robert, prefer leaving you to the man Shrig, to justice and the hangman's rope——"

As this dread word was uttered, the leafy screen was torn apart and a man came leaping through,—yet in this moment the hunted man, snatching a second pistol from its hiding-place, fired point-blank, and Viscount Twily, reeling back to the wall, leaned there watching two men who fought like brute beasts, a life-and-death struggle that ended suddenly as it had begun. . . .

"All . . . right, Jarsper!" a hoarse voice panted. "No need . . .t'shoot. He's . . . done!"

"A toughish customer, Dan'l. But he lays very still now. You ain't killed him, I hope?"

"Not as I knows on, Jarsper."

"If you do happen to have doused his glim 'tis a pity, for he's a Capital as should dance the Tyburn Jig, Dan'l."

"He will, Jarsper."

"You're pretty bloody, Dan'l."

"Ar, though 'tis mostly his."

"Better get the darbies on him."

"I will so, Jarsper."

The business thus successfully concluded, Mr. Shrig now turned to their silent spectator.

"My lord," said he, "it seemed as how Wiciousness yonder took a shot at you just as my Dan'l tackled same. No harm done, I hope?"

"Nothing to mention," answered the Viscount, smiling. "I shall do . . . very well. And now, by your leave, I'll go."

"I shall need your testimoney later on, my lord."

"That is quite understood."

"Werry good, my lord, I am dooly grateful."

"Mr. Shrig," said the Viscount, glancing back at the prostrate misery that had once been his friend, "it has given me such . . . extremity of joy that I . . . shall grieve if I . . . am unable to see him hanged."

Being come where his horse stood tethered, the Viscount seemed to experience some difficulty in mounting, but this he accomplished at last and set off very purposefully in a certain direction, urging his mare to an easy canter though he seemed rather more languid than usual and was, moreover, afflicted by a thin, intermittent cough, at which times he shivered, though the day was very warm and still.

Reaching a certain cottage gate, he reined up and sat to view the sunny garden, bright with many-hued flowers; then dismounting with an effort, he thrust closely folded handkerchief against the pulsing agony in his side, rebuttoned waistcoat and coat to hide that which must soon become too manifest, and walked swiftly and jauntily as possible along the flagged path, then paused to bow with graceful flourish of hat, saying, and with smiling lips but odd catches in his voice:

"Mrs. Jennings, madam, may I crave a few minutes' speech with Lady Scrope; it is . . . very important! And do pray believe me I . . . shall not keep her long." Now why did this gentle lady, knowing from Cecily what manner of man he was, why should she, instead of refusing him, stand hesitant? For though perhaps a little paler than usual, his bearing was gallant, his smile ready as ever and his close-fitting coat as yet betrayed no sign of the life that was ebbing from him with every heart-beat; then why, instead of bidding him away, did she move towards him with hands outstretched instinctively to aid and comfort him? Perhaps because she had borne one who had sinned, suffered and died young, or perhaps because she was just a natural born mother, that gentlest, most patient and forgiving of all creatures.

However, she reached forth both hands to this stricken man, saying:

"Sir, I think you had better come in—indeed I beg you will."

"Madam," he answered, faint-smiling, "you are very gracious . . . such great kindness, I . . . from my heart I thank you, but . . . I am better out here in your garden. How . . . pretty it is. I have . . . always loved flowers, but . . . never knew how much . . . till now." Then, walking leisurely, he came to a garden seat and sank down there like one very weary; and he seemed almost asleep when Cecily came speeding to him.

"My dearest says you are ill—hurt—and, yes, I see you are . . . Oh, what is it?" And, faint-smiling, he answered:

"Merely death, Cecily, a very commonplace, everyday occurrence. This is why I dared see you again . . . to make my confession to your sweet purity and . . . undo as much evil . . . as I may. For your Ralph's brutal folly, blame me! I would have ruined him gladly . . . body and soul . . . to win you. For those vile anonymous letters . . . blame me! For the . . . actual stealing of . . . Wrybourne's child—blame me! For aiding and abetting in . . . two attempted murders . . . blame me! But for loving you . . . so truly and . . . honourably at last . . . as I do, Cecily, forgive and praise me, for this is . . . the best thing I . . . ever did. Now I must go for . . . I think my time is short and . . . I must not die here. But, Cecily, if there is a God and if He will listen to . . . such as I, then . . . in this last hour I . . . pray God bless you . . . and Ralph . . . with happiness, now and . . . hereafter . . . if there is a hereafter. Now I must go——" Before she might aid him he got to his feet, but with the effort he coughed again, choked, sank back and—the horror was manifest at last. . . . Then Cecily was beside him on her knees and Mrs.

Jennings also, together doing all they might to keep the life in him. Thus presently recovering a little, he looked up from one gentle anxious face to the other and whispered, faint-smiling again:

"Angels . . . of mercy . . . you make me . . . almost believe in a heaven . . . though its gates would be . . . shut and barred . . . against me . . . and . . . very rightly——"

"My dear soul," murmured Mrs. Jennings, wiping this moist brow, "the gate of God's clemency will open to every knock."

"A comforting thought . . . dear lady. But . . . oh, Cecily . . . I had rather . . . the sweet heaven of . . . your arms . . . these last . . . brief moments of . . . my life. So . . . can you have . . . such mercy for me . . . Cecily?"

"Oh, my dear, yes—yes!" she sobbed. "You are so young to die! Come then, and as I take you now, I do pray God will take you home to His everlasting love."

"Tears . . . for me, Cecily?" he whispered very faintly. "Now if you . . . can show such mercy . . . then now . . . at last . . . I . . . believe——" The feeble voice hushed, the eyes closed wearily, the pale lips smiled and parted as if for speech.

"Yes?" she questioned, bending nearer—and then she saw, and knew he would speak nevermore.

CHAPTER XXXIX

HOW MR. STANDISH RETURNED

WITH SPADE, rake, shears and pruning-knife, Sam was about to start work in the old rose garden known from time immemorial as "My Lady's Plaisaunce" and which in these days Andromeda had made her own,—when his head gardener, rendered thus bold by desperation, dared to confront him, a hard-breathing man who, sweating at his own temerity, touched his hat and enquired:

"By y'r leave, my lord, but if you please—why for the spade?" And my lord, a very lonely, bitterly disappointed man and therefore prone to sudden wrath, replied:

"To dig with, y'fool!"

"Ay! And, if y' please—they shears?"

"To shear with, dolt! And this rake is to rake with, and this knife to prune with."

"Ay, so they be, for sure, my lord," said this desperate man, this intrepidly devoted soul. "Ar, so they be, sure-ly, but—not here!" My lord dropped these tools with a clatter,— he too now breathed deep; he also clenched powerful fists and demanded:

"Well, now—damme! Who commands here?"

"I do, my lord. 'Tis for this as you pays me, and ef I now lets you dig and rake, and chip and chop, this yere gardin 'll be a ruination when my leddy do come back home."

My lord unclenched his fists, glanced away to the Great House that was indeed no home, scowled at it, and said:

"You are George Ash, the head gardener, I believe. How long have you gardened here?"

"Arl my days, my lord."

"What are you paid?"

Mopping troubled brow, George Ash, trembling now, mentioned a sum.

"Absurd!" exclaimed my lord. "Not enough for such devilish determined gardener as George Ash; he is worth another two guineas a week. See to it!" And away strode my lord, leaving the head gardener to stare dazedly at the spade, the rake, the shears and pruning-knife as if he had never beheld such things in all his long gardening career.

My lord's horticultural effort thus quelled and ruthlessly nipped in the bud, he was wandering back towards his great, desolate house when, hearing faint, blithe jingle, he glanced round and beheld Mr. Standish approaching, lithe graceful and immaculate as ever from crown of modish hat to spurred heels of his gleaming riding boots.

"Ha!" exclaimed my lord, halting to stare.

"Yes!" replied Mr. Standish, halting to bow. "Do I surprise your lordship?"

"You do! Damme if you don't!"

"Agreeably, I hope. Though I fear not, judging by your lordship's dooced forbidding scowl."

"Are you from London?"

"This moment, my lord."

"From—the Countess?"

"No, my lord."

"Then why the devil are you here?"

"Simply to inform your lordship there is no longer any reason or need for me to shoot your lordship as promised."

"So? More damned shooting, hey!"

"I repeat there is no longer any need. For though your lordship's sudden, and I affirm, extremely unjust dismissal of me so afflicted my Rowena that she nearly died, yet by the . . . the mercy of God, she came back . . . out of the very shadow of death, bearing . . . our little daughter in her arms. And so——"

Striding forward, Sam grasped the speaker's hand, saying no word, and, linked thus, they gazed at one another, and still neither spoke; then drawing the suddenly-nerveless arm of Mr. Standish within his own, Sam began his quarter-deck walk, leading his companion up and down and both still mute until Sam halted at last to say:

"So . . . it's a daughter?"

"Yes!"

"Ha . . . well, if not otherwise engaged, there are business papers needing attention in your 'office', Harry." And after a moment Mr. Standish answered, rather huskily:

"Why then . . . old f'lo' . . . the sooner I'm at 'em, the better."

"Ay, ay!" quoth Sam, almost cheerily. "But first, how are things and—everyone—in Town?"

"Blooming, m'dear old Earl, especially the infant!"

"Yours or mine, Harry?"

"Both, thank God!"

"And—she—Andromeda?"

"Not so well."

"How so?"

"Mopish, old f'lo', yes, moping like a confoundedly, dooced, lovely owl! Too much solitude and so on! No *joie de vivre*! Shuns all society's glamour—assemblies, routs, balls and glittering functions, all dust and ashes, dry bones, tinsel and sawdust! Needs country air and—so forth, most especially, y'know."

"What 'so forth', Harry?"

"Her husband, Sam."

"Then why the devil doesn't she return?"

"Dooce only knows! Perhaps she awaits for him to call her or, better still—fetch her!"

"Then she'll wait in vain! Yes, damme, in London she'll stay."

"D'you—actually—mean that?"

"I do! And finally!"

"Then I'll go and have a look at those dooced papers. Business for me and, for you, this!" said Mr. Standish and from the breast of his exquisite coat he drew a letter.

"From—Andromeda, Harry?"

"No. Her Grace of Camberhurst."

Sam frowned, and, thrusting the missive into pocket, led Mr. Standish to a seat nearby, saying:

"By the way, I have Sir Robert Chalmers here, upstairs in

bed." Mr. Standish, having just sat down, shot up again, staring in blank astonishment.

"Chalmers—here?" he gasped, "In bed——?"

"Yes, though by this time he's probably dead. I'm waiting news of the doctors now."

"Dead?" whispered Mr. Standish. "Goo' Lord! You don't . . . you never mean . . . you and he . . . a duel?"

"No, murder. I found him in the woods three days ago and brought him in. And, Harry, you were quite wrong in suspecting him of that first attempt to kill me, because, d'ye see, someone had a second go at me! Ay, someone or other attacked me from the rear and bludgeoned me into that Old Mill pool, and I was drowning, but Chalmers came in after me and hauled me out."

"But Sam, how do you know he hadn't first pitched you in?"

"I taxed him with it, Harry, though pretty sure he hadn't, because 'twixt you and me, I suspected my damned cousin, Ralph, remembering how he had threatened me and his known violence, and, d'ye see, as Chalmers reminded me, murder runs in my family—we accursed Scropes!"

"Do you still believe it was your cousin, Sam?"

"I'm not so sure, now. Though it seems the fool is insanely jealous of me. But d'ye see, Harry, there are others as likely, or even more so! One is that Viscount fellow, Twily, and the other a foul ruffian I thrashed for frightening little Jane—ay, I half-killed the brute and I'm wondering if either of them shot Sir Robert, mistaking him for me? We are the same height, he and I, and much alike in build."

"And when they discover their mistake, Sam, they'll be after you again! Well, I'm beside you again and dooced glad of it! Yes, here am I, yours again most devotedly—fostering care, the ever watchful eye! Yes, I'm no end glad to be with you again, m'dear old lord!"

"And I'm heartily glad of you, Harry, for I'll—ah, yonder comes the doctor at last! You'll remember him, I suppose?"

"Yes, but he looks dooced impressive!"

"He always does."

"And most confoundedly solemn, Sam!"

"Ay, his patient is dead, I expect! Well, doctor," enquired Sam, rising. "What news?"

Doctor Little, looming rather larger than usual, perhaps by reason of the tidings he bore, or so thought Sam, bowed to them each in turn, cleared his throat, shook his large, shaggy head and folded his arms.

"My lord," said he unctuously, "the two surgeons, the physician and the eminent Doctor Stowe of London, all favour my opinion that, everything having now been done the which art of medicine, and the craft of surgery can do for our sore-stricken patient, nature must now operate and do her share."

"Is Sir Robert still alive?"

"He exists, but no more. Thanks to your lordship's rough though adequate surgery and his own mag-nificent constitution, he yet breathes, he persists, he lingers tarrying on the very brink of dissolution!"

"Can he live?"

"Nature, my lord, alone can say. At present he hovers, he flits 'twixt life and death, now in raving delirium, anon with brief periods of semi-awareness, but always through these three long days and nights, ever and always, sirs, he cries for—a woman! The woman——"

"But isn't she still with him? I sent for Mistress McGregor at once."

"Indeed, my lord, and her care has been inveterate, tireless! She is an inspiration to my professional nurses, she has been life to him! But though a woman, and such woman, she is not—the woman, no! The woman he constantly yearns for is one named 'Jane'. His wife, I opined, and ordered her to be sent for. But, sirs, it seems he has no wife, hence we can but suppose she is—a—an irregular connection. However, she, this woman, must if possible be found; her mere presence would soothe, satisfy and bring peace to a mind distraught which thus threatens to undo all our handiwork and challenges even Mother Nature herself."

"You believe he might then recover?"

"Wrybourne," said the doctor, unfolding his arms and spreading them wide, "nature is potent! I am not unskilled and our patient is blessed with the vitality of a—a horse, nay —an elephant! But his mind must be set at rest, in fine—this Jane woman must be found."

"I'll send for her at once. What is her address?"

"Alas, my lord, this is where fear smites us! For my patient gives no clue and Mistress McGregor affirms she don't know and never heard of any such woman. So that is the problem!"

"And sounds hopeless, doctor."

"My lord, it is, and, friend Sam, it—fairly gravels me!"

"Why then—of course!" quoth Sam. "A glass of wine! You too, Harry!" So indoors they went and, their glasses charged, Sam proposed: "A speedy recovery to your patient, doctor, health and long life to Sir Robert Chalmers!" Mr. Standish blinked, hesitated, but the toast was honoured, the glasses quickly refilled, slowly emptied; and then, with sigh of beatitude, upstairs to his patient went Doctor Little, off to his "office" strode Mr. Standish, glad of eye and light of foot, and Sam, thus alone, drew out her Grace's missive, broke the seals, unfolded it and read:

> "Camberhurst House,
> London.
> July 27, 18—.

DEAR SAM,

That Andromeda should expect you to be an Archangel in boots and buckskins, and other garments of course, is her own foolish fault. But young wives will be so ridiculous as to endow their new spouses with wings and haloes,—so very awkward for the poor wretches!

However, my dear Sam, that you should be so clumsy in your amours as to obtrude them upon the notice of your too-adoring wife, is your fault and most reprehensible. Andromeda, being your wife,—and herself as well,—is quite naturally shocked and grieved and thus has acted on impulse and of course very unwisely in thus deserting you.

For myself, as your friend, I am quite surprisingly surprised by your conduct both as man and husband, since even I was foolish enough to believe you other than you are and slightly better than most other he creatures. How extremely silly of me! Nevertheless, a longish life, of much experience in the foibles and follies of others, has made me a latitudinarian. Hence, though surprised and perhaps a little disappointed, I am still your friend, and, as such, here suggest you visit me (and Andromeda) for all our sakes and in the not too far distant future. Thus with truest wishes for your future happiness,

I rest,

Your much enduring friend,
ANASTASIA,
CAMBOURNE."

Having pondered this letter some while, Sam took quill, trimmed it and wrote:

"Wrybourne Feveril,
July 28, 18—.

MY DEAREST DUCHESS AND KIND FRIEND,

Though a mere man and coarse-grained male totally unfit for wing or halo, yet I am not an amorist except as regards my lawful wife. But her all too ready belief in my guilt,—no, turpitude is a better word,—and lack of faith in my honour and probity, angers and disgusts me because it so dishonours our past love and herself so much more. Therefore, since of her own free will she left me and with no word spoken or written, of her own free will she must and shall return to this place of roof and walls called Wrybourne Feveril, but—nevermore to the arms and heart of her husband until she has abased her hateful pride and made all atonement for her cruelty and base injustice. And this is final.

Here in my peaceful loneliness I abide and, on the whole, do very well. Pray tell Rowena I am truly glad to have Harry with me again, and that the Dower House shall be ready to welcome her and her small daughter, and myself to congratulate her, so soon as she is able for the journey.

And now, Duchess, dear and good friend, why not visit your very truly loving Sam who would welcome you, literally, with open arms and sincerest joy. However, pray know me now and ever for

Your grateful, loving,
WRYBOURNE,
SAM."

CHAPTER XL

HOW SIR ROBERT WAS COMFORTED

FOR ANOTHER long week, the invalid had, to use Doctor Little's phrase, "hovered between life and death". But day and night, with fitful dozings and brief interludes of sleep, Elspeth McGregor, this devoted more-than-mother, had watched over him. Soft of voice, quick of eye, ready of hand, she overawed the four nurses and moved Doctor Little to reiterate praise, as upon this midsummer afternoon.

"Wrybourne, my dear lord, she is a treasure, the perfect answer to a conscientious medico's prayerful supplication! I have just suggested, and she has agreed, to an hour's drive in this balmy, vitalizing air."

"Good!" nodded the Earl. "She shall have an open carriage. I'll order it now." This done, he enquired: "How is Sir Robert today?"

"No, no! Here comes Mistress McGregor herself. She can inform you as well—or better than myself. Come your ways, ma'am, and tell our good friend the Earl how our patient begins to give us hope. Meantime I'll to him while you enjoy your well-merited rest."

Mistress Elspeth seemed a little thinner and paler than of yore, but vital as ever.

"Aweel, m'lord," sighed she, sinking into the easy chair he placed for her, "and 'deed 'tis ye'sel is the guid friend, Sam, and 'tis the grateful soul I am. For truly and indeed I do begin to hope your enemy will live, and if so, will it be to hate you still? 'Twas this I asked him the morn's morn, telling him all you have done for him and me, ay I did so! And . . . Oh, friend Sam, all the answer he made was to—show me his stump!"

"And does he still ask for this mysterious woman?"

"Not now the fever has left him, and when I ask of her who she is and where she bides he just looks at me and frowns or smiles as the mood takes him. Ah, puir body, he's sadly changed! So vera pale and weak as a wean! Yourself hasna' seen him yet, I'm thinking?"

"No, Elspeth, nor shall I unless he asks for me, which he never will, of course."

"How do you feel towards him, friend Sam?"

"Pity, Elspeth."

"Which goes beyond expectation, considering his past wickedness to you . . . that kidnapping——"

"So you know of this?"

"Oh, man, why wouldn't I, and himself raving of his hate of you and schemes for your ruin! Ay, for . . . God forgive him . . . he planned . . . and lived only to break your heart and kill your soul! And 'tis yourself kept him in life—and how, ah, how will he use it, if he does not die?"

"You have good hope then, Elspeth, that he will perfectly recover?"

"No, Sam, no! I can but hope—and pray! And yet 'tis with dread I do pray, lest my petition be answered and Robert live—to your future hurt——"

"My dear," said Sam, taking her thin hand and holding it because of her greatly troubled look, "this is for the Almighty to decide, I suppose. However, I shall be prepared, for indeed there's little more he can do to harm me—now. So, Elspeth, don't grieve——"

At this juncture a footman knocked to say the carriage waited; so, giving her his arm, Sam led her thitherwards. But upon the terrace they were greeted by a joyous-barking Esau who bounded towards them, trailing Jane on the end of his lead.

"Unclesam . . . dear," she cried breathlessly, "I'm bringing Esau to show you . . . his new collar . . . all knobs an' spikes . . . what I bought for him wiv some of . . . my birfday money what you gave me, it's frighflee . . . expensive, but . . . isn't it lovely an' fine?"

"Magnificent, sweetheart!" replied Sam, bending to kiss her and pat the great dog.

"Well, so now, Unclesamdear, will you take him for a walk an' me for a ride on my pony,—will you, please, like a dear pet?"

"Not today, my Jane, but tomorrow, we——"

Mistress Elspeth loosed Sam's big arm to clasp Jane's little one, saying and also breathlessly:

"Oh . . . I wonder . . . are you . . . the Jane? Tell me, little Jane, do you know . . . a tall gentleman with . . . only one hand . . . do you?"

"Yes, ma'am," replied Jane, very politely and with her best, though rather wobbly, curtsey, "he's my fairy Uncle Robin Goodfellow, only I've lost him for days an' days——"

"Would you like to . . . find him again?"

"Ooh—yes! 'Cause I've got some more pomes for him—an' you too, UncleSamdear——"

"Come then, ma bonnie, wee lassie—go with me, little Jane, and you shall find him and help him to get well, to grow strong . . . and good, I pray God! Come with me, ma dearie."

So presently up the great stair they went, hand in hand, along a wide passage to a certain door that opened softly upon a spacious, dim-lit room, though all Jane saw was the vast bed, its silk curtains back-drawn showing upon snowy pillows a face framed in jet-black hair and whiskers, yet so thin, so pale that Jane shrank away; but a faint voice spoke, a feeble hand beckoned:

"Jane . . . oh, little Jane! Won't you come to . . . your fairy uncle . . . your poor Robin Goodfellow . . ."

Then, hesitating no longer, she ran to the great bed, both small hands outstretched in joyous greeting.

"Ooh!" cried she. "So I've found you again at last! I've looked for you an' looked, an' waited an' waited, an' here you are—all nice an' safe in bed!"

"Yes!" he whispered, clasping her small vital hands in his large, feeble one, "Here I am, little Jane, safe . . . at last."

CHAPTER XLI

IN WHICH THE DUCHESS WRITES A LETTER

THE RESPONSE of the Duchess to Sam's letter was prompt: for, speedily as relays of horses could bring her, she came in person.

With liveried coachman, footmen and outriders, in huge four-horsed vehicle she rumbled ponderously into the wide, echoing courtyard of Wrybourne Feveril, there to be greeted by the Earl with the chief of his many servants, male and female, behind him; he bowed profoundly to this small, great lady, kissed her little, mittened hand gallantly, then led her within doors to that spacious glory of carved panelling and gilded ceiling known as "The Queen's Chamber".

"Well," said the Duchess, loosing the strings of her plumed bonnet, "so much for the Earl's greeting! How will mere Sam welcome me I won——" She was picked up, kissed heartily in mid air, squeezed and set down again, all in as many moments.

"Goodness! Gracious! Me!" she gasped, as she straightened her bonnet and smoothed frills and flounces. "My poor, injured innocent! My wretched, misjudged, ill-used lamb, how brutally nice and strong you are—as a bull! Yes, Sam, you are absurdly like a bullish donkey or assinine bull! And, dear me,—how bronzed that cheek! How bright those eyes! How completely masterful and complacently assured your aspect! Wifeless solitude appears to agree with you. Does it, Sam, does it?"

"Why, d'ye see, my dear, I'm very busy these days. Instead of fighting the French at sea, as I should have preferred, I'm farming my lands against them and seeing my tenants do the like. Sometimes I'm in the saddle all day, and now that Harry is back with me——"

"Back with you indeed! The poor, dear wretch was in such state of mind about you and the perils threatening your

precious person that just as soon as the baby was born and
Rowena out of danger—she had a bad time, poor child—she
and I insisted he should return to you. So here he came and
found you in your right mind—so far as he was concerned.
But now, what of our darling, yours and mine, what of Andromeda?" Sam frowned, but ere he might reply came a discreet
knock at the door which opened to a procession of gorgeous
footmen bearing all essentials for tea and commanded by Mr.
Perkins, himself also arrayed and adorned in honour of this
noble visitor, a superb Perkins from powdered head to gleaming shoe-buckles, who, silent of tongue but stately of gesture,
marshalled his splendid cohort until, his and their parts duly
performed, he announced in subdued, dulcet tone and with
profound obeisance:

"Your Grace—My Lord, tea awaits you."

"How nice!" exclaimed the Duchess, removing her bonnet
and tossing it at a chair which it missed. "There is nothing
like tea, except ale strong and nappy—in a pot!" Mr. Perkins
on his knees in the act of retrieving the bonnet, almost dropped
it, but commanded himself and, rising, set it in place of safety
so reverently that he very nearly bowed to it; instead he
retreated softly to the door and, bowing himself out, closed it
soundlessly.

"Sam, d'you remember," enquired Her Grace, busy with
the teapot, "that first occasion we drank tea together, when
you told me of your love for Andromeda, believing she was a
poor gipsy, and when I laughed, how you actually berated me
and bade me not mock your sacred ardour? Ah, how you
loved her—then!"

"Yes, I did!" he sighed. "I did indeed! Though even
then she grieved and troubled me——"

"And quite rightly! For love, Sam, without grief is no
better than merest passion. So all true lovers should mope
and pine grievously as possible of course, and they should
suffer constantly and yearn consumedly. I hope you do and
are! Do and are you?"

"I'm much too busy!"

"Now, Sam, I hope you are a liar."

"Well, no!" he answered, with grim smile. "The Scropes, though scoundrels, have never been liars, I understand."

"And are you trying to tell me, as a scoundrelly Scrope, that your love is dead?"

"Oh no, merely in abeyance for the time."

"Ah, drink your tea—and choke!" Sam drank and smiled, saying:

"Surely you know I'm not one to grieve idly in corners, to make a pet of trouble when there are so many better things waiting to be done? What with the French threatening us overseas, and with doctors and nurses and that dying man above stairs—who probably won't die after all."

"What man?"

"Sir Robert Chalmers."

"That brute you fought? Here? Dying? My gracious! Tell me what's been happening, all about everything, this moment!" And when in few words as possible he had done so, speech seemed beyond her, though only for a moment or so, then:

"Now were it not for your perfectly heartless usage of our darling, I should indeed look to see if wings were sprouting on those big shoulders and a halo forming on that dogged brow! To think that you can be so angelic as to love your enemy—and such an enemy!"

"But I don't! I have the utmost contempt for him, d'ye see."

"Fudge and a fiddlestick, Sam! You cherished this wretch who has been your plague, this wicked brute who stole your babe and wrecked your home——"

"I didn't tell you so."

"Of course not, you wouldn't! But it could be none other and is quite in accord with his vindictive nature. I knew him long before you did and consequently know I do! Now tell me, are you going to allow him to triumph, living or dead,—will you permit the evil of him to come between you and Andromeda? How much longer are you going to make her suffer?"

"Not I!" he answered, gently, but with a smile that shocked his hearer. "Not I, my dear kind soul; say, rather, her own

merciless pride. She has made it a weapon to wound me . . .
rather desperately, and it has so transformed her that she
has made of me that right pitiful mockery—a deserted husband! Which poor figure of scorn now ventures to ask for
another cup of tea." The Duchess gazed at Sam disbelievingly,
saying:

"This is not, this cannot be you, Sam?"

"This," he retorted, white teeth agleam in that same sardonic grin, "this is what wedlock has made of me, and, what's
more, I——"

Here was a discreet tapping on the door and, receiving permission, a perturbed Mr. Perkins appeared to bow and say
in voice anxious as his look:

"My lord, you . . . you are asked for by . . . by your
lordship's cousin, Lord Ralph, my lord."

"Oh? Well, say I'm engaged—yet, no, I'd better see him.
In the long gallery, Perkins."

"Y—yes, my lord." And the personage bowed himself out,
a very nervous Perkins indeed who, lifting hands and eyes
ceilingwards, murmured: "More shootings and fightings—
ho-ly heavens!"

"Your Grace," said my lord, rising, "will pray excuse
me for brief while?"

"Gladly and for a long!" she snapped. "Your noble lordship has become so un-Sam-like that I shall be glad of a
respite. So, noble sir, take your time, and when you return
let it be as Sam!" My lord bowed ceremoniously but with
Sam's flashing grin as he departed. Scarcely had he gone
than Her Grace tugged the bell-rope and sent urgently for
Mr. Standish, who no sooner appeared than she rose, saying:

"Harry, take me where I can talk and you listen without
interruption!"

"My office!" said he and thither forthwith conducted her.

"Harry," said she, seating herself at his paper-strewn
writing-table, "it seems our lordly Sam is as set in his pride-
ful folly as Andromeda in hers! She is breaking her heart
for him and admits it—to me, and he's breaking his for her
but pretends he isn't! They yearn for reunion, yet this can

never be while their silly pride, this ever-growing giant, looms
between, forbidding and hiding them from each other. Could
she now see him or him her, all would be well. But she will
not, and he won't. Her pride is like a flint, and his as hard
as—as the Devil's forehead! Both are so perfectly immovable
that move them I will by hook or crook! The only question
is—how? There is a way, and find it I shall, soon or late.
Have you any suggestions, Harry?"

"'Fraid not," he sighed. "Unless I go to her and try to
get her to return with me on some pretext or other, though
I don't suppose she——"

"Ha!" exclaimed the Duchess, thumping the table resound-
ingly and instantly sucking her knuckles. "A pretext! Certainly that is an idea! a . . . pretext! Our loving fools are
both such heroic personalities, so dominating and headstrong,
they must be met by strength more compelling, so forceful they
must be forced and their silly, loving heads knocked together
till she weeps, he kisses her and they are in each other's arms!
And only a pretext can do it, but what, who, or how? A pretext, a subterfuge, a fib, a tarradiddle, a white or black lie,
a tale of cock-and-bull . . ." The Duchess stared hard at the
carpet beneath her little, pretty feet, up at the carved ceiling
above her small but very stately head, at Mr. Standish, nodded
suddenly and said:

"By Heavens, Harry, I have it! I mean 'him' of course.
Robert Chalmers shall be our pretext, fib tarradiddle and all
the rest! Yes, I will make this wicked wretch do good in spite
of himself. He shall bring happiness at last instead of misery;
he shall actually crown his hated enemy with joy! What do
you think of that?"

"Stu-pendous!" answered Mr. Standish, rising from chair
the better to say it. "Doo-ced marvellous and exactly like
your Grace! But—how on earth?"

"Oh, very easily! By a wile, Harry, feminine guile and
duplicity, artful craftiness and yet not one lie or even the
whitest of fibs. I shall write Andromeda such letter of chaotic
woe she shall think, poor dear, Sam is Robert and Robert
Sam! Sam at death's door and Robert hale and triumphant!

Give me a pen—quick! If common sense and reasoned argument won't do it, trickery shall! Pen, Harry, a pen!"

"Here, you small, wonderful Duchess!"

"Thank you, Harry. And I do believe I am rather marvellous, but then I always was. But, aha, I shall love using Robert, this man-killing, arrogant, vindictive wretch to such noble purpose! Now the letter . . . how best to phrase it? To succeed it must afflict . . . it must compel . . . and it shall! Let me think!" She nibbled the feather of her pen, stared very hard at nothing in particular, nodded suddenly, dipped pen and began to write so speedily and with such vigour that the quill squeaked. . . . A fateful though not very lengthy epistle, for presently she sank back, twiddled her pen, flourished it, tossed it aside and read aloud:

> "At Wrybourne Feveril,
> July 30.

OH, MY POOR ANDROMEDA!

My dearest child, what horrors leap when least expected! One attempted murder, one horrid assassination should be enough, nay all too much for one life-time. Yet here is another and this, I fear, promises to be dreadfully successful. That hateful man and most vindictive wretch, Robert Chalmers—your poor Sam refused to be warned and would not beware of him as you know. He was shot in a wood days ago and has lain here at death's door ever since. I do and am now doing all I may for him, but with things in such dreadful turmoil, doctors and nurses and the shadow of death over all, he needs you now as never before. I suggest post-horses, leaving our precious babe and your women to follow later.

Whatever happens now, and however you suffer and agonize over this news, yet at some future day you will be eternally grateful to

> Your devoted, harassed
> GODMOTHER.

P.S. If this letter seems confused, as it most certainly is, blame the circumstances in which it is written and in such desperation of mind and haste."

"Ye-es!" said the Duchess, nodding complacently at her handiwork. "I think this will do! It should bring her back home—fast as wheels can turn and hoofs gallop! Should it torment her with remorse and anxiety, as I'm sure it will,— and slay her pride—for the time being at least,—so much the better. Lord! How she will fly to those nice, strong arms of his! How ardently she will kiss him in the passion of her relief! And, oh, Harry, what an artful, crafty *deus*— no, *dea ex machina* sort of creature I am. Do you not admire me, Harry?"

"I do!" he answered fervently. "Yes, by heaven, that I do——"

"So do I!" said the Duchess.

CHAPTER XLII

HOW AND WHY RALPH CALLED JAPHET, SAM

MEANWHILE, Sam, on his way to the Long Gallery where hung so many portraits of his hated ancestors, was accosted by Mr. Perkins who, murmurous and in moist anxiety, enquired:

"My lord, having regard to the violent and fiery nature of your lordly cousin, would not your lordship be well advised to meet him—forearmed?" and with the word he proffered a brace of horse-pistols. Sam laughed, patted Mr. Perkins on the crown of his powdered head and entering the Long Gallery, beheld Ralph at the further end, gazing up at portrait of a scowling gentleman in black half-armour and full-bottomed wig, and labelled: "Admiral, Lord Japhet Scrope. 1658"; turning from this, as Sam approached, he nodded, saying:

"Yes, b'gad! Judging by your likeness to this old fellow, you're a Scrope, sure enough—Sam!"

"Too true!" he admitted and with a scowl black as the Admiral's. "But, Ralph, if you happen to have come after my blood as you threatened, I must ask you to wait, for, d'ye see, there's been all too much o' that, lately."

"Just what do you mean,—Sam?"

"First, the murderous attack on me at the Old Mill pool,— d'you chance to have heard of it?"

"No! How the devil should I?"

"And now this shooting of Sir Robert Chalmers—is this news to you also?"

"Eh—news? Good gad, yes! Sir Robert Chalmers—and shot, you say?"

"Was he a friend of yours, Ralph?"

"Oh no. Don't think I ever met him."

"Though you knew his friends, especially Viscount Twily."

"Yes. Yes, I knew him. But that's over. I'm done with the fellow for good, Sam."

"Ah! May I ask why?"

"For the same reason that I now call you 'Sam'—as maybe you didn't notice."

"I did, and wondered why?"

"Because, Sam, instead of being here after your blood, as you put it, I came to—ask your pardon and—confess myself a fool, yes and also a damned brute and beast. I think now there must have been some curse on me."

"Ay," nodded Sam, "the curse of the Scropes! Ours has been a very damnable family."

"Yes, Sam, and left a devilish black record! Yes, the Scropes have been a vile race, but 'what's bred in the bone comes out in the flesh'. So what chances have we, since every Scrope seems born for and predestined to evil, eh, Sam?"

"Never think it, Ralph! No, damme, for there have been good Scropes, one or two exceptions, d'ye see."

"Yes, but very few, Sam."

"However, I'm hoping we also may prove exceptions, you and I, and break this curse. What say you, Ralph?"

"Perhaps, Sam. Yes, maybe, for I'm done with the cursed . . . sottish past; no more of that for me, I've sworn off because of—Cecily!"

"Does she know you are here with me?"

"Of course, Sam. When she explained those meetings with you in the wood and showed me how and why and what a perfect dam'-fool I'd been, there was nothing I could do but come and tell you so, as I told her and she agreed. 'Though,' said I to her, 'cousin Japhet is such a grimly gruff and tough customer he's like enough to floor me or be at my throat before I can say a word.' 'Yes, he is,' said she——"

"Did she, by Jingo!" exclaimed Sam.

"She did so, Japhet—I mean, Sam, but then she added, 'though really Sam is the gentlest, kindest man I ever knew, so, Ralph, instead of naming him "damned Japhet", begin by calling him "Sam".' So, Sam, this is why I've been 'Samming' you so repeatedly."

"And, Ralph, this is why I can now venture to enquire how your shoulder is, that stab——"

"Wonderfully well, thanks."

"And now, Ralph, I will even dare to thank you, ay, with all my heart, for the rescue of my little son——"

"Oh, as to that," said Ralph, self-conscious as a boy, "think you should know I could never have managed it without the help of a right good friend, a gipsy, Sam, a Romany and a scholar, and not only that but a tip-top fighting man, once known as 'The Fibbing Gipsy', and would have been champion but for Jessamy Todd, and not only all this, but such a man as I am devilish proud to call 'friend'. So your thanks are equally due to him."

"Who is this good friend?"

"Name of Lovel, Tawno Lovel. They say you are one of the few landowners who are kind to them,—though your keepers have begun hounding 'em lately. So now I ask you to be gentle with all Lovels for the sake of one, my friend, Tawno."

"I will, Ralph."

"Thanks! And now I think that's about all I have to say . . . except . . . if you care to take it . . . here's my hand."

"First, Ralph, it's my turn to ask pardon of you for the harsh things I've said of you and to you in the past. As for your Cecily, who is and always has been so truly your own, I so love and honour her sweet purity and gentleness,—ay, and that noble simplicity of hers, that love of any other sort is perfectly unthinkable for her or myself. So now, Ralph——"

But just then, as if conjured thither by mention of her name, Cecily herself came towards them, her plumed hat and riding-habit dusty with speed of travel.

"Why," cried Ralph, hands outstretched in eager welcome, "hey—what's this? You've been crying!"

"Yes, Ralph dear, yes, I have . . . for, oh, Sam, I've come to tell you . . . poor Viscount Twily was shot and killed! He died in my arms, and as he died, confessed to . . . anonymous letters . . . to stealing your baby . . . to helping in murder. . . . But I think, yes I know he grieved and repented at the last. . . . And so it was I could pray God, our merciful Father, to take him to His forgiveness and everlasting love. And now . . . oh,

now I'm praying for you too, both of you, my dears, that God
shall learn you to love each other instead of hate . . . to be
brothers 'stead of foes. So now, for our dear Lord's sake and
all our sakes, take each other's hands—do, like the dears you
are, come now!"

Then, with her strong, shapely arms about each, she drew
them—to new understanding and a fellowship that was to
endure.

CHAPTER XLIII

TELLS HOW JANE WROTE A POLITE INVITATION

JANE WAS talking (of course) perched upon the great bed on throne of pillows within easy reach of her invalid, Sir Robert, whose deep-sunken eyes, bright with return of life, watched her so intently while he listened to her inconsequent chatter and every intonation of her sweetly-clear, young voice with a quite pathetic eagerness.

For, as a certain blackbird had once tuned his pipe and sung the abiding joy and blessedness of simple things, so now Jane, in her childish innocence, was changing his outlook on life and the order of its values, showing him how the first should often be last, and last first; teaching him those ancient, long-known, little-heeded truths, that glory and fame, riches and power, could of themselves be a weariness, and how the love and faith of one simple heart is far better than the adulation of multitudes or the favour of kings.

Thus today Sir Robert, new risen from death, knew that the best and greatest blessing this new life could bestow was the love for and faith in him of Jane herself.

Therefore his pallid cheek showed a tinge of colour as, leaning suddenly towards him, she enquired and very earnestly :

"Uncle Robin, 'cause we love each other such lots, will you please tell me something what I want to know—please?"

"Yes, my dearest, if I can."

"Well, the other day my Granny was reading to me out of the Bible like she always does before I go to bed and she came where it says: 'If thy hand offend thee cut it off.' So what I want to know is—did 'thy hand offend thee'?"

Now, gazing at his small questioner's grave face, Sir Robert answered, after breathless pause :

"Yes, Jane . . . yes, it did."

"So then," she persisted, leaning nearer yet, "did you . . . oh, did you cut it off wiv a knife or chop it wiv a chopper?"

And after another brief pause, he answered very gravely: "Something of the sort, Jane."

"Ooh!" she whispered, in hushed ecstasy. "How . . . frighflee . . . brave of you! So now I'm going to kiss you!" Which she did, and with his handless arm close about her. "You 'member, Uncle Robin, how in Fairy Dell I kissed the place to make it well—ooh, and there's a rhyme for another pome! Only it didn't make it well 'cause I suppose I'm only Jane. But if you had died yourself into a nangel, God would have gave your hand back an' made it well like He did poor Lord Nelson's hand an' arm an' eye, like my Granny says."

"She must be a wonderful person, Jane!"

"Yes, she is, only she makes me do sums what I don't like, an' write pothooks an' hangers on my slate 'stead of real pen an' ink."

"I have tried my hand at pothooks and hangers, Jane dear——"

"Yes, but not on a slate what squeaks! I suppose," sighed she, nestling instinctively within his clasping arm, "it's lovely to be a bright angel of God like my mother is an' Lord Nelson an' everybody what's gone up to heaven, but—oh—I'm glad you didn't!"

"Are you . . . really, my darling?" he asked very wistfully, and tightening his clasp.

"Yes, 'cause I want to keep you for my uncle what I found while I sat under that tree giving my Batilda a lesson with Esau what barked at you at first. Do you 'member?"

"Yes, Jane, I shall always remember."

"Though I didn't think I quite liked you at first 'cause your hair looked so black as your whiskers—they're frightflee black, aren't they?"

"Yes, dear, I'm afraid they are."

"An' your eyes looked so big at me like your teef—you've got such big, sharp, gobbly teef, you know! But when Esau barked at you an' I made him hush and be p'lite, you smiled an' I knew."

"What, what did you know, Jane?"

"That I liked you lots, 'cause your eyes smiled too, so then I didn't mind your gobbly teef or your whiskers so black. An' when you said you were Robin I knew you were Goodfellow too an' my fairy Uncle like Auntie Mee's my fairy Aunt."

"Oh? And who is she, Jane dear?"

"Well, her name's An-drom-e-da, such a big name to say, an' now she b'longs to my UncleSamdear what married her into his wife."

"And who is your Uncle Sam?"

"Oh, he's the man what everything b'longs to 'cause he's a nearl."

"Ah!" murmured the invalid. "So, your Uncle Sam is Lord Wrybourne, is he?"

"Yes, didn't you know that?"

"I ought to have guessed."

"Well, Uncle Robin, I'm 'fraid he doesn't quite like you——"

"Which does not surprise me, Jane dear."

"Oh, but it surprised me lots, 'cause he's so nice an' kind an' likes everybody 'cept that nasty man in the wood what took my necklace, an' you're not a bit like him, so why doesn't he like you?"

"There are reasons, my dear!"

"That's jest what he said when I asked him to come an' see you."

"Just what did he say, Jane?" And she, heedless of commas, semicolons or full-stops, answered:

"He said no Jane there are reasons an' S'Robert doesn't want me or he'd have asked for me so I said he didn't have to be asked 'cause you were only my Uncle Robin an' my poor inv'leed an' he said too many uncles were bad for me so I said didn't he like you an' he said no he didn't then I said I was surprised at him 'cause you had nearly died yourself into a nangel an' all angels b'long to God so then he asked me if I loved you an' I said lots an' so he shook his head at me an' said Jane I b'leeve you love him more than me so I said no I didn't only you were a poor invaleed wiv only one hand an' he wasn't an' had two so then I made him kiss me an' promise to be p'lite an' visit you if you wanted him to an' asked him so do you an' will you—please?" Here (and no wonder) Jane drew a deep breath, so did Sir Robert, and, looking down into the eager eyes of his little suppliant, he smiled and, kissing her bright hair, murmured tenderly:

"Yes, Jane, to please you, I will."

"Ooh!" she exclaimed. "Shall I go an' tell him; shall I fetch him—now?"

"No, dear! Oh no, we must do it properly and very, very p'litely. You will have to write him an invitation."

"Yes—yes, I will!" said she. "In my copy-book an'—oh, now where's my pencil?"

"Not your pencil, Jane; you must write with pen and ink and on a proper sheet of paper."

"Ink!" she cried rapturously, and lisping in her excitement. "An' a real pen wiv a fevver onto it!"

Thus presently, seated at the bedside table, Jane wrote at her invalid's dictation, with the utmost care and only one very small blot:

"Mistress Jane presents her compliments to my Lord the Earl of Wrybourne and begs the pleasure of his company to meet her Fairy Uncle Robin Goodfellow at four-thirty for tea."

This polite missive, duly sealed and superscribed, was handed to a nurse, who in turn passed it to a footman, who instantly hastened to deliver it to my lord, just now dusty and rather weary from a very long day in the saddle. Breaking the enormous seal, he opened and, having read it, rang the bell and said to the bowing Perkins:

"Find Mistress McGregor and say I desire word with her, yes, and the Duchess also."

"My lord, Her Grace is abroad taking the air."

"Very well—Mistress McGregor."

So presently came Mistress Elspeth, fresh from one of her catnaps, to whom my lord in turn handed this very polite note;

she read it and for a moment words seemed beyond her. Then, clasping her worn, so capable hands, she looked up through a glitter of tears.

"Now," she murmured, "Lord God bless our wee lassie, our little Jane, this very child of God! For she has wrought the miracle I have worked and prayed for . . . she has touched my Rabbie's hard heart and waked his soul at last. . . . And you, my lord . . . Sam, good friend, will ye forgive and try to forget—ah, ye'll no refuse? You'll go?"

"Of course!" answered Sam, rising somewhat wearily. "I've just time to be dusted and made presentable."

CHAPTER XLIV

HOW JANE POURED TEA FOR TWO ENEMIES

IT WAS "Mistress" Jane who opened to Sam's knock and with her most gracious, though rather wobbly curtsey, saying:

"My lord UncleSamdear, you are very welcome."

Sam acknowledged her curtsey with a stately bow, then, picking her up, kissed her, put her down, whereat she took his hand and led him to the bed where, pale and feeble, lay his inveterate enemy; thus for a moment they surveyed each other, neither speaking.

"Well, Wrybourne," said Jane's invalid at last, with something of mockery in his smile, "it seems I am to live. Jane tells me so and the doctors so pronounce."

"I'm glad!" answered Sam.

"I wonder!" murmured Sir Robert. "Jane, do you think he is truly glad?"

"Yes, I do, 'cause my UncleSamdear never tells lies or even fibs, an' so am I an' so is my Batilda an' Esau an' everybody 'cause we all love you, don't we, Uncle Sam?"

"And that," murmured the invalid, with ghost of a chuckle, "is a leading question, my lord, which need not be answered. Jane, pray show his lordship where he may sit at table."

"There!" said Jane, with flourish of the spoon she chanced to be holding, then, "Ooh," she exclaimed, "Granny says it's rude to point an' I must be very p'lite 'cause I'm going to pour out tea. So, please, Uncle Sam, take that chair by the bed, an' do you take milk an' sugar, both uncles, do you please?"

"Yes please, Jane."

"Thanks, sweetheart." Ensued now a silence, both men avoiding each other's eyes, watching instead their small hostess and she far too intent on the proper manage of teapot, milk-jug and sugar-tongs, for mere speech.

"There!" sighed she, at last. "I've only spilt the teeniest

268

drop, so please, Uncle Sam, will you give my inv'leed his cup an' stir it for him 'cause he's got only one hand." Obediently, Sam plied spoon and held the saucer while his enemy sipped, gazing up at him the while with more than a hint of mockery in those dark, glowing eyes of his.

"Thanks, Wrybourne!" said he. "But I can manage very well if you will be good enough to draw the bed-table nearer."

So this strange meal began, the two men so near in body yet so remote in sentiment that they seldom looked at or addressed each other, content to watch their small, eager hostess, who talked for both.

And now Sam noted with what care and quite motherly solicitude Jane waited upon her invalid, folding his bread and butter, spreading jam for him, tending his one-handed awkwardness,—and how the invalid, in turn, followed with his eyes and the ghost of a smile ever upon his pale lips, and how surprisingly gentle his voice whenever he uttered her name. And she, having now supplied their immediate needs, glanced from one to other, saying:

"UncleSamdear, when Robin Goodfellow is all well again I want you to take him an' me riding to show him our old Magic-y Tree what first magiced you till you kissed my Auntie Meda before you married her into your wife, because I've been thinking it might magic Uncle Robin's hand back for him like it did my Batilda for me an' my lovely cradle an' dolls' house, —do you suspose it might?"

"And there," murmured the invalid, viewing Sam askance and with wry smile, "there, my poor Wrybourne, is question better avoided—if possible."

"Don't you suspose it might?" Jane repeated.

"No, sweetheart, I'm afraid it wouldn't," Sam replied, very conscious of the watching eyes and smiling mouth so near him.

"But don't you think we ought to try, 'cause he's a fairy too, so don't you?"

"Yes, of course we can try, my dear."

"An' to have only one hand must be a bit trying, don't you think?"

"Oh no," answered the invalid, before Sam could reply,

"not when one gets used to it, Jane. But didn't you say you had a poem for me?"

"Yes, yes I have, only it isn't quite finished 'cause I can't find a nice word what rhymes with 'whiskers'."

"No wonder!" smiled the invalid. "That is such an awkward word. But we should like to hear as much as you have written, if we may."

"Very well," said Jane, and, reaching for her rather dog's-eared copy-book, she opened it at a certain smudgy page, saying with the despondency of true authorship: "I don't think it's quite so good as what I hoped it would be when I began it."

"Things seldom are—in this world, Jane!" said her invalid, wistfully.

"Does that mean in heaven they will be?"

"We hope so, Jane. But now, pray read to us." And so, obediently and naturally as any bird ever sang, Jane read:

" 'With Batilda my child an' with Esau an' me
    I went for a walk an' sat under a tree,
    Then came Uncle Robin upon a fine horse
    Like the lady what rode her to Banbury Cross.
    Though he hadn't got any bells on his toes
    So he can't make music wherever he goes.
    An' I didn't quite like him at first, 'cause I saw
    Such very black whiskery whiskers he wore
    An' his gobbly teef were so sharp an' so white
    An' his eyes were so big an' so shiny an' bright,
    But he said he was Robin an' smiled, so I knew
    He was Robin Goodfellow an' so he would do
    For a nice fairy uncle although all his whiskers
    Are so frighflee black I don't mind——' "

"An' that's where I have to stop because of his whiskers. But I've done a bit more on the next page,—shall I read it for you?"

"Yes, sweetheart, do."

"Pray go on, Jane," said her invalid, "for your poem describes me—to a hair."

"No, only your whiskers, Uncle Robin, an' I end my pome like this:

> 'An' I know he's as clever as clever can be
> For only an' only just one hand has he
> 'Cause with that one hand I suppose he can do
> As much as all people can do with their two.'

"An' that's all!" said Jane, closing her book. "So now, 'cause you're both growed so nice and big, find me a proper word what rhymes with 'whiskers' please?"

"A rhyme!" murmured Sir Robert, glancing round about as if in search of one.

"'Whiskers'!" repeated the Earl, doing the same, and thus it chanced their glances met; Sir Robert smiled, the Earl grinned. . . . And it was in this fateful moment that Mistress Elspeth thought proper to appear from the adjacent dressing-room where she had been spying so prayerfully.

"Oh, Jane," said she, radiant of look and with a glad ring in her voice, "Jane, my precious, your Granny wants you, so come with me, my dearie."

"Oh dear, dear!" sighed Jane, woefully. "Jest when I'm reely happy it's bedtime; it always is!"

"Not just yet. I think she wants to—to give you something and I'm sure I do! So, ma bonnie wee lassie give me your hand." Jane obeyed, bobbed a polite curtsey to each uncle, and with a last, lingering look at the teapot, departed.

"And there," sighed Sir Robert as the door closed, "there goes my salvation, Wrybourne, my new and blessed interest in life! Dare I believe you will not deprive me of it?"

"How do you mean, Chalmers?"

"May I hope you will allow her to visit me and . . . perhaps stay with me occasionally?"

"This is for Mrs. Leet, her grandmother, to decide."

"Then will you . . . can you be so generous as to persuade Mrs. Leet?" Up rose Sam and began his quarter-deck walk, scowling very blackly the while.

"Sir Robert," said he, at last halting beside the bed, "this rather wonderful child is quite inexpressibly dear to me!"

"And to me!" said Sir Robert, with fervour. "She is my hope, and one you can snatch from me if you will because I am—your enemy!"

"Yes, Chalmers, and how merciless you were I am too bitterly conscious,—my ruined home is a constant reminder. Well, now, does my present unhappiness content you? Is your remorseless vengeance sated at last?"

Sir Robert lay very still and mute.

"Tell me, Chalmers, and this is my last question, are you still my enemy? Well? Why don't you answer?"

"Because," said Sir Robert, turning to look up at him at last, "upon my soul, Wrybourne, I don't know! As I lay here, swaying between life and death, I have had visions— and not delirium, nor sick-fancies, for I have been haunted by you—from our first hostile meeting in the Duchess's garden. I have fought you again, every thrust and parry of our duel. I have stared in horror again at my bloody wrist and my severed hand upon the grass, sprawled like a great, white spider. I have nursed my hate, cherished my hope of vengeance, schemed the destruction of your happiness. I have seen you again smitten to your death in that pool and gloated on your dying there in the mud. Yet why—why did I then plunge after you, risking the same ghastly end? Wrybourne, I don't know! Why then did I strive, as never before, to win you to the air, to support you to the bank, to haul you to safety, fighting for you till I thought my heart would burst with the effort—why? And I tell you still, I do not know. I said then I had preserved you for my future vengeance,—was this truly so? I cannot tell. Had I ceased to hate you then, or long before? Had I ever hated you or was this but the expression of extreme disgust for myself? I don't know. Yet this I can tell you—the vile scheme I had laid for the stealing of your child, the sending of anonymous letters, these I abandoned and utterly forbade. Yet they were done and without my knowledge by those who vainly attempted my life in London and here again plotted my death, first by means of you, and, when this failed, by shooting me from ambush. These are the facts, Wrybourne, briefly and badly expressed, I fear.

But whether I have hated or admired you, scorning myself, I don't know. But of this I am perfectly sure, there can be no forgiveness for such ruthless enemy as I have been, nor do I ask it. . . . Only I do beg of you that, since I am to live, you will not forbid me altogether the society of this child whose precious innocence has been and . . . is to me . . . far more than I can say or know how to express. So now, Wrybourne, you are quits with me for the pool, you have given me a new chance of life—and this child, our little Jane, a light which I . . . I am hoping you will not take quite away to leave me in outer darkness."

Sam took another brief quarter-deck walk, then, sitting down beside the bed, folded his arms, saying:

"Now, Robert Chalmers, hear my side! When you forced that duel upon me, I chose a cutlass because I had used such frequently aboard ship and I meant to so damage that too-deadly pistol-hand of yours that it should never kill again. When I saw you reel back and your hand off-clutching the grass at my feet, your horror was no greater than mine. The wound you gave me was no great matter, but the memory of your loss haunted me and helped to delay my recovery. For, pray believe me, during our assault, the longer we fought the more I esteemed you, vindictive though you were. And afterwards, pray believe me, despite your so often avowed hate—and, yes, in spite of myself, I wished for your friendship. Twice I proffered it and twice you refused. . . . So now I'm wondering, will you refuse again, will you deny me this third time . . . Robert?"

In the great house, clocks, near and far, began to chime and strike the hour of six, tuneful chimes all and all softly mellowed by distance; but in this luxurious bedchamber, where more than one royal personage had slept, was a hush, a silence becoming with every heart-beat the more painful. . . . Then slowly, wearily Sir Robert turned, hiding his face among the many pillows, but slowly, almost timidly, his only hand stirred, lifted, stole forward—and was clasped firmly in Sam's right. And so again, for a while, was silence; when at last Sam spoke, it was in hearty, everyday tone:

"Robert, old foeman, I'll send our Jane to kiss you good night."

CHAPTER XLV

IN WHICH MY LORD ASKS A VERY PERSONAL QUESTION

SWEAT-STREAKED horses at full gallop and dusty postilion urging them on; dusty chaise that rocks and swings and out from the window a bonneted head, a face beautiful though very pale, and a voice that cries against rush of wind:

"Faster! Oh, faster! . . ."

Sam, astride his horse at Willowmead before that open, ever-hospitable door, taking leave of these loved and long familiar friends. But as he turns and rides through the fragrant rick-yard bright with the mellow radiance of sunset, Captain Ned walks beside him; two very thoughtful men they are, though the face of one is glad and radiant as the evening, the other dark and gloomy.

"By the way, Sam," says Radiance, looking up at Gloom, "I may as well let you know, old shipmate, and you'll be the very first, but we're expecting, messmate, hoping!"

"Oh?" says Gloom, lost in his own unhappy thoughts. "Why so, Ned, what for?"

"Another, Sam."

"Ah?" sighs Gloom. "Another—what?"

"Child, y'numbskull!"

"Ha!" exclaims Gloom, sighing deeper than ever and looking very wistful. "Another child, d'ye say?" Here, rousing, he claps his old friend on the shoulder, saying heartily: "Good man! I'm glad of it, Ned! Congratulations and loving wishes to you and Kate. God bless you both! I only wish——"

"What's your wish, Sam?"

"Oh—nothing!"

"So do I, old shipmate!"

"What, Ned?"

"I wish you the same."

"Thanks, but that's not likely. No, that will probably never be—now!"

"Nonsense, Sam! She'll come back!"

"Ay, maybe. But—even so——"

"Shipmate, were I a betting man, which I'm not, I'd lay you odds on it, ay, and within the year."

"And I'd take you, Ned—that neither this year, no, nor any other can such ever be. . . . You and Kate have made joyful success of your marriage—mine's gone a-wrack, a sheer hulk dragging her anchors with rocks in her lee and the water shoaling—soon to strike and beat to drifting wreckage."

"Good Lord, Sam, what nonsense! Remember your old, favourite mottoes—'never say die' and 'while there's life there's hope——' "

"Damme, Ned, what a lubberly fool I was in those days!"

"Not you, Sam! Oh no! In those days you became my best friend and first officer, ay, and an inspiration to every man aboard."

"And would to God I were aboardship now. Ay, and maybe I shall yet——"

"Not you!" said the Captain, halting, for they had reached the wide gate with the highroad beyond. "You were never the sort to run from trouble, Sam, 'twas always the reverse. So now, since your trouble is at home, face it there and give it battle as you did at sea. . . . And now, Sam, to refer to what's been in my mind ever since Kate told me,—if it happens to be a girl, we want her named Katharine,—spelt with a 'K', mind you, Katherine Andromeda, if your Andromeda agrees. I must ask her——"

"Of course she'll agree, take it from me, for I don't suppose you'll have a chance to see and ask her."

"However, I will, Sam, just as soon as she returns, which I predict will be so soon as you—fetch her."

"Never in this world!" growled Sam. "She must come back to me of her own will or not at all! She knows this, Ned, yet all these weeks she's let me wait—and no message, never one word:"

"It's hardly a month, Sam. And I still think 'tis you should make the first advance."

"Well, that's where we differ, Ned. To be misjudged was bad, to be deserted was worse, but—to be thus utterly neglected and ignored is unforgivable, yes, damme if it isn't! And, Ned, 'twixt you and me, I've decided on my future course,—in another week I'm off to sea again——"

"Easy, shipmate! Now haul your wind and listen! Your properest and only true course is to 'bout ship and bear away for London and Andromeda——"

"No! In a week's time I shall bear away to fight the French."

"And what o' your tenantry?"

"Harry Standish shall take charge——"

"He will not have the same influence or——"

"However, Ned, my mind is made up at last, d'ye see, and so—well—good night, old friend!" Then with fervent handclasp, Sam rode away, leaving the Captain to gaze after him distressfully.

Thus, Gloom rides on through a fragrant dusk, so lost in mournful reflection that at the cross-roads he is nearly run down by—sweat-streaked horses at full gallop, dusty postilion urging them on, a dusty chaise that rocks and swings, a bonneted head, a beautiful face, while against rush of wind a voice cries:

"Stop! Oh—stop!"

So, with much clattering of hoofs, the vehicle is pulled up and the amazed postilion beholds his fare, this great lady, throw open the door, leap into the road and, heedless of dust, careless of dainty silks and laces, run towards that solitary horseman. . . .

"Sam! Oh, Sam . . . my darling!"

The postilion, eyes wide and mouth agape, sees her caught up in this horseman's arms that lift and fold her close—a horseman who, uttering no word, kisses her instead and so rides slowly away with her.

The stupefied postilion gazes after them until, recovering his wits somewhat, he follows, but, being one of some experience and hence regarding himself as a "knowing covey", keeps at a respectful distance.

"Oh, but . . . Sam, darling," sighed Andromeda, recovering breath, "this seems quite impossible!"

"Yes!" he answered, tightening his clasp. "Yes, it does! Too good to be true. Yet true it is, thank God!"

"Yes, thank God! But, Sam, how can it be true? How can you be in bed dying if I am really in your dear arms and you are kissing me with such . . . such violence?"

"Did I hurt you?"

"No, of course not. I loved it, but——" Here he, of course, was instantly violent again. "Oh, but . . . Sam dearest, what does it mean? You are in bed . . . shot and dangerously wounded! So how can I possibly be here in your arms that feel so very . . . so extremely vital and . . . compelling? And you are not even wounded, are you?"

"Not the slightest! Does this disappoint you?"

"No, silly man! But you are supposed to be lying in bed between life and death! You ought to be—I mean, I believed you were."

"Oh?" said he, pondering this. "Why?"

"Godmother's letter, of course. She wrote the most dreadful news—how you had been shot in the wood by Sir Robert Chalmers——"

"Ah!" exclaimed Sam, stooping to peer under the brim of her bonnet. "So you came back to me . . . at once . . . at breakneck speed?"

"And breaking my heart, too, Sam, my poor, grieving heart! For in all the world is only one Sam and, oh, had I lost him . . . I should have been lost too, and ready for death."

"So ho!" quoth my lord. "Then, madam, my poor, purblind creature, you still love this coarse, brutal Sam fellow in spite of all his shameful infidelities, do you?"

"Yes, my lord. I do and shall love him in spite of everything, for ever and ever."

"Now, God love us all!" exclaimed Sam. "Here is my wife again! Ay, here is my own Andromeda bringing all joy and happiness back to her meek, adoring Sam!"

"And—here," she murmured, drawing him to her lips, "here is my own Sam who never was meek but who will always adore me—I hope! Yes, but strong and well, thank God, in spite of Godmother's awful letter!"

"Aha, our Duchess!" exclaimed Sam, kissing his wife. "God bless her, she's done it again! Ay, as she did before! She first brought us together by a trick and she has reunited us by another——"

"So then," cried Andromeda, indignantly, trying to sit up quite unsuccessfully, "so then, her letter was a—a wicked hoax."

"Ay, a right blessed hoax, seemingly!"

"Did you know of it?"

"No."

"Well, it was cruel, a—a basely cruel deception that nearly drove me frantic with grief and anxiety."

"So God bless her again!"

"How can you say that?"

"Because grief and anxiety have melted your icy pride and made you my own Andromeda again. But . . . are you glad to be here in my arms, are you?"

"Far more than glad!" she sighed, nestling to him. "To lie here upon your breast—where I so truly belong! . . . But now, Sam, because you will have me to kiss how and when you will . . . oh, pray stop doing it on the public highway . . . suffer your lady to return to her chaise that she drive home with the dignity befitting your lordship's wife—now do, Sam!"

"Excellent!" he laughed rapturously. "We will take the chaise and drive home—home, mark you—with a capital letter —together and with what dignity love will allow us. Hi— Postboy!" he bellowed. "Postboy!"

"But, Sam, your horse?"

"Steady old Rufus will find his way home, ay, home, my lady—as well or better without me."

So they dismounted, and, with a clap on glossy flank, away trotted Rufus stable-wards. The postilion, this extremely knowing covey, now approached, and, saluting with whip, reined the chaise to a standstill; in stepped his passengers and away they drove.

Now had the postilion turned his dusty head, which he was far too knowing to do, he would most certainly have envied this tall horseman, for:

"Into my arms, now!" Sam commanded, and was instantly obeyed. "Off with this bonnet! Your dear, lovely head upon my shoulder! Now, first I must tell you there is a man at home, —home, mind you,—in bed and dangerously wounded, but he is Sir Robert Chalmers. No! Keep your head where it is and listen to me. Sir Robert is going to live, but his hate for me is dead,—slaughtered, I believe, by your fairy niece, our blessed small Jane. So now I pray God bless Jane! Say 'Amen'!"

"Amen!" repeated Andromeda, with fervour.

"And now, madam, there is—us! My wickedly unfaithful lordship and your cruelly jealous self! Oh yes, you were furiously, blindly jealous and all too ready to doubt me. Well now, why don't you demand to hear of Cecily and myself, ay, and those anonymous letters? Come, ask me!"

"No, my lord."

"Then I'll tell you they were written by Viscount Twily with the intention of doing exactly what they did, creating doubt and suspicion between us."

"Oh, what wicked wretch!"

"Yet he tried his best to undo their evil with his last breath, just before he died,—killed by that one-time friend of his who will answer for it——"

"But, oh, Sam,—yes, I did lose faith in you! Can you forgive me? Because now I see you—my own Sam again . . . these dear, truthful eyes that cannot lie. Oh, I know I should never have doubted you! Oh, Sam dear——"

"Madam, your present un-Andromeda-like humility charms me and mightily becomes you. Know then that cousin Ralph also has no longer any unworthy doubts of that sweet wife of his and—has become my friend. Cecily, by her own simple goodness, has won her battle at last and her husband for good and all, ay, and brought peace between him and me. So now I say 'God bless Cecily'! And what says your ladyship to all this?"

"I pray God bless them both,—and my Sam's forgiveness that I ever doubted his love."

"So, my lady," he enquired, holding her away, the better to look into her face, even more lovely now because of its gentleness and humility, "you plead my forgiveness, do you?"

"Yes, my dear lord."

"Then you shall have it fully and freely—on a condition."

"Oh?" she demanded, losing much of her meekness. "Indeed, and what pray?"

"First—my shoulder!" said he, drawing her nearer. "Your beloved head again! Now! Are you listening with both those pretty ears, are you?"

"Yes, yes, of course I am."

"Very well,—you must know this very evening I was talking with my old messmate, Ned——"

"A very ordinary occurrence, Sam."

"Yes, it is. But this evening, d'ye see, he told me something rather . . . well . . . out of the ordinary . . . he told me that Kate and he were hoping for and expecting another child, and he suggested——"

Here Sam made such a long pause that Andromeda enquired at last:

"What did he suggest?"

"That I, with your ladyship's kind assistance, should do likewise. . . . And so . . . pray, madam, how says your ladyship?"

And now it was she who hesitated, until:

"Well?" he demanded. Still she was mute, nor was it until the postilion slowed his horses to enter the great gates of Wrybourne Feveril that the Countess replied and with the very sweetest humility.

"As you will, my lord!" And then, with no humility whatever: "Oh, Sam, you dear, gentle, silly man, of cour——"
His lips silenced her until the postilion reined to a final stop.

Thus Sam brought his Andromeda back to this place of roof and walls which, through long, eventful years, she was to make for him, and others, that most sacred of all blessed places:

HOME.